Richard F Burton

Supplemental Nights to the Book of the Thousand and one Nights with

Notes Anthropological...

Vol. Four

Richard F Burton

Supplemental Nights to the Book of the Thousand and one Nights with Notes Anthropological...
Vol. Four

ISBN/EAN: 9783743417595

Manufactured in Europe, USA, Canada, Australia, Japa

Cover: Foto ©Andreas Hilbeck / pixelio.de

Manufactured and distributed by brebook publishing software (www.brebook.com)

Richard F Burton

Supplemental Nights to the Book of the Thousand and one Nights with

Notes Anthropological...

SUPPLEMENTAL NIGHTS

TO·THE·BOOK·OF·THE·THOUSAND
AND·ONE·NIGHTS·WITH·NOTES
ANTHROPOLOGICAL·AND
EXPLANATORY

BY

RICHARD·F·BURTON

VOLUME
FOUR

PRIVATELY·PRINTED
BY·THE·BURTON·CLUB

TO WILLIAM H. CHANDLER, ESQ.,

Pembroke College, Oxford.

MY DEAR MR. CHANDLER,

As without your friendly and generous aid this volume could never have seen the light, I cannot resist the temptation of inscribing it to you—and without permission, for your modesty would have refused any such acknowledgment.

I am, ever,

Yours sincerely,

RICHARD F. BURTON.

TRIESTE, *March 10th,* 1888.

CONTENTS OF THE FOURTEENTH VOLUME.

———◆———

VOL. XIV.

CONTENTS.

Contents.

THE TRANSLATOR'S FOREWORD.

---◇---

AS MY first and second volumes (Supplemental) were composed of translated extracts from the Breslau Edition of The Nights, so this tome and its successor (vols. iv. and v.) comprise my version from the (Edward) Wortley Montague Codex immured in the old Bodleian Library, Oxford.

Absence from England prevents for the present my offering a satisfactory description of this widely known manuscript; but I may safely promise that the hiatus shall be filled up in vol. v., which is now ready for the press.

The contents of the Wortley Montague text are not wholly unfamiliar to Europe. In 1811 Jonathan Scott, LL.D. Oxon. (for whom see my vols. i., ix. and x. 434), printed with Longmans and Co. his "Arabian Nights Entertainments" in five substantial volumes 8vo, and devoted a sixth and last to excerpts entitled

TALES

SELECTED FROM THE MANUSCRIPT COPY

OF THE

1001 NIGHTS

BROUGHT TO EUROPE BY EDWARD WORTLEY MONTAGUE, ESQ.

Translated from the Arabic

By JONATHAN SCOTT, LL.D.

Unfortunately for his readers Scott enrolled himself amongst the acolytes of Professor Galland, a great and original genius in the line *Raconteur*, and a practical Orientalist whose bright example was destined to produce disastrous consequences. The Frenchman, however unscrupulous he might have been about casting down and building up in order to humour the dead level of Gallican *bon goût*, could, as is shown by his "Aladdin," translate literatim and verbatim when the story-stuff is of the right species and acceptable to the average European taste. But, as generally happens in such cases, his servile suite went far beyond their master and model. Petis de la Croix ("Persian and Turkish Tales"), Chavis and Cazotte ("New Arabian Nights"), Dow ("Ináyatu llah") and Morell ("Tales of the Genii"), with others manifold whose names are now all but forgotten, carried out the Gallandian liberties to the extreme of licence and succeeded in producing a branchlet of literature, the most vapid, frigid and insipid that can be imagined by man,—a bastard Europeo-Oriental, pseudo-Eastern world of Western marionettes garbed in the gear which Asiatic are (or were) supposed to wear, with sentiments and opinions, manners and morals to match; the whole utterly lacking life, local colour, vraisemblance, human interest. From such abortions, such monstrous births, libera nos, Domine!

And Scott out-gallanded Galland:—

> Diruit, ædificat, mutat quadrata rotundis.

It is hard to quote a line which he deigned textually to translate. He not only commits felony on the original by abstracting whole sentences and pages *ad libitum*, but he also thrusts false goods into his author's pocket and patronises the unfortunate Eastern story-teller by foisting upon him whatever he, the "translator and traitor," deems needful. On this point no more need be said: the curious reader has but to compare any one of Scott's "translations" with the original or, for that matter, with the present version.

I determined to do that for Scott which Lane had done partly and imperfectly, and Payne had successfully and satisfactorily done for Galland. But my first difficulty was about the text. It was impossible to face without affright the prospect of working for months amid the discomforts and the sanitary dangers of Oxford's learned atmosphere and in her obsolete edifices the Bodleian and the Radcliffe. Having ascertained, however, that in the so-called "University" not a scholar could be found to read the text, I was induced to apply for a loan—not to myself personally for I should have shunned the responsibility—but in the shape of a temporary transfer of the seven-volumed text, tome by tome, to the charge of Dr. Rost, the excellent Librarian of the India Office.

My hopes, however, were fated to be deferred. Learned bodies, Curators and so forth, are ponderous to move and powerless to change for

> The trail of the slow-worm is over them all.

My official application was made on September 13th, 1886. The tardiest steps were taken as if unwillingly and, when they could no longer decently be deferred, they resulted in the curtest and most categorical but not most courteous of refusals, under circumstances of peculiar disfavour, on November 1st of the same year. Here I shall say no more: the correspondence has been relegated to Appendix A. My subscribers, however, will have no reason to complain of these "Ineptiæ Bodleianæ." I had pledged myself in case of a loan "not to translate Tales that might be deemed offensive to propriety:" the Curators have kindly set me free from that troublesome condition and I thank them therefor.

Meanwhile I had not been idle. Three visits to Oxford in September and October had enabled me to reach the DIVth Night. But the laborious days and inclement evenings, combined with the unsanitary state of town and libraries—the Bodleian and the Rotunda—brought on a serious attack of "lithiasis" as it is now called, and prostrated me for two months, until it was time to leave England en route for my post.

Under these circumstances my design threatened to end in failure. As often befalls to men out of England, every move ventured by me menaced only check-mate. I began by seeking a copyist at Oxford, one who would imitate the text as an ignoramus might transcribe music: an undergraduate volunteered for the task and after a few days dropped it in dumb disgust. The attempt was presently repeated by a friend with the unsatisfactory result that three words out of four were legible. In London several Easterns were described as able and willing for the work; but they also were found wanting; one could not be trusted with the MS. and another was marriage-mad. Photography was lastly proposed, but considerations of cost seemed to render it unavailable. At last, when matters were at the worst, the proverbial amendment appeared. Mr. Chandler, whose energetic and conscientious opposition to all "Bodleian loans," both of books and of manuscripts, had mainly caused the passing of the prohibitory statute, came forward in the most friendly and generous way: with no small trouble to himself he superintended the "sunpictures," each page of the original being reduced to half-size, and he insisted upon the work being done wholly and solely at his own expense. I know not how to express my gratitude.

The process was undertaken by Mr. Percy Notcutt, of Kingsbury and Notcutt, 45, St. George's Place, Knightsbridge, and the four hundred and odd pages were reproduced in most satisfactory style.

Being relegated to a port-town which never possessed even an Arabic lexicon, I have found some difficulty with the Wortley Montague MS. as it contains a variety of local words unknown to the common dictionaries. But I have worked my best to surmount the obstacle by consulting many correspondents, amongst whom may be mentioned the name of my late lamented friend, the Reverend George Percy Badger; and, finally, by submitting my proofs to the corrections and additions of the lexicologist Dr. Steingass.

Appendix B will require no apology to the numerous admirers of Mr. E. J. W. Gibb's honest and able work, "The History of the Forty Vezirs" (London, Redway, MDCCCLXXXVI). The writer in a book intended for the public was obliged to leave in their original Turkish, and distinguished only by italics, three "facetious" tales which, as usual, are some of the best in the book. These have been translated for me and I offer them to my readers on account of their curious analogies with many in The Nights.

RICHARD F. BURTON.

TRIESTE, *April 10th,* 1888.

SUPPLEMENTAL NIGHTS

TO THE BOOK OF THE

THOUSAND NIGHTS AND A NIGHT

STORY OF THE SULTAN OF AL-YAMAN AND HIS THREE SONS.[1]

THERE was erewhile in the land of Al-Yaman a man which was a Sultan and under him were three Kinglets whom he overruled. He had four children; to wit, three sons and a daughter: he also owned wealth and treasures greater than reed can pen or page may contain; as well as animals such as horses and camels, sheep and black cattle; and he was held in awe by all the sovrans. But when his reign had lasted for a length of time, Age[2] brought with it ailments and infirmities and he became incapable of faring forth his Palace to the Divan, the hall of audience; whereupon he summoned his three sons to the presence and said to them, "As for me, 'tis my wish to divide among you all my substance ere I die, that ye may be equal in circumstance and live in accordance with whatso I shall command." And they said, "Hearkening and obedience." Then quoth the Sultan, "Let the eldest of you become sovereign after me: let the cadet succeed to my moneys and treasures[3] and as for the youngest let him inherit my animals

---

[1] From the Wortley Montague MS. vol. iii. pp. 80–96. J. Scott: vol. vi. pp. 1–7. *Histoire du Sulthan d'Yemen et de ses trois fils;* Gauttier vol. vi. pp. 158–165.

[2] The worst disease in human life, now recognised as "Annus Domini."

[3] Arab. "Mál wa Ghawál": in Badawi parlance "Mál" would = flocks and herds (pecunia, pecus); and amongst the burghers = ready money, coin. Another favourite jingle of similar import is "Mál wa Nawál."

There is an older form of the Sultan of Al Yaman and his three sons, to be found in M. Zotenberg's 'Chronique de Tabari," vol. ii. pp. 357–61.

VOL. XIV.

of every kind. Suffer none to transgress against other; but each aid each and assist his co-partner." He then caused them to sign a bond and agreement to abide by his bequeathal; and, after delaying a while, he departed to the mercy of Allah. Thereupon his three sons got ready the funeral gear and whatever was suited to his estate for the mortuary obsequies such as cerements and other matters: they washed the corpse and enshrouded it and prayed over it: then, having committed it to the earth they returned to their palaces where the Wazirs and the Lords of the Land and the city-folk in their multitudes, high and low, rich and poor, flocked to condole with them on the loss of their father. And the news of his decease was soon bruited abroad in all the provinces; and deputations from each and every city came to offer condolence to the King's sons. These ceremonies duly ended, the eldest Prince demanded that he should be seated as Sultan on the steatl of his sire in accordance with the paternal will and testament; but he could not obtain it from his two brothers as both and each said, "I will become ruler in room of my father." So enmity and disputes for the government now arose amongst them and it was not to be won by any; but at last quoth the eldest Prince, "Wend we and submit ourselves to the arbitration of a Sultan of the tributary sultans; and let him to whom he shall adjudge the realm take it and reign over it." Quoth they " 'Tis well!" and thereto agreed, as did also the Wazirs; and the three set out without suite seeking the capital of one of the subject Sovrans.——And Shahrázád[1] was surprised by the dawn of day[2] and fell silent and ceased to say her permitted say. Then quoth her sister Dunyázád, "How sweet is thy story, O sister mine, and how enjoyable and delectable!" Quoth she, "And where is this compared with that I would relate to you on the coming night, an the King suffer me to survive?" Now when it was the next night and that was

The Three Hundred and Thirtieth Night,

DUNYAZAD said to her, "Allah upon thee, O my sister, an thou be other than sleepy, finish for us thy tale that we may cut short

---

[1] In the W. M. MS. the sisters are called "Shahrzádeh" (= City born) and "Dinár-zádeh" (= ducat born) and the royal brothers Shahrbáz (= City player or City falcon) and Kahramán (vol. i. p. 1) alias Samarbán (*ibid.*). I shall retain the old spelling.

[2] I have hitherto translated "wa adraka (masc.) Shahrázáda al-Sabáh," as = And

the watching of this our latter night!" She replied, "With love
and good will!" It hath reached me, O auspicious King, the
director, the right-guiding, lord of the rede which is benefiting
and of deed fair-seeming and worthy celebrating, that the three
Princes fared seeking a Sultan of the sultans who had been under
the hands of their sire, in order that they might take him to
arbitrator. And they stinted not faring till the middle way, when
behold, they came upon a mead abounding in herbage and in rain-
water lying sheeted.[1] So they sat them down to rest and to eat
of their victual, when one of the brothers, casting his eye upon
the herbage, cried, "Verily a camel hath lately passed this way
laden half with Halwá-sweetmeats and half with Hámiz-pickles."[2]
"True," cried the second, "and he was blind of an eye." Exclaimed the third, " 'Tis sooth; and indeed he hath lost his tail."
Hardly, however, had they ended their words when lo! the
owner of the camel came upon them (for he had overheard their
speech and had said to himself, "By Allah, these three fellows
have driven off my property, inasmuch as they have described
the burthen and eke the beast as tail-less and one-eyed"), and
cried out, "Ye three have carried away my camel!"[3] "By Allah
we have not seen him," quoth the Princes, "much less have we
touched him;" but quoth the man, "By the Almighty, who can
have taken him except you? and if you will not deliver him to me,
off with us, I and you three, to the Sultan." They replied, "By
all manner of means; let us wend to the Sovran." So the four
hied forth, the three Princes and the Cameleer, and ceased not

Shahrazad *perceived* the dawn of day; but it is more correct as well as more picturesque
to render the phrase "was surprised (or overtaken) by the dawn."
    [1] Arab. "'Adrán," = much and heavy rain.
    [2] For "Halwá" see vol. ii. pp. 47–212. Scott (vol. vi. 413) explains "Hámiz" as "a
species of small grain," probably confounding it with Hummus (or Himmis) = vetches.
It is the pop. term for pickles, "sour meat" as opposed to "sweetmeats." The Arabs
divide the camel's pasture into "Khullah" which means sweet food called bread and
into "Hámiz" termed fruit: the latter is composed mainly of salsolaceæ, and as camels
feed upon it during the hot season it makes them drink. Hence in Al Hariri (Preface)
"I change the pasture," *i.e.*, I pass from grave to gay, from light to dignified style. (Chenery,
p. 274).
    [3] This is the modern version of the tale which the author of "Zadig" has made familiar
to Europe. The hero is brought before the King and Queen of Babylon for stealing a
horse and a dog; and, when held by the chief "Destour" (priest) to be a thief, justifies
himself. I have given in full the older history from Tabari, the historian (vixit A.D. 839–
923). For the tracker ("Paggí") and the art of tracking see Sind Revisited, i. 180–183.
I must again express my wonder that the rural police of Europe still disdain the services
of trained dogs when these are about to be introduced into the army.

faring till they reached the capital of the King. There they took seat without the wall to rest for an hour's time and presently they arose and pushed into the city and came to the royal Palace. Then they craved leave of the Chamberlains, and one of the Eunuchs caused them enter and signified to the sovereign that the three sons of Such-and-such a Sultan had made act of presence. So he bade them be set before him and the four went in and saluted him, and prayed for him and he returned their salams. He then asked them, "What is it hath brought you hither and what may ye want in the way of enquiry?" Now the first to speak was the Cameleer and he said, "O my lord the Sultan; verily these three men have carried off my camel by proof of their own speech."——And Shahrazad perceived the dawn of day and fell silent and ceased saying her permitted say. Then quoth her sister Dunyazad, "How sweet and tasteful is thy tale, O sister mine, and enjoyable and delectable!" Quoth she, "And where is this compared with that I would relate to you on the coming night an the Sovran suffer me to survive?" Now when it was the next night and that was

The Three Hundred and Thirty-first Night,

DUNYAZAD said to her, "Allah upon thee, O my sister, an thou be other than sleepy, finish for us thy tale that we may cut short the watching of this our latter night!" She replied, "With love and good will!" It hath reached me, O auspicious King, the director, the right-guiding, lord of the rede which is benefiting and of deeds fair-seeming and worthy celebrating, that the Cameleer came forward between the Sultan's hands and said, "O my lord, verily these men have carried away the camel which belongeth to me,[1] for they have indeed described him and the burthen he bore! And I require of our lord the Sultan that he take from these wights and deliver to me the camel which is mine as proved by their own words." Presently asked the Sultan, "What say ye to the claims of this man and the camel belonging to him?" Hereto the Princes made answer, "By Allah, O King of the Age, we have not seen the camel, much less have we stolen him." Thereupon the Cameleer exclaimed, "O my

---

[1] Arab. "Bitá'í" == my own. I have already noticed that this is the Egypt. form and the Nilotes often turn the 'Ayn into an H, e.g. Bitáht for Bitá'at, e.g. Ash Shabakah bitáht as-Sayd, thy net for fishing. (Spitta Bey, Contes Arabes Modernes, p. 43.)

lord, I heard yonder one say that the beast was blind of an eye;
and the second said that he was tail-less, and the third said that
half his load was of sour stuff and the other half was of sweet
stuff." They replied, "True, we spake these words;" and the
Sultan cried to them, "Ye have purloined the beast by this proof."
They rejoined, "No, by Allah, O my lord. We sat us in such a
place for repose and refreshment and we remarked that some of
the pasture had been grazed down, so we said, 'This is the graz-
ing of a camel; and he must have been blind of one eye as the
grass was eaten only on one side.' But as for our saying that he
was tail-less, we noted the droppings lying heaped[1] upon the
ground which made us agree that the tail must have been cut off,
it being the custom of camels at such times to whisk their tails
and scatter the dung abroad. So 'twas evident to us that the
camel had lost his tail. But as for our saying that the load was
half Halwá and half Hámiz, we saw on the place where the camel
had knelt the flies gathering in great numbers while on the other
were none: so the case was clear to us (as flies settle on naught
save the sugared) that one of the panniers must have contained
sweets and the other sours." Hearing this the Sultan said to the
Cameleer, "O man, fare thee forth and look after thy camel; for
these signs and tokens prove not the theft of these men, but only
the power of their intellect and their penetration."[2] And when
the Cameleer heard this, he went his ways. Presently the Sultan
cleared a place in the Palace and allotted to it the Princes for their
entertainment: he also directed they be supplied with a banquet
and the eunuchs did his bidding. But when it was eventide and
supper was served up, the trio sat down to it purposing to eat;
the eldest, however, having hent in hand a bannock of bread
exclaimed, "By Allah, verily this cake was baked by a woman in
blood, to wit, one with the menses." The cadet tasting a bit of
kid exclaimed, "This kid was suckled by a bitch"; and the youngest exclaimed, "Assuredly this Sultan must be a son of shame, a
bastard." All this was said by the youths what while the Sultan
had hidden himself in order to hear and to profit by the Princes'

---

[1] Arab. "Mukabbab;" prop. vaulted, arched, domed in Kubbah (or cupola)-shape.
[2] Arab. "Firásah." "Sciences are of three kinds: one the science of Faith, another
the science of Physiognomy (Firásah), and another the science of the Body; but unless
there be the science of Physiognomy, other science availeth not." So says "The Forty
Vizirs:" Lady's vith story and Vizir's xxxist story. For a note on "Firásah" see vol.
viii. 326.

words. So he waxed wroth and entered hastily crying, "What be these speeches ye have spoken?" They replied, "Concerning all thou hast heard enquire within and thou wilt find it wholly true." The Sultan then entered his women's apartments and after inquisition found that the woman who had kneaded the bread was sick with her monthly courses. He then went forth and summoned the head-shepherd and asked him concerning the kid he had butchered. He replied, "By Allah, O my lord, the nanny-goat that bare the kid died and we found none other in milk to suckle him; but I had a bitch that had just pupped and her have I made nourish him." The Sultan lastly hent his sword in hand and proceeded to the apartments of the Sultánah-mother and cried, "By Allah, unless thou avert my shame[1] we will cut thee down with this scymitar! Say me whose son am I?" She replied, "By Allah, O my child, indeed falsehood is an excuse, but fact and truth are more saving and superior. Verily thou art the son of a cook!"——And Shahrazad was surprised by the dawn of day and fell silent and ceased to say her permitted say. Then quoth her sister Dunyazad, "How sweet is thy story, O sister mine, and how enjoyable and delectable!" Quoth she, "And where is this compared with that I would relate to you on the coming night, an the King suffer me to survive?" Now when it was the next night and that was

The Three Hundred and Thirty-second Night.

DUNYAZAD said to her, "Allah upon thee, O my sister, an thou be other than sleepy, finish for us thy tale that we may cut short the watching of this our latter night!" She replied, "With love and good will!" It hath reached me, O auspicious King, the director, the right-guiding, lord of the rede which is benefiting and of deeds fair-seeming and worthy celebrating, that the Sultan's mother said to him, "Verily thou art a cook's son. Thy sire could not beget boy-children and I bare him only a single daughter. But it so fortuned that the kitchener's wife lay in of a boy (to wit, thyself); so we gave my girl-babe to the cook and took thee as the son of the Sultan, dreading for the realm after thy sire's death." The King went forth from his mother in

---

[1] Arab. "In lam tazidd Kayní" = *lit.* unless thou oppose my forming or composition.

astonishment at the penetration of the three youths and, when he had taken seat in his Palace, he summoned the trio and as soon as they appeared he asked them; "Which of you was it that said, 'She who kneaded the bread was in blood'?" Quoth the eldest, "That was I;" and quoth the King, "What led thee to suspect that she was menstruous?" He replied, "O my lord, when I took the bannock and broke off a bittock, the flour fell out in lumps.[1] Now had the kneader been well, her strength of hand would have remained and the bread would have been wrought by all the veins; but, when the blood came, her powers were minished for women's force is in their hands; and as soon as the monthly period cometh upon them their strength is lost. Their bodies contain three hundred and sixty veins all lying hard by one another and the blood of the catamenia floweth from them all; hence their force becometh feebleness. And this was my proof of the woman which was menstruous." Quoth the Sultan, " 'Tis well. We accept as certain thy saying upon this evidence, for it is agreeable to man's understanding nor can any challenge it; this being from the power of insight into the condition of womankind. And we are assured of its soothfastness, for 'tis evident to us without concealment. But which is he who said of the kid's meat that the beast was suckled by a bitch? What proof had he of this? How did he learn it and whence did his intelligence discover it to him?" Now when the deceased Sultan's second son heard these words, he made answer. "I, O King of the Age, am he who said that say!" The King replied, " 'Tis well;" and the Prince resumed, "O my lord, that which showed me the matter of the meat which was to us brought is as follows. I found the fat of the kid all hard by the bone, and I knew that the beast had sucked bitch's milk; for the flesh of dogs lieth outside and their fat is on their bones, whereas in sheep and goats the fat lieth upon the meat. Such, then, was my proof wherein there is nor doubt nor hesitation; and when thou shalt have made question and inquiry thou wilt find this to be fact." Quoth the Sultan, " 'Tis well; thou hast spoken truth and whatso thou sayest is soothfast. But which is he who declared that I am a bastard and what was his proof and what sign in me exposed it

---

[1] Arab. "Faráfish," a word which I cannot find in the dictionary, and so translate according to the context. Dr. Steingass remarks that the nearest approach to it would be "Faráfik" (plur. of Furfák) = fine, thin or soft bread.

to him?" Quoth the youngest Prince, "I am he who said it;" and
the Sultan rejoined, "There is no help but that thou provide me
with a proof." The Prince rejoined, "'Tis well!"——And
Shahrazad perceived the dawn of day and fell silent and ceased
saying her permitted say. Then quoth her sister Dunyazad,
"How sweet and tasteful is thy tale, O sister mine, and enjoyable
and delectable!" Quoth she, "And where is this compared with
that I would relate to you on the coming night an the Sovran
suffer me to survive?" Now when it was the next night and
that was

The Three Hundred and Thirty-third Night,

DUNYAZAD said to her, "Allah upon thee, O my sister, an thou
be other than sleepy, finish for us thy tale that we may cut short
the watching of this our latter night!" She replied, "With love
and good will!" It hath reached me, O auspicious King, the
director, the right-guiding lord of the rede which is benefiting
and of deeds fair-seeming and worthy celebrating, that the
youngest Prince said to the Sultan, "O my lord, I have evidence
that thou art the son of a cook and a base-born in that thou
didst not sit at meat with us and this was mine all-sufficient
evidence. Every man hath three properties which he inheriteth
at times from his father, at times from his maternal uncle and at
times from his mother.[1] From his sire cometh generosity or
niggardness; from his uncle courage or cowardice; from his
mother modesty or immodesty; and such is the proof of every
man." Then quoth to him the Sultan, "Sooth thou speakest;
but say me, men who like you know all things thoroughly by
evidence and by your powers of penetration, what cause have
they to come seeking arbitration at my hand? Beyond yours there
be no increase of intelligence. So fare ye forth from me and
manage the matter amongst yourselves, for 'tis made palpable
to me by your own words that naught remaineth to you save to

---

[1] See, in the "Turkish Tales" by Petis de la Croix (Weber, Tales of the East, vol. iii.
196), the History of the Sophi of Baghdad, where everything returns to (or resembles)
its origin. Thus the Wazir who proposed to cut up a criminal and hang him in the shambles
was the self-convicted son of a butcher; he who advised boiling him down and giving his
flesh to the dogs was the issue of a cook, and the third who proposed to pardon him was
nobly born. See Night cccxli.

speak of mysterious subjects;[1] nor have I the capacity to adjudge
between you after that which I have heard from you. In fine
an ye possess any document drawn up by your sire before his
decease, act according to it and contrary it not." Upon this the
Princes went forth from him and made for their own country and
city and did as their father had bidden them do on his death-bed.
The eldest enthroned himself as Sultan; the cadet assumed possession and management of the moneys and treasures and the
youngest took to himself the camels and the horses and the
beeves and the muttons. Then each and every was indeed equal
with his co-partner in the gathering of good. But when the new
year came, there befel a drought among the beasts and all belonging to the youngest brother died nor had he aught of property
left: yet his spirit brooked not to take anything from his brethren
or even to ask of them aught. This then is the Tale of the King
of Al-Yaman in its entirety; yet is the Story of the Three
Sharpers[2] more wondrous and marvellous than that just recounted.——And Shahrazad was surprised by the dawn of day
and fell silent and ceased to say her permitted say. Then quoth
her sister Dunyazad, "How sweet is thy story, O sister mine,
and how enjoyable and delectable!" Quoth she, "And where is
this compared with that I would relate to you on the coming
night, an the King suffer me to survive." Now when it was the
next night and that was

The Three Hundred and Thirty-fourth Night,

DUNYAZAD said to her, "Allah upon thee, O my sister, an thou
be other than sleepy, finish for us thy tale that we may cut short

---

[1] Arab. "Al-Mafyaat," lit. = a shady place; a locality whereupon the sun does not rise.
[2] Arab. "Ja'idíyah," a favourite word in this MS. "Ja'ad" = a curl, a liberal man:
Ja'ad al-yad = miserly, and Abú ja'dah = father of curls, = a wolf. Scott (*passim*) translates the word "Sharper;" Gore Ouseley "Labourer;" and De Sacy (Chrestomathie ii.
369, who derives it from Ju'd = *avoir les cheveux crépus*): in Egypt, *homme de la populace,
canaille.* He finds it in the Fabrica Linguæ Arab. of Germanus of Silesia (p. 786) = ignavis,
hebes, stupidus, esp. a coward. Ibrahim Salamah of Alexandria makes the term signify
in Syria, impudent, thieving, wicked. Spitta Bey translates this word *musicien ambulant*
in his Gloss. to Contes Arabes, p. 171. According to Dr. Steingass, who, with the *Muhit
al-Muhit*, reads "Ju'aydíyah," Ju'ayd is said to be the P. N. of an Egyptian clown, who,
with bell-hung cap and tambourine in hand, wandered about the streets singing laudatory
doggrel and pestering the folk for money. Many vagabonds who adopted this calling
were named after him and the word was generalised in that sense.

the watching of this our latter night!" She replied, "With love
and good will! It hath reached me, O auspicious King, the
director, the right-guiding, lord of the rede which is benefiting
and of deeds fair-seeming and worthy celebrating;" and she
began to recount

THE STORY OF THE THREE SHARPERS.[1]

SAYING, "Verily their adventure is wondrous and their actions
delightsome and marvellous," presently adding——There were
in time of yore three Sharpers who were wont every day in early
morning to prowl forth and to prey, rummaging[2] among the
mounds which outlay the city. Therein each would find a silver
bit of five parahs or its equivalent, after which the trio would forgather and buy whatso sufficed them for supper: they would also
expend two Nusfs[3] upon Bast,[4] which is Bhang, and purchase a
waxen taper with the other silver bit. They had hired a cell in
the flank of a Wakálah, a caravanserai without the walls, where
they could sit at ease to solace themselves and eat their Hashísh
after lighting the candle and enjoy their intoxication and conse-
quent merriment till the noon o' night. Then they would sleep,
again awaking at day-dawn when they would arise and seek for
spoil, according to their custom, and ransack the heaps where at
times they would hit upon a silverling of five dirhams and at
other times a piece of four; and at eventide they would meet to
spend together the dark hours, and they would expend everything they came by every day. For a length of time they pursued
this path until, one day of the days, they made for the mounds
as was their wont and went round searching the heaps from
morning to evening without finding even a half-parah; wherefore
they were troubled and they went away and nighted in their cell
without meat or drink. When the next day broke they arose and
repaired for booty, changing the places wherein they were wont

---

[1] MS. vol. iii. pp. 96-121. Scott, "Story of the Three Sharpers and the Sultan," pp.
7-17; Gauttier, *Histoire des trois filous et d'un Sulthan*, vi. 165-176.

[2] Arab. Yasrahú == roaming, especially at early dawn; hence the wolf is called "Sirhán,"
and Yaklishu (if I read it aright) is from Kulsh, and equivalent to "kicking" (their heels).

[3] Nusf == half a dirham, drachma or franc, see ii. 37; vi. 214, etc.

[4] Bast, a preparation of Bhang (*Cannabis Sativa*), known in Egypt but not elsewhere:
see Lane, M. E., chapt. xv. Here it is made synonymous with "Hashísh" == Bhang in
general.

to forage; but none of them found aught; and their breasts were straitened for lack of a find of dirhams wherewith to buy them **supper.** This lasted for three full-told and following days until hunger waxed hard upon them and vexation; **so** they said one **to** other, "Go we to the Sultan and let us serve him with a sleight, and each of us three shall claim to be a past master of some craft: haply Allah Almighty may incline his heart uswards and he may largesse us with something to expend upon our necessities." Accordingly all three agreed to do on this wise and they sought the Sultan whom they found in the palace-garden. They asked leave to go in to him, but the Chamberlains refused admission: **so** they stood afar off unable to approach the presence. Then quoth they one to other, " 'Twere better we fall to and each smite his comrade and cry aloud and make a clamour,[1] and as soon as he **shall hear** us he will send to summon us." Accordingly they jostled one another and each took to frapping his fellow, making the while loud outcries. The Sultan hearing this turmoil said, "Bring me yonder wights;" and the Chamberlains and Eunuchs ran out to them and seized them **and** set them between the hands of the Sovran. As soon as they stood in the presence he asked them, "What be the cause of your wrath one against other?" They answered, "O King of the Age, we are **past masters** of crafts, each of us weeting an especial art." **Quoth the** Sultan, "What be your crafts?" and quoth one of the trio, **"O** our lord, as for my art I am a jeweller by trade." The King exclaimed, "Passing strange! a sharper and a jeweller:[2] this is a wondrous **matter.**" And he questioned the second——And Shahrazad perceived the dawn of day and fell silent and ceased saying her permitted say. Then quoth her sister Dunyazad, "How sweet and tasteful is thy tale, O sister mine, and enjoyable and delectable!" Quoth she, "And **where** is this compared with

---

[1] Ghaushah, a Persianism for which "Ghaughá" is a more common form. "Ghaush" is a tree of hard wood whereof musical instruments were made; hence the mod. words "Ghásha" and "Ghawwasha" = he produced a sound, and "Ghaushah" = tumult, quarrel. According to Dr. Steingass, the synon. in the native dicts. are "Khisám," "Laghat," "Jalabah," etc.

[2] Said *ironicè*, the jeweller being held to be one of the dishonest classes, like the washerman, the water-carrier, the gardener, etc. In England we may find his representative in the "silversmith," who will ask a pound sterling for a bit of metal which cost him perhaps five shillings or even less, and who hates to be bought by weight. The Arab. has "Jauhar-ji," a Turkish form for Jauhari; and here "jauhar" apparently means a pearl, the stone once peculiar to royalty in Persia, but the kind of gem is left undetermined.

that I would relate to you on the coming night an the Sovran suffer me to survive?" Now when it was the next night which was

The Three Hundred and Thirty-fifth Night.

DUNYAZAD said to her, "Allah upon thee, O my sister, an thou be other than sleepy, finish for us thy tale that we may cut short the watching of this our latter night!" She replied, "With love and good will!" It hath reached me, O auspicious King, the director, the right-guiding, lord of the rede which is benefiting and of deeds fair-seeming and worthy celebrating, that the Sultan asked the second Sharper saying, "And thou, the other, what may be thy craft?" He answered, "I am a genealogist[1] of the horse-kind." So the King glanced at him in surprise and said to himself, "A sharper yet he claimeth an astounding knowledge!" Then he left him and put the same question to the third who said to him, "O King of the Age, verily my art is more wondrous and marvellous than aught thou hast heard from these twain: their craft is easy but mine is such that none save I can discover the right direction thereto or know the first of it from the last of it." The Sultan enquired of him, "And what be thy craft?" Whereto he replied, "My craft is the genealogy of the sons of Adam." Hearing these words the Sovran wondered with extreme wonderment and said in himself, "Verily He informeth with His secrets the humblest of His creatures! Assuredly these men, an they speak truth in all they say and it prove soothfast, are fit for naught except kingship. But I will keep them by me until the occurrence of some nice contingency wherein I may test them; then, if they approve themselves good men and trustworthy of word, I will leave them on life; but if their speech be lying I will do them die." Upon this he set apart for them apartments and rationed them with three cakes of bread and a dish of roast meat[2] and set over them his sentinels dreading lest they fly. This case continued for a while till behold, there came to the Sultan from the land of 'Ajam a present of rarities, amongst which were two gems whereof one was clear of water and the other was

---

[1] Arab. "Sáza, yasízu," not a dictionary word. Perhaps it is a clerical error for "Sása," he groomed or broke in a horse, hence understood all about horses.

[2] In the orig. "Shorbah," Pers. = a mess of pottage: I have altered it for reasons which will presently appear.

clouded of colour.[1] The Sultan hent them in hand for a time and fell to considering them straitly for the space of an hour; after which he called to mind the first of the three Sharpers, the self-styled jeweller, and cried, "Bring me the jeweller-man." Accordingly they went and brought him and set him before the Sovran who asked him, "O man, art thou a lapidary?" And when the Sharper answered "Yes" he gave him the clear-watered stone, saying, "What may be the price of this gem?"——And Shahrazad was surprised by the dawn of day and fell silent and ceased to say her permitted say. Then quoth her sister Dunyazad, "How sweet is thy story, O sister mine, and how enjoyable and delectable!" Quoth she, "And where is this compared with that I would relate to you on the coming night, an the Sovran suffer me to survive?" Now when it was the next night and that was

The Three Hundred and Thirty-sixth Night,

DUNYAZAD said to her, "Allah upon thee, O my sister, an thou be other than sleepy, finish for us thy tale that we may cut short the watching of this our latter night!" She replied, "With love and good will!" It hath reached me, O auspicious King, the director, the right-guiding, lord of the rede which is benefiting and of deeds fair-seeming and worthy celebrating, that the Sharper took the jewel in hand and turned it rightwards and leftwards and considered the outside and pried into the inside; after which he said to the Sultan, "O my lord, verily this gem containeth a worm[2] bred within the heart thereof." Now when the King heard these words he waxed wroth with exceeding wrath and commanded the man's head to be stricken off, saying, "This jewel is clear of colour and free of flaw or other default; yet thou chargest it falsely with containing a worm!" Then he summoned the Linkman[3] who laid hands on the Sharper and pinioned his elbows and trussed up his legs[4] like a camel's and was about

---

[1] Arab. "Ghabasah," from Ghabas = obscure, dust-coloured.
[2] Arab. "Súsah" = a weevil, a moth, a worm. It does not mean simply a flaw, but a live animal (like our toads in the rock); and in the popular version of the tale the lapidary discovers its presence by the stone warming in his hand.
[3] Arab. "Mashá'ili" the cresset-bearer who acted hangman: see vol. i. 259, etc.
[4] Arab. "Ta'kíl," tying up a camel's foreleg above the knee; the primary meaning of Akl, which has so many secondary significations.

to smite his neck when behold, the Wazir entered the presence and, seeing the Sovran in high dudgeon and the Sharper under the scymitar, asked what was to do. The Sultan related to him what had happened when he drew near to him and said, "O my lord, act not after this fashion! An thou determine upon the killing of yonder man, first break the gem and, if thou find therein a worm, thou wilt know the wight's word to have been veridical; but an thou find it sound then strike off his head." "Right is thy rede," quoth the King: then he took in hand the gem and smote it with his mace[1] and when he brake behold, he found therein the worm amiddlemost thereof. So he marvelled at the sight and asked the man, "What proved to thee that it harboured a worm?" "The sharpness of my sight," answered the Sharper. Then the Sultan pardoned him and, admiring his power of vision, addressed his attendants saying, "Bear him back to his comrades and ration him with a dish of roast meat and two cakes of bread." And they did as he bade them. After some time, on a day of the days, there came to the King the tribute of 'Ajam-land accompanied with presents amongst which was a colt whose robe black as night[2] showed one shade in the sun and another in the shadow When the animal was displayed to the Sultan he fell in love with it and set apart for it a stall and solaced himself at all times by gazing at it and was wholly occupied with it and sang its praises till they filled the whole country side. Presently he remembered the Sharper who claimed to be a genealogist of the horse-kind and bade him be summoned. So they fared forth and brought him and set him between the hands of the Sovran who said to him, "Art thou he who knoweth the breed and descent of horses?" "Yea verily," said the man. Then cried the King, "By the truth of Him who set me upon the necks of His servants and who sayeth to a thing 'Be' and it becometh, an I find aught of error or confusion in thy words, I will strike off thy head." "Hearkening and obedience," quoth the Sharper. Then they led him to the colt that he might consider its gene-alogy. He called aloud to the groom[3]——And Shahrazad per-ceived the dawn of day and fell silent and ceased saying her per-mitted say. Then quoth her sister Dunyazad, "How sweet and

---

[1] Arab. "Suwán," lit. = rock, syenite, hard stone, flint; here a *marteau de guerre*.
[2] Arab. "Hálik" = intensely black, so as to look blue under a certain angle of light.
[3] Arab. "Rikáb" (= stirrup) + "dár" Pers. (= holder).

tasteful is thy tale, O sister mine, and enjoyable and delectable!"
Quoth she, "And where is this compared with that I would
relate to you on the coming night an the Sovran suffer me to survive?" Now when it was the next night and that was

The Three Hundred and Thirty-seventh Night.

DUNYAZAD said to her, "Allah upon thee, O my sister, an thou
be other than sleepy, finish for us thy tale that we may cut short
the watching of this our latter night!" She replied, "With love
and good will!" It hath reached me, O auspicious King, the
director, the right-guiding, lord of the rede which is benefiting
and of deeds fair-seeming and worthy celebrating, that the
Sharper called aloud to the stirrup-holder and when they brought
him he bade the man back the colt for his inspection. So he
mounted the animal and made it pace to the right and to the left
causing it now to prance and curvet and then to step leisurely,
while the connoisseur looked on and after a time quoth he to
the groom, "'Tis enough!" Then he went in to the presence and
stood between the hands of the King who enquired, "What hast
thou seen in the colt, O Kashmar?"[1] Replied the Sharper, "By
Allah, O King of the Age, this colt is of pure and noble blood on
the side of the sire: its action is excellent and all its qualities are
praiseworthy save one; and but for this one it had been perfect
in blood and breed nor had there been on earth's face its fellow
in horseflesh. But its blemish remaineth a secret." The Sultan
asked, "And what is the quality which thou blamest?" and the
Sharper answered, "Its sire was noble, but its dam was of other
strain: she it was that brought the blemish and if thou, O my
lord, allow me I will notify it to thee." "'Tis well, and needs
must thou declare it," quoth the Sultan. Then said the Sharper,
"Its dam is a buffalo-cow."[2] When the King heard these words

---

[1] I have ransacked dictionaries and vocabularies but the word is a mere blank.

[2] Arab. "Jámúsah." These mules are believed in by the Arabs. Shaw and other travellers mention the Mauritanian "Jumart," the breed between a bull and a mare (or jenny-
ass) or an ass and a cow. Buffon disbelieved in the mongrel, holding it to be a mere *bardeau*,
got by a stallion horse out of an ass. Voltaire writes "Jumarre" after German fashion,
and Littré derives it from jument + art (finale péjorative), or the Languedoc "Gimere"
which according to Diez suggests "Chimæra." Even in London not many years ago
a mule was exhibited as the issue of a horse and a stag. No Indian ever allows his colt
to drink buffalo's milk, the idea being that a horse so fed will lie down instead of fording
or swimming a stream.

he was wroth with wrath exceeding and he bade the Linkman take the Sharper and behead him, crying, "O dog! O accursed! How can a buffalo-cow bear a horse?" The Sharper replied, "O my lord, the Linkman is in the presence; but send and fetch him who brought thee the colt and of him make enquiry. If my words prove true and rightly placed, my skill shall be stablished; but an they be lies let my head pay forfeit for my tongue. Here standeth the Linkman and I am between thy hands: thou hast but to bid him strike off my head!" Thereupon the King sent for the owner and breeder of the colt and they brought him to the presence.——And Shahrazad was surprised by the dawn of day and fell silent and ceased to say her permitted say. Then quoth the sister Dunyazad, "How sweet is thy story, O sister mine, and how enjoyable and delectable!" Quoth she, "And where is this compared with that I would relate to you on the coming night, an the Sovran suffer me to survive?" Now when it was the next night and that was

The Three Hundred and Thirty-eighth Night,

DUNYAZAD said to her, "Allah upon thee, O my sister, an thou be other than sleepy, finish for us thy tale that we may cut short the watching of this our latter night!" She replied, "With love and good will!" It hath reached me, O auspicious King, the director, the right-guiding, lord of the rede which is benefiting and of deeds fair-seeming and worthy celebrating, that the Sultan sent for the owner and breeder of the colt and asked him saying, "Tell me the truth anent the blood of this colt. Didst thou buy it or breed it so that it was a rearling of thy homestead?" Said he, "By Allah, O King of the Age, I will speak naught which is not sooth, for indeed there hangeth by this colt the strangest story: were it graven with graver-needles upon the eye-corners it had been a warning to whoso would be warned. And this it is. I had a stallion of purest strain whose sire was of the steeds of the sea;[1] and he was stabled in a stall apart for fear of the evil eye, his service being entrusted to trusty servants. But one day in springtide the Syce took the horse into the open and there picquetted him when behold, a buffalo-cow walked into the

---

[1] See Sindbad the Seaman, vol. vi. 9.

enclosed pasture where the stallion was tethered, and seeing her he brake his heel-ropes and rushed at her and covered her. She conceived by him and when her days were completed and her throwing-time came she suffered sore pains and bare yonder colt. And all who have seen it or have heard of it were astounded," said he, presently adding, "by Allah, O King of the Age, had its dam been of the mare-kind the colt would have had no equal on earth's surface or aught approaching it." Hereat the Sultan took thought and marvelled; then, summoning the Sharper he said to him when present, "O man, thy speech is true and thou art indeed a genealogist in horseflesh and thou wottest it well. But I would know what proved to thee that the dam of this colt was a buffalo-cow?" Said he, "O King, my proof thereof was palpable nor can it be concealed from any wight of right wits and intelligence and special knowledge; for the horse's hoof is round whilst the hooves of buffaloes are elongated and duck-shaped,[1] and hereby I kenned that this colt was a jumart, the issue of a cow-buffalo." The Sultan was pleased with his words and said, "Ration him with a plate of roast meat and two cakes of bread;" and they did as they were bidden. Now for a length of time the third Sharper was forgotten till one day the Sultan bethought him of the man who could explain the genealogy of Adam's sons. So he bade fetch him and when they brought him into the presence he said, "Thou art he that knowest the caste and descent of men and women?" and the other said, "Yes." Then he commanded the Eunuchs take him to his wife[2] and place him before her and cause him declare her genealogy. So they led him in and set him standing in her presence and the Sharper considered her for a while looking from right to left; then he fared forth to the Sultan who asked him, "What hast thou seen in the Queen?" Answered he, "O my lord, I saw a somewhat adorned with loveliness and beauty and perfect grace, with fair stature of symmetrical trace and with modesty and fine manners and skilful case; and she is one in whom all good qualities appear on every side, nor is aught of accomplishments or knowledge concealed from her and haply in her centre all desirable attributes. Natheless, O King of the Age, there is a curious point that dishonoureth

---

[1] Arab. "Mubattat" from batt = a duck: in Persia the Batt-i-May is a wine-glass shaped like the duck. Scott (vi. 12) translates "thick and longish."

[2] Arab. "his Harim"; see vol. i. 165; iv. 126.

her from the which were she free none would outshine her of all
the women of her generation." Now when the Sultan heard the
words of the Sharper, he sprang hastily to his feet and clapping
hand upon hilt bared his brand and fell upon the man purposing
to slay him;——And Shahrazad perceived the dawn of day and
fell silent and ceased saying her permitted say. Then quoth her
sister Dunyazad, "How sweet and tasteful is thy tale, O sister
mine, and enjoyable and delectable!" Quoth she, "And where is
this compared with that I would relate to you on the coming
night an the Sovran suffer me to survive?" Now when it was
the next night and that was

The Three Hundred and Thirty-ninth Night,

DUNYAZAD said to her, "Allah upon thee, O my sister, an thou be
other than sleepy, finish for us thy tale that we may cut short the
watching of this our latter night!" She replied, "With love
and good will!" It hath reached me, O auspicious King, the
director, the right-guiding, lord of the rede which is benefiting
and of deeds fair-seeming and worthy celebrating, that the
Sultan fell upon the Sharper with his sword purposing to slay
him; but the Chamberlains and the Eunuchs prevented him
saying, "O our lord, kill him not until his falsehood or his fact
shall have been made manifest to thee." The Sultan said to him,
"What then appeared to thee in my Queen?" "He[1] is ferly
fair," said the man, "but his mother is a dancing-girl, a gypsey."[2]
The fury of the King increased hereat and he sent to summon the
inmates of his Harem and cried to his father-in-law, "Unless thou
speak me sooth concerning thy daughter and her descent and
her mother I"——[3] He replied, "By Allah, O King of the Age,
naught saveth a man save soothfastness! Her mother indeed
was a Gháziyah: in past time a party of the tribe was passing by
my abode when a young maid strayed from her fellows and was
lost. They asked no questions concerning her; so I lodged her
and bred her in my homestead till she grew up to be a great girl
and the fairest of her time. My heart would not brook her

---

[1] Again "he" for she. See vol. ii. 179.
[2] Arab. "Gháziyah": for the plur. "Ghawázi" see vol. i. 214; also Lane (M.E.) index
under "Ghazeeyehs."
[3] The figure prothesis without apodosis. Understand "will slay thee": see vol. vi. 203.

wiving with any other; so I wedded her and she bare me this daughter whom thou, O King, hast espoused." When the Sultan heard these words the flame in his heart was quenched[1] and he wondered at the subtlety of the Sharper man; so he summoned him and asked him saying, "O wily one, tell me what certified to thee that my Queen had a dancing girl, a gypsey, to mother?" He answered, "O King of the Age, verily the Ghaziyah race hath eye-balls intensely black and bushy brows whereas other women than the Ghaziyah have the reverse of this." On such wise the King was convinced of the man's skill and he cried, "Ration him with a dish of roast meat and two scones." They did as he bade and the three Sharpers tarried with the Sultan a long time till one day when the King said to himself, "Verily these three men have by their skill solved every question of genealogy which I proposed to them: first the jeweller proved his perfect knowledge of gems; secondly the genealogist of the horse-kind showed himself as skilful, and the same was the case with the genealogist of mankind, for he discovered the origin of my Queen and the truth of his words appeared from all quarters. Now 'tis my desire that he do the same with me that I also may know my provenance." Accordingly they set the man between his hands and he said to him, "O fellow, hast thou the power to tell me mine origin?" Said the Sharper, "Yes, O my lord, I can trace thy descent, but I will so do only upon a condition; to wit, that thou promise me safety[2] after what I shall have told thee; for the saw saith, 'Whilst Sultan sitteth on throne 'ware his despite, inasmuch as none may be contumacious when he saith 'Smite.'" Thereupon the Sultan told him, "thou hast a promise of immunity, a promise which shall never be falsed."———And Shahrazad was surprised by the dawn of day and fell silent, and ceased to say her permitted say. Then quoth her sister Dunyazad, "How sweet is thy story, O sister mine, and how enjoyable and delectable!" Quoth she, "And where is this compared with that I would relate to you on the coming night an the Sovran suffer me to survive?" Now when it was the next night, and that was

---

[1] Because the girl had not been a professional dancer, *i.e.* a public prostitute.
[2] Arab. "Amán" = quarter, mercy: see vol. i. 342.

The Three Hundred and Fortieth Night,

DUNYAZAD said to her, "Allah upon thee, O my sister, an thou be other than sleepy, finish for us thy tale that we may cut short the watching of this our latter night!" She replied, "With love and good will!" It hath reached me, O auspicious King, the director, the right-guiding, lord of the rede which is benefiting and of deeds fair-seeming and worthy celebrating, that the Sultan pledged his word for the safety of the Sharper with the customary kerchief[1] and the man said, "O King of the Age, whenas I acquaint thee with thy root and branch, let it be between us twain lest these present hear us." "Wherefore O man?" asked the Sultan, and the Sharper answered, "O my lord, Allah of All-might hath among His names 'The Veiler';"[2] wherefore the King bade his Chamberlains and Eunuchs retire so that none remained in the place save those two. Then the Sharper came forward and said, "O my lord, thou art a son of shame and an issue of adultery." As soon as the King heard these words his case changed and his colour waxed wan and his limbs fell loose:[3] he foamed at the mouth;[4] he lost hearing and sight; he became as one drunken without wine and he fell fainting to the ground. After a while he recovered and said to the Sharper, "Now by the truth of Him who hath set me upon the necks of His servants, an thy words be veridical and I ascertain their sooth by proof positive, I will assuredly abdicate my Kingdom and resign my realm to thee, because none deserveth it save thou and it becometh us least of all and every. But an I find thy speech lying I will slay thee." He replied, "Hearing and obeying;" and the Sovran, rising up without stay or delay, went inside to his mother with grip on glaive, and said to her, "By the truth of Him who uplifted the lift above

---

[1] For the "Mandíl" of mercy see vol. i. 343; for that of dismissal x. 47 and Ibn Khall. iv. 211. In Spitta Bey's "Contes Arabes" (p. 223), I find throwing the kerchief (tarammá al mahramah) used in the old form of choosing a mate. In the Tale of the Sultan of Al-Yaman and his three Sons (Supplem. Nights, vol. iv.) the Princesses drop their kerchiefs upon the head of the Prince who had saved them, by way of pointing him out.

[2] Arab. "Sattár;" see vols. i. 258 and iii. 41.

[3] In the text "Arghá" for "Arkhá" = he "brayed" (like an ostrich, etc.) for "his limbs relaxed." It reminds one of the German missionary's fond address to his flock, "My prethren, let us bray!"

[4] Arab. "Azbad," from Zbd (Zabd) = foaming, frothing, etc., whence "Zubaydah," etc.

the earth, an thou answer me not with the whole truth in whatso I ask thee, I will cut thee to little bits with this blade." She enquired, "What dost thou want with me?" and he replied, "Whose son am I, and what may be my descent?" She rejoined, "Although falsehood be an excuse, fact and truth are superior and more saving. Thou art indeed the very son of a cook. The Sultan that was before thee took **me to wife** and **I cohabited with** him a while of time without my becoming pregnant **by him or** having issue; and he would mourn and groan from the **core of his** heart for that he had no seed, **nor** girl nor **boy; neither could he** enjoy aught of sweet food or **sleep.** Now we had **about the** Palace many caged birds; and **at last,** one day of the **days, the** King longed to eat somewhat of poultry, so he went into **the court** and sent for the Kitchener to slaughter[1] one of the fowls; **and the** man applied himself to catching it. At that time I had taken **my** first bath after the monthly ailment and quoth I to myself, 'If this case continue with the King he will perish **and the** Kingdom pass from us.' And the Shaytan tempted me **to that** which displeased Allah"——And Shahrazad perceived **the dawn of** day and fell silent and ceased saying her permitted say. Then quoth her sister Dunyazad, "How sweet and tasteful is thy tale, O sister mine, and enjoyable and delectable!" Quoth she, "And where is this compared with that I would relate to you on the coming night an the Sovran suffer me to survive?" Now when it was the next night and that was

The Three Hundred and Forty-first Night,

DUNYAZAD said to her, "Allah upon thee, O my sister, an thou be other than sleepy, finish for us thy tale that we may cut short the watching of this our latter night!" She replied, "With love and good will!" It hath reached me, O auspicious King, the director, the right-guiding, lord of the rede which is benefiting and of deeds fair-seeming and worthy celebrating, that the Queen continued, "And Satan tempted me and made the sin fair in my sight. So I went up to the Kitchener, attired and adorned as I

---

[1] Arab. "Zabh" (Zbh) = the ceremonial killing of animals for food: see vols. v. 391; viii. 44. I may note, as a proof of how modern is the civilisation of Europe that the domestic fowl was unknown to Europe till about the time of Pericles (ob. B.C. 429).

was in my finest apparel and I fell a-jesting with him and provok-
ing him and disporting with him till his passions were excited by
me: so he tumbled me at that very hour, after which he arose and
slaughtered one of the birds and went his ways. Then I bade the
handmaids sprinkle water on the fowl and clean it and cook it;
and they did my bidding. After a while symptoms of pregnancy
declared themselves in me and became evident; and when the
King heard that his Queen was with child, he waxed gladsome and
joyful and gave alms and scattered gifts and bestowed robes upon
his Officers of State and others till the day of my delivery and I
bare a babe—which is thyself. Now at that time the Sultan was
hunting and birding and enjoying himself about the gardens all of
his pleasure at the prospect of becoming a father; and when the
bearer of good news went to him and announced the birth of a
man-child he hurried back to me and forthright bade them decorate the capital and he found the report true; so the city adorned
itself for forty days in honour of its King. Such is my case and my
tale."[1] Thereupon the King went forth from her to the Sharper
and bade him doff his dress and when this had been done he
doffed his own raiment and habited the man in royal gear and
hooded him with the Taylasán[2] and asked him saying, "What
proof hast thou of my being a son of adultery?" The Sharper
answered, "O my lord, my proof was thy bidding our being
rationed, after showing the perfection of our skill, with a dish of
roast meat and two scones of bread, whereby I knew thee to be of
cook's breed, for the Kings be wont in such case to make presents
of money and valuables, not of meat and bread as thou didst, and
this evidenced thee to be a bastard King." He replied, "Sooth
thou sayest," and then robed him with the rest of his robes including the Kalansuwah or royal head-dress under the hood[3] and
seated him upon the throne of his estate.——And Shahrazad was

---

[1] See in "The Forty Vizirs" (Lady's ivth Tale) how Khizr tells the King the origin of his
Ministers from the several punishments which they propose for the poor man. I have
noticed this before in Night cccxxxiii. Boethius, translated by Chaucer, explains the under-
lying idea, "All thynges seken ayen to hir propre course and all thynges rejoysen in hir
returninge agayne to hir nature."

[2] For the Taylasán hood see vol. iv. 286.

[3] The "Kalansuwah"-cap is noted by Lane (A. N. chapt. iii. 22) as "Kalensuweh." In
M. E. (Supplement i. "The Copts") he alters the word to Kalás'weh and describes it as a
strip of woollen stuff, of a deep blue or black colour, about four inches wide, attached
beneath the turban and hanging down the back to the length of about a foot. It is the dis-
tinguishing mark of the Coptic regular clergy.

surprised by the dawn of day and fell silent and ceased to say her permitted say. Then quoth her sister Dunyazad, "How sweet is thy story, O sister mine, and how enjoyable and delectable!" Quoth she, "And where is this compared with that I would relate to you on the coming night, an the Sovran suffer me to survive." Now when it was the next night and that was

The Three Hundred and Forty-second Night,

DUNYAZAD said to her, "Allah upon thee, O my sister, an thou be other than sleepy, finish for us thy tale that we may cut short the watching of this our latter night!" She replied, "With love and good will!" It hath reached me, O auspicious King, the director, the right-guiding, lord of the rede which is benefiting and of deeds fair-seeming and worthy celebrating, that the Sultan enthroned the Sharper upon the throne of estate and went forth from him after abandoning all his women to him and assumed the garb of a Darwaysh who wandereth about the world and formally abdicated his dominion to his successor. But when the Sharper-king saw himself in this condition, he reflected and said to himself, "Summon thy whilome comrades and see whether they recognize thee or not." So he caused them be set before him and conversed with them; then, perceiving that none knew him he gifted them and sent them to gang their gait. And he ruled his realm and bade and forbade and gave and took away and was gracious and generous to each and every of his lieges; so that the people of that region who were his subjects blessed him and prayed for him. Such was the case with the Sharper; but as for

The Sultan who Fared Forth in the Habit of a Darwaysh,[1]

HE ceased not wayfaring, as become a wanderer, till he came to Cairo[2] city whose circuit was a march of two and a half days and

[1] W. M. MS. vol. iii. pp. 121-141. Scott, "The Adventures of the abdicated Sultan," pp. 18-19; including the "History of Mahummud, Sultan of Cairo," pp. 20-30.

[2] "Káhirah." I repeat my belief (Pilgrimage i. 171) that "Káhirah," whence our "Cairo" through the Italian corruption, means not *la victorieuse* (Mediant al Káhirah) as D'Herbelot has it; but City of Káhir or Mars the planet. It was so called because as Richardson informed the world (*sub voce*) it was founded in A.H. 358 (= A.D. 968) when the warlike planet was in the ascendant by the famous General Jauhar a Dalmatian renegade (not a "Greek slave") for the first of the Fatimite dynasty Al-Mu'izz li 'l-díni 'lláh.

which then was ruled by her own King Mohammed hight. He
found the folk in safety and prosperity and good ordinance; and
he solaced himself by strolling about the streets to the right and
left and he diverted his mind by considering the crowds and the
world of men contained in the capital, until he drew near the
palace when suddenly he sighted the Sultan returning from the
chase and from taking his pleasure. Seeing this the Darwaysh
retired to the wayside, and the King happening to glance in that
direction, saw him standing and discerned in him the signs of
former prosperity. So he said to one of his suite, "Take yon man
with thee and entertain him till I send for him." His bidding
being obeyed he entered the Palace and, when he had rested from
the fatigues of the way, he summoned the Fakír to the presence
and questioned him of his condition, saying, "Thou, from what
land art thou?" He responded, "O my lord, I am a beggar man;"
and the other rejoined, "There is no help but that thou tell me
what brought thee hither." The Darwaysh retorted, "O my
lord, this may not be save in privacy," and the other exclaimed,
"Be it so for thee." The twain then arose and repaired to a
retired room in the Palace and the Fakir recounted to the Sultan
all that had befallen him since the loss of his kingship and also
how he, a Sultan, had given up the throne of his realm and had
made himself a Darwaysh. The Sovran marvelled at his self-denial
in yielding up the royal estate and cried, "Laud be to Him who
degradeth and upraiseth, who honoureth and humbleth by the
wise ordinance of His All-might," presently adding, "O Darwaysh, I have passed through an adventure which is marvellous;
indeed 'tis one of the Wonders of the World[1] which I needs must
relate to thee nor from thee withhold aught thereof." And he
fell to telling——. And Shahrazad perceived the dawn of day
and fell silent and ceased saying her permitted say. Then quoth
her sister Dunyazad, "How sweet and tasteful is thy tale, O sister
mine, and enjoyable and delectable!" Quoth she, "And where
is this compared with that I would relate to you on the coming
night an the Sovran suffer me to survive?" Now when it was
the next night and that was

---

[1] According to Caussin de Perceval (père) in his translation of the "Contes Arabes,"
there are four wonders in the Moslem world: (1) the Pharos of Alexandria; (2) the Bridge
of Sanjia in Northern Syria; (3) The Church of Rohab (Edessa); and (4) the Amawi
Mosque of Damascus.

The Three Hundred and Forty-third Night,

DUNYAZAD said to her, "Allah upon thee, O my sister, an thou be other than sleepy, finish for us thy tale that we may cut short the watching of this our latter night!" She replied, "With love and good will!" It hath reached me, O auspicious King, the director, the right-guiding, lord of the rede which is benefiting and of deeds fair-seeming and worthy celebrating, that the King fell to telling the beggar man

The History of Mohammed, Sultan of Cairo.

I BEGAN my career in the world as a Darwaysh, an asker, owning naught of the comforts and conveniences of life, till at length, one day of the days, I became possessor of just ten silverlings[1] (and no more) which I resolved to expend upon myself. Accordingly I walked into the Bazar purposing to purchase somewhat of provaunt. While I was looking around, I espied a man passing by and leading in an iron chain a dog-faced baboon and crying "Haráj!"[2] this ape is for sale at the price of ten faddahs." The folk jibed at the man and jeered at his ape; but quoth I to myself, "Buy this beast and expend upon it the ten silverlings." Accordingly I drew near the seller and said to him, "Take these ten faddahs;" whereupon he took them and gave me the ape which I led to the cell wherein I dwelt. Then I opened the door and went in with my bargain but began debating in my mind what to do and said, "How shall I manage a meal for the baboon and myself?" While I was considering behold, the beast was suddenly transformed, and became a young man fair of favour who had no equal in loveliness and stature and symmetric grace, perfect as the moon at full on the fourteenth night; and he addressed me saying, "O Shaykh Mohammed, thou hast bought me with ten faddahs, being all thou hadst and art debating how we shall feed, I and thou." Quoth I, "What art thou?" and quoth he, "Query me no questions, concerning whatso thou shalt see, for good luck

---

[1] Arab. "Faddah," lit. = silver, because made of copper alloyed with nobler metal; the smallest Egyptian coin = Nuss (i.e. Nusf, or half a dirham) and the Turk. paráh. It is the fortieth of the piastre and may be assumed at the value of a quarter-farthing.

[2] This word, in Egypt. "Harág," is the cry with which the Dallál (broker) announces each sum bidden at an auction.

hath come to thee." Then he gave me an Ashrafi[1] and said,
"Take this piece of gold and fare thee forth to the Bazar and get
us somewhat to eat and drink." I took it from him and repairing
to the market purchased whatso food our case required; then returning to the cell set the victual before him and seated myself
by his side. So we ate our sufficiency and passed that night, I and
he, in the cell, and, when Allah caused the morn to dawn, he
said to me, "O man, this room is not suitable to us: hie thee and
hire a larger lodging." I replied, "To hear is to obey;" and, rising without stay or delay, went and took a room more roomy in
the upper part of the Wakálah.[2] Thither we removed, I and the
youth, and presently he gave me ten dinars more and said, "Go to
the Bazar and buy thee furniture as much as is wanted." Accordingly, I went forth and bought what he ordered and on my return
I found before him a bundle containing a suit of clothes suitable
for the Kings. These he gave to me desiring that I hie me to the
Hammam and don them after bathing, so I did his bidding and
washed and dressed myself and found in each pocket of the many
pockets an hundred gold pieces; and presently when I had donned
the dress I said to myself, "Am I dreaming or wide awake?"[3]
Then I returned to the youth in the room and when he saw me he
rose to his feet and commended my figure and seated me beside
him. Presently he brought up a bigger bundle and bade me take
it and repair to the Sultan of the City and at the same time ask
his daughter in marriage for myself.——And Shahrazad was surprised by the dawn of day and fell silent and ceased to say her
permitted say. Then quoth her sister Dunyazad, "How sweet is
thy story, O sister mine, and how enjoyable and delectable!"
Quoth she, "And where is this compared with that I would relate
to you on the coming night, an the Sovran suffer me to survive?"
Now when it was the next night and that was

The Three Hundred and Forty-fourth Night.

Dunyazad said to her, "Allah upon thee, O my sister, an thou
be other than sleepy, finish for us thy tale that we may cut short
the watching of this our latter night!" She replied, "With love

---

[1] The Portuguese Xerafim: Supplemental Nights, vol. iii. 166.
[2] A Khan or caravanserai: see vol. i. 266 and Pilgrimage i. 60.
[3] Arab. "Hilm" (vision) "au 'Ilm" (knowledge) a phrase peculiar to this MS.

and good will!" It hath reached me, O auspicious King, the
director, the right-guiding, lord of the rede which is benefiting
and of deeds fair-seeming and worthy celebrating, that the Sultan
of Cairo continued:[1]—So I took it and repaired with it to the
King of that city, and a slave whom the youth had bought bore
the bundle. Now when I approached the Palace I found there-
about the Chamberlains and Eunuchs and Lords of the Land: so I
drew near them and when they saw me in that suit they approved
my appearance and questioned me saying, "What be thy business
and what dost thou require?" I replied, "My wish is to have
audience of the King," and they rejoined, "Wait a little while till
we obtain for thee his permission." Then one of the ushers went
in and reported the matter to the Sultan who gave orders to
admit me; so the man came out and led me within and on entering
the presence I salamed to the Sovran and wished him welfare and
presently set before him the bundle, saying, "O King of the Age,
this be in the way of a gift which besitteth my station not thine
estate." The Sultan bade the package be spread out, and he
looked into it and saw a suit of royal apparel whose like he never
had owned. So he was astonished at the sight and said in his
mind, "By Allah, I possess naught like this, nor was I ever master
of so magnificent a garment;" presently adding, "It shall be
accepted, O Shaykh, but needs must thou have some want or
requisition from me." I replied, "O King of the Age, my wish is
to become thy connection through that lady concealed and pearl
unrevealed, thy daughter." When the Sultan heard these words,
he turned to his Wazir and said, "Counsel me as to what I should
do in the matter of this man?" Said he, "O King of the Age,
show him thy most precious stone and say him, 'An thou have
a jewel evening this one it shall be my daughter's marriage-
dowry.'" The King did as he was advised, whereat I was wild
with wonderment and asked him, "An I bring thee such a gem
wilt thou give me the Princess?" He answered, "Yea, verily!"
and I took my leave bearing with me the jewel to the young man
who was awaiting me in the room.[2] He enquired of me, "Hast

---

[1] The careless scribe forgets that the Sultan is speaking and here drops into the third
person. This "Enallage of persons" is, however, Koranic and therefore classical: Arab
critics aver that in such cases the "Hikáyah" (= literal reproduction of a discourse, etc.)
passes into an "Ikhbár" = mere account of the same discourse). See Al Mas'údi iii. 216.
I dare not reproduce this figure in English.

[2] Arab. "Auzah," the Pers. Oták and the Turk. Otah (vulg. "Oda" whence "Odalisque"),
a popular word in Egypt and Syria.

thou proposed for the Princess?" and I replied, "Yes: I have spoken with the Sultan concerning her, when he brought out this stone, saying to me, 'An thou have a jewel evening this one, it shall be my daughter's marriage-dowry;' nor hath the Sultan power to false his word." The youth rejoined, "This day I can do naught, but to-morrow (Inshallah!) I will bring thee ten jewels like it and these thou shalt carry and present to the Sovran." Accordingly when the morning dawned he arose and fared forth and after an hour or so he returned with ten gems which he gave me. I took them and repaired with them to the Sultan and, entering the presence, I presented to him all the ten. When he looked upon the precious stones he wondered at their brilliant water and turning to the Wazir again asked him how he should act in this matter. Replied the Minister, "O King of the Age, thou requiredst of him but one jewel and he hath brought thee ten; 'tis therefore only right and fair to give him thy daughter."——And Shahrazad perceived the dawn of day and fell silent and ceased saying her permitted say. Then quoth her sister Dunyazad, "How sweet and tasteful is thy tale, O sister mine, and enjoyable and delectable!" Quoth she, "And where is this compared with that I would relate to you on the coming night an the Sovran suffer me to survive?" Now when it was the next night and that was

The Three Hundred and Forty-fifth Night,

DUNYAZAD said to her, "Allah upon thee, O my sister, an thou be other than sleepy, finish for us thy tale that we may cut short the watching of this our latter night!" She replied, "With love and good will!" It hath reached me, O auspicious King, the director, the right-guiding, lord of the rede which is benefiting and of deeds fair-seeming and worthy celebrating, that the Minister said to the Monarch, "Give him thy daughter." Accordingly the Sultan summoned the Kazis and the Efendis[1] who wrote out the marriage-contract between me and the Princess. Then I returned to the youth who had remained in the room and told him all that had occurred when he said, " 'Twere best to conclude the

---

[1] Arab. "Al Afandiyah" showing the late date or reduction of the tale. The Turkish word derives from the Romaic Afentis (ἀφέντης) the corrupted O.G. αὐθέντης = an absolute commander, and "authentic." The word should not be written as usual "Effendi," but "Efendi," as Prof. Galland has been careful to do.

wedding-ceremony and pay the first visit to thy bride at once;
but thou shalt on no wise consummate the nuptials until I bid
thee go in unto her, after somewhat shall have been done by me."
"Hearing and obeying," replied I; and, when the night of going
in[1] came, I visited the Sultan's daughter but sat apart from her by
the side of the room during the first night and the second and the
third; nor did I approach her although every day her mother came
and asked her the usual question[2] and she answered, "He hath
never approached me." So she grieved with sore grief for that
'tis the wont of womankind, when a maid is married and her
groom goeth not in unto her, to deem that haply folk will attribute
it to some matter which is not wholly right. After the third
night the mother reported the case to her father who cried, "This
night except he abate her pucelage I will slay him!" The tidings
reached my bride who told all to me, so I repaired to the young
man and acquainted him therewith. He cried, "When thou shalt
visit her say, 'By Allah, I will not enjoy thee unless thou give
me the amulet-bracelet hanging to thy right shoulder.'" I replied,
"To hear is to obey;" and, when I went in to her at nightfall, I
asked her, "Dost thou really desire me to futter thee?" She
answered, "I do indeed;" so I rejoined, "Then give me the
amulet-bracelet hanging over thy right shoulder." She arose
forthright and unbound it and gave it to me, whereupon I bled
her of the hymeneal blood[3] and going to the young man gave him
the jewel. Then I returned to my bride and slept by her side till
the morning when I awoke and found myself lying outstreched
in my own caravanserai-cell. I was wonderstruck and asked myself, "Am I on wake or in a dream?" and I saw my whilome garments, the patched gabardine[4] and tattered shirt alone with my
little drum;[5] but the fine suit given to me by the youth was not

---

[1] Arab. "Al dakhlah"; repeatedly referred to in The Nights. The adventure is a replica of that in "Abu Mohammed hight Lazybones," vol. iv., pp. 171-174.

[2] Usual in the East, not in England, where some mothers are idiots enough not to tell their daughters what to expect on the wedding night. Hence too often unpleasant sur-prises, disgust and dislike. The most modern form is that of the chloroform'd bride upon whose pillow the bridegroom found a paper pinned and containing the words, "Mamma says you're to do what you like."

[3] Arab. "Akhaztu dam wajhhi há."

[4] Arab. "Dilk" more commonly "Khirkah," the tattered and pieced robe of a religious mendicant.

[5] Arab. "Darbálah." Scott (p. 24) must have read "Gharbálah" when he translated "A turban full of holes as a sieve." In classical Arabic the word is written "Darbalah," and seems to correspond with the Egyptian "Darábukkah," a tabor of wood or earthenware

on my body nor did I espy any sign of it anywhere. So with fire burning in my heart after what had befallen me, I wandered about crowded sites and lone spots and in my distraction I knew not what to do, whither to go or whence to come; when lo and behold! I found sitting in an unfrequented part of the street a Maghrabi,[1] a Barbary man, who had before him some written leaves and was casting omens for sundry bystanders. Seeing this state of things, I came forward and drew near him and made him a salam which he returned; then, after considering my features straitly, he exclaimed, "O Shaykh, hath that Accursed done it and torn thee from thy bride?" "Yes," I replied. Hereupon he said to me, "Wait a little while," and seated me beside him; then, as soon as the crowd dispersed he said, "O Shaykh, the baboon which thou boughtest for ten silver bits and which was presently transformed into a young man of Adam's sons, is not a human of the sons of Adam but a Jinni who is enamoured of the Princess thou didst wed. However, he could not approach her by reason of the charmed bracelet hanging from her right shoulder, where-fore he served thee this sleight and won it and now he still weareth it. But I will soon work his destruction to the end that Jinnkind and mankind may be at rest from his mischief; for he is one of the rebellious and misbegotten imps who break the law of our lord Solomon (upon whom be the Peace!)." Presently the Maghrabi took a leaf and wrote upon it as it were a book.——— And Shahrazad was surprised by the dawn of day and fell silent and ceased to say her permitted say. Then quoth her sister Dun-yazad, "How sweet is thy story, O sister mine, and how enjoy-able and delectable!" Quoth she, "And where is this compared with that I would relate to you on the coming night, an the Sov-ran suffer me to survive?" Now when it was the next night and that was

The Three Hundred and Forty-sixth Night,

DUNYAZAD said to her, "Allah upon thee, O my sister, an thou be other than sleepy, finish for us thy tale that we may cut short

---

figured by Lane (M.E. chapt. xviii.). It is, like the bowl, part of the regular Darwaysh's begging gear.

[1] Vulg. Maghribi. For this word see the story of Alaeddin, Supplem., vol. iii. 31. Ac-cording to Heron, "History of Maugraby," the people of Provence, Languedoc and Gascony use *Maugraby* as a term of cursing: *Maugrebleu* being used in other parts of France.

the watching of this our latter night!" She replied, "With love and good will!" It hath reached me, O auspicious King, the director, the right-guiding, lord of the rede which is benefiting and of deeds fair-seeming and worthy celebrating, that the Maghrabi wrote a writ and signed his name within and sealed it; after which he handed it to me saying, "O Shaykh, take this missive and hie thee herewith to a certain spot where thou must wait and observe those who pass by. Hearten thy heart and when thou shalt see approaching thee a man attended by a numerous train, present to him this scroll for 'tis he who will win for thee thy wish." I took the note from the Barbary man and fared forth to the place which he had described and ceased not faring till I reached it after travelling all that night and half the next day; then I sat down until darkness set in to await whatso might befal me. When a fourth part of the night had passed, a dazzling glare of lights suddenly appeared from afar advancing towards me; and as it shone nearer, I made out men bearing flambeaux[1] and lanthorns, also a train of attendants befitting the Kings. They looked on and considered me whilst my heart fluttered with fear, and I was in sore affright. But the procession defiled and drew off from before me, marching two after two, and presently appeared the chief cortège wherein was a Sultan[2] of the Jánn. As he neared me I heartened my heart and advanced and presented to him the letter which he, having halted, opened and read aloud; and it was:——"Be it known to thee, O Sultan of the Jann, that the bearer of this our epistle hath a need which thou must grant him by destroying his foe; and if opposition be offered by any we will do the opponent die. An thou fail to relieve him thou wilt know to seek from me relief for thyself." When the King of the Jann had read the writ and had mastered its meaning and its mysteries, he forthwith called out to one of his serjeants[3] who at once came forward and bade him bring into his presence without

---

[1] In text "Fanárát"; the Arab. plur. of the Pers. "Fanár" = a light-house, and here equiv. to the Mod. Gr. φανός, a lantern, the Egypt. "Fánús."

[2] This Sultan of the Jann preceded by sweepers, flag-bearers and tent-pitchers always appears in the form of second-sight called by Egyptians "Darb al Mandal" = striking the magic circle in which the enchanter sits when he conjures up spirits. Lane (M. E. chapt. xii.) first made the "Cairo Magician" famous in Europe, but Herklots and others had described a cognate practice in India many years before him.

[3] Arab. "Jáwúsh" for Cháwush (vulg. Chiaush) Turk. = an army serjeant, a herald or serjeant at arms; an apparitor or officer of the Court of Chancery (not a "Mace-bearer or Messenger," Scott). See vol. vii. 327.

delay such-and-such a Jinni who by his spells had wrought round the daughter of the Cairene Sultan. The messenger replied, "Hearing and obeying," and departed from him and disappearing was absent an hour or thereabouts; after which he and others returned with the Jinni and set him standing before the King who exclaimed, "Wherefore, O Accurst, hast thou wrought ill to this man and done on this wise and on that wise?" He replied, "O my lord, all came of my fondness for the Princess who wore a charm in her armlet which hindered my approaching her and therefore I made use of this man to effect my purpose. I became master of the talisman and won my wish but I love the maiden and never will I harm her." Now when the Sultan heard these words he said, "Thy case can be after one of two fashions only. Either return the armlet that the man may be reunited with his wife and she with her husband as whilome they were; or contrary me and I will command the headsman strike thy neck." Now when the Jinni heard this speech (and 'twas he who had assumed the semblance of a dog-faced baboon), he refused and was rebellious to the King and cried, "I will not return the armlet nor will I release the damsel, for none can possess her save myself." And having spoken in this way he attempted to flee. ——And Shahrazad perceived the dawn of day and fell silent and ceased saying her permitted say. Then quoth her sister Dunyazad, "How sweet and tasteful is thy tale, O sister mine, and enjoyable and delectable!" Quoth she, "And where is this compared with that I would relate to you on the coming night an the Sovran suffer me to survive?" Now when it was the next night and that was

The Three Hundred and Forty-seventh Night,

DUNYAZAD said to her, "Allah upon thee, O my sister, an thou be other than sleepy, finish for us thy tale, that we may cut short the watching of this our latter night!" She replied, "With love and good will!" It hath reached me, O auspicious King, the director, the right-guiding, lord of the rede which is benefiting and of deeds fair-seeming and worthy celebrating, that the Márid would fain have fled from before the King of the Jann, but the Sovran bade other Marids and more forceful arrest him; so they seized him and pinioned him and bound him in chains and collar and dragged him behind the King of the Jann till the latter had reached his place and had summoned him and had taken from him the armlet. Then the Sultan gave order for him to be slain and they slew him. When this was done, I prayed for the charm-armlet and I recovered it after the Marid's death; they also restored to me my fine suit. So I proceeded to the city which I entered, and as soon as the guards and courtiers saw me, they cried out for joy and said, "This is the son-in-law of the Sultan who was lost!" Hereat all the lieges hurried up to me and received me with high respect and greeted me. But after entering the Palace I proceeded forthright till I reached the apartment set apart by them for myself and my spouse whom I found in a deep sleep and stupefied, as it were; a condition in which she had lain ever since I took from her the talismanic armlet. So I replaced the jewel upon her right shoulder and she awoke and arose and ordered herself; whereat her father and family and the Lords of the Land and all the folk joyed with exceeding joy. After this we lived together in all happiness till the death of her sire who, having no son, named me his successor so that I became what I am. Now when the Darwaysh-Sultan heard all this he was astounded at what happeneth in this world of marvels and miracles; upon which I said to him, "O my brother wonder not; for whatso is predetermined shall perforce be carried out. But thou needs must become my Wazir; because thou art experienced in rule and governance and, since what time my sire-in-law the Sultan died, I have been perplexed in my plight being unable to find me a Minister who can administer the monarchy. So do thou become my Chief Counsellor in the realm." Thereupon the Darwaysh replied, "Hearkening and obedience." The Sultan then robed him in a sumptuous robe of honour and committed to him his seal-ring and all other matters pertinent to his office, at the same time setting apart for him a palace, spacious of corners, which he furnished with splendid furniture and wadded carpets and *vaiselle* and other such matters. So the Wazir took his seat of office and held a Divan or Council of State forthright and commanded and countermanded, and bade and forbade according as he saw just and equitable; and his fame for equity and justice was dispread abroad; insomuch that who ever had a cause or request or other business he would come to the Wazir for ordering whatso he deemed advisable. In this condition he continued for many years till, on a day of the days, the Sultan's mind was

depressed. Upon this he sent after the Minister who attended
at his bidding, when he said, "O Wazir, my heart is heavy!"
"Enter then," replied the Minister, "O King, into thy treasury
of jewels and rubies and turn them over in thy hands and thy
breast will be broadened." The Sultan did accordingly but it
took no effect upon his ennui; so he said, "O Wazir, I cannot win
free of this melancholic humour and nothing pleasureth me in my
palace; so let us fare forth, I and thou, in disguise." "Hearing is
obeying," quoth the Minister. The twain then retired into a
private chamber to shift their garb and habited themselves as
Darwayshes, the Darwayshes of Ajam-land, and went forth and
passed through the city right and left till they reached a Máristán, a hospital for lunatics.[1] Here they found two young men,
one reading the Koran[2] and the other hearkening to him, both
being in chains like men Jinn-mad; and the Sultan said in his
mind, "By Allah, this is a marvel-case," and bespake the men
asking, "Are ye really insane?" They answered saying, "No, by
Allah; we are not daft but so admirable are our adventures that
were they graven with needle-gravers upon the eye-corners they
had been warners to whoso would be warned." "What are
they?" quoth the King, and quoth they, "Each of us, by Allah,
hath his own story;" and presently he who had been reading
exclaimed, "O King of the Age, hear my tale."——And Shahrazad was surprised by the dawn of day and fell silent and ceased
to say her permitted say. Then quoth her sister Dunyazad,
"How sweet is thy story, O sister mine, and how enjoyable and
delectable!" Quoth she, "And where is this compared with that
I would relate to you on the coming night, an the Sovran suffer
me to survive?" Now when it was the next night, and that was

The Three Hundred and Forty-eighth Night,

DUNYAZAD said to her, "Allah upon thee, O my sister, an thou
be other than sleepy finish for us thy tale that we may cut short
the watching of this our latter night!" She replied, "With love
and good will!" It hath reached me, O auspicious King, the

---

1 Arab. from Persian "Bímáristán," a "sick-house," hospital, a mad-house: see vol. i. 288.
2 The text says only that "he was reading:" sub. the Holy Volume.

director, the right-guiding, lord of the rede which is benefiting
and of deeds fair-seeming and worthy celebrating, that the youth
began relating to the Sultan

The Story of the First Lunatic.[1]

I WAS a merchant and kept a shop wherein were Hindi goods of
all kinds and colours, highmost priced articles; and I sold and
bought with much profit. I continued in this condition a while
of time till one day of the days as I, according to my custom, was
sitting in my shop an old woman came up and gave me the good
morning and greeted me with the salam. I returned her salute
when she seated her upon the shopboard and asked me saying,
"O master, hast thou any pieces of choice Indian stuffs?" I
replied, "O my mistress, I have with me whatso thou wantest;"
and she rejoined, "Bring me forth one of them." Accordingly
I arose and fetched her a Hindi piece of the costliest price and
placed it in her hands. She took it and examining it was greatly
pleased by its beauty and presently said to me, "O my lord, for
how much is this?" Said I, "Five hundred dinars;" whereupon
she pulled forth her purse and counted out to me the five hundred
gold pieces. Then she took the stuff and went her ways; and I,
O our lord the Sultan, had sold to her for five hundred sequins a
piece of cloth worth at cost price three hundred and fifty gold
pieces. She came to me again, O my lord, on the next day and
asked me for another piece; so I rose up and brought her the
bundle and she paid me once more five hundred dinars: then she
took up her bargain and ganged her gait. She did the same, O my
lord, on the third and the fourth day and so on to the fifteenth,
taking a piece of stuff from me and paying me regularly five hundred golden pieces for each bargain. On the sixteenth behold,
she entered my shop as was her wont, but she found not her
purse; so she said to me, "O Khwájah,[2] I have left my purse at

---

[1] MS. vol. iii., pp. 142-168. Scott, "Story of the First Lunatic," pp. 31-44. Gauttier,
Histoire du Premier Fou, vol. vi. 187. It is identical with No. ii. of Chavis and Cazotte,
translated by C. de Perceval, *Le Bimaristan (i.e.* the Hospital), *ou Histoire du jeune Mar-
chand de Bagdad et de la Dame inconnue* (vol. viii. pp. 179-180). Heron terms it the
"Story of Haiechalbe (Ali Chelebi?) and the Unknown Lady," and the narrative is provided with a host of insipid and incorrect details, such as "A gentleman enjoying his pipe."
The *motif* of this tale is common in Arab. folk lore, and it first appears in the "Tale of Aziz
and Azízah," ii. 328. A third variant will occur further on.
[2] Spelt in vol. iii. 143 and elsewhere, "Khwájá" for "Khwájah."

home." Said I, "O my lady, an thou return 'tis well and if not thou art welcome to it." She sware she would not take it and I, on the other hand, sware her to carry it off as a token of love and friendship.[1] Thereupon debate fell between us, and I, O our lord the Sultan, had made muchel of money by her and, had she taken two pieces gratis, I would not have asked questions anent them. At last she cried, "O Khwajah, I have sworn an oath and thou hast sworn an oath, and we shall never agree except thou favour me by accompanying me to my house so thou mayest receive the value of the stuff, when neither of us will have been forsworn: therefore lock up thy shop lest anything be lost in thine absence." Accordingly I bolted my door and went with her, O our lord the Sultan, and we ceased not walking, conversing the while we walked, I and she, until we neared her abode when she pulled out a kerchief from her girdle and said, " 'Tis my desire to bind this over thine eyes." Quoth I, "For what cause?" and quoth she, "For that on our way be sundry houses whose doors are open and the women are sitting in the vestibules of their homes, so that haply thy glance may alight upon some one of them, married or maid, and thy heart become engaged in a love-affair and thou abide distraight, because in this quarter of the town be many fair faces, wives and virgins, who would fascinate even a religious, and wherefore we are alarmed for thy peace of mind." Upon this I said in myself, "By Allah, this old woman is able of advice;" and I consented to her requirement, when she bound the kerchief over my eyes and blindfolded me. Then we walked on till we came to the house she sought; and when she rapped with the door-ring a slave-girl came out and opening the door let us in. The old body then approached me and unbound the kerchief from over my eyes; whereupon I looked around me, holding myself to be a captive, and I found me in a mansion having sundry separate apartments in the wings and 'twas richly decorated resembling the palaces of the Kings.——— And Shahrazad perceived the dawn of day and fell silent and ceased saying her permitted say. Then quoth her sister Dunyazad, "How sweet and tasteful is thy tale, O sister mine, and how

---

[1] Arab. "Hubban li-raasik," = out of love for thy head, i.e. from affection for thee. Dr. Steingass finds it analogous with the Koranic "Hubban li 'llahi" (ii. 160), where it is joined with "Ashaddu" = stronger, as regards love to or for Allah, more Allah loving. But it can stand adverbially by itself = out of love for Allah, for Allah's sake.

enjoyable and delectable!" Quoth she, "And where is this compared with that I would relate to you on the coming night an
the Sovran suffer me to survive?" Now when it was the next
night and that was

The Three Hundred and Forty-ninth Night,

DUNYAZAD said to her "Allah upon thee, O my sister, an thou be
other than sleepy, finish for us thy tale that we may cut short the
watching of this our latter night!" She replied, "With love and
good will!" It hath reached me, O auspicious King, the director,
the right-guiding, lord of the rede which is benefiting and of
deeds fair-seeming and worthy celebrating, that the youth pursued:——By Allah, O our lord the Sultan, of that house I never
saw the fellow. She then bade me hide within a room and I did
her bidding in a corner place where beside me I beheld heaped
together and cast down in that private site all the pieces of stuff
which the ancient dame had purchased of me. Seeing this I
marvelled in my mind and lo! appeared two damsels as they were
moons and came down from an upper story till they stood on the
ground-floor; after which they cut a piece of cloth into twain and
each maiden took one and tucked up her sleeves. They then
sprinkled the court of that palace with water of the rose and of
the orange-flower,[1] wiping the surface with the cloth and rub-
ing it till it became as silver; after which the two girls retired
into an inner room and brought out some fifty chairs[2] which they
set down, and placed over each seat a rug[3] with cushions of
brocade. They then carried in a larger chair of gold and placed
upon it a carpet with cushions of orfrayed work and after a time
they withdrew. Presently, there descended from the staircase,
two following two, a host of maidens in number till they evened
the chairs and each one of them sat down upon her own, and at
last suddenly appeared a young lady in whose service were ten
damsels, and she walked up to and they seated her upon the
great chair. When I beheld her, O my lord the Sultan, my right

---

[1] Arab. "Zahr," lit. and generically a blossom; but often used in a specific sense throughout The Nights.

[2] Arab. "Kursí" here = a square wooden seat without back and used for sitting cross-
legged. See Suppl. vol. i. 9.

[3] Arab. "Sujjádah" = lit. a praying carpet, which Lane calls "Seggádeh."

senses left me and my wits fled me and I was astounded at her
loveliness and her stature and her symmetric grace as she swayed
to and fro in her pride of beauty and gladsome spirits amongst
those damsels and laughed and sported with them. At last she
cried aloud, "O mother mine!" when the ancient dame answered
her call and she asked her, "Hast thou brought the young man?"
The old woman replied, "Yes, he is present between thy hands;"
and the fair lady said, "Bring him hither to me!" But when I
heard these words I said to myself, "There is no Majesty and
there is no Might, save in Allah, the Glorious, the Great!
Doubtless when this damsel shall have discovered my being in
such hiding place she will bid them do me die." The old woman
then came forwards to me and led me before the young lady
seated on the great chair; and, when I stood in her presence, she
smiled in my face and saluted me with the salam and welcomed
me; after which she signed for a seat to be brought and when her
bidding was obeyed set it close beside her own. She then commanded me to sit and I seated me by her side.——And Shahrazad was surprised by the dawn of day and fell silent and ceased
to say her permitted say. Then quoth her sister Dunyazad,
"How sweet is thy story, O sister mine, and how enjoyable and
delectable!" Quoth she, "And where is this compared with that
I would relate to you on the coming night, an the Sovran suffer
me to survive?" Now when it was the next night and that was

The Three Hundred and Fiftieth Night,

DUNYAZAD said to her, "Allah upon thee, O my sister, an thou be
other than sleepy, finish for us thy tale that we may cut short the
watching of this our latter night!" She replied, "With love and
good will!" It hath reached me, O auspicious King, the director,
the right-guiding, lord of the rede which is benefiting and of
deeds fair-seeming and worthy celebrating, that the youth pursued:——She seated me beside her, O our lord the Sultan, and
fell to talking and joking with me for an hour or so when she said,
"O youth, what sayest thou of me and of my beauty and my
loveliness? Would Heaven that I could occupy thy thought and
please thee so that I might become to thee wife and thou be to me
man." When I heard these her words I replied, "O my lady,
how dare I presume to attain such honour? Indeed I do not

deem myself worthy to become a slave between thy hands."
Hereupon said she, "Nay, O young man, my words have in them
nor evasion nor alteration; so be not disheartened or fearful of
returning me a reply, for that my heart is fulfilled of thy love."
I now understood, O our lord the Sultan, that the damsel was
desirous of marrying me; but I could not conceive what was the
cause thereof or who could have given her intelligence concerning
me. She continued to enjoy herself in the gladsomest way till at
length I was emboldened to say to her, "O my lady, an thy words
to me be after the fashion of thy will, remember the proverb,
'When a kindness is to be done, this is its time.' " "By Allah, O
youth, there cannot be a more fortunate day than this present."
"O my lady, what shall I apportion to thee for dowry?" "The
dowry hath been paid to me in the value of the stuffs which thou
entrustedst to this ancient dame who is my mother!" "That
cannot suffice." "By Allah, naught shall be added; but, O youth,
'tis my intention forthright to send after the Kazi and his Assessors and I will choose me a trustee[1] that they may tie together us
twain without delay; and thou shalt come in to me this coming
evening. But all such things be upon one condition." "And
what may be thy condition?" "This, that thou swear never to
address or to draw near any woman save myself." And I, O our
lord the Sultan, being unmarried and eager to possess so beautiful
a bride, said to her, "This be thine; and I will never contrary thee
by word or by deed." She then sent to summon the Kazi and
his witnesses and appointed an agent; upon which they knotted
the knot. After the marriage ceremony was ended she ordered
coffee[2] and sherbets and gave somewhat of dirhams to the Kazi
and a robe of honour to her trustee; and this done, all went their
several ways. I was lost in astonishment and said in my mind,
"Do I dream or am I on wake?" She then commanded her
damsels to clear the Hammam-bath and cleanse it and fill it
afresh and get ready towels and waist-cloths and silken napkins[3]
and scented woods and essences, as virgin ambergris and ottars
and perfumes of vari-coloured hues and kinds. And when they
had executed her orders, she ordered the Eunuchry standing in

---

[1] Arab. "Wakíl," lit. = agent: here the woman's representative, corresponding roughly
with the man who gives away the bride amongst ourselves.
[2] The mention of coffee and sherbet, here and in the next page, makes the tale syn-
chronous with that of Ma'arúf or the xviith. century.
[3] The MS. writes "Zardakát" for "Zardakhán": see below.

her service to take me and bear me to the Bath, largessing each
one with a sumptuous dress. They led me into a Hammam which
had been made private and I saw a place tongue is powerless to
portray. And as we arrived there they spread vari-coloured carpets upon which I sat me down and doffed what clothing was
upon me: then I entered the hot rooms and smelt delicious scents
diffused from the sides of the hall, sandal-wood, Comorin lign-
aloes and other such fragrant substances. Here they came up to
me and seated me, lathering me with perfumed soaps and sham-
poo'd me till my body became silver-bright; when they fetched
the metal tasses and I washed with water luke-warm after which
they brought me cold water mingled with rose water and I
sprinkled it over me. After this they supplied me with silken
napkins and drying-towels of palm-fibre[1] wherewith I rubbed me
and then repaired to the cool room outside the calidarium[2] where
I found a royal dress. The Eunuchry arrayed me therein and
after fumigating me with the smoke of lign-aloes served up somewhat of confections[3] and coffee and sherbets of sundry sorts; so
I drank after eating the Ma'jún. About eventide I left the
Baths with all the Eunuchry in attendance on me and we walked
till we entered the Palace and they led me into a closet spread
with kingly carpets and cushions. And behold, she came up to
me attired in a new habit more sumptuous than that I had seen
her wearing erewhile.——And Shahrazad perceived the dawn
of day and fell silent and ceased saying her permitted say. Then
quoth her sister Dunyazad, "How sweet and tasteful is thy
tale, O sister mine, and enjoyable and delectable!" Quoth she,
"And where is this compared with that I would relate to you
on the coming night an the Sovran suffer me to survive?" Now
when it was the next night and that was

---

[1] Scott (p. 36) has "mahazzim (for maházim), al Zerdukkaut (for al-Zardakhán)" and
"munnaskif (for manáshif) al fillfillee." Of the former he notes (p. 414) "What this
composition is I cannot define: it may be translated compound of saffron, yoke of egg or
of yellowish drugs." He evidently confounds it with the Pers. Zard-i-Kháyah = yoke of
egg. Of the second he says "compound of peppers, red, white and black." Lane (The
Nights, vol. i. p. 8) is somewhat scandalised at such misrepresentation; translating the
first "apron-napkins of thick silk," and the second "drying towels of Lif or palm-fibre,"
further suggesting that the text may have dropped a conjunction = drying towels and
fibre.

[2] Arab. "Líwán al-barrání," lit. = the outer bench in the "Maslakh" or apodyterium.

[3] Arab. "Ma'jún," pop. applied to an electuary of Bhang (*Cannabis sativa*): it is the
"Maagoon" sold by the "Maagungee" of Lane (M.E. chapt. xv.). Here, however, the term
may be used in the sense of "confections" generally, the sweetmeats eaten by way of
restoratives in the Bath.

The Three Hundred and Fifty-first Night,

DUNYAZAD said to her, "Allah upon thee, O my sister, an thou be other than sleepy, finish for us thy tale that we may cut short the watching of this our latter night!" She replied, "With love and good will!" It hath reached me, O auspicious King, the director, the right-guiding, lord of the rede which is benefiting and of deeds fair-seeming and worthy celebrating, that the youth continued:——And I, O our lord the Sultan, went into the closet and behold, she met me wearing a habit of the most sumptuous: so when I sighted her she seemed to me from the richness of her ornaments like an enchanted hoard wherefrom the talisman had been newly removed. She sat down beside me and bent lovingly over me and I rose up for I could no longer contain my passion and wrought that work which was to be worked.[1] Presently she again disappeared but soon returned in vestments even richer than the last and she did with me as before and I embraced her once more. In short, O our lord the Sultan, we ceased not dwelling together, I and she, in joyaunce and enjoyment, laughter and disport and delicious converse for a space of twenty days. At the end of this time I called to mind my lady-mother, and said to the dame I had espoused, "O my lady, 'tis long since I have been absent from home and 'tis long since my parent hath seen me or wotteth aught concerning me: needs must she be pining and grieving for my sake. So do thou give me leave to visit her and look after my mother and also after my shop." Quoth she, "No harm in that: thou mayst visit thy mother daily and busy thyself about thy shop-business; but this ancient dame (my mother) is she who must lead thee out and bring thee back." Whereto I replied, " 'Tis well." Upon this the old woman came in and tied a kerchief over my eyes according to custom and fared forth with me till we reached the spot where she had been wont to remove the bandage. Here she unbound it saying, "We'll expect thee to-morrow about noontide and when thou comest

---

[1] He speaks of taking her maidenhead as if it were porter's work and so defloration was regarded by many ancient peoples. The old Nilotes incised the hymen before congress; the Phœnicians, according to Saint Athanasius, made a slave of the husband's abate it. The American Chibchas and Caribs looked upon virginity as a reproach, proving that the maiden had never inspired love. For these and other examples see p. 72, chap. iii. "L'Amour dans l'Humanité," by P. Mantegazza, a civilised and unprejudiced traveller.

to this place, thou shalt see me awaiting thee." I left her and
repaired to my mother whom I found grieving and weeping at
my absence; and upon seeing me she rose up and threw her
arms round my neck with tears of joy. I said, "Weep not, O my
mother, for the cause of my absence hath been a certain matter
which be thus and thus." I then related to her my adventure and
she on hearing it was rejoiced thereby and exclaimed, "O my son,
may Allah give thee gladness; but I pray thee solace me[1] at least
every two days with a visit that my longing for thee may be
satisfied." I replied, "This shall be done;" and thenceforth, O
our lord the Sultan, I went to my shop and busied myself as was
my wont till noontide, when I returned to the place appointed
and found the old woman awaiting me. Nor did I ever fare forth
from the mansion without her binding my eyes with the kerchief
which she loosed only when we reached my own house; and
whenever I asked her of this she would answer, "On our way be
sundry houses whose doors are open and the women sitting in the
vestibules of their homes, so that haply thy glance may alight
upon some one of them, matron or maid: all sniff up love like
water,[2] and we fear for thee lest thy heart be netted in the net
of amours." For thirty days, a whole month, I continued to go
and come after this fashion but, O our lord the Sultan, at all
times and tides I was drowned in thought and wondered in my
mind, saying, "What chance caused me forgather with this
damsel? What made me marry her? Whence this wealth which
is under her hand? How came I to win union with her?" For
I knew not the cause of all this. Now, on a day of the days, I
found an opportunity of being private with one of her black slave
girls[3] and questioned her of all these matters that concerned her
mistress. She replied, "O my lord, the history of my lady is
marvellous; but I dare not relate it to thee in fear lest she hear
thereof and do me die." So I said to her, "By Allah, O handmaid of good, an thou wilt say me sooth I will veil it darkly for in
the keeping of secrets there is none like myself: nor will I reveal it
at any time." Then I took oath of secrecy when she said, "O
my lord,"——And Shahrazad was surprised by the dawn of day
and fell silent and ceased to say her permitted say. Then quoth

---

[1] Arab. "Zill," lit. "shadow me."

[2] Arab. "Istinshák," one of the items of the "Wuzú" or lesser ablution: see vol. v. 198.

[3] In Chavis her name is "Zaliza" and she had "conceived an unhappy passion" for her master, to whom she "declared her sentiments without reserve."

her sister Dunyazad, "How sweet is thy story, O sister mine, and how enjoyable and delectable!" Quoth she, "And where is this compared with that I would relate to you on the coming night, an the Sovran suffer me to survive?" Now when it was the next night and that was

The Three Hundred and Fifty-second Night,

DUNYAZAD said to her, "Allah upon thee, O my sister, an thou be other than sleepy, finish for us thy tale that we may cut short the watching of this our latter night!" She replied, "With love and good will!" It hath reached me, O auspicious King, the director, the right-guiding, lord of the rede which is benefiting and of deeds fair-seeming and worthy celebrating, that the youth continued:——Then the handmaiden said to me, "O my lord, my lady went forth one day of the days to the Hammam with the object of pleasuring and of diverting herself, for which purpose she made goodly preparation including gifts and presents,[1] matters worth a mint of money.[2] After leaving the baths she set out upon an excursion to eat the noon-day meal in a flower garden where she enjoyed herself with exceeding joy and enjoyment, eating and drinking till the evening; and when she designed to depart she collected the fragments of the feast and distributed them amongst the mean and the mesquin. On her return she passed through the Bazar-street wherein standeth thy shop, and it was a Friday when thou wast sitting, adorned with thy finest dress, in converse with the nearest neighbour. And suddenly as she fared by, she beheld thee in such state and her heart was stricken with sore stroke of love albeit none of us observed her condition and what affection she had conceived for thee. However, no sooner had she reached her palace than her melancholy began to grow upon her with groans and her cark and care, and her colour left her: she ate and drank little and less and her sleep forsook her and her frame was sorely enfeebled till at last she took to her bed. Upon this her mother went to summon a learned man[3] or a mediciner that he might consider the condition of her

---

[1] Arab. "Armaghánát," the Arab. plur. of "Armaghán," Pers. = a present.
[2] In the text, "jumlatun min al-mál," which Scott apparently reads "Hamlat al-jamal" and translates (p. 38) "a camel's load of treasure."
[3] The learned man was to exorcise some possible "evil spirit" or "the eye," a superstition which seems to have begun, like all others, with the ancient Egyptians.

daughter and what sickness had gotten about her: she was absent for an hour and returned with an ancient dame who took
seat beside her and putting forth her hand felt the patient's
pulse. But she could perceive in her no bodily ailment or pain,
upon which the old woman understood her case, but she durst
not bespeak her of it nor mention to her mother that the girl's
heart was distraught by love. So she said, 'There is no harm to
thee! and (Inshallah!) to-morrow I will return hither to thee and
bring with me a certain medicine.' She then went forth from us
and leading the mother to a place apart, said to her, 'O my lady,
Allah upon thee, pardon me for whatso I shall mention and be
thou convinced that my words are true and keep them secret nor
divulge them to any.' The other replied, 'Say on and fear not
for aught which hath become manifest to thee of my daughter's
unweal: haply Allah will vouchsafe welfare.' She rejoined,
'Verily, thy daughter hath no bodily disorder or malady of the
disease kind but she is in love and there can be no cure for her
save union with her beloved.' Quoth the mother, 'And how
about the coming of her sweetheart? This is a matter which may
not be managed except thou show us some contrivance whereby
to bring this youth hither and marry him to her. But contrivance is with Allah.' Then the old lady went her ways forthright
and the girl's mother sought her daughter and said to her after
kindly fashion, 'O my child, as for thee thy disorder is a secret
and not a bodily disease. Tell me of him thou requirest and fear
naught from me; belike Allah will open to us the gate of contrivance whereby thou shalt win to thy wish.' Now when the
maiden heard these words she was abashed before her parent and
kept silence, being ashamed to speak; nor would she return any
reply for the space of twenty days. But during this term her
distraction increased and her mother ceased not to repeat the
same words, time after time, till it became manifest to the parent
that the daughter was madly in love with a young man; so at
last quoth she, 'Describe him to me.' Quoth the other, 'O
mother mine, indeed he is young of years and fair of favour; also
he woneth in such a Bazar, methinks on its southern side.'
Therewith the dame arose without stay or delay and fared forth
to find the young man and 'tis thyself, O youth! And when the
mother saw thee she took from thee a piece of cloth and brought
it to her daughter and promised thou shouldst visit her. Thence-
forwards she ceased not repeating her calls to thee for the period

thou wottest well until by her cunning she brought thee hither;
and that happened which happened and thou didst take the
daughter to wife. Such is her tale and beware lest thou reveal
my disclosure." "No, by Allah," replied I. Then the lunatic
resumed speaking to the Sultan: —— O my lord, I continued to
cohabit with her for the space of one month, going daily to see
my mother and to sell in my shop and I returned to my wife every
evening blindfolded and guided as usual by my mother-in-law.
Now one day of the days as I was sitting at my business, a damsel
came into the Bazar-street. —— And Shahrazad perceived the
dawn of day and fell silent and ceased saying her permitted say.
Then quoth her sister Dunyazad, "How sweet and tasteful is thy
tale, O sister mine, and enjoyable and delectable!" Quoth she,
"And where is this compared with that I would relate to you on
the coming night an the Sovran suffer me to survive?" Now
when it was the next night and that was

The Three Hundred and Fifty-third Night,

DUNYAZAD said to her, "Allah upon thee, O my sister, an thou be
other than sleepy, finish for us thy tale that we may cut short the
watching of this our latter night!" She replied, "With love
and good will!" It hath reached me, O auspicious King, the
director, the right-guiding, lord of the rede which is benefiting
and of deeds fair-seeming and worthy celebrating, that the youth
continued: —— A damsel came into the Bazar-street bearing the
image of a cock made of precious ore and crusted with pearls and
rubies and other gems; and she offered it to the goodmen[1] of the
market for sale. So they opened the biddings at five hundred
dinars and they ceased not contending[2] thereanent till the price
went up to nine hundred and fifty gold pieces. All this time and
I looked on nor did I interfere by speaking a syllable or by adding
to the biddings a single bit of gold. At last, when none would
offer aught more, the girl came up to me and said, "O my lord,
all the gentlemen have increased their biddings for the cock; but
thou hast neither bidden nor heartened my heart by one kind

---

[1] The MS., I have said, always writes "Khwájá" instead of "Khwájah" (plur. "Khwá-
ját"): for this word, the modern Egyptian "Howájah," see vol. vi. 46. Here it corresponds
with our "goodman."

[2] Arab. "Yatazáwadú" = increasing.

word." Quoth I, "I have no need thereof;" and quoth she, "By Allah, needs must thou bid somewhat more than the others." I replied, "Since there is no help for it, I will add fifty dinars which will fill up the thousand." She rejoined, "Allah gar thee gain!"[1] So I fared into my shop to fetch the money, saying in my mind, "I will present this curiosity to my Harim: haply 'twill pleasure her." But when I was about, O my lord the Sultan, to count out the thousand ducats, the damsel would not accept aught of me but said, "I have a request to make of thee, O youth! to wit, that I may take one kiss from thy cheek." I asked her, "For what purpose?" and she answered, "I want one kiss of thy cheek which shall be the price of my cock, for I need of thee naught else." I thought to myself, "By Allah, a single kiss of my cheek for the value of a thousand sequins were an easy price;" and I gave my consent thereto, O my lord. Then she came up to me and leaned over me and bussed my cheek, but after the kiss she bit me with a bite which left its mark:[2] then she gave me the cock and went her ways in haste. Now when it was noon I made for my wife's house and came upon the old woman awaiting me at the customed stead and she bound the kerchief over my eyes and after blindfolding them fared with me till we reached our home when she unbound it. I found my wife sitting in the saloon dressed from head to foot in cramoisy[3] and with an ireful face, whereupon I said to myself, "O Saviour,[4] save me!" I then went up to her and took out the cock which was covered with pearls and rubies, thinking that her evil humour would vanish at the sight of it and said, "O my lady, accept this cock for 'tis curious and admirable to look upon; and I bought it to pleasure thee." She put forth her hand and taking it from me examined it by turning it rightwards and leftwards; then exclaimed, "Didst thou in very sooth buy this on my account?" Replied I, "By Allah, O my lady, I bought it for thee at a thousand gold pieces." Hereupon she shook her head at me, O my lord the Sultan, and cried out after a long look at my face, "What meaneth that bite on thy cheek?"

---

[1] By which she accepted the offer.

[2] This incident has already occurred in the tale of the Portress (Second Lady of Baghdad, vol. i. 179), but here the consequences are not so tragical. In Chavis the vulgar cock becomes "a golden Censer ornamented with diamonds, to be sold for two thousand sequins" (each = 9 shill.).

[3] A royal sign of wrath generally denoting torture and death. See vols. iv. 72; vi. 250.

[4] Arab. "Yá Sallám," addressed to Allah.

Then with a loud and angry voice she called to her women who
came down the stairs forthright bearing the body of a young girl
with the head cut off and set upon the middle of the corpse;[1] and
I looked and behold, it was the head of the damsel who had sold
me the cock for a kiss and who had bitten my cheek. Now my
wife had sent her with the toy by way of trick, saying to her,
"Let us try this youth whom I have wedded and see if he hold
himself bound by his plighted word and pact or if he be false
and foul." But of all this I knew naught. Then she cried a
second cry and behold, up came three handmaids bearing with
them three cocks like that which I had brought for her and she
said, "Thou bringest me this one cock when I have these three
cocks; but inasmuch as, O youth, thou hast broken the covenant
that was between me and thee, I want thee no more: go forth!
wend thy ways forthright!" And she raged at me and cried to
her mother, "Take him away!"[2] —— And Shahrazad was surprised by the dawn of day and fell silent and ceased to say her
permitted say. Then quoth her sister Dunyazad, "How sweet is
thy story, O sister mine, and how enjoyable and delectable!"
Quoth she, "And where is this compared with that I would
relate to you on the coming night, an the Sovran suffer me to
survive?" Now when it was the next night and that was

The Three Hundred and Fifty-fourth Night,

DUNYAZAD said to her, "Allah upon thee, O my sister, an thou
be other than sleepy, finish for us thy tale that we may cut short
the watching of this our latter night!" She replied, "With love
and good will!" It hath reached me, O auspicious King, the
director, the right-guiding, lord of the rede which is benefiting and
of deeds fair-seeming and worthy celebrating, that the Youth
continued to the King: —— Hereupon the old woman, O my
lord, hent me by the hand and bound the kerchief over my eyes

---

[1] Here more is meant than meets the eye. When a Moslem's head was struck off, in
the days of the Caliphate, it was placed under his armpit, whereas that of a Jew or a Christian was set between his legs, close to the seat of dishonour.

[2] In Chavis and Cazotte the lady calls to "Morigen, her first eunuch, and says, Cut off
his head!" Then she takes a theorbo and "composed the following couplets" — of which
the first may suffice:

> Since my swain unfaithful proves,
> Let him go to her he loves, etc., etc.

as was her wont and led me to the customed place when she loosed the bandage saying, "Begone!" and disappeared. But I, O my lord, became like a madman and ran through the streets as one frantic crying, "Ah her loveliness! Ah her stature! Ah her perfect grace! Ah her ornaments!" Hereupon the folk seeing me and hearing me say these words shouted out, "Yonder is a lunatic;" so they seized me perforce and jailed me in the mad-house as thou hast seen me, O our lord the Sultan. They say, "This man is Jinn-mad;" but, by Allah, I am no maniac, O my lord, and such is my tale. Hereat the King marvelled and bowed his brow groundwards for a while in deep thought over this affair: then he raised his head and turning to his Minister said, "O Wazir, by the truth of Him who made me ruler of this realm, except thou discover the damsel who married this youth, thy head shall pay forfeit." The Wazir was consterned to hear the case of the young man; but he could not disobey the royal com-mandment so he said, "Allow me three days of delay, O our lord the Sultan;" and to this much of grace the King consented. Then the Wazir craved dismissal and would have taken the Youth with him; when the Sultan cried, "As soon as thou shalt have hit upon the house, the young man will go into it and come forth it like other folk." He replied, "Hearkening and obedience." So he took the Youth and went out with aching head and giddy as a drunken man, perplexed and unknowing whither he should wend; and he threaded the city streets from right to left and from east to west, tarrying at times that he might privily ques-tion the folk. But naught discovered himself to him and he made certain of death. In this condition he continued for two days and the third till noontide, when he devised him a device and said to the Youth, "Knowest thou the spot where the old woman was wont to blindfold thine eyes?" He replied, "Yes." So the Minister walked on with him till the young man ex-claimed, "Here, 'tis this!"[1] The Wazir then said, "O Youth, knowest thou the door-ring wherewith she was wont to rap and canst thou distinguish its sound?" He said, "I can." Accord-ingly, the Wazir took him and went the round of all the houses in that quarter and rapped with every door-ring asking him, "Is't this?" and he would answer, "No." And the twain ceased not to do after such fashion until they came to the door where

---

[1] The device has already occurred in "Ali Baba."

the appointment had taken place without risk threatened;[1] and
the Wazir knocked hard at it and the Youth, hearing the knock,
exclaimed, "O my lord, verily this be the ring without question
or doubt or uncertainty." So the Minister knocked again with
the same knocker and the slave-girls threw open the door and the
Wazir, entering with the Youth, found that the palace belonged
to the daughter of the Sultan who had been succeeded by his
liege lord.[2] But when the Princess saw the Minister together
with her spouse, she adorned herself and came down from the
Harem and salam'd to him. Thereupon he asked her, "What
hath been thy business with this young man?" So she told him
her tale from first to last and he said, "O my lady, the King commandeth that he enter and quit the premises as before and that
he come hither without his eyes being bandaged with the kerchief." She obeyed and said, "The commandments of our lord
the Sultan shall be carried out." Such was the history of that
youth whom the Sultan heard reading the Koran in the Máristán,
the public madhouse: but as regards the second Lunatic who sat
listening, the Sultan asked him, "And thou, the other, what be
thy tale?" So he began to relate the

Story of the Second Lunatic.[3]

"O MY LORD," quoth the young man, "my case is marvellous, and
haply thou wilt desire me to relate it in order continuous;" and
quoth the Sultan, "Let me hear it." —— And Shahrazad perceived the dawn of day and fell silent and ceased saying her
permitted say. Then quoth her sister Dunyazad, "How sweet
and tasteful is thy tale, O sister mine, and enjoyable and delectable!" Quoth she, "And where is this compared with that
I would relate to you on the coming night an the Sovran suffer
me to survive?" Now when it was the next night and that was

---

[1] Arab. "Al-ma'húd min ghayr wa'd."

[2] In Chavis and Cazotte the king is Harun al-Rashid and the masterful young person
proves to be Zeraida, the favourite daughter of Ja'afar Bermaki, whilst the go-between
is not the young lady's mother but Nemana, an old governess. The over-jealous husband
in the Second Lady of Baghdad (vol. i. 179) is Al-Amin, son and heir of the Caliph Harun
al-Rashid.

[3] Vol. iii. pp. 168–179; and Scott's "Story of the Second Lunatic," pp. 45–51. The
name is absurdly given as the youth was anything but a lunatic; but this is Arab symme-
tromania. The tale is virtually the same as "Women's Wiles," in Supplemental Nights,
vol. ii. 99–107.

The Three Hundred and Fifty-fifth Night,

DUNYAZAD said to her, "Allah upon thee, O my sister, an thou be other than sleepy, finish for us thy tale that we may cut short the watching of this our latter night!" She replied, "With love and good will!" It hath reached me, O auspicious King, the director, the right-guiding, lord of the rede which is benefiting and of deeds fair-seeming and worthy celebrating, that the second youth said: —— O my lord the Sultan, I am by calling a merchant man and none of the guild was younger, I having just entered my sixteenth year. Like my fellows I sold and bought in the Bazar every day till, one day of the days, a damsel came up to me and drew near and handed to me a paper which I opened; and behold, it was full of verses and odes in praise of myself, and the end of the letter contained the woman's name professing to be enamoured of me. When I read it I came down from my shop-board, in my folly and ignorance, and putting forth my hand seized the girl and beat her till she swooned away.[1] After this I let her loose and she went her ways and then I fell into a brown study saying to myself, "Would Heaven I wot whether the girl be without relations or if she have kith and kin to whom she may complain and they will come and bastinado me." And, O our lord the Sultan, I repented of what I had done whenas repentance availed me naught and this lasted me for twenty days. At the end of that time as I was sitting in my shop according to my custom, behold, a young lady entered and she was sumptuously clad and sweetly scented and she was even as the moon in its fullness on the fourteenth night. When I gazed upon her my wits fled and my sane senses and right judgment forsook me and I was incapable of attending to aught save herself. She then came up and said, "O youth, hast thou by thee a variety of metal ornaments?" and said I, "O my lady, of all kinds thou canst possibly require." Hereupon she wished to see some anklets which I brought out for her, when she put forth her feet to me and showing me the calves of her legs said, "O my lord, try them on me." This I did. Then she asked for a necklace[2] and I pro-

---

[1] This forward movement on the part of the fair one is held to be very insulting by the modest Moslem. This incident is wanting in "Women's Wiles."

[2] Arab. "Labbah," usually the part of the throat where ornaments are hung or camels are stabbed.

duced one when she unveiled her bosom and said, "Take its
measure on me:" so I set it upon her and she said, "I want a
fine pair of bracelets," and I brought to her a pair when, extend-
ing her hands and displaying her wrists to me she said, "Put them
on me." I did so and presently she asked me, "What may be the
price of all these?" when I exclaimed, "O my lady, accept them
from me in free gift;" and this was of the excess of my love to her,
O King of the Age, and my being wholly absorbed in her. Then
quoth I to her, "O my lady, whose daughter art thou?" and quoth
she, "I am the daughter of the Shaykh al-Islám."[1] I replied,
"My wish is to ask thee in marriage of thy father," and she
rejoined, " 'Tis well: but, O youth, I would have thee know that
when thou askest me from my sire he will say, 'I have but one
daughter and she is a cripple and deformed even as Satíh was.'[2]
Do thou, however, make answer that thou art contented to accept
her and if he offer any remonstrance cry, 'I'm content, content!' " I then enquired, "When shall that be?" and she replied,
"Tomorrow about undurn hour[3] come to our house and thou
wilt find my sire, the Shaykh al-Islam, sitting with his companions and intimates. Then ask me to wife." So we agreed
upon this counsel and on the next day, O our lord the Sultan, I
went with several of my comrades and we repaired, I and they,
to the house of the Shaykh al-Islam, whom I found sitting with
sundry Grandees about him. We made our salams which they
returned and they welcomed us and all entered into friendly and
familiar conversation. When it was time for the noon-meal the
tablecloth[4] was spread and they invited us to join them, so we
dined with them and after dinner drank coffee. I then stood up
saying, "O my lord, I am come hither to sue and solicit thee for
the lady concealed and the pearl unrevealed, thy daughter."
But when the Shaykh al-Islam heard from me these words he
bowed his head for awhile groundwards —— And Shahrazad
was surprised by the dawn of day and fell silent and ceased to
say her permitted say. Then quoth her sister Dunyazad, "How

---

[1] The chief of the Moslem Church. For the origin of the office and its date (A.D. 1453)
see vols. ix. 289, and x. 81.
[2] Arab. "Satíhah" = a she-Satíh: this seer was a headless and neckless body, with face
in breast, lacking members and lying prostrate on the ground. His fellow, "Shikk," was a
half-man, and both foretold the divine mission of Mohammed. (Ibn Khall. i. 487.)
[3] Arab. "Wakt al-Zuhà;" the division of time between sunrise and midday.
[4] In the text "Sufrah" = the cloth: see vol. i. 178, etc.

sweet is thy story, O sister mine, and how enjoyable and delectable!" Quoth she, "And where is this compared with that
I would relate to you on the coming night, an the Sovran suffer
me to survive?" Now when it was the next night and that was

The Three Hundred and Fifty-sixth Night,

DUNYAZAD said to her, "Allah upon thee, O my sister, an thou be
other than sleepy, finish for us thy tale that we may cut short the
watching of this our latter night!" She replied, "With love
and good will!" It hath reached me, O auspicious King, the
director, the right-guiding, lord of the rede which is benefiting
and of deeds fair-seeming and worthy celebrating, that the youth
resumed: —— Now when the Shaykh al-Islam heard from me
those words he bowed his brow groundwards for a while in deep
thought concerning the case of his daughter who was a cripple
and wondrously deformed. For the damsel who had told me of
her had played me a trick and served me a sleight, I all the time
knowing nothing about her guile. Presently he raised his head
and said to me, "By Allah, O my son, I have a daughter but she
is helpless." Quoth I, "I am content;" and quoth he, "An thou
take her to wife after this description, 'tis on express condition
that she be not removed from my house and thou also shalt pay
her the first visit and cohabit with her in my home." I replied,
"To hear is to obey;" being confident, O King of the Age, that
she was the damsel who had visited my shop and whom I had
seen with my own eyes. Thereupon the Shaykh al-Islam
married his daughter to me and I said in my mind, "By Allah,
is it possible that I am become master of this damsel and shall
enjoy to my full her beauty and loveliness?" But when night
fell they led me in procession to the chamber of my bride;
and when I beheld her I found her as hideous as her father had
described her, a deformed cripple. At that moment all manner
of cares mounted my back and I was full of fury and groaned
with grief from the core of my heart; but I could not say a
word, for that I had accepted her to wife of my own free will
and had declared myself contented in presence of her sire. So
I took seat silently in a corner of the room and my bride in
another, because I could not bring myself to approach her, she
being unfit for the carnal company of man and my soul could not

accept cohabitation with her. And at dawntide, O my lord the
Sultan, I left the house and went to my shop which I opened
according to custom and sat down with my head dizzy like one
drunken without wine; when lo! there appeared before me the
young lady who had caused happen to me that mishap. She came
up and salam'd to me but I arose with sullenness and abused her
and cried, "Wherefore, O my lady, hast thou put upon me such
a piece of work?" She replied, "O miserable,[1] recollect such a
day when I brought thee a letter and thou after reading it didst
come down from thy shop and didst seize me and didst trounce
me and didst drive me away." I replied, "O my lady, prithee
pardon me for I am a true penitent;" and I ceased not to soften
her with soothing[2] words and promised her all weal if she would
but forgive me. At last she deigned excuse me and said, "There
is no harm for thee; and, as I have netted thee, so will I unmesh
thee." I replied, "Allah! Allah![3] O my lady, I am under thy
safeguard;" and she rejoined, "Hie thee to the Aghá of the
Janákilah,[4] the gypsies, give him fifty piastres and say him,
'We desire thee to furnish us with a father and a mother and
cousins and kith and kin, and do thou charge them to say of me,
This is our cousin and our blood relation.' Then let him send
them all to the house of the Shaykh al-Islam and repair thither
himself together with his followers, a party of drummers and a
parcel of pipers. When they enter his house and the Shaykh
shall perceive them and exclaim, 'What's this we've here?' let
the Agha reply, 'O my lord, we be kinsmen with thy son-in-law
and we are come to gladden his marriage with thy daughter and
to make merry with him.' He will exclaim, 'Is this thy son a
gypsey musician?' and do thou explain, saying, 'Aye, verily I am
a Jankali;' and he will cry out to thee, 'O dog, thou art a gypsey
and yet durst thou marry the daughter of the Shaykh al-Islam?'
Then do thou make answer, 'O my lord, 'twas my ambition to be
ennobled by thine alliance and I have espoused thy daughter
only that the mean name of Jankali may pass away from me and

---

[1] Arab. "Ya Tinjír," lit. = O Kettle.

[2] Arab. "Tari," lit. = wet, with its concomitant suggestion, soft and pleasant like
desert-rain.

[3] Here meaning "Haste, haste!" See vol. i. 46.

[4] The chief man (Aghá) of the Gypsies, the Jink of Egypt whom Turkish soldiers call
Ghiovendé, a race of singers and dancers; in fact professional Nautch-girls. See p. 222,
"Account of the Gypsies of India," by David MacRitchie (London, K. Paul, 1886), a
most useful manual.

that I may be under the skirt of thy protection.'" Hereat, O my
lord the Sultan, I arose without stay and delay and did as the
damsel bade me and agreed with the Chiefs of the Gypsies for
fifty piastres.[1] On the second day about noon lo and behold!
all the Janákilah met before the house of the Shaykh al-Islam
and they, a-tom-toming and a-piping and a-dancing, crowded
into the courtyard of the mansion. —— And Shahrazad perceived the dawn of day and fell silent and ceased saying her
permitted say. Then quoth her sister Dunyazad, "How sweet
and tasteful is thy tale, O sister mine, and enjoyable and delectable!" Quoth she, "And where is this compared with that
I would relate to you on the coming night an the Sovran suffer me
to survive?" Now when it was the next night and that was

The Three Hundred and Fifty-seventh Night,

DUNYAZAD said to her, "Allah upon thee, O my sister, an thou
be other than sleepy, finish for us thy tale that we may cut short
the watching of this our latter night!" She replied, "With love
and good will!" It hath reached me, O auspicious King, the
director, the right-guiding, lord of the rede which is benefiting and
of deeds fair-seeming and worthy celebrating, that the youth
continued: — So the Janákilah entered the house of the Shaykh
al-Islam all a-drumming and a-dancing. Presently the family
came out and asked, "What is to do? And what be this hub-
bub?" The fellows answered, "We are gypsey-folk and our son
is in your house having wedded the daughter of the Shaykh al-
Islam." Hearing these words the family went up and reported
to its head, and he, rising from his seat, descended to the courtyard which he found full of Jankalis. He enquired of them their
need and they told him that the youth, their kinsman, having
married the daughter of the house, they were come to make
merry at the bride-feast. Quoth the Shaykh, "This indeed be a
sore calamity that a gypsey should espouse the daughter of the
Shaykh al-Islam. By Allah, I will divorce her from him." So
he sent after me, O our lord the Sultan, and asked me saying,

---

[1] Arab. "Kurúsh," plur of. "Kirsh" (pron. "Girsh"), the Egyptian piastre = one-fifth
of a shilling. The word may derive from Karsh = collecting money; but it is more probably a corruption of Groschen, primarily a great or thick piece of money and secondarily a
small silver coin = 3 kreuzers = 1 penny.

"What is thy breed and what wilt thou take to be off with thy-self?" Said I, "A Jankali; and I married thy daughter with one design namely to sink the mean name of a gypsey drummer in the honour of connection and relationship with thee." He replied, " 'Tis impossible that my daughter can cohabit with thee: so up and divorce her." I rejoined, "Not so: I will never repudiate her." Then we fell to quarrelling but the folk interposed be-tween us and arranged that I should receive forty purses[1] for putting her away. And when he paid me the moneys I gave her the divorce and took the coin and went to my shop, rejoicing at having escaped by this contrivance. On the next day, behold, came the damsel who had taught me the sleight and saluted me and wished me good morning. I returned her salam and indeed, O our lord the Sultan, she was a model of beauty and loveliness, stature and symmetrical grace and my heart was enmeshed in her love for the excess of her charms and the limpid flow of her speech and the sweetness of her tongue. So I said to her, "And when this promise?" and said she, "I am the daughter of Such-and-such, a cook in such a quarter; and do thou go ask me in mar-riage of him." So I rose up with all haste and went to her father and prayed that he would give her to me. And presently I wedded her and went in unto her and found her as the full moon of the fourteenth night and was subjugated by her seemli-head. Such, then, is the adventure which befel me; but, O my lord the Sultan, the Story of the Sage Such-an-one and his Scholar is more wonderful and delectable; for indeed 'tis of the marvels of the age and among the miracles which have been seen by man. Thereupon the Sovran bade him speak, and the Second Lunatic proceeded to recount the

Story of the Sage and the Scholar.[2]

THERE was in times of yore and in ages long gone before a learned man who had retired from the world secluding himself in an upper cell of a Cathedral-mosque, and this place he left not for

---

[1] The purse ("Kís") is = 500 piastres (kurúsh) = £5; and a thousand purses compose the Treasury ("Khaznah") = £5,000.

[2] MS. vol. iii. pp. 179–303. It is Scott's "Story of the Retired Sage and his Pupil, related to the Sultan by the Second Lunatic," vi. pp. 52–67; and Gauttier's *Histoire du Sage*, vi. 199–214. The scene is laid in Cairo.

many days save upon the most pressing needs.   At last a beautiful boy whose charms were unrivalled in his time went in to
him and salam'd to him.   The Shaykh returned the salute and
welcomed him with the fairest welcome and courteously entreated him seating him beside himself.   Then he asked him of
his case and whence he came and the boy answered, "O my lord,
question me not of aught nor of my worldly matters, for verily I
am as one who hath fallen from the heavens upon the earth[1]
and my sole object is the honour of tending thee."   The Sage
again welcomed him and the boy served him assiduously for a
length of time till he was twelve years old.   Now on one day
of the days[2] the lad heard certain of his fellows saying that the
Sultan had a daughter endowed with beauty whose charms were
unequalled by all the Princesses of the age.   So he fell in love
with her by hearsay. —— And Shahrazad was surprised by the
dawn of day and fell silent and ceased to say her permitted say.
Then quoth her sister Dunyazad, "How sweet is thy story, O
sister mine, and how enjoyable and delectable!"   Quoth she,
"And where is this compared with that I would relate to you
on the coming night, an the Sovran suffer me to survive?"   Now
when it was the next night, and that was

The Three Hundred and Fifty-eighth Night,

DUNYAZAD said to her, "Allah upon thee, O my sister, an thou
be other than sleepy, finish for us thy tale that we may cut short
the watching of this our latter night!"   She replied, "With love
and good will!"   It hath reached me, O auspicious King, the
director, the right-guiding, lord of the rede which is benefiting
and of deeds fair-seeming and worthy celebrating, that the lad
who served the Sage fell in love with the Sultan's daughter by
hearsay.   Presently he went in to his master and told him
thereof adding, "O my lord, verily the King hath a daughter
beautiful and lovesome and my soul longeth to look upon her an
it be only a single look."   The Shaykh asked him saying, "Wherefore, O my son?   What have the like of us to do with the daughters of Sovrans or others?   We be an order of eremites and self-

---

[1] Meaning that he was an orphan and had, like the well-known widow, "seen better days."

[2] The phrase, I have noted, is not merely pleonastic: it emphasises the assertion that it was a chance day.

contained and we fear the Kings for our own safety." And the
Sage continued to warn the lad against the shifts of Time and to
divert him from his intent; but the more words he uttered to
warn him and to deter him, the more resolved he became to win
his wish, so that he abode continually groaning and weeping.
Now this was a grievous matter to the good Shaykh who loved
him with an exceeding love passing all bounds; and when he
saw him in this condition he exclaimed, "There is no Majesty
and there is no Might save in Allah, the Glorious, the Great."
And his heart was softened and he had ruth upon the case of his
scholar and pitied his condition, and at last said to him, "O my
son, dost thou truly long to look but a single look at the Sultan's
daughter?" Quoth he, "Yes, O my lord," and quoth the other,
"Come hither to me." Accordingly he came up to him and the
Shaykh produced a Kohl-pot and applied the powder to one of
his scholar's eyes, who behold, forthright became such that all
who saw him cried out, "This is a half-man."[1] Then the Sage
bade him go about the city and the youth obeyed his commands
and fared forth; but whenas the folk espied him they cried out,
"A miracle! a miracle! this be a half-man!" And the more the
youth walked about the streets the more the folk followed him
and gazed upon him for diversion and marvelled at the spectacle;
and as often as the great men of the city heard of him they sent to
summon him and solaced themselves with the sight and said,
"Laud to the Lord! Allah createth whatso He wisheth and
commandeth whatso He willeth as we see in the fashioning of

---

[1] An old Plinian fable long current throughout the East. It is the Pers. Ním-chihreh,
and the Arab Shikk and possibly Nasnás = nisf al-Nás (?) See vol. v. 333. Shikk had
received from Allah only half the form of a man, and his rival diviner Satíh was a shapeless
man of flesh without limbs. They lived in the days of a woman named Tarífah, daughter
of Al-Khayr al-Himyarí and wife of Amrú bin 'Amir who was famous for having intercourse
with the Jann. When about to die she sent for the two, on account of their deformity and
the influence exercised upon them by the demons; and, having spat into their mouths,
bequeathed to them her Jinni, after which she departed life and was buried at Al-Johfah.
Presently they became noted soothsayers; Shikk had issue but Satíh none; they lived 300
(some say 600) years, and both died shortly before the birth of the Prophet concerning
whom they prophesied. When the Tobba of Al-Yaman dreamed that a dove flew from a
holy place and settled in the Tihámah (lowland-seaboard) of Meccah, Satíh interpreted
it to signify that a Prophet would arise to destroy idols and to teach the best of faiths.
The two also predicted (according to Tabari) to Al-Rabí'ah, son of Nasr, a Jewish king
of Al-Yaman, that the Habash (Abyssinians) should conquer the country, govern it, and
be expelled, and after this a Prophet should arise amongst the Arabs and bring a new reli-
gion which all should embrace and which should endure until Doomsday. Compare this
with the divining damsel in Acts xvi. 16–18.

this half-man." The youth also looked freely upon the Haríms of the Grandees, he being fairer than any of them; and this case continued till the report reached the Sultan who bade him be brought into the presence, and on seeing him marvelled at the works of the Almighty. Presently the whole court gathered together to gaze at him in wonderment and the tidings soon reached the Queen who sent an Eunuch to fetch him and intro-duce him into the Serraglio. The women all admired the prodigy and the Princess looked at him and he looked at her; so his fascination increased upon him and he said in his secret soul, "An I wed her not I will slay myself!" After this the youth was dismissed by the Sultan's Harim and he, whose heart burned with love for the King's daughter, returned home. The Shaykh asked him, "Hast thou, O my son, seen the Princess?" and he answered, "I have, O my master; but this one look suf-ficeth me not, nor can I rest until I sit by her side and fill myself with gazing upon her." Quoth he, "O my child, we be an ascetic folk that shun the world nor have we aught to do with enmeshing ourselves in the affairs of the Sultan, and we fear for thee, O my son." But the youth replied, "O my lord, except I sit by her side and stroke her neck and shoulders with these my hands, I will slay myself." Hereupon the Sage said in his mind, "I will do whatso I can for this good youth and perchance Allah may enable him to win his wish." He then arose and brought out the Kohl-pot and applied the powder to his scholar's either eye; and, when it had settled therein, it made him invisible to the ken of man. Then he said, "Go forth, O my son, and indulge thy desire; but return again soon and be not absent too long." Accordingly the youth hastened to the Palace and entering it looked right and left, none seeing him the while, and proceeded to the Harem where he seated himself beside the daughter of the Sultan. Still none perceived him until, after a time, he put forth his hand and softly stroked her neck. But as soon as the Princess felt the youth's touch, she shrieked a loud shriek heard by all ears in the Palace and cried "I seek refuge with Allah from Satan, the stoned!" At this proceeding on the girl's part all asked her saying, "What is to do with thee?" Whereto she answered, "Verily some Satan hath this instant touched me on the neck." Upon this her mother was alarmed for her and sent for her nurse[1]

---

[1] Arab. "Kahramánah;" the word has before been explained as a nurse, a duenna, an

and when informed of what had befallen the girl the old woman
said, "If there be aught of Satans here naught is so sovereign a
specific to drive them away and keep them off as the smoke of
camel's dung."[1]   Then she arose and brought thereof a quantity
which was thrown into the fire and presently it scented and per-
vaded the whole apartment.   All this and the Youth still sat
there without being seen.   But when the dung-smoke thickened,
his eyes brimmed and he could not but shed tears, and the more
smoke there was the more his eyes watered and big drops flowed
till at last all the Kohl was washed off and trickled down with
the tears.   So he became visible a-middlemost the royal Harem;
and, when the dames descried him, all shrieked one shriek, each
at other, upon which the Eunuchry rushed in; then, finding the
young man still seated there, they laid hands upon him and haled
him before the Sultan to whom they reported his crime and
how he had been caught lurking in the King's Serraglio a-sitting
beside the Princess.   Hearing this, the Sovran bade summon the
Headsman and committed to him the criminal bidding him take
the youth and robe him in a black habit bepatched with flame-
colour;[2] then, to set him upon a camel and, after parading him
through Cairo city and all the streets, to put him to death.   Accordingly the executioner took the Youth. —— And Shahrazad
perceived the dawn of day and fell silent and ceased saying her
permitted say.   Then quoth her sister Dunyazad, "How sweet
and tasteful is thy tale, O sister mine, and enjoyable and delectable!"   Quoth she, "And where is this compared with that I
would relate to you on the coming night an the Sovran suffer me
to survive?"   Now when it was the next night and that was

The Three Hundred and Fifty-ninth Night,

DUNYAZAD said to her, "Allah upon thee, O my sister, an thou be
other than sleepy, finish for us thy tale that we may cut short

---

Amazon guarding the Harem.   According to C. de Perceval (père) it was also the title
given by the Abbasides to the Governess of the Serraglio.

[1] So in the Apocrypha ("Tobias" vi. 8).   Tobit is taught by the Archangel Raphael to
drive away evil spirits (or devils) by the smoke of a bit of fish's heart.   The practice may
date from the earliest days when "Evil Spirits" were created by man.   In India, when
Europeans deride the existence of Jinns and Rakshasas, and declare that they never saw
one, the people receive this information with a smile which means only, "I should think
not! you and yours are worse than any of our devils."

[2] An Inquisitorial costume called in the text "Shámiyát bi al-Nár."

the watching of this our latter night!" She replied, "With love and good will!" It hath reached me, O auspicious King, the director, the right-guiding, lord of the rede which is benefiting and of deeds fair-seeming and worthy celebrating, that the Link-man took the youth and fared forth with him from the palace: then he looked at him and found him fair of form and favour, a sans peer in loveliness, and he observed that he showed no fear nor shrinking from death. So he had pity upon him and his heart yearned to him and he said in his mind, "By Allah, attached to this young man is a rare history." Then he brought a leathern gown which he put upon him, and the flamey black habit which he passed over his arms: and setting him upon a camel as the Sultan had commanded, at last carried him in procession crying out the while, "This is the award and the least award of him who violateth the Harem of the King;" and he threaded the streets till they came to the square before the great Mosque wherein was the Shaykh. Now as all the folk were enjoying the spectacle, the Sage looked out from the window of his cell and beheld the condition of his scholar. He was moved to ruth and reciting a spell he summoned the Jánn and bade them snatch the young man off the camel's back with all care and kindness and bring him to his cell; and he also commanded an 'Aun of the 'Auns[1] to seize some oldster and set him upon the beast in lieu of the Youth. They did as he bid them for that he had taken fealty of the Jánn and because of his profound studies in the Notaricon[2] and every branch of the art magical. And when all the crowd saw the youth suddenly transformed into a grey-beard they were awe-stricken and cried, "Alhamdolillah — laud to the Lord — the young man hath become an old man!" They then looked again and behold, they saw a person well-known amongst the lieges, one who had long been wont to sell greens and colocasia at the hostelry gate near the Cathedral-mosque. Now the headsman noting this case was confounded with sore affright; so he returned to the palace with the oldster seated on the camel and went in to the Sultan followed by all the city-folk

---

[1] A tribe of the Jinn sometimes made synonymous with "Márid" and at other times contrasted with these rebels, as in the Story of Ma'aruf and J. Scott's "History of the Sultan of Hind" (vol. vi. 195). For another note see The Nights, iv. 88.

[2] Arab. "'Ilm al-Hurúf," not to be confounded with the "'Ilm al-Jumal," or "Hisáb Al-Jumal," a notation by numerical values of the alphabet. See Lumsden's Grammar of the Persian Language, i. 37.

who were gazing at the spectacle. Then he stood before the
King and the eunuchry and did homage and prayed for the
Sovran and said, "O our lord the Sultan, verily the Youth hath
vanished, and in lieu of him is this Shaykh well known to the
whole city." Hearing these words the King was startled; sore
fear entered his heart and he said to himself, "Whoso hath been
able to do this deed can do e'en more: he can depose me from my
kingship or he can devise my death." So his affright increased
and he was at a loss how to contrive for such case. Presently
he summoned his Minister and when he came into the presence
said to him, "O Wazir, advise me how to act in the affair of this
Youth and what measures should be taken." The Minister
bowed his brow groundwards in thought for a while, then raising it he addressed the Sultan and said, "O King of the Age, this
be a thing beyond experience, and the doer must be master of a
might we comprehend not and haply he may work thee in the
future some injury and we fear from him for thy daughter.
Wherefore the right way is that thou issue a royal autograph
and bid the Crier go round about the city and cry saying, 'Let
him who hath wrought this work appear before the King under
promise of safety and again safety — safety on the word of a
Sultan which shall never be falsed.' Should the Youth then
surrender himself, O King of the Age, marry him to thy daughter
when perhaps his mind may be reconciled to thee by love of her.
He hath already cast eyes upon her and he hath seen the inmates
of thy Harem unrobed, so that naught can save their honour
but his being united with the Princess." Hereupon the Sultan
indited an autographic rescript and placed it in the Crier's
hands even as the Wazir had counselled: and the man went about
the streets proclaiming, "By Command of the just King! whoso
hath done this deed let him discover himself and come to the
Palace under promise of safety and again safety, the safety of
sovereigns — safety on the word of a Sultan which shall never be
falsed." And the Crier ceased not crying till in fine he reached
the square fronting the great Mosque. The Youth who was
standing there heard the proclamation and returning to his
Shaykh said, "O my lord, the Crier hath a rescript from the
Sultan and he crieth saying, 'Whoso hath done this deed let him
discover himself and come to the Palace under promise of safety
and again safety — safety on the word of a Sultan which shall
never be falsed.' And, I must go to him perforce." Said the

Sage, "O my son, why shouldst thou do on such wise? Hast
thou not already suffered thy sufficiency?" But the young man
exclaimed, "Nothing shall prevent my going;" and at this the
Shaykh replied, "Go then, O my son, and be thy safeguarding
with the Living, the Eternal." Accordingly, the Youth repaired to the Hammam and having bathed attired himself in the
richest attire he owned, after which he went forth and discovered
himself to the Crier who led him to the Palace and set him before
the Sovran. He salamed to the Sultan and did him obeisance
and prayed for his long life and prosperity in style the most
eloquent, and proffered his petition in verse the most fluent.
The Sultan looked at him (and he habited in his best and with all
of beauty blest), and the royal mind was pleased and he enquired
saying, "Who art thou, O Youth?" The other replied, "I am
the Half-man whom thou sawest and I did the deed whereof
thou wottest." As soon as the King heard this speech he
entreated him with respect and bade him sit in the most honourable stead, and when he was seated the twain conversed together.
The Sultan was astounded at his speech and they continued their
discourse till they touched upon sundry disputed questions of
learning, when the Youth proved himself as superior to the
Sovran as a dinar is to a dirham: and to whatever niceties of
knowledge the monarch asked, the young man returned an all-
sufficient answer, speaking like a book. So the Sultan abode
confounded at the eloquence of his tongue and the purity of his
phrase and the readiness of his replies; and he said in his mind,
"This Youth is as worthy to become my daughter's mate as she
is meet to become his helpmate." Then he addressed him in
these words, "O Youth, my wish is to unite thee with my
daughter and after thou hast looked upon her and her mother
none will marry her save thyself." The other replied, "O King
of the Age, I am ready to obey thee, but first I must take counsel
of my friends." The King rejoined, "No harm in that: hie thee
home and ask their advice." The Youth then craved leave to
retire and repairing to his Shaykh, —— And Shahrazad was
surprised by the dawn of day and fell silent and ceased to say
her permitted say. Then quoth her sister Dunyazad, "How
sweet is thy story, O sister mine, and how enjoyable and delectable!" Quoth she, "And where is this compared with that
I would relate to you on the coming night, an the Sovran suffer
me to survive?" Now when it was the next night and that was

The Three Hundred and Sixtieth Night,

DUNYAZAD said to her, "Allah upon thee, O my sister, an thou be other than sleepy, finish for us thy tale that we may cut short the watching of this our latter night!" She replied, "With love and good will!" It hath reached me, O auspicious King, the director, the right-guiding, lord of the rede which is benefiting and of deeds fair-seeming and worthy celebrating, that the Youth then craved leave to retire and, repairing to his Shaykh, informed him of what had passed between himself and the Sultan and said to him, " 'Tis also my wish, O my lord, to marry his daughter." The Sage replied, "There be no fault herein if it be lawful wedlock: fare thee forth and ask her in marriage." Quoth the Youth, "But I, O my lord, desire to invite the King to visit us;" and quoth the Sage, "Go invite him, O my son, and hearten thy heart." The Youth replied, "O my lord, since I first came to thee and thou didst honour me by taking me into thy service, I have known none other home save this narrow cell wherein thou sittest, never stirring from it by night or by day. How can we invite the King hither?" The Sage rejoined, "O my son, do thou go invite him relying upon Allah, the Veiler who veileth all things, and say to him, 'My Shaykh greeteth thee with the salam and inviteth thee to visit him next Friday.' " Accordingly, the Youth repaired to the King and saluted him and offered his service and blessed him with most eloquent tongue and said, "O King of the Age, my Shaykh greeteth thee and sayeth to thee, 'Come eat thy pottage[1] with us next Friday,' " whereto the Sultan replied, "Hearing is consenting." Then the Youth returned to the Sage and waited upon him according to custom, longing the while for the coming of Friday. On that day the Sage said to the Youth, "O my son, arise with me and I will show thee what house be ours, so thou mayst go fetch the King." Then he took him and the two walked on till they came upon a ruin in the centre of the city and the whole was in heaps, mud, clay, and stones. The Sage looked at it and said, "O my son, this is our mansion; do thou hie thee to the King and bring him hither." But the Youth exclaimed, "O my lord, verily

---

[1] Like our "Cut your mutton," or *manger la soupe* or *die suppe einzunehmen.* For this formula meaning like the Brazilian "cup of water," a grand feast, see vol. vii. 168.

this be a ruinous heap! How then can I invite the Sultan and
bring him to such an ill place? This were a shame and a disgrace to us." Quoth the Sage, "Go and dread thou naught."
Upon this the Youth departed saying in himself, "By Allah, my
Shaykh must be Jinn-mad and doubtless he confoundeth in his
insanity truth and untruth." But he stinted not faring till he
reached the Palace and went in to the Sultan whom he found
expecting him; so he delivered the message, "Deign honour us,
O my lord, with thy presence."[1] Hereupon the King arose without stay or delay and took horse, and all the lords of the land also
mounted, following the Youth to the place where he told them
his Shaykh abode. But when they drew near it they found a
royal mansion and eunuchry standing at the gates in costliest
gear as if robed from a talismanic hoard. When the young man
saw this change of scene, he was awe-struck and confounded in
such way that hardly could he keep his senses, and he said to
himself, "But an instant ago I beheld with mine own eyes this
very place a ruinous heap: how then hath it suddenly become on
this same site a Palace such as belongeth not to our Sultan? But
I had better keep the secret to myself." Presently the King
alighted as also did his suite, and entered the mansion, and whenas he inspected it he marvelled at the splendour of the first
apartment, but the more narrowly he looked the more magnificent he found the place, and the second more sumptuous than
the first. So his wits were bewildered thereat till he was ushered
into a spacious speak-room where they found the Shaykh sitting
on one side of the chamber[2] to receive them. The Sultan salam'd
to him whereupon the Sage raised his head and returned his
greeting but did not rise to his feet. The King then sat him
down on the opposite side when the Shaykh honoured him by
addressing him and was pleased to converse with him on various
themes; all this while the royal senses being confounded at the
grandeur around him and the rarities in that Palace. Presently
the Shaykh said to his Scholar, "Knock thou at this door and
bid our breakfast be brought in." So the young man arose and
rapped and called out, "Bring in the breakfast;" when lo! the

---

[1] Arab. "Tafazzal," a most useful word employed upon almost all occasions of invitation
and mostly equivalent to "Have the kindness," etc. See vol. ii. 103.

[2] The Shaykh for humility sits at the side, not at the "Sadr," or top of the room; but
he does not rise before the temporal power. The Sultan is equally courteous and the
Shaykh honours him by not keeping silence.

door was opened and there came out of it an hundred Mame-
lukes[1] of the Book, each bearing upon his head a golden tray,
whereon were set dishes of precious metals; and these, which
were filled with breakfast-meats of all kinds and colours, they
ranged in order before the Sultan. He was surprised at the
sight for that he had naught so splendid in his own possession;
but he came forwards and ate, as likewise did the Shaykh and all
the courtiers until they were satisfied. And after this they
drank coffee and sherbets, and the Sultan and the Shaykh fell to
conversing on questions of lore: the King was edified by the
words of the Sage who on his part sat respectfully between the
Sovran's hands. Now when it was well nigh noon, the Shaykh
again said to his Scholar, "Knock thou at that door and bid our
noonday-meal be brought in." He arose and rapped and called
out, "Bring in the dinner;" when lo! the door opened of itself
and there came out of it an hundred white slaves all other than
the first train and each bearing a tray upon his head. They
spread the Sufrah-cloth before the Sultan and ranged the dishes,
and he looked at the plates and observed that they were of precious metals and stones; whereat he was more astonished than
before and he said to himself, "In very deed this be a miracle!"
So all ate their sufficiency when basins and ewers, some of gold
and others of various noble ores, were borne round and they
washed their hands, after which the Shaykh said, "O King, at
how much hast thou valued for us the dower of thy daughter?"
The Sovran replied, "My daughter's dower is already in my
hands." This he said of his courtesy and respect, but the
Shaykh replied, "Marriage is invalid save with a dower." He
then presented to him a mint of money and the tie of wedlock
was duly tied; after which he rose and brought for his guest a
pelisse of furs such as the Sultan never had in his treasury and
invested him therewith and he gave rich robes to each and every
of his courtiers according to their degree. The Sultan then took
leave of the Shaykh and accompanied by the Scholar returned
to the Palace. —— And Shahrazad perceived the dawn of day
and fell silent and ceased saying her permitted say. Then quoth
her sister Dunyazad, "How sweet and tasteful is thy tale, O
sister mine, and enjoyable and delectable!" Quoth she, "And

---

[1] Arab. "Miat Mamlúk kitábí," the latter word meaning "one of the Book, a Jew" (especially), or a Christian.

where is this compared with that I would relate to you on the coming night an the Sovran suffer me to survive?" Now when it was the next night and that was

The Three Hundred and Sixty-first Night,

DUNYAZAD said to her, "Allah upon thee, O my sister, an thou be other than sleepy, finish for us thy tale that we may cut short the watching of this our latter night!" She replied, "With love and good will!" It hath reached me, O auspicious King, the director, the right-guiding, lord of the rede which is benefiting and of deeds fair-seeming and worthy celebrating, that the Sultan took with him the Scholar and they fared till they reached the citadel and entered the Palace, during which time the King was pondering the matter and wondering at the affair. And when night came he bade them get ready his daughter that the first visit might be paid to her by the bridegroom. They did his bidding and carried the Youth in procession to her and he found the apartment bespread with carpets and perfumed with essences; the bride, however, was absent. So he said in his mind, "She will come presently albeit now she delayeth;" and he ceased not expecting her till near midnight, whilst the father and the mother said, "Verily the young man hath married our daughter and now sleepeth with her." On this wise the Youth kept one reckoning and the Sultan and his Harem kept another till it was hard upon dawn —— all this and the bridegroom watched in expectation of the bride. Now when the day brake, the mother came to visit her child expecting to see her by the side of her mate; but she could not find a trace of her, nor could she gather any clear tidings of her. Accordingly she asked the Youth, her son-in-law, who answered that since entering the apartment he had expected his bride but she came not to him nor had he seen a sign of her. Hereupon the Queen shrieked and rose up calling aloud upon her daughter, for she had none other child save that one. The clamour alarmed the Sultan who asked what was to do and was informed that the Princess was missing from the Palace and had not been seen after she had entered it at eventide. Thereupon he went to the Youth and asked him anent her, but he also told him that he had not found her when the procession led him into the bridal chamber. Such was the case with these; but as regards the Princess, when they conducted her to the bridal room before the coming of the bridegroom, a Jinni[1] of the Márids, who often visited the royal Harem, happened to be there on the marriage-night and was so captivated by the charms of the bride that he took seat in a corner, and upon her entering and before she was ware snatched her up and soared with her high in air. And he flew with her till he reached a pleasant place of trees and rills some three months' journey from the city, and in that shady place he set her down But he wrought her no bodily damage and every day he would bring her whatso she wanted of meat and drink and solaced her by showing her the rills and trees. Now this Jinni had changed his shape to that of a fair youth fearing lest his proper semblance affright her, and the girl abode in that place for a space of forty days. But the father, after failing to find his daughter, took the Youth and repaired to the Shaykh in his cell, and he was as one driven mad as he entered and complained of the loss of his only child. The Shaykh hearing these words dove into the depths of meditation for an hour: then he raised his head and bade them bring before him a chafing-dish of lighted charcoal. They fetched all he required and he cast into the fire some incenses over which he pronounced formulæ of incantation, and behold! the world was turned topsy-turvy and the winds shrieked and the earth was canopied by dust-clouds whence descended at speed winged troops bearing standards and colours.[2] And amiddlemost of them appeared three Sultans of the Jánn all crying out at once "Labbayka! Labbayk! Adsumus, hither we speed to undertake thy need." The Shaykh then addressed them, saying, "My commandment is that forthright ye bring me the Jinni who hath snatched away the bride of my son," and they said, "To hear is to obey," and at once commanded fifty of their dependent Jinns to reconduct the Princess to her chamber and to hale the culprit before them. These orders were obeyed: they disappeared for an hour or so and suddenly returned, bringing the delinquent Jinni in person; but as for the Sultan's daughter, ten of them conveyed her to her Palace, she wotting naught of them and not feeling aught of fear. And when they set the Jinni before the Shaykh, he bade the three Sultans of the Jann

---

[1] This MS. prefers the rare form "Al-Jánn" for the singular.
[2] These flags, I have noticed, are an unfailing accompaniment of a Jinn army.

burn him to death and so they did without stay or delay. All
this was done whilst the Sovran sat before the Shaykh, looking
on and listening and marvelling at the obedience of that host
and its Sultans and their subjection and civil demeanour in
presence of the Elder. Now as soon as the business ended after
perfectest fashion, the Sage recited over them a spell and all went
their several ways; after which he bade the King take the Youth
and conduct him to his daughter. This bidding was obeyed and
presently the bridegroom abated the maidenhead of the bride,
what while her parents renewed their rejoicings over the recovery of their lost child. And the Youth was so enamoured of
the Princess that he quitted not the Harem for seven consecutive
days. On the eighth the Sultan was minded to make a marriage-
banquet and invited all the city-folk to feast for a whole month
and he wrote a royal rescript and bade proclaim with full publicity that, according to the commands of the King's majesty, the
wedding-feast should continue for a month, and that no citizen,
be he rich or be he poor, should light fire or trim lamp in his own
domicile during the wedding of the Princess; but that all must
eat of the royal entertainment until the expiry of the fête. So
they slaughtered beeves and stabbed camels in the throat and the
kitcheners and carpet-spreaders were commanded to prepare the
stables, and the officers of the household were ordered to receive
the guests by night and by day. Now one night King Mohammed
of Cairo said to his Minister, "O Wazir, do thou come with me
in changed costume and let us thread the streets and inspect and
espy the folk: haply some of the citizens have neglected to appear
at the marriage-feast." He replied, "To hear is to obey." So the
twain after exchanging habits for the gear of Persian Darwayshes
went down to the city and there took place

The Night-Adventure of Sultan Mohammed of Cairo.[1]

THE Sultan and the Wazir threaded the broadways of the city
and they noted the houses and stood for an hour or so in each and
every greater thoroughfare, till they came to a lane, a cul-de-sac
wherethrough none could pass, and behold, they hit upon a house

---

[1] MS. vol. iii. pp. 203–210; Scott, "Night Adventure of the Sultan," pp. 68–71. Gauttier,
Aventure nocturne du Sulthan, vi. 214.

containing a company of folk. Now these were conversing and saying, "By Allah, our Sultan hath not acted wisely nor hath he any cause to be proud, since he hath made his daughter's bride-feast a vanity and a vexation and the poor are excluded therefrom. He had done better to distribute somewhat of his bounty amongst the paupers and the mesquin, who may not enter his palace nor can they obtain aught to eat." Hearing this the Sultan said to the Wazir, "By Allah, needs must we enter this place;" and the Minister replied, "Do whatso thou willest." Accordingly the King went up to the door and knocked, when one came out and asked, "Who is at the door?" The Sultan answered, "Guests;" and the voice rejoined, "Welcome to the guests;" and the door was thrown open. Then they went in till they reached the sitting-room where they found three men of whom one was lame, the second was broken-backed and the third was split-mouthed.[1] And all three were sitting together in that place. So he asked them, "Wherefore sit ye here, ye three, instead of going to the Palace?" and they answered him, "O Darwaysh, 'tis of the weakness of our wits!" The King then turned to his Minister and said, "There is no help but thou must bring these three men into my presence, as soon as the wedding-fêtes be finished, that I may enquire into what stablished their imbecility."——And Shahrazad was surprised by the dawn of day and fell silent and ceased to say her permitted say. Then quoth her sister Dunyazad, "How sweet is thy story, O sister mine, and how enjoyable and delectable!" Quoth she, "And where is this compared with that I would relate to you on the coming night, an the Sovran suffer me to survive?" Now when it was the next night and that was

The Three Hundred and Sixty-second Night,

DUNYAZAD said to her, "Allah upon thee, O my sister, an thou be other than sleepy, finish for us thy tale that we may cut short the watching of this our latter night!" She replied, "With love and good will!" It hath reached me, O auspicious King, the director, the right-guiding, lord of the rede which is benefiting

---

[1] Arab. "Mashrút shadak." Ashdak is usually applied to a wide-chapped face, like that of Margaret Maultasch or Mickle-mouthed Meg. Here, however, it alludes to an accidental deformity which will presently be described.

and of deeds fair-seeming and worthy celebrating, that the Sultan said to the Wazir, "Needs must thou bring these three men into my presence, as soon as the wedding-fêtes be finished, and we will enquire into what proved their imbecility." Then quoth the King to them, "Wherefore fare ye not, ye three, and eat of the royal banquet day by day?" and quoth they, "O Darwaysh, we are crippled folk who cannot go and come, for this be grievous to us; but, an the Sultan would assign to us somewhat of victual, and send it hither, we would willingly eat thereof." He rejoined, "What knoweth the Sultan that ye sit in this place?" and they retorted, "Ye be Darwayshes who enter everywhere: so when ye go in to him, tell him our tale; haply shall Almighty Allah incline his heart uswards." The King asked them, "Be you three ever sitting together in this stead?" and they answered, "Yea, verily: we never leave one another by night or by day." Then the King and the Minister rose up and having presented them with a few silvers took leave and departed. Now it was midnight when they reached a tenement wherein sat three girls with their mother spinning and eating; and each one appeared fairer than her fellows, and at times they sang and then they laughed and then they talked. The Sultan said to the Wazir, "There is no help but we enter to these damsels;" whereto the Minister replied "What have we to do with going near them? Let them be as they are!" The Sultan, however, rejoined, "Needs must we enter," and the Wazir retorted, "Hearkening and obedience;" and he rapped at the door when one of the sisterhood cried out, "Who knocketh in this gloom of the night?" The Minister answered, "We are two Darwayshes, guests and strangers;" and the girl rejoined, "We are maidens with our mother and we have no men in our house who can admit you; so fare ye to the marriage-feast of the Sultan and become ye his guests." The Minister continued, "We are foreigners and we know not the way to the Palace and we dread lest the Chief of Police happen upon us and apprehend us at this time o' night. We desire that you afford us lodging till daylight when we will go about our business and you need not expect from us aught save respect and honourable treatment." Now when the mother heard this, she pitied them and bade one daughter open the door. So the damsel threw it open and the Sultan and Wazir entered and salam'd and sat down to converse together; but the King gazed upon the sisters and marvelled at their beauty and their loveliness, and said in his mind, "How cometh it that these maidens dwell by themselves unmated and they in such case?" So quoth he to them, "How is it ye lack husbands, you being so beautiful, and that ye have not a man in the house?" Quoth the youngest, "O Darwaysh, hold thy tongue[1] nor ask us of aught, for our story is wondrous and our adventures marvellous. But 'ware thy words and shorten thy speech; verily hadst thou been the Sultan and thy companion the Wazir an you heard our history haply ye had taken compassion upon our case." Thereupon the King turned to the Minister and said, "Up with us and wend we our ways; but first do thou make sure of the place and affix thy mark upon the door." Then the twain rose up and fared forth but the Wazir stood awhile and set a sign upon the entrance and there left his imprint; after which the twain returned to the Palace. Presently the youngest sister said to her mother, "By Allah, I fear lest the Darwayshes have made their mark upon our door to the end that they may recognise it by day; for haply the twain may be the King and his Minister." "What proof hast thou of this?" asked the mother, and the daughter answered, "Their language and their questioning which were naught save importunity!" And saying this she went to the door where she found the sign and mark. Now besides the two houses to the right and to the left were fifteen doors, so the girl marked them all with the same mark set by the Wazir.[2] But when Allah had caused the day to dawn, the King said to the Minister, "Go thou and look at the sign and make sure of it." The Wazir went as he was commanded by the Sultan, but he found all the doors marked in the same way, whereat he marvelled and knew not nor could he distinguish the door he sought. Presently he returned and reported the matter of the door-marks to the King who cried, "By Allah, these girls must have a curious history! But when the bride-feast is finished we will enquire into the case of the three men who are weak-witlings and then we will consider that of the damsels who are not." As soon as the thirtieth feast-day passed by, he invested with robes of honour all the Lords of his land and the high Officers of his estate and matters returned to their customed course. Then he sent to summon the three men who had professed them-

---

[1] Arab. "Amsik lisána-k": the former word is a standing "chaff" with the Turks, as in their tongue it means cunnus-penis and nothing else. I ever found it advisable when speaking Arabic before Osmanlis, to use some such equivalent as Khuz = take thou.

[2] This is the familiar incident in "Ali Baba": Supplem. vol. iii. 231, etc.

selves weak of wits and they were brought into the presence, each saying of himself, "What can the King require of us?" When they came before him he bade them be seated and they sat; then he said to them, "My requirement is that ye relate to me proofs of the weakness of your minds and the reason of your maims." Now the first who was questioned was he of the broken back, and when the enquiry was put to him he said, "Deign to favour me with an answer O our Lord the Sultan, on a matter which passed through my mind." He replied, "Speak out and fear not!" So the other enquired, "How didst thou know us and who told thee of us and of our weakly wits?" Quoth the King, " 'Twas the Darwaysh who went in to you on such a night;" and quoth the broken-backed man, "Allah slay all the Darwayshes who be tattlers and tale-carriers!" Thereupon the Sultan turned to the Wazir and laughing said, "We will not reproach them for aught: rather let us make fun of them," adding to the man, "Recite, O Shaykh." So he fell to telling

The Story of the Broke-Back Schoolmaster.[1]

I BEGAN life, O King of the Age, as a Schoolmaster and my case was wondrous.——And Shahrazad perceived the dawn of day and fell silent and ceased saying her permitted say. Then quoth her sister Dunyazad, "How sweet and tasteful is thy tale, O sister mine, and enjoyable and delectable!" Quoth she, "And where is this compared with that I would relate to you on the coming night an the Sovran suffer me to survive?" Now when it was the next night and that was

The Three Hundred and Sixty-third Night,

DUNYAZAD said to her, "Allah upon thee, O my sister, an thou be other than sleepy, finish for us thy tale that we may cut short the watching of this our latter night!" She replied, "With love

---

[1] MS. iii. 210-214. Scott's "Story of the broken-backed Schoolmaster," vi. pp. 72–75, and Gauttier's "*Histoire du Maître d'école éreinté*," vi. 217. The Arabic is "Muaddib al-Atfál" = one who teacheth children. I have before noted that amongst Moslems the Schoolmaster is always a fool. So in Europe of the 16th century probably no less than one-third of the current jests turned upon the Romish clergy and its phenomenal ignorance compared with that of the pagan augur. The Story of the First Schoolmaster is one of the most humorous in this MS.

and good will!" It hath reached me, O auspicious King, the
director, the right-guiding, lord of the rede which is benefiting
and of deeds fair-seeming and worthy celebrating, that the Shaykh
continued.——I began life, O my lord, as a Schoolmaster, and
my tale with the boys was wondrous. They numbered from
sixty to seventy, and I taught them to read and I inculcated due
discipline and ready respect esteeming these a part of liberal
education; nor did I regard, O King of the Age, the vicissitudes
of Time and Change; nay, I held them with so tight a rein that
whenever the boys heard me sneeze[1] they were expected to lay
down their writing-tablets and stand up with their arms crossed
and exclaim, "Allah have ruth upon thee, O our lord!" whereto
I would make reply, "Allah deign pardon us and you!" And
if any of the lads failed or delayed to join in this prayer I was
wont to bash him with a severe bashing. One day of the days
they asked leave to visit the outskirts of the town for liberty and
pleasuring[2] and when I granted it they clubbed their pittances
for a certain sum of money to buy them a noonday meal. So we
went forth to the suburbs and there found verdure and water, and
we enjoyed ourselves that day with perfect enjoyment until mid-
afternoon when we purposed to return homewards. Accordingly, the boys collected their belongings and laded them upon an
ass and we walked about half-way when behold, the whole party,
big and little, stood still and said to me, "O our lord, we are
athirst and burning with drowthiness, nor can we stir from this
spot and if we leave it without drinking we shall all die." Now
there was in that place a draw-well, but it was deep and we had
nor pitcher nor bucket nor aught wherein to draw water and the
scholars still suffered from exceeding thirst. We had with us,
however, cooking-gear such as chauldrons and platters; so I said
to them, "O boys, whoso carrieth a cord or hath bound his belongings with one let him bring it hither!" They did my bidding
and I tied these articles together and spliced them as strongly as
I could: then said I to the lads, "Bind me under the arm-pits."
Accordingly they made me fast by passing the rope around me
and I took with me a chauldron, whereupon they let me down
bucket-wise into the well till I reached the water. Then I loosed

---

[1] For the usual ceremony when a Moslem sneezes, see vol. ix. 220.
[2] The "day in the country," lately become such a favourite with English schools, is an
old Eastern custom.

the bandage from under my armpits and tied it to the chauldron
which I filled brim-full and shook the rope for a signal to the boys
above. They haled at the vessel till they pulled it up and began
drinking and giving drink; and on this wise they drew a first
chauldron and a second and a third and a fourth till they were
satisfied and could no more and cried out to me, "We have had
enough, quite enough." Hereupon I bound the bandage under
my armpits, as it was when I went down, and I shook it as a
signal and they haled me up till I had well-nigh reached the kerb-
stone of the well when a fit of sneezing seized me and I sneezed
violently. At this all let go their hold and carrying their arms
over their breasts, cried aloud, "Allah have ruth upon thee, O
our lord!" but I, as soon as they loosed hold, fell into the depths
of the well and brake my back. I shrieked for excess of agony
and all the boys ran on all sides screaming for aid till they were
heard by some wayfaring folk; and these haled at me and drew
me out. They placed me upon the ass and bore me home: then
they brought a leach to medicine me and at last I became even
as thou seest me, O Sultan of the Age. Such, then, is my story
showing the weakness of my wits; for had I not enjoined and
enforced over-respect the boys would not have let go their hold
when I happened to sneeze nor would my back have been broken.
"Thou speakest sooth, O Shaykh," said the Sultan, "and indeed
thou hast made evident the weakness of thy wit." Then quoth
he to the man who was cloven of mouth. "And thou, the other,
what was it split thy gape?" "The weakness of my wit, O my
lord the Sultan," quoth he, and fell to telling the

Story of the Split-Mouthed Schoolmaster.[1]

I ALSO began life, O King of the Age, as a Schoolmaster and had
under my charge some eighty boys. Now I was strict with such
strictness that from morning to evening I sat amongst them and
would never dismiss them to their homes before sundown. But
'tis known to thee, O our lord the King, that boys' wits be short
after the measure of their age, and that they love naught save
play and forgathering in the streets and quarter. Withal, I took

---

[1] MS. iii. 214–219. Scott's "Story of the wry-mouthed Schoolmaster," vi. pp. 74–75:
Gauttier's *Histoire du Second Estropié*, vi. p. 220.

no heed of this and ever grew harder upon them till one day all
met and with the intervention of the eldest Monitor they agreed
and combined to play me a trick. He arranged with them that
next morning none should enter the school until he had taught
them, each and every, to say as they went in, "Thy safety, O our
lord, how yellow is thy face!" Now the first who showed himself was the Monitor and he spoke as had been agreed; but I was
rough with him and sent him away; then a second came in and
repeated what the first had said; then a third and then a fourth,
until ten boys had used the same words. So quoth I to myself,
"Ho, Such-an-one! thou must be unwell without weeting it:"
then I arose and went into the Harem and lay down therein when
the Monitor, having collected from his school-fellows some hun-
dred-and-eighty Nusfs,[1] came in to me and cried, "Take this, O
our lord, and expend the money upon thy health." Thereupon I
said to myself, "Ho, Such-an-one! every Thursday[2] thou dost not

---

[1] In these days the whole would be about 10d.

[2] Pay-day for the boys in Egypt. The Moslem school has often been described but it
always attracts the curiosity of strangers. The Moorish or Maroccan variety is a simple
affair; "no forms, no desks, few books. A number of boards about the size of foolscap,
whitewashed on either side, whereon the lessons — from the alphabet to sentences of the
Koran — are plainly written in large black letters; a pen and ink, a book and a switch
or two, complete the paraphernalia. The dominie, squatting on the ground, tailor-fashion,
like his pupils, who may number from ten to thirty, repeats the lesson in a sonorous sing-
song voice, and is imitated by the urchins, who accompany their voices by a rocking to
and fro which sometimes enables them to keep time. A sharp application of the cane is
wonderfully effectual in recalling wandering attention; and lazy boys are speedily expelled. On the admission of a pupil, the parents pay some small sum, varying according
to their means, and every Wednesday, which is a half-holiday, a payment is made from
¼d. to 2d. New moons and feasts are made occasions for larger payments, and are also
holidays, which last ten days during the two greater festivals. Thursdays are whole holidays, and no work is done on Friday mornings, that day being the Mohammedan 'Sab-
bath,' or at least 'meeting day,' as it is called. When the pupils have mastered the first
short chapter of the Koran, it is customary for them to be paraded round the town on
horseback, with ear-splitting music, and sometimes charitably disposed persons make
small presents to the youngster by way of encouragement. After the first, the last is
learned, then the last but one, and so on, backwards, as, with the exception of the first,
the longest chapters are at the beginning. Though reading and a little writing are taught,
at the same time, all the scholars do not arrive at the pitch of perfection necessary to
indite a polite letter, so that consequently there is plenty of employment for the numerous
scribes or Tá'libs who make a profession of writing. These may frequently be seen in small
rooms opening on to the street, usually very respectably dressed in a white flowing haik
and large turban, and in most cases of venerable appearance, their noses being adorned
with huge goggles. Before them are their appliances, — pens made of reeds, ink, paper,
and sand in lieu of blotting paper. They usually possess also a knife and scissors, with a
case to hold them all. In writing, they place the paper on the knee, or upon a pad of paper
in the left hand." The main merit of the village school in Eastern lands is its noises which

collect sixty Faddahs from the boys," and I cried to him, "Go,
let them forth for a holiday." So he went and dismissed them
from school to the playground. On the next day he collected as
much as on the first and came in to me and said, "Expend these
moneys, O our lord, upon thy health." He did the same on the
third day and the fourth, making the boys contribute much coin
and presenting it to me; and on such wise he continued till the
tenth day, when he brought the money as was his wont. At
that time I happened to hold in my hand a boiled egg which I
purposed eating, but on sighting him I said in myself, "An he see
thee feeding he will cut off the supplies." So I crammed the egg
into my chops——And Shahrazad was surprised by the dawn of
day and fell silent and ceased to say her permitted say. Then
quoth her sister Dunyazad, "How sweet is thy story, O sister
mine, and how enjoyable and delectable!" Quoth she, "And
where is this compared with that I would relate to you on the
coming night, an the Sovran suffer me to survive?" Now when
it was the next night and that was

Œbe Œbree Hundred and Sixty-fourth Night,

DUNYAZAD said to her, "Allah, upon thee, O my sister, an thou
be other than sleepy, finish for us thy tale that we may cut short
the watching of this our latter night!" She replied, "With love
and good will!" It hath reached me, O auspicious King, the
director, the right-guiding, lord of the rede which is benefiting
and of deeds fair-seeming and worthy celebrating, that the
Schoolmaster said to himself, "If the Monitor see thee eating the
egg now in thy hand he will cut off the supplies and assert thee
to be sound." So (continued he) I crammed the egg into my
chops and clapped my jaws together. Hereupon the lad turned
to me and cried, "O my lord, thy cheek is much swollen;" and I,
" 'Tis only an imposthume." But he drew a whittle[1] forth his
sleeve and coming up to me seized my cheek and slit it, when the
egg fell out and he said, "O my lord, this it was did the harm
and now 'tis passed away from thee." Such was the cause of the

---

teach the boy to concentrate his attention. As Dr. Wilson of Bombay said, the young
idea is taught to shout as well as to shoot, and this vivâ voce process is a far better mne-
monic than silent reading. Moreover it is fine practice in the art of concentrating attention.

[1] Arab. "Mikshat," whose root would be "Kasht" = skinning (a camel).

splitting of my mouth, O our lord the Sultan. Now had I cast away greed of gain and eaten the egg in the Monitor's presence, what could have been the ill result? But all this was of the weakness of my wit; for also had I dismissed the boys every day about mid-afternoon, I should have gained naught nor lost aught thereby. However the Dealer of Destiny is self-existent, and this is my case. Then the Sultan turned to the Wazir and laughed and said, "The fact is that whoso schooleth boys is weak of wit;" and said the other, "O King of the Age, all pedagogues lack perceptives and reflectives; nor can they become legal witnesses before the Kazi because verily they credit the words of little children without evidence of the speech being or factual or false. So their reward in the world to come must be abounding!"[1] Then the Sultan asked the limping man, saying, "And thou, the other, what lamed thee?" So he began to tell

The Story of the Limping Schoolmaster.[2]

My tale, O my lord the Sultan, is marvellous and 'twas as follows. My father was by profession a schoolmaster and, when he fared to the ruth of Almighty Allah, I took his place in the school and taught the boys to read after the fashion of my sire. Now over the schoolroom was an upper lattice whereto planks had been nailed and I was ever casting looks at it till one chance day I said to myself, "By Allah, this lattice thus boarded up needs must contain hoards or moneys or manuscripts which my father stored there before his decease; and on such wise I am deprived of them." So I arose and brought a ladder and lashed it to another till the two together reached the lattice and I clomb them holding a carpenter's adze[3] wherewith I prized up the planks until all were removed. And behold, I then saw a large fowl, to wit, a kite,[4] setting upon her nestlings. But when she saw me she flew sharply in my face and I was frightened by her and thrown back; so I tumbled from the ladder-top to the ground and brake both

---

[1] Evidently said ironicè as of innocents. In "The Forty Vezirs" we read, "At length they perceived that all this tumult arose from their trusting on this wise the words of children." (Lady's XXth Tale.)

[2] MS. iii. 219–220. For some unaccountable reason it is omitted by Scott (vi. 76), who has written English words in the margin of the W. M. Codex.

[3] In text "Kádúm," for "Kudúm," a Syrian form.

[4] Arab. "Hidyah," which in Egypt means a falcon; see vol. iii. 138.

knee-caps. Then they bore me home and brought a leach to heal
me; but he did me no good and I fell into my present state.
Now this, O our lord the Sultan, proveth the weakness of my wit
and the greatness of my greed; for there is a saw amongst men
that saith "Covetise aye wasteth and never gathereth: so 'ware
thee of covetise." Such, O lord of the Age and the Time, is my
tale. Hereupon the King bade gifts and largesse be distributed
to the three old schoolmasters, and when his bidding was obeyed
they went their ways. Then the Sultan turned to the Minister
and said, "O Wazir, now respecting the matter of the three
maidens and their mother, I would have thee make enquiry and
find out their home and bring them hither; or let us go to them
in disguise and hear their history, for indeed it must be wonderful. Otherwise how could they have understood that we served
them that sleight by marking their door and they on their part set
marks of like kind upon all the doors of the quarter that we
might lose the track and touch of them. By Allah, this be rare
intelligence on the part of these damsels; but we, O Wazir, will
strive to come upon their traces." Then the Minister fared
forth, after changing his dress and demeanour, and walked to the
quarter in question, but found all the doors similarly marked.
So he was sore perplext concerning his case and fell to questioning
all the folk wont to pass by these doors but none could give him
any information; and he walked about sore distraught until eventide, when he returned to the Sultan without aught of profit. As
he went in to the presence, his liege lord asked him saying, "What
bringest thou of tidings?" and he answered, "O King, I have not
found the property,[1] but there passed through my mind a
stratagem which, an we carry it out, peradventure shall cause us
to happen upon the maidens." Quoth the Sultan, "What be
that?" and quoth he, "Do thou write me an autograph-writ and
give it to the Crier that he may cry about the city, 'Whoso
lighteth wick after supper-tide shall have his head set under his
heels.'" The Sultan rejoined, "This thy rede is right." Accordingly, on the next day the King wrote his letter and gave it to
the Crier bidding him fare through the city and forbid the lighting of lamps after night-prayers; and the man took the royal
rescript and set it in a green bag. Then he went forth and cried
about the street saying, "According to the commandment of our

---

[1] Arab. "Sifah," = lit. a quality.

King, the Lord of prosperity and Master of the necks of God's servants, if any light wick after night-prayers his head shall be set under his heels, his good shall be spoiled and his women shall be cast into jail." And the Crier stinted not crying through the town during the first day and the second and the third, until he had gone round the whole place; nor was there a citizen but who knew the ordinance. Now the King waited patiently till after the proclamation of the third day; but on the fourth night he and his Minister went down from the palace in disguise after supper-tide to pry about the wards and espy into the lattices of the several quarters. They found no light till they came to the ward where the three damsels lived, and the Sultan, happening to glance in such a direction, saw the gleam of a lamp in one of the tenements. So he said to the Wazir, "Ho! there is a wick alight." Presently they drew near it and found that it was within one of the marked houses; wherefore they came to a stand and knocked at the door,——And Shahrazad perceived the dawn of day and fell silent and ceased saying her permitted say. Then quoth her sister Dunyazad, "How sweet and tasteful is thy tale, O sister mine, and enjoyable and delectable!" Quoth she, "And where is this compared with that I would relate to you on the coming night an the Sovran suffer me to survive?" Now when it was the next night and that was

The Three Hundred and Sixty-fifth Night,

DUNYAZAD said to her, "Allah upon thee, O my sister, an thou be other than sleepy, finish for us thy tale that we may cut short the watching of this our latter night!" She replied, "With love and good will!" It hath reached me, O auspicious King, the director, the right-guiding, lord of the rede which is benefiting and of deeds fair-seeming and worthy celebrating, that when the Sultan and the Wazir stood over against the door behind which was the light and knocked at it, the youngest of the sisters cried out, "Who is at the door?" and they replied, "Guests and Darwayshes." She rejoined, "What can you want at this hour and what can have belated you?" And they, "We be men living in a Khan; but we have lost our way thither and we fear to happen upon the Chief of Police. So of your bountiful kindness open ye to us and house us for the remnant of the night; and

such charity shall gain you reward in Heaven." Hereto the
mother added, "Go open to them the door!" and the youngest
of the maidens came forward and opened to them and admitted
them. Then the parent and her children rose up and welcomed
them respectfully and seated them and did them honour and set
before them somewhat of food which they ate and were gladdened.
Presently the King said, "O damsels, ye cannot but know that
the Sultan proclaimed forbiddal of wick-burning; but ye have
lighted your lamps and have not obeyed him when all the citizens
have accepted his commandment." Upon this the youngest
sister accosted him saying, "O Darwaysh, verily the Sultan's
order should not be obeyed save in commandments which be
reasonable; but this his proclamation forbidding lights is sinful to
accept; and indeed the right direction[1] wherein man should walk
is according to Holy Law which saith, 'No obedience to the
creature in a matter of sin against the Creator.' The Sultan
(Allah make him prevail!) herein acteth against the Law and
imitateth the doings of Satan. For we be three sisters with our
mother, making four in the household, and every night we sit
together by lamp-light and weave a half-pound weight of linen
web[2] which our mother taketh in the morning for sale to the
Bazar and buyeth us therewith half a pound of raw flax and
with the remainder what sufficeth us of victual." The Sultan
now turned to his Minister and said, "O Wazir, this damsel
astonisheth me by her questions and answers. What case of
casuistry can we propose to her and what disputation can we set
up? Do thou contrive us somewhat shall pose and perplex her."
"O my lord," replied the Wazir, "we are here in the guise of Darwayshes and are become to these folk as guests: how then can
we disturb them with troublesome queries in their own home?"
Quoth the Sultan, "Needs must thou address them;" so the
Wazir said to the girl, "O noble one, obedience to the royal
orders is incumbent upon you as upon all lieges." Said she,
"True, he is our Sovran; but how can he know whether we be
starving or full-fed?" "Let us see," rejoined the Wazir, "when
he shall send for you and set you before the presence and question
you concerning your disobeying his orders, what thou wilt say?"

---

[1] Arab. "Istiláh" = specific dialect, idiom. See De Sacy, Chrestomathie, i. 443, where
the learned Frenchman shows abundant learning, but does very little for the learner.
[2] In the text "Kattán" = linen, flax.

She retorted, "I would say to the Sultan, 'Thou hast contraried Holy Law.'" At this the Minister resumed, "An he ask thee sundry questions wilt thou answer them?" and she replied, "Indeed I will." Hereat the Minister turned to the King and said, "Let us leave off question and answer with this maiden on points of conscience and Holy Law and ask if she understand the fine arts." Presently the Sultan put the question when she replied, "How should I not understand them when I am their father and their mother?" Quoth he, "Allah upon thee, O my lady, an thou wouldst favour us, let us hear one of thine airs and its words." So she rose and retired but presently returning with a lute sat down and set it upon her lap and ordered the strings and smote it with a masterly touch: then she fell to singing amongst other verses these ordered couplets:—

"Do thou good to men and so rule their necks: * Long reigns who by benefit rules mankind:
And lend aid to him who for aidance hopes: * For aye grateful is man with a noble mind:
Who brings money the many to him will incline * And money for tempting of man was designed:
Who hindereth favour and bounties, ne'er * Or brother or friend in creation shall find:
With harsh looks frown not in the Sage's face; * Disgusteth the freeman denial unkind:
Who frequenteth mankind all of good unknow'th: * Man is lief of rebellion, of largesse loath."

When the Sultan heard these couplets, his mind was distraught and he was perplext in thought; then turning to his Wazir, he said, "By Allah, these lines were surely an examination of and an allusion to our two selves; and doubtless she weeteth of us that I am the Sultan and thou art the Wazir, for the whole tenor of her talk proveth her knowledge of us." Then he turned to the maiden and said, "Right good are thy verse and thy voice, and thy words have delighted us with exceeding delight." Upon this she sang the following two couplets:—

"Men seek for them sorrow, and toil * Thro' long years as they brightly flow;
But Fate, in the well like the tank[1] * Firm-fixt, ruleth all below."

---

[1] Arab. "Fí Jifán ka'l-Jawábí!" which, I suppose, means small things (or men) and great.

Now as soon as the Sultan heard these last two couplets he made certain that the damsel was aware of his quality. She did not leave off her lute-playing till near daylight, when she rose and retired and presently brought in a breakfast befitting her degree (for indeed she was pleased with them); and when she had served it up they ate a small matter which sufficed them. After this she said, "Inshallah, you will return to us this night before supper-tide and become our guests;" and the twain went their ways marvelling at the beauty of the sisters and their loveliness and their fearlessness in the matter of the proclamation; and the Sultan said to the Wazir, "By Allah, my soul inclineth unto that maiden." And they stinted not walking until they had entered the palace. But when that day had gone by and evening drew nigh, the Monarch made ready to go, he and the Minister, to the dwelling of the damsels——And Shahrazad was surprised by the dawn of day and fell silent and ceased to say her permitted say. Then quoth her sister Dunyazad, "How sweet is thy story, O sister mine, and how enjoyable and delectable!" Quoth she, "And where is this compared with that I would relate to you on the coming night an the Sovran suffer me to survive." Now when it was the next night and that was

The Three Hundred and Sixty-sixth Night,

DUNYAZAD said to her, "Allah upon thee, O my sister, an thou be other than sleepy, finish for us thy tale that we may cut short the watching of this our latter night!" She replied, "With love and good will!" It hath reached me, O auspicious King, the director, the right-guiding, lord of the rede which is benefiting and of deeds fair-seeming and worthy celebrating, that the King and the Councillor made ready to go to the dwelling of the damsels taking with them somewhat of gold pieces, the time being half an hour after set of sun; and presently they repaired to the house of the sisters whither they had been invited on the past night. So they rapped at the door when the youngest maiden came to it and opened and let them in: then she salam'd to them and greeted them and entreated them with increased respect saying, "Welcome to our lords the Darwayshes." But she eyed them with the eye of the physiognomist[1] and said in herself, "Verily these two men are

---

[1] This form of cleverness is a favourite topic in Arabian folk-lore. The model man was

on no wise what they seem and, unless my caution and intelligence and power of knowledge have passed away from me, this must be the Sultan and that his Wazir, for grandeur and majesty are evident on them." Then she seated them and accosted them even more pleasantly and set before them supper, and when they had eaten enough, she brought basins and ewers for handwashing and served up coffee causing them to enjoy themselves and to give and take in talk till their pleasure was perfect. At the time of night-orisons they arose and, after performing the Wuzú-ablution, prayed, and when their devotions were ended the Sultan hent in hand his purse and gave it to the youngest sister saying, "Expend ye this upon your livelihood." She took the bag which held two thousand dinars and kissed his right hand, feeling yet the more convinced that he must be the Sultan: so she proved her respect by the fewness of her words as she stood between his hands to do him service. Also she privily winked at her sisters and mother and said to them by signs, "Verily this be the Monarch and that his Minister." The others then arose and followed suit as the sister had done, when the Sultan turned to the Wazir and said, "The case is changed: assuredly they have comprehended it and ascertained it;" presently adding to the girl, "O damsel, we be only Darwaysh folk and yet you all stand up in our service as if we were sovrans. I beseech you do not on

---

Iyás al-Muzani, al-Kazi (of Bassorah), in the 2nd century A.H., mentioned by Al-Haríri in his 7th Ass. and noted in Arab. Prov. (i. 593) as "more intelligent than Iyás." Ibn Khallikan (i. 233) tells sundry curious tales of him. Hearing a Jew ridicule the Moslem Paradise where the blessed ate and drank ad libitum but passed nothing away, he asked if all his food were voided: the Jew replied that God converted a part of it into nourishment and he rejoined, "Then why not the whole?" Being once in a courtyard he said that there was an animal under the bricks and a serpent was found: he had noted that only two of the tiles showed signs of dampness and this proved that there was something underneath that breathed. Al-Maydáni relates of him that hearing a dog bark, he declared that the beast was tied to the brink of a well; and he judged so because the bark was followed by an echo. Two men came before him, the complainant claimed money received by the defendant who denied the debt. Iyás asked the plaintiff where he had given it, and was answered, "Under a certain tree." The judge told him to go there by way of refreshing his memory and in his absence asked the defendant if his adversary could have reached it. "Not yet," said the rogue, forgetting himself; " 'tis a long way off" — which answer convicted him. Seeing three women act upon a sudden alarm, he said, "One of them is pregnant, another is nursing, and the third is a virgin." He explained his diagnosis as follows: "In time of danger persons lay their hands on what they most prize. Now I saw the pregnant woman in her flight place her hand on her belly, which showed me she was with child; the nurse placed her hand on her bosom, whereby I knew that she was suckling, and the third covered her parts with her hand proving to me that she was a maid." (Chenery's Al-Haríri, p. 334.)

this wise." But the youngest sister again came forwards and kissed the ground before him and blessed him and recited this couplet:

"Fair fate befal thee to thy foe's despite: * White be thy days and his be black as night.[1]

By Allah, O King of the Age, thou art the Sultan and that is the Minister." The Sovran asked, "What cause hast thou for supposing this?" and she answered, "From your grand demeanour and your majestic mien; for such be the qualities of Kings which cannot be concealed." Quoth the Monarch, "Thou hast spoken sooth; but, tell me, how happeneth it that you wone here without men protectors?" and quoth she, "O my lord the King, our history is wondrous and were it graven with graver-needles upon the eye-corners it were a warning to whoso would be warned." He rejoined, "What is it?" and she began the

Story of the Three Sisters and Their Mother.[2]

I AND my sisters and my mother are not natives of this city but of a capital in the land Al-Irák where my father was Sovran having troops and guards, Wazirs and Eunuch-chamberlains; and my mother was the fairest woman of her time insomuch that her beauty was a proverb throughout each and every region. Now it chanced that when I and my sisters were but infants, our father would set out to hunt and course and slay beasts of raven and take his pleasure in the gardens without the city. So he sent for his Wazir and appointed and constituted him Viceregent in his stead with full authority to command and be gracious to his lieges: then he got him ready and marched forth and the Viceroy entered upon his office. But it happened that it was the hot season and my mother betook herself to the terrace-roof of the palace in order to smell the air and sniff up the breeze. At that very hour, by the decree of the Decreer, the Wazir was sitting in the Kiosk or roofed balcony hanging to his upper mansion and holding in hand a mirror; and, as he looked therein, he saw the reflection of my mother, a glance of eyes which bequeathed him a

---

1 Such an address would be suited only to a King or a ruler.
2 MS. iii. 231-240; Scott's "Story of the Sisters and the Sultana their mother," vi. 82; Gauttier's *Histoire de la Sulthane et de ses trois Filles*, vi. 228.

thousand sighs. He was forthright distracted by her beauty and loveliness and fell sick and took to his pillow. Presently a confidential nurse came in and feeling his pulse, which showed no malady, said to him, "No harm for thee! thou shalt soon be well nor ever suffer from aught of sorrow." Quoth he, "O my nurse, canst thou keep a secret?" and quoth she, "I can." Then he told her all the love he had conceived for my mother and she replied, "This be a light affair nor hath it aught of hindrance: I will manage for thee such matter and I will soon unite thee with her." Thereupon he packed up for her some of the most sumptuous dresses in his treasury and said, "Hie thee to her and say, 'The Wazir hath sent these to thee by way of love-token and his desire is either that thou come to him and converse, he and thou, for a couple of hours,[1] or that he be allowed to visit thee.'" The nurse replied with "Hearkening and obedience," and fared forth and found my mother (and we little ones were before her) all unknowing aught of that business. So the old woman saluted her and brought forwards the dresses, and my mother arose and opening the bundle beheld sumptuous raiment and, amongst other valuables, a necklace of precious stones. So she said to the nurse, "This is indeed ornamental gear, especially the collar;" and said the nurse, "O my lady, these are from thy slave the Wazir by way of love-token, for he doteth on thee with extreme desire and his only wish is to forgather with thee and converse, he and thou, for a couple of hours, either in his own place or in thine whither he will come." Now when my mother heard these words from the nurse she arose and drew a scymitar which lay hard by and of her angry hastiness made the old woman's head fall from her body and bade her slave-girls pick up the pieces and cast them into the common privy of the palace. So they did her bidding and wiped away the blood. Now the Wazir abode expecting his nurse to return to him but she returned not; so next day he despatched another handmaid who went to my mother and said to her, "O my lady, our lord the Wazir sent thee a present of dress by his nurse; but she hath not come back to him." Hereupon my mother bade her Eunuchs take the slave and strangle her, then cast the corpse into the same house of easement where they had thrown the nurse. They did her bidding; but she said in her mind, "Haply the Wazir will return from the road of unright:"

---

[1] Arab. "Darajatáni" = lit. two astronomical degrees: the word is often used in this MS.

and she kept his conduct a secret. He however fell every day to sending slave-girls with the same message and my mother to slaying each and every, nor deigned show him any signs of yielding. But she, O our lord the Sultan, still kept her secret and did not acquaint our father therewith, always saying to herself, "Haply the Wazir will return to the road of right." And behold my father presently came back from hunting and sporting and pleasuring, when the Lords of the land met him and salam'd to him, and amongst them appeared the Minister whose case was changed. Now some years after this, O King of the Age, our sire resolved upon a Pilgrimage to the Holy House of Meccah—— And Shahrazad perceived the dawn of day and fell silent and ceased saying her permitted say. Then quoth her sister Dunyazad, "How sweet and tasteful is thy tale, O sister mine, and enjoyable and delectable." Quoth she, "And where is this compared with that I would relate to you on the coming night an the sovran suffer me to survive?" Now when it was the next night and that was

The Three Hundred and Sixty-seventh Night,

DUNYAZAD said to her "Allah upon thee, O my sister, an thou be other than sleepy, finish for us thy tale that we may cut short the watching of this our latter night." She replied, "With love and good will!" It hath reached me, O auspicious King, the director, the right-guiding, lord of the rede which is benefiting and of deeds fair-seeming and worthy celebrating, that the youngest sister continued to the Sultan:——So our sire, O King of the Age, resolved upon a Pilgrimage to the Holy House of Meccah and stablished the same Wazir Viceregent in his stead to deal commandment and break off and carry out. So he said in his heart, "Now have I won my will of the Sultan's Harem." So the King gat him ready and fared forth to Allah's Holy House after committing us to the charge of his Minister. But when he had been gone ten days, and the Wazir knew that he must be far from the city where he had left behind him me and my sisters and my mother, behold, an Eunuch of the Minister's came in to us and kissed ground before the Queen and said to her "Allah upon thee, O my lady, pity my lord the Wazir, for his heart is melted by thy love and his wits wander and his right mind; and he is now become as one annihilated. So do thou have ruth upon him and revive his heart and restore his health." Now when my mother heard these words, she bade her Eunuchs seize that Castrato and carry him from the room to the middle of the Divan-court and there slay him; but she did so without divulging her reasons. They obeyed her bidding; and when the Lords of the land and others saw the body of a man slain by the eunuchry of the palace, they informed the Wazir, saying, "What hateful business is this which hath befallen after the Sultan's departure?" He asked, "What is to do?" and they told him that his Castrato had been slain by a party of the palace eunuchry. Thereupon he said to them, "In your hand abideth testimony of this whenas the Sultan shall return and ye shall bear witness to it." But, O King, the Wazir's passion for our mother waxed cool after the deaths of the nurse and the slave-girls and the eunuch; and she also held her peace and spake not a word there anent. On this wise time passed and he sat in the stead of my sire till the Sultan's return drew near when the Minister dreaded lest our father, learning his ill deeds, should do him die. So he devised a device and wrote a letter to the King saying, "After salutation be it known to thee that thy Harem hath sent to me, not only once but five several times during thine absence, soliciting of me a foul action, to which I refused consent and replied, By Allah, however much she may wish to betray my Sovran, I by the Almighty will not turn traitor; for that I was left by thee guardian of the realm after thy departure." He added words upon words; then he sealed the scroll and gave it to a running courier with orders to hurry along the road. The messenger took it and fared with it to the Sultan's camp when distant eight days' journey from the capital; and, finding him seated in his pavilion,[1] delivered the writ. He took it and opened it and read it and when he understood its secret significance, his face changed, his eyes turned backwards and he bade his tents be struck for departure. So they fared by forced marches till between him and his capital remained only two stations. He then summoned two Chamberlains with orders to forego him to the city and take my mother and us three girls a day's distance from it and there put us to death. Accordingly, they led us four to the open country purposing to kill us, and my mother knew not what intent was in their minds until they

---

[1] Arab. "Síwan;" plur. "Síwáwín."

reached the appointed spot. Now the Queen had in times past heaped alms-deeds and largesse upon the two Chamberlains, so they held the case to be a grievous and said each to other, "By Allah we cannot slaughter them; no, never!" Then they told my mother of the letter which the Wazir had written to our father saying such-and-such, upon which she exclaimed, "He hath lied, by Allah, the arch-traitor; and naught happened save so-and-so." Then she related to them all she had done with the exactest truth. The men said, "Sooth thou hast spoken;" then arising without stay or delay they snared a gazelle and slaughtered it and filled with its blood four flasks; after which they broiled some of the flesh over the embers and gave it to my mother that we might satisfy our hunger. Presently they farewelled us saying, "We give you in charge of Him who never disappointed those committed to His care;" and, lastly, they went their ways leaving us alone in the wild and the wold. So we fell to eating the desert-grasses and drinking of the remnants of the rain, and we walked awhile and rested awhile without finding any city or inhabited region; and we waxed tired, O King of the Age, when suddenly we came upon a spot on a hill-flank abounding in vari-coloured herbs and fair fountains. Here we abode ten days and behold, a caravan drew near us and encamped hard by us, but they did not sight us for that we hid ourselves from their view until night fell. Then I went to them and asked of sundry eunuchs and ascertained that there was a city at the distance of two days' march from us; so I returned and informed my mother who rejoiced at the good tidings. As soon as it was morn the caravan marched off, so we four arose and walked all that day through at a leisurely pace, and a second day and so forth; until, on the afternoon of the fifth, a city rose before our sight fulfilling all our desires[1] and we exclaimed, "Alhamdolillah, laud be to the Lord who hath empowered us to reach it." We ceased not faring till sunset when we entered it and we found it a potent capital. Such was our case and that of our mother;[2] but as regards our sire the Sultan, as he drew near his home after the return-journey from the Hajj, the Lords of the land and the Chiefs of the city flocked out to meet him, and the town-folk followed one another like men riding on

---

[1] Arab. " 'Alà hudúd (or Alà ha-dd) al-Shauk," repeated in MS. iii. 239.

[2] Here the writer, forgetting that the youngest sister is speaking, breaks out into the third person — "their case" — "their mother," etc.

pillions[1] to salute him, and the poor and the mesquin congratulated him on his safety and at last the Wazir made his appearance.
The Sultan desired to be private with the Minister———And
Shahrazad was surprised by the dawn of day and fell silent and
ceased to say her permitted say. Then quoth her sister Dunyazad, "How sweet is thy story, O sister mine, and how enjoyable
and delectable!" Quoth she, "And where is this compared with
that I would relate to you on the coming night an the Sovran
suffer me to survive?" Now when it was the next night and
that was

The Three Hundred and Sixty-eighth Night,

DUNYAZAD said to her, "Allah upon thee, O my sister, an thou
be other than sleepy, finish for us thy tale that we may cut short
the watching of this our latter night!" She replied, "With love
and good will!" It hath reached me, O auspicious King, the
director, the right-guiding, lord of the rede which is benefiting
and of deeds fair-seeming and worthy celebrating, that the King
desired to be private with the Minister and when they were left
alone he said, "O Wazir, how was it between thee and that
Harim of mine?" Said the other, "O King of the Age, she sent to
me not only once but five several times and I refrained from her
and whatsoever eunuch she despatched I slew, saying, Haply she
may cease so doing and abandon her evil intent. But she did not
repent, so I feared for thine honour and sent to acquaint thee
with the matter." The Sultan bowed his head groundwards for
a while, then raising it he bade summon the two Chamberlains
whom he had sent to slay his wife and three children. On their
appearing he asked them, "What have you done in fulfilling my
commandment?" They answered, "We did that which thou
badest be done," and showed him the four flasks they had filled
with the blood and said, "This be their blood, a flask-full from
each." The Sultan hent them in hand and mused over what had
taken place between him and his wife of love and affection and
union; so he wept with bitter weeping and fell down in a fainting
fit. After an hour or so he recovered and turning to the Wazir
said, "Tell me, hast thou spoken sooth?" and the other replied,

---

[1] The idea is that of the French anonyma's "Mais, Monsieur, vous me suivez comme
un lavement."

"Yes, I have." Then the Sultan addressed the two Chamberlains and asked them, "Have ye put to death my daughters with their mother?" But they remained silent nor made aught of answer or address. So he exclaimed, "What is on your minds that ye speak not?" They rejoined, "By Allah, O King of the Age, the honest man cannot tell an untruth for that lying and leasing are the characteristics of hypocrites and traitors." When the Wazir heard the Chamberlains' speech his colour yellowed, his frame was disordered and a trembling seized his limbs, and the King turned to him and noted that these symptoms had been caused by the words of the two officials. So he continued to them, "What mean ye, O Chamberlains, by your saying that lies and leasing are the characteristics of hypocrites and traitors? Can it be that ye have not put them to death? And as ye claim to be true men either ye have killed them and ye speak thus or you are liars. Now by Him who hath set me upon the necks of His lieges, if ye declare not to me the truth I will do you both die by the foulest of deaths." They rejoined, "By Allah, O King of the Age, whenas thou badest us take them and slay them, we obeyed thy bidding and they knew not nor could they divine what was to be until we arrived with them at the middlemost and broadest of the desert; and when we informed them of what had been done by the Wazir, thy Harem exclaimed, 'There is no Majesty and there is no Might save in Allah, the Glorious, the Great. Verily we are Allah's and unto Him are we returning. But an ye kill us you will kill us wrongfully and ye wot not wherefor. By the Lord, this Wazir hath foully lied and hath accused us falsely before the Almighty.' So we said to her, O King of the Age, 'Inform us of what really took place,' and said the mother of the Princesses, 'Thus and thus it happened.' Then she fell to telling us the whole tale from first to last of the nurse who was sent to her and the handmaids and the Eunuch."[1] Hereupon the Sultan cried, "And ye, have ye slain them or not?" and the Chamberlains replied, "By Allah, O King of the Age, whenas the loyalty of thy Harem was made manifest to us we snared a gazelle and cut its throat and filled these four flasks with its blood; after which we broiled some of the flesh upon the embers and offered it to thy Harem and her children saying to them, 'We give thee in charge to Him who never disappointeth those committed to His care,'

---

[1] The text (p. 243) speaks of two eunuchs, but only one has been noticed.

and we added, 'Your truth shall save you.' Lastly we left them in the midmost of the waste and we returned hither." When the Sultan heard these words he turned to the Wazir and exclaimed, "Thou hast estranged from me my wife and my children;" but the Minister uttered not a word nor made any address and trembled in every limb like one afflicted with an ague. And when the King saw the truth of the Chamberlains and the treachery of the Minister he bade fuel be collected and set on fire and they did his bidding. Then he commanded them to truss up the Wazir, hand tied to foot, and bind him perforce upon a catapult[1] and cast him into the middle of the fiery pyre which made his bones melt before his flesh. Lastly he ordered his palace to be pillaged, his good to be spoiled and the women of his Harem to be sold for slaves. After this he said to the Chamberlains, "You must know the spot wherein you left the Queen and Princesses;" and said they, "O King of the Age, we know it well; but when we abandoned them and returned home they were in the midst of the wolds and the wilds nor can we say what befel them or whether they be now alive or dead." On this wise fared it with them; but as regards us three maidens and our mother, when we entered the city——And Shahrazad perceived the dawn of day and fell silent and ceased saying her permitted say. Then quoth her sister Dunyazad, "How sweet and tasteful is thy tale, O sister mine, and enjoyable and delectable?" Quoth she, "And where is this compared with that I would relate to you on the coming night an the Sovran suffer me to survive?" Now when it was the next night and that was

The Three Hundred and Sixty-ninth Night,

DUNYAZAD said to her, "Allah upon thee, O my sister, an thou be other than sleepy, finish for us thy tale that we may cut short the watching of this our latter night!" She replied, "With love and good will!" It hath reached me, O auspicious King, the director, the right-guiding, lord of the rede which is benefiting and of deeds fair-seeming and worthy celebrating, that the

---

[1] Arab. "Manjaník;" there are two forms of this word from the Gr. Μάγγανον, or Μηχανή, and it survives in our mangonel, a battering engine. The idea in the text is borrowed from the life of Abraham whom Nimrod cast by means of a catapult (which is a bow worked by machinery) into a fire too hot for man to approach.

youngest sister continued her tale:——So when we three
maidens and our mother entered the city about sunset I the
youngest said to them, "We be three Princesses and a Queen-
mother: so we cannot show ourselves in this our condition and
needs must we lodge us in a Khan: also 'tis my rede that we
should do best by donning boys' dress." All agreeing hereto we
did accordingly and, entering a Caravanserai, hired us a retired
chamber in one of the wings. Now every day we three fared
forth to service and at eventide we forgathered and took what
sufficed us of sustenance; but our semblance had changed with
the travails of travel and all who looked at us would say, These
be lads. In this plight we passed the space of a year full-told till,
one day of the days, we three fared forth to our chares, as was
our wont, and behold, a young man met us upon the way and
turning to me asked, "O lad, wilt thou serve in my house?"
Quoth I, "O my uncle,[1] I must ask advice," and quoth he, "O
my lad, crave counsel of thy mother and come and serve in our
home." He then looked at my sisters and enquired, "Be these
thy comrades, O lad?" and I replied "No, they are my brothers."
So we three went to our mother in the Khan and said to her,
"This young man wisheth to hire the youngest of us for service,"
and said she, "No harm in that." Thereupon the youth arose
and taking me by the hand guided me to his home and led me
in to his mother and his wife, and when the ancient dame saw
me, her heart was opened to me. Presently quoth the young man
to his parent, "I have brought the lad to serve in our house and
he hath two brothers and his mother dwelling with them."
Quoth she, "May it be fortunate to thee, O my son."[2] So I
tarried there serving them till sunset and when the evening-
meal was eaten, they gave me a dish of meat and three large
bannocks of clean bread. These I took and carried to my mother
whom I found sitting with my sisters and I set before them the
meat and bread; but when my parent saw this she wept with
sore weeping and cried, "Time hath overlooked us; erst we gave
food to the folk and now the folk send us food." And cried I,
"Marvel not at the works of the Creator; for verily Allah hath
ordered for us this and for others that and the world endureth

---

[1] Showing that he was older; otherwise she would have addressed him, "O my cousin."
A man is "young," in Arab speech, till forty and some say fifty.
[2] The little precatory formula would keep off the Evil Eye.

not for any one;" and I ceased not soothing my mother's heart till
it waxed clear of trouble and we ate and praised Almighty Allah.
Now every day I went forth to serve at the young man's house
and at eventide bore to my mother and sisters their sufficiency
of food for supper,[1] breakfast and dinner; and when the youth
brought eatables of any kind for me I would distribute it to the
family. And he looked well after our wants and at times he
would supply clothing for me and for the youths, my sisters, and
for my parent; so that all hearts in our lodgings were full of affection for him. At last his mother said, "What need is there for the
lad to go forth from us every eventide and pass the night with his
people? Let him lie in our home and every day about afternoon-
time carry the evening meal to his mother and brothers and then
return to us and keep me company." I replied, "O my lady, let
me consult my mother, to whom I will fare forthright and acquaint her herewith." But my parent objected saying, "O my
daughter, we fear lest thou be discovered, and they find thee out
to be a girl." I replied, "Our Lord will veil our secret;" and she
rejoined, "Then do thou obey them." So I lay with the young
man's mother nor did any divine that I was a maid, albeit from
the time when I entered into that youth's service my strength
and comeliness had increased. At last, one night of the nights, I
went after supper to sleep at my employer's and the young man's
mother chanced to glance in my direction when she saw my
loosed hair which gleamed and glistened many-coloured as a pea-
cock's robe. Next morning I arose and gathering up my locks
donned the Tákiyah[2] and proceeded, as usual, to do service about
the house never suspecting that the mother had taken notice of
my hair. Presently she said to her son, " 'Tis my wish that thou
buy me a few rose-blossoms which be fresh." He asked, "To
make conserve?" and she answered, "No." Then he enquired;
"Wherefore wantest thou roses?" and she replied, "By Allah, O
my son, I wish therewith to try this our servant whom I suspect
to be a girl and no boy; and under him in bed I would strew rose-
leaves, for an they be found wilted in the morning he is a lad,
and if they remain as they were he is a lass."[3] So he fared forth

---

[1] Supper comes first because the day begins at sundown.
[2] Calotte or skull-cap; vol. i. 224; viii. 120.
[3] This is a new "fact" in physics and certainly to be counted amongst "things not generally known." But Easterns have a host of "dodges" to detect physiological differences
such as between man and maid, virgin and matron, imperfect castratos and perfect eunuchs

and presently returned to his mother with the rose-blossoms;
and, when the sleeping-hour came, she went and placed them in
my bed. I slept well and in the morning when I arose she came
to me and found that the petals had not changed for the worse;
nay, they had gained lustre. So she made sure that I was a girl.
——And Shahrazad was surprised by the dawn of day and fell
silent and ceased to say her permitted say. Then quoth her
sister Dunyazad, "How sweet is thy story, O sister mine, and
how enjoyable and delectable!" Quoth she, "And where is this
compared with that I would relate to you on the coming night
an the Sovran suffer me to survive?" Now when it was the next
night and that was

The Three Hundred and Seventieth Night,

DUNYAZAD said to her, "Allah upon thee, O my sister, an thou be
other than sleepy, finish for us thy tale that we may cut short the
watching of this our latter night!" She replied, "With love and
good will!" It hath reached me, O auspicious King, the director,
the right-guiding, lord of the rede which is benefiting and of
deeds fair-seeming and worthy celebrating, that the damsel continued:——So the young man's mother made certain that her
servant lad was a virgin lass. But she concealed her secret from
her son and was kind to me and showed me respect and, of the
goodness of her heart, sent me back early to my mother and
sisters. Now one day of the days the youth came home about
noon as was his wont; and he found me with sleeves tucked up
to the elbows engaged in washing a bundle of shirts and tur-
bands; and I was careless of myself so he drew near me and noted
my cheeks that flushed rosy red and eyes which were as those of
the thirsty gazelle and my scorpion locks hanging adown my side
face. This took place in summertide; and when he saw me thus
his wits were distraught and his sound senses were as naught and
his judgment was in default: so he went in to his parent and said
to her, "O my mother, indeed this servant is no boy, but a
maiden girl and my wish is that thou discover for me her case and
make manifest to me her condition and marry me to her, for that

---

and so forth. Very Eastern, *mutatis mutandis*, is the tale of the thief-catcher, who discovered a fellow in feminine attire by throwing an object for him to catch in his lap and
by his closing his legs instead of opening them wide as the petticoated ones would do.

my heart is fulfilled of her love." Now by the decree of the
Decreer I was privily listening to all they said of me; so presently
I arose, after washing the clothes and what else they had given
me; but my state was changed by their talk and I knew and felt
certified that the youth and his mother had recognised me for a
girl. I continued on this wise till eventide when I took the food
and returned to my family and they all ate till they had eaten
enough, when I told them my adventure and my conviction. So
my mother said to me, "What remaineth for us now to do?" and
said I, "O my mother, let us arise, we three, before night shall set
in and go forth ere they lock the Khan upon us;[1] and if the door-
keeper ask us aught let us answer, 'We are faring to spend the
night in the house of the youth where our son is serving.'" My
mother replied, "Right indeed is thy rede." Accordingly, all
four of us went forth at the same time and when the porter asked,
"This is night-tide and whither may ye be wending?" we
answered, "We have been invited by the young man whom our
son serveth for he maketh a Septena-festival[2] and a bridal-feast:
so we purpose to night with him and return a-morn." Quoth he,
"There is no harm in that." So we issued out and turned aside
and sought the waste lands, the Veiler veiling us, and we ceased
not walking till the day brake and we were sore a-wearied. Then
we sat for rest till the rise of sun and when it shone we four
sprang up and strave with our wayfare throughout the first day
and the second and the third until the seventh. (Now all this
was related to Mohammed the Sultan of Cairo and his Wazir by
the youngest Princess and they abode wondering at her words.)
On the seventh day we reached this city and here we housed
ourselves; but to this hour we have no news of our sire after
the Minister was burnt nor do we know an he be whole or dead.
Yet we yearn for him: so do thou, of thine abundant favour, O
King of the Age, and thy perfect beneficence, send a messenger
to seek tidings of him and to acquaint him with our case, when
he will send to fetch us. Here she ceased speaking and the
Monarch and Minister both wondered at her words and exclaimed, "Exalted be He who decreeth to His servants severance
and reunion." Then the Sultan of Cairo arose without stay or

---

[1] She did not wish to part with her maidenhead at so cheap a price.
[2] Arab. "Subú'" (for "Yaum al-Subú'") a festival prepared on the seventh day after a
birth or a marriage or return from pilgrimage. See Lane (M. E. passim) under "Subooa."

delay and wrote letters to the King of Al-Irák, the father of the lamsels, telling him that he had taken them under his safeguard, ᵗhem and their mother, and gave the writ to the Shaykh of the Cossids¹ and appointed for it a running courier and sent him forth with it to the desert. After this the King took the three maidens and their mother and carried them to his Palace where he set apart for them an apartment and he appointed for them what sufficed of appointments. Now, as for the Cossid who fared forth with the letter, he stinted not spanning the waste for the space of two months until he made the city of the bereaved King of Al-Irák, and when he asked for the royal whereabouts they pointed out to him a pleasure-garden. So he repaired thither and went in to him, kissed ground before him, offered his services, prayed for him and lastly handed to him the letter. The King took it and brake the seal and opened the scroll; but when he read it and comprehended its contents, he rose up and shrieked a loud shriek and fell to the floor in a fainting fit. So the high officials flocked around him and raised him from the ground, and when he recovered after an hour or so they questioned him con-cerning the cause of this. He then related to them the adventures of his wife and children; how they were still in the bonds of life whole and hearty; and forthright he ordered a ship to be got ready for them and stored therein gifts and presents for him who had been the guardian of his Queen and her daughters. But he knew not what lurked for them in the future. So the ship sailed away, all on board seeking the desired city, and she reached it without delay, the winds blowing light and fair. Then she fired the cannon of safe arrival² and the Sultan sent forth to enquire concerning her,——And Shahrazad perceived the dawn of day and fell silent and ceased saying her permitted say. Then quoth her sister Dunyazad, "How sweet and tasteful is thy tale, O sister mine, and enjoyable and delectable!" Quoth she, "And where is this compared with that I would relate to you on the coming night an the Sovran suffer me to survive?" Now when it was the next night and that was

---

¹ For this Anglo-Indian term, ═ a running courier, see vol. vii. 340. It is the gist of the venerable Joe Miller in which the father asks a friend to name his seven-months child. "Call him 'Cossid' for verily he hath accomplished a march of nine months in seven months."

² Arab. "Madáfi al-Salámah," a custom showing the date of the tale to be more modern than any in the ten vols. of The Nights proper.

The Three Hundred and Seventy-first Night,

DUNYAZAD said to her, "Allah upon thee, O my sister, an thou be other than sleepy, finish for us thy tale that we may cut short the watching of this our latter night!" She replied, "With love and good will!" It hath reached me, O auspicious King, the director, the right-guiding, lord of the rede which is benefiting and of deeds fair-seeming and worthy celebrating, that the Sultan made enquiries concerning that ship, when behold! the Rais[1] came forth from her to the land and accosting the King handed to him the letter and acquainted him with the arrival of the gifts and presents. Whereupon he bade all on board her come ashore and be received in the guest-house for a space of three days until the traces of travel should disappear from them. After that time the Sultan gat ready whatso became his high degree of offerings evening those despatched to him by the father of the damsels and stowed them in the vessel, where he also embarked as much of victual and provaunt as might suffice for all the voyagers. On the fourth day after sunset the damsels and their mother were borne on board and likewise went the master after they had taken leave of the King and had salam'd to him and prayed for his preservation. Now in early morning the breeze blew free and fair so they loosed sail and made for the back[2] of the sea and voyaged safely for the first day and the second. But on the third about mid-afternoon a furious gale came out against them; whereby the sails were torn to tatters and the masts fell overboard; so the crew made certain of death, and the ship ceased not to be tossed upwards and to settle down without mast or sail till midnight, all the folk lamenting one to other, as did the maidens and their mother, till the wreck was driven upon an island and there went to pieces. Then he whose life-term was short died forthright and he whose life-term was long survived; and some bestrode planks and others butts and others again bulks of timber whereby all were separated each from other. Now the mother and two of the daughters clomb upon planks they chanced find and sought their safety; but the youngest of the maidens, who had mounted a keg,[3] and who knew nothing of

---

[1] Master, captain, skipper (not owner): see vols. i. 127; vi. 112.
[2] Zahr al-Bahr = the surface which affords a passage to man.
[3] Arab. "Batiyah," gen. = a black jack, a leathern flagon.

her mother and sisters, was carried up and cast down by the
waves for the space of five days till she landed upon an extensive
sea-board where she found a sufficiency to eat and drink. She sat
down upon the shore for an hour of time until she had taken rest
and her heart was calmed and her fear had flown and she had recovered her spirits: then she rose and paced the sands, all unknowing whither she should wend, and whenever she came upon
aught of herbs she would eat of them. This lasted through the
first day and the second till the forenoon of the third, when lo
and behold! a Knight advanced towards her, falcon on fist and
followed by a greyhound. For three days he had been wandering
about the waste questing game either of birds or of beasts, but he
happened not upon either when he chanced to meet the maiden,
and seeing her said in his mind, "By Allah, yon damsel is my
quarry this very day." So he drew near her and salam'd to her
and she returned his salute; whereupon he asked her of her condition and she informed him of what had betided her; and his heart
was softened towards her and taking her up on his horse's crupper
he turned him homewards. Now of this youngest sister (quoth
Shahrazad) there is much to say, and we will say it when the tale
shall require the telling. But as regards the second Princess, she
ceased not floating on the plank for the space of eight days, until
she was borne by the set of the sea close under the walls of a
city; but she was like one drunken with wine when she crawled
up the shore and her raiment was in rags and her colour had
wanned for excess of affright. However, she walked onwards at a
slow pace till she reached the city and came upon a house of low
stone walls. So she went in and there finding an ancient dame
sitting and spinning yarn, she gave her good evening and the
other returned it adding, "Who art thou, O my daughter, and
whence comest thou?" She answered, "O my aunt, I'm fallen
from the skies and have been met by the earth: thou needest not
question me of aught, for my heart is clean molten by the fire of
grief. An thou take me in for love and kindness 'tis well and if
not I will again fare forth on my wanderings." When the old
woman heard these words she compassioned the maiden and her
heart felt tender towards her, and she cried, "Welcome to thee, O
my daughter, sit thee down!" Accordingly she sat her down
beside her hostess and the two fell to spinning yarn whereby to
gain their daily bread: and the old dame rejoiced in her and said,
"She shall take the place of my daughter." Now of this second

Princess (quoth Shahrazad) there is much to say and we will say
it when the tale shall require the telling. But as regards the eldest
sister, she ceased not clinging to the plank and floating over the
sea till the sixth day passed, and on the seventh she was cast upon
a stead where lay gardens distant from the town six miles. So
she walked into them and seeing fruit close-clustering she took
of it and ate and donned the cast-off dress of a man she found
nearhand. Then she kept on faring till she entered the town and
here she fell to wandering about the Bazars till she came to the
shop of a Kunáfah[1]-maker who was cooking his vermicelli; and
he, seeing a fair youth in man's habit, said to her, "O younker,
wilt thou be my servant!" "O my uncle," she said, "I will
well;" so he settled her wage each day a quarter farthing,[2] not
including her diet. Now in that town were some fifteen shops
wherein Kunafah was made. She abode with the confectioner the
first day and the second and the third to the full number of ten,
when the traces of travel left her and fear departed from her
heart, and her favour and complexion were changed for the better
and she became even as the moon, nor could any guess that the lad
was a lass. Now it was the practice of that man to buy every
day half a quartern[3] of flour and use it for making his vermicelli;
but when the so-seeming youth came to him he would lay in each
morning three quarterns; and the townsfolk heard of this change
and fell to saying, "We will never dine without the Kunafah of
the confectioner who hath in his house the youth." This is what
befel the eldest Princess of whom (quoth Shahrazad) there is
much to say and we will say it when the tale shall require the
telling. But as regards the Queen-mother,——And Shahrazad
was surprised by the dawn of day and fell silent and ceased to
say her permitted say. Then quoth her sister Dunyazad, "How
sweet is thy story, O sister mine, and how enjoyable and delectable!" Quoth she, "And where is this compared with that I
would relate to you on the coming night an the Sovran suffer me
to survive?" Now when it was the next night and that was

---

[1] "Kunafáh" = a vermicelli cake often eaten at breakfast: see vol. x. 1: "Kunafáni" is
the baker or confectioner. Scott (p. 101) converts the latter into a "maker of cotton
wallets for travelling."

[2] In the text (iii. 260) "Mídí," a clerical error for "Mayyidí," an abbreviation of "Muay-
yadí," the Faddah, Nuss or half-dirham coined under Sultan al-Muayyad, A.H. ixth
cent. = A.D. xvth.

[3] Arab. "Rub'" (plur. "Arbá'") = the fourth of a "Waybah," the latter being the
sixth of an Ardabb (Irdabb) = 5 bushels. See vol. i. 263.

The Three Hundred and Seventy-second Night.

DUNYAZAD said to her, "Allah upon thee, O my sister, an thou be other than sleepy, finish for us thy tale that we may cut short the watching of this our latter night!" She replied, "With love and good will!" It hath reached me, O auspicious King, the director, the right-guiding, lord of the rede which is benefiting and of deeds fair-seeming and worthy celebrating, that as regards the mother of the maidens, when the ship broke up under them and she bestrode the bulk of timber, she came upon the Rais in his boat manned by three of the men; so he took her on board and they ceased not paddling for a space of three days when they sighted a lofty island which fulfilled their desire, and its summit towered high in air. So they made for it till they drew near it and landed on a low side-shore where they abandoned their boat; and they ceased not walking through the rest of that day and those that followed till one day of the days behold, a dust-cloud suddenly appeared to them spireing up to the skies. They fared for it and after a while it lifted, showing beneath it a host with swords glancing and lance-heads' gleams lancing and war steeds dancing and prancing, and these were ridden by men like unto eagles and the host was under the hands of a Sultan around whom ensigns and banners were flying. And when this King saw the Rais and the sailors and the woman following, he wheeled his charger themwards to learn what tidings they brought and rode up to the strangers and questioned them; and the castaways informed them that their ship had broken up under them. Now the cause of this host's taking the field was that the King of Al-Irak, the father of the three maidens, after he appointed the ship and saw her set out, felt uneasy at heart, presaging evil, and feared with sore fear the shifts of Time. So he went forth, he and his high Officials and his host, and marched adown the longshore till, by decree of the Decreer, he suddenly and all unexpectedly came upon his Queen who was under charge of the ship's captain. Presently, seeing the cavalcade and its ensigns the Rais went forward and recognising the King hastened up to him and kissed his stirrup and his feet. The Sultan turned towards him and knew him; so he asked him of his state and the Rais answered by relating all that had befallen him. Thereupon the King commanded his power to alight in that place and they

did so and set up their tents and pavilions. Then the Sultan took
seat in his Shámiyánah[1] and bade them bring his Queen and they
brought her, and when eye met eye the pair greeted each other
fondly and the father asked concerning her three children. She
declared that she had no tidings of them after the shipwreck and
she knew not whether they were dead or alive. Hereat the King
wept with sore weeping and exclaimed, "Verily we are Allah's
and unto Him we are returning!" after which he gave orders to
march from that place upon his capital. Accordingly they stinted
not faring for a space of four days till they reached the city and he
entered his citadel-palace. But every time and every hour he was
engrossed in pondering the affair of the three Princesses and kept
saying, "Would heaven I wot are they drowned or did they
escape the sea; and, if they were saved, Oh, that I knew whether
they were scattered or abode in company one with other and
whatever else may have betided them!" And he ceased not
brooding over the issue of things and kept addressing himself in
speech; and neither meat was pleasant to him nor drink. Such
were his case and adventure; but as regards the youngest sister
whenas she was met by the Knight and seated upon the crupper
of his steed, he ceased not riding with her till he reached his city
and went into his citadel-palace. Now the Knight was the son
of a Sultan who had lately deceased, but a usurper had seized the
reins of rule in his stead and Time had proved a tyrant to the
youth, who had therefore addicted himself to hunting and sporting. Now by the decree of the Decreer he had ridden forth to the
chase where he met the Princess and took her up behind him, and
at the end of the ride, when he returned to his mother, he was
becharmed by her charms; so he gave her in charge to his parent
and honoured her with the highmost possible honour and felt for
her a growing fondness even as felt she for him. And when the
girl had tarried with them a month full-told she increased in
beauty and loveliness and symmetrical stature and perfect grace;
then, the heart of the youth was fulfilled with love of her and on
like wise was the soul of the damsel who, in her new affection,
forgot her mother and her sisters. But from the moment that
maiden entered his Palace the fortunes of the young Knight
amended and the world waxed propitious to him nor less did the

---

[1] A royal pavilion; according to Shakespear (Hind. Dict. *sub voce*) it is a corruption of
the Pers. "Sayabán." = canopy.

hearts of the lieges incline to him; so they held a meeting and said, "There shall be over us no Sovran and no Sultan save the son of our late King; and he who at this present ruleth us hath neither great wealth nor just claim to the sovereignty." Now all this benefit which accrued to the young King was by the auspicious coming of the Princess. Presently the case was agreed upon by all the citizens of the capital that on the morning of the next day they would make him ruler and depose the usurper. ——And Shahrazad perceived the dawn of day and fell silent and ceased saying her permitted say. Then quoth her sister Dunyazad, "How sweet and tasteful is thy tale, O sister mine, and enjoyable and delectable!" Quoth she, "And where is this compared with that I would relate to you on the coming night an the Sovran suffer me to survive?" Now when it was the next night and that was

The Three Hundred and Seventy-third Night,

DUNYAZAD said to her, "Allah upon thee, O my sister, an thou be other than sleepy, finish for us thy tale that we may cut short the watching of this our latter night!" She replied, "With love and good will!" It hath reached me, O auspicious King, the director, the right-guiding, lord of the rede which is benefiting and of deeds fair-seeming and worthy celebrating, that the citizens in early morning held a meeting whereat were present the Lords of the land and the high Officials, and they went in to the usurping Sultan determined to remove and depose him. But he refused and forswore consent, saying, "By Allah, such thing may not be except after battle and slaughter." Accordingly they fared forth and acquainted the young King who held the matter grievous and was overridden by cark and care: however he said to them, "If there must perforce be fighting and killing, I have treasures sufficient to levy a host." So saying he went away and disappeared; but presently he brought them the moneys which they distributed to the troops. Then they repaired to the Maydán, the field of fight outside the city, and on like guise the usurping Sultan rode out with all his power. And when the two opposing hosts were ranged in their forces, each right ready for the fray, the usurper and his men charged home upon the young King and either side engaged in fierce combat and sore slaughter befel. But the usurper had the better of the battle and purposed

to seize the young King amidst his many when, lo and behold!
appeared a Knight backing a coal-black mare; and he was armed
cap-à-pie in a coat of mail, and he carried a spear and a mace.
With these he bore down upon the usurper and shore off his
right forearm so that he fell from his destrier, and the Knight
seeing this struck him a second stroke with the sword and parted
head from body. When his army saw the usurper fall, all sought
safety in flight and *sauve qui peut;* but the army of the young
King came up with them and caused the scymitar to fall upon
them so that were saved of them only those to whom length of
life was foreordained. Hereupon the victors lost no time in
gathering the spoils and the horses together; but the young King
stood gazing at the Knight and considering his prowess; yet he
failed to recognise him and after an hour or so the stranger disappeared leaving the conqueror sorely chafed and vexed for that
he knew him not and had failed to forgather with him. After
this the young King returned from the battle-field with his band
playing behind him and he entered the seat of his power, and was
raised by the lieges to the station of his sire. Those who had
escaped the slaughter dispersed in all directions and sought safety
in flight and the partizans who had enthroned the young King
thronged around him and gave him joy as also did the general
of the city, whose rejoicings were increased thereby. Now the
coming of the aforesaid Knight was a wondrous matter. When
the rightful King made ready for battle the Princess feared for his
life and, being skilled in the practice of every weapon, she escaped
the notice of the Queen-dowager and after donning her war-garb
and battle-gear she went forth to the stable and saddled her a
mare and mounted her and pushed in between the two armies.
And as soon as she saw the usurper charge down upon the young
King as one determined to shed his life's blood, she forestalled
him and attacked him and tore out the life from between his ribs.
Then she returned to her apartment nor did any know of the deed
she had done. Presently, when it was eventide the young King
entered the Palace after securing his succession to royalty; but
he was still chafed and vexed for that he knew not the Knight.
His mother met him and gave him joy of his safety and his acces-
sion to the Sultanate, whereto he made reply, "Ah! O my
mother, my length of days was from the hand of a horseman who
suddenly appearing joined us in our hardest stress and aided me
in my straitest need and saved me from Death." Quoth she, "O

my son, hast thou recognised him?" and quoth he, " 'Twas my
best desire to discover him and to stablish him as my Wazir, but
this I failed to do." Now when the Princess heard these words
she laughed and rejoiced and still laughing said, "To whoso will
make thee acquainted with him what wilt thou give?" and said
he, "Dost thou know him?" So she replied, "I wot him not"
and he rejoined, "Then what is the meaning of these thy words?"
when she answered him in these prosaic rhymes:[1]—

"O my lord, may I prove thy sacrifice * Nor exult at thy sorrows thine
　　enemies!
　Could unease and disease by others be borne * The slave should bear load on
　　his lord that lies:
　I'll carry whatever makes thee complain * And be my body the first that
　　dies."

When he heard these words he again asked, "Dost thou know
him?" and she answered, "He? Verily we wot him not;"[2] and
repeated the saying to him a second time: withal he by no means
understood her. So quoth she, "How canst thou administer the
Sultanate and yet fail to comprehend my simple words? For
indeed I have made the case clear to thee." Hereupon he
fathomed the secret of the saying and flew to her in his joy and
clasped her to his bosom and kissed her upon the cheeks. But
his mother turned to him and said, "O my son, do not on this
wise, for everything hath its time and season;"———And Shahrazad was surprised by the dawn of day and fell silent and ceased
to say her permitted say. Then quoth her sister Dunyazad, "How
sweet is thy story, O sister mine, and how enjoyable and delectable!" Quoth she, "And where is this compared with that I
would relate to you on the coming night an the Sovran suffer me
to survive?" Now when it was the next night and that was

The Three Hundred and Seventy-fourth Night,

Dunyazad said to her, "Allah upon thee, O my sister, an thou
be other than sleepy, finish for us thy tale that we may cut short

---

[1] Arab. "Musajja' " = rhymed prose: for the Saj'a, see vol. i. 116, and Terminal Essay,
vol. x. p. 220. So Chaucer: —

　　　　　　In rhyme or ellès in cadence.

[2] Arab. "Huwa inná na'rifu-h" lit. = He, verily we wot him not: the juxtaposition of
the two first pronouns is intended to suggest "I am he."

the watching of this our latter night!" She replied, "With love and good will!" It hath reached me, O auspicious King, the director, the right-guiding, lord of the rede which is benefiting and of deeds fair-seeming and worthy celebrating, that the Sultan's mother said, "O my son, everything hath its time and season; and whoso hurrieth a matter before opportunity befit shall be punished with the loss of it." But he replied, "By Allah, O my mother, thy suspicion be misplaced: I acted thus only on my gratitude to her, for assuredly she is the Knight who came to my aidance and who saved me from death." And his mother excused him. They passed that night in converse and next day at noontide the King sought the Divan in order to issue his commandments; but when the assembly filled the room and became as a garden of bloom the Lords of the land said to him, "O King of the Age, 'twere not suitable that thou become Sultan except thou take to thee a wife; and Alhamdolillah—laud to the Lord who hath set thee on the necks of His servants and who hath restored the realm to thee as successor of thy sire. There is no help but that thou marry." Quoth he, "To hear is to consent;" then he arose without stay or delay and went in to his mother and related to her what had happened. Quoth she, "O my son, do what becometh thee and Allah prosper thy affairs!" He said to her, "O my mother, retire thou with the maiden and persuade her to marriage for I want none other and I love not aught save herself," and said she, "With joy and gladness." So he went from her and she arose and was private with the damsel when she addressed her, "O my lady, the King desireth to wed thee and he wanteth none other and he seeketh not aught save thee." But the Princess hearing this exclaimed, "How shall I marry, I who have lost my kith and kin and my dear ones and am driven from my country and my birth-place? This were a proceeding opposed to propriety! But if it need must be and I have the fortune to forgather with my mother and sisters and father, then and then only it shall take place." The mother replied, "Why this delay, O my daughter? The Lords of the land have stood up against the King in the matter of marriage, and in the absence of espousals we fear for his deposition. Now maidens be many and their relations long to see each damsel wedded to my son and become a Queen in virtue of her husband's degree: but he wanteth none other and loveth naught save thyself. Accordingly, an thou wouldst take compassion on him and protect him

by thy consent from the insistence of the Grandees, deign accept
him to mate." Nor did the Sultan's mother cease to speak soothing words to the maiden and to gentle her with soft language
until her mind was made up and she gave consent.[1] Upon this
they began to prepare for the ceremony forthright, and summoned the Kazi and witnesses who duly knotted the knot of
wedlock and by eventide the glad tidings of the espousals were
bruited abroad. The King bade spread bride-feasts and banquet-
ing tables and invited his high Officials and the Grandees of the
kingdom and he went in to the maiden that very night and the
rejoicings grew in gladness and all sorrows ceased to deal sadness.
Then he proclaimed through the capital and all the burghs that
the lieges should decorate the streets with rare tapestries and
multiform in honour of the Sultanate. Accordingly, they adorned
the thoroughfares in the city and its suburbs for forty days and
the rejoicings increased when the King fed the widows and the
Fakirs and the mesquin and scattered gold and robed and gifted
and largessed till all the days of decoration were gone by. On
this wise the sky of his estate grew clear by the loyalty of the
lieges and he gave orders to deal justice after the fashion of the
older Sultans, to wit, the Chosroës and the Cæsars; and this condition endured for three years, during which Almighty Allah
blessed him by the Princess with two men-children as they were
moons. Such was the case with the youngest Princess; but as
regards the cadette, the second sister,——And Shahrazad perceived the dawn of day and fell silent and ceased saying her permitted say. Then quoth her sister Dunyazad, "How sweet and
tasteful is thy tale, O sister mine, and enjoyable and delectable!"
Quoth she, "And where is this compared with that I would
relate to you on the coming night an the Sovran suffer me to survive?" Now when it was the next night and that was

The Three Hundred and Seventy-fifth Night,

DUNYAZAD said to her, "Allah upon thee, O my sister, an thou
be other than sleepy, finish for us thy tale that we may cut short

---

[1] In Moslem tales decency compels the maiden, however much she may be in love, to
show extreme unwillingness in parting with her maidenhead especially by marriage; and
this farce is enacted in real life (see vol. viii. 40). The French tell the indecent truth,

Désir de fille est un feu qui dévore:
Désir de femme est plus fort encore.

the watching of this our latter night!" She replied, "With love
and good will!" It hath reached me, O auspicious King, the
director, the right-guiding, lord of the rede which is benefiting
and of deeds fair-seeming and worthy celebrating, that as regards
the case of the cadette, the second damsel, when she was adopted
to daughter by the ancient dame she fell to spinning with her and
living by the work of their hands. Now there chanced to govern
that city a Báshá[1] who had sickened with a sore sickness till he
was near unto death; and the wise men and leaches had com-
pounded for him of medicines a mighty matter which, however,
availed him naught. At last the tidings came to the ears of the
Princess who lived with the old woman and she said to her, "O
my mother, I desire to prepare a tasse of broth and do thou bear
it to the Basha and let him drink of it; haply will Almighty Allah
vouchsafe him a cure whereby we shall gain some good." Said
the other, "O my daughter, and how shall I obtain admittance
and who shall set the broth before him?" The maiden replied,
"O my mother, at the Gate of Allah Almighty!"[2] and the dame
rejoined, "Do thou whatso thou willest." So the damsel arose
and cooked a tasse of broth and mingled with it sundry hot spices
such as pimento[3] and she had certain leaflets taken from the so-

---

[1] The Arab. form (our old "bashaw") of the Turk. "Pasha," which the French and many
English write Pacha, thus confusing the vulgar who called Ibrahim Pacha "Abraham
Parker." The origin of the word is much debated and the most fanciful derivations have
been proposed. Some have taken it from the Sansk. "Paksha" == a wing: Fuerst from
Pers. Páigáh == rank, dignity; Von Hammer (History) from Pái-Sháh == foot of the king;
many from "Pádisháh" == the Sovran, and Mr. E. T. W. Gibb suspects a connection with
the Turk. "Básh" == a head. He writes to me that the oldest forms are "Bashah" and
"Báshah"; and takes the following quotation from Colonel Jevád Bey, author of an excellent work on the Janissaries published a few years ago. "As it was the custom of the
(ancient) Turks to call the eldest son 'Páshá,' the same style was given to his son Alá
al-Din (Aladdin) by Osmán Gházi, the founder of the Empire; and he kept this heir at
home and beside him, whilst he employed the cadet Orkhan Bey as his commander-in-
chief. When Orkhán Gházi ascended the throne he conferred the title of Páshá upon his
son Sulayman. Presently reigned Murád (Amurath), who spying signs of disaffection in
his first-born Sáwújí Bey about the middle of his reign created Kárá Khalíl (his Kází-
Askar or High Chancellor) Wazir with the title Kazyr al-Dín Pasha; thus making him,
as it were, an adopted son. After this the word passed into the category of official titles
and came to be conferred upon those who received high office." Colonel Jevád Bey then
quotes in support of his opinion the "History of Munajjim Pasha" and the "Fatáyah
al-Wukú'at" == Victories of Events. I may note that the old title has been sadly pros-
tituted in Egypt as well as in Turkey: in 1851 Páshás could be numbered on a man's fingers;
now they are innumerable and of no account.

[2] Arab. " 'Alá bábi 'lláh" == for the love of the Lord, gratis, etc., a most popular phrase.

[3] Arab. "Bahár," often used for hot spices generally.

called Wind tree,[1] whereof she inserted a small portion deftly
mingling the ingredients. Then the old woman took it and set
forth and walked till she reached the Basha's mansion where the
servants and eunuchs met her and asked her of what was with
her. She answered, "This is a tasse of broth which I have brought
for the Basha that he drink of it as much as he may fancy; haply
Almighty Allah shall vouchsafe healing to him." They went in
and reported that to the Basha who exclaimed, "Bring her to me
hither." Accordingly, they led her within and she offered to him
the tasse of broth, whereupon he rose and sat upright and removed the cover from the cup which sent forth a pleasant savour:
so he took it and sipped of it a spoonful and a second and a third,
when his heart opened to her and he drank of it till he could no
more. Now this was in the forenoon and after finishing the soup
he gave the old woman a somewhat of dinars which she took and
returned therewith to the damsel rejoicing, and handed to her the
gold pieces. But the Basha immediately after drinking the broth
felt drowsy and he slept a restful sleep till mid-afternoon and
when he awoke health had returned to his frame beginning from
the time he drank. So he asked after the ancient dame and sent
her word to prepare for him another tasse of broth like the first;
but they told him that none knew her dwelling-place. Now
when the old woman returned home the maiden asked her
whether the broth had pleased the Basha or not; and she said
that it was very much to his liking; so the girl got ready a second
portion but without all the stronger ingredients[2] of the first.
Then she gave it to the dame who took it and went forth with it
and whilst the Basha was asking for her behold, up she came and
the servants took her and led her in to the Governor. On seeing
her he rose and sat upright and called for other food and when it
was brought he ate his sufficiency, albeit for a length of time he
could neither rise nor walk. But from the hour he drank all the
broth he sniffed the scent of health and he could move about as
he moved when hale and hearty   So he asked the old dame saying,
"Didst thou cook this broth?" and she answered, "O my lord, my
daughter made it and sent me with it to thee." He exclaimed,
"By Allah this maiden cannot be thy daughter, O old woman;
and she can be naught save the daughter of Kings. But bid her

---

[1] In the text Shajarat Ríh.
[2] Arab. "Ma'ádin" = minerals, here mentioned for the first time.

every day at morning-tide cook me a tasse of the same broth."
The other replied, "To hear is to obey," and returned home with
this message to the damsel who did as the Basha bade the first day
and the second to the seventh day. And the Basha waxed
stronger every day and when the week was ended he took horse
and rode to his pleasure-garden. He increased continually in
force and vigour till, one day of the days, he sent for the dame
and questioned her concerning the damsel who lived with her; so
she acquainted him with her case and what there was in her of
beauty and loveliness and perfect grace. Thereupon the Basha
fell in love with the girl by hearsay and without eye-seeing[1]:——
And Shahrazad was surprised by the dawn of day and fell silent
and ceased to say her permitted say. Then quoth her sister Dunyazad, "How sweet is thy story, O sister mine, and how enjoyable and delectable!" Quoth she, "And where is this compared
with that I would relate to you on the coming night an the
Sovran suffer me to survive?" Now when it was the next night
and that was

The Three Hundred and Seventy-sixth Night,

DUNYAZAD said to her, "Allah upon thee, O my sister, an thou
be other than sleepy, finish for us thy tale that we may cut short
the watching of this our latter night!" She replied, "With love
and good will!" It hath reached me, O auspicious King, the
director, the right-guiding, lord of the rede which is benefiting
and of deeds fair-seeming and worthy celebrating, that the Basha
fell in love with the girl by hearsay and without eye-seeing: so he
changed his habit and donning a dress of Darwaysh-cut left his
mansion and threaded the streets passing from house to house
until he reached that of the old woman. He then knocked at the
entrance and she came behind it and asked "Who's at the door?"
"A Darwaysh and a stranger," answered he, "who knoweth no
man in this town and who is sore anhungered." Now the ancient
dame was by nature niggardly and she had lief put him off, but the
damsel said to her, "Turn him not away," and quoting "Honour
to the foreigner is a duty," said, "So do thou let him in." She
admitted him and seated him when the maiden brought him a
somewhat of food and stood before him in his service. He ate

---

[1] For the ear conceiving love before the eye (the basis of half these love-stories), see vol
iii. 9.

one time and ten times he gazed at the girl until he had eaten his
sufficiency when he washed his hands and rising left the house
and went his ways. But his heart flamed with love of the Princess
and he was deeply enamoured of her and he ceased not walking
until he reached his mansion whence he sent for the old woman.
And when they brought her, he produced a mint of money and a
sumptuous dress in which he requested and prayed her to attire
the damsel: then the old woman took it and returned to her
protegée, saying to herself, "By Allah, if the girl accept the Basha
and marry him she will prove sensible as fortunate; but an she
be not content so to do I will turn her out of my door." When
she went in she gave her the dress and bade her don it, but the
damsel refused till the old woman coaxed her and persuaded her
to try it on. Now when the dame left the Basha, he privily
assumed a woman's habit and followed in her footsteps; and at
last he entered the house close behind her and beheld the Princess
in the sumptuous dress. Then the fire of his desire flamed higher
in his heart and he lacked patience to part from her, so he returned
to his mansion with mind preoccupied and vitals yearning.
Thither he summoned the old woman and asked her to demand
the girl in marriage and was instant with her and cried, "No help
but this must be." Accordingly she returned home and acquainted
the girl with what had taken place adding, "O my daughter,
verily the Basha loveth thee and his wish is to wed thee: he hath
been a benefactor to us, and thou wilt never meet his like; for
that he is deeply enamoured of thee and the byword saith, 'Reward of lover is return of love.'" And the ancient dame ceased
not gentling her and plying her with friendly words till she was
soothed and gave consent. Then she returned to the Basha and
informed him of her success, so he joyed with exceeding joy, and
without stay or delay bade slaughter beeves and prepare bridal
feasts and spread banquets whereto he invited the notables of his
government: after which he summoned the Kazi who tied the
knot and he went in to her that night. And of the abundance of
his love he fared not forth from her till seven days had sped; and
he ceased not to cohabit with her for a span of five years during
which Allah vouchsafed to him a man-child by her and two
daughters. Such was the case with the cadette Princess; but as
regards the eldest sister, when she entered the city in youth's
attire she was accosted by the Kunáfah-baker and was hired for a
daily wage of a Mídí of silver besides her meat and drink in his

house. Now 'twas the practice of that man every day to buy half a quartern of flour and thereof make his vermicelli; but when the so-seeming youth came to him he would buy and work up three quarterns; and all the folk who bought Kunafah of him would flock to his shop with the view of gazing upon the beauty and loveliness of the Youth and said, "Exalted be He who created and perfected what He wrought in the creation of this young man!" Now by the decree of the Decreer the baker's shop faced the lattice-windows of the Sultan's Palace and one day of the days the King's daughter chanced to look out at the window and she saw the Youth standing with sleeves tucked up from arms which shone like ingots[1] of silver. Hereat the Princess fell in love with the Youth,——And Shahrazad perceived the dawn of day and fell silent and ceased saying her permitted say. Then quoth her sister Dunyazad, "How sweet and tasteful is thy tale, O sister mine, and enjoyable and delectable!" Quoth she, "And where is this compared with that I would relate to you on the coming night an the Sovran suffer me to survive?" Now when it was the next night and that was

The Three Hundred and Seventy-seventh Night,

DUNYAZAD said to her, "Allah upon thee, O my sister, an thou be other than sleepy finish for us thy tale that we may cut short the watching of this our latter night!" She replied, "With love and good will!" It hath reached me, O auspicious King, the director, the right-guiding, lord of the rede which is benefiting and of deeds fair-seeming and worthy celebrating, that when the Sultan's daughter looked out at the window she fell in love with the youth, and she knew not how to act that she might forgather with him: so desire afflicted her and extreme fondness and presently she took to her pillow all for her affection to that young man. Thereupon her nurse went in to her and found her lying upon the carpet-bed a-moaning and a-groaning "Ah!" So she exclaimed, "Thy safety from all whereof thou hast to complain!" Then she took her hand and felt her pulse but could find in it no

---

[1] According to Dr. Steingass "Mirwad" = the iron axle of a pulley or a wheel for drawing water or lifting loads, hence possibly a bar of metal, an ingot. But he is more inclined to take it in its usual sense of "Kohl-pencil." Here "Mirwád" is the broader form like "Miftáh" for "Miftah," much used in Syria.

symptoms of sickness bodily, whereupon she said, "O my lady, thou hast no unease save what eyesight hath brought thee." She replied, "O my mother, do thou keep sacred my secret, and if thy hand can reach so far as to bring me my desire, prithee do so;" and the nurse rejoined, "O my lady, like me who can keep a secret? therefore confide to me thy longing and Allah vouchsafe thee thy dearest hope." Said the Princess, "O my mother, my heart is lost to the young man who worketh in the vermicelli-baker's shop and if I fail to be united with him I shall die of grief." The nurse replied, "By Allah, O my lady, he is the fairest of his age and indeed I lately passed by him as his sleeves were tucked up above his forearms and he ravished my wits: I longed to accost him but shame overcame me in presence of those who were round him, some buying Kunafah and others gazing on his beauty and loveliness, his symmetric stature and his perfect grace. But I, O my lady, will do thee a service and cause thee forgather with him ere long." Herewith the heart of the Princess was solaced and she promised the nurse all good. Then the old woman left her and fell to devising how she should act in order to bring about a meeting between her and the youth or carry him into the Palace. So she went to the baker's shop and bringing out an Ashrafi[1] said to him, "Take, O Master, this gold piece and make me a platter[2] of vermicelli meet for the best and send it for me by this Youth who shall bring it to my home that be near hand: I cannot carry it myself." Quoth the baker in his mind, "By Allah, good pay is this gold piece and a Kunafah is worth ten silverlings; so all the rest is pure profit." And he replied, "On my head and eyes be it, O my lady;" and taking the Ashrafi made her a plate of vermicelli and bade his servant bear it to her house. So he took it up and accompanied the nurse till she reached the Princess's palace when she went in and seated the Youth in an out-of-the-way closet. Then she repaired to her nursling and said, "Rise up, O my lady, for I have brought thee thy desire." The Princess sprang to her feet in hurry and flurry and fared till she came to the closet; then, going in she found the Youth who had set down the Kunafah and who was standing in expectation of the nurse's return that he and she might wend homewards. And suddenly the

---

[1] For the Ashrafi, a gold coin of variable value, see vol. iii. 294. It is still coined; the Calcutta Ashrafi worth £1 11s. 8d. is ⅙₀th (about 5s. to the oz.) better than the English standard, and the Regulations of May, 1793, made it weigh 190.894 grs. Troy.

[2] In text "Anjar" = a flat platter; Pers.

Sultan's daughter came in and bade the Youth be seated beside her, and when he took seat she clasped him to her bosom of her longing for him and fell to kissing him on the cheeks and mouth ever believing him to be a male masculant, till her hot desire for him was quenched.[1] Then she gave to him two golden dinars and said to him, "O my lord and coolth of my eyes, do thou come hither every day that we may take our pleasure, I and thou." He said, "To hear is to obey," and went forth from her hardly believing in his safety, for he had learnt that she was the Sultan's daughter, and he walked till he reached the shop of his employer to whom he gave the twenty dinars. Now when the baker saw the gold, affright and terror entered his heart and he asked his servant whence the money came; and, when told of the adventure, his horror and dismay increased and he said to himself, "An this case of ours continue, either the Sultan will hear that this youth practiseth upon his daughter, or she will prove in the family way and 'twill end in our deaths and the ruin of our country. The lad must quit this evil path." Thereupon quoth he to the Youth, "From this time forwards do thou cease faring forth thereto," whereat quoth the other, "I may not prevent myself from going and I dread death an I go not." So the man cried, "Do whatso may seem good to thee." Accordingly, the Princess in male attire fell to going every morning and meeting the Sultan's daughter, till one day of the days she went in and the twain sat down and laughed and enjoyed themselves, when lo and behold! the King entered. And as soon as he espied the youth and saw him seated beside his daughter, he commanded him be arrested and they arrested him;———And Shahrazad was surprised by the dawn of day and fell silent and ceased to say her permitted say. Then quoth her sister Dunyazad, "How sweet is thy story, O sister mine, and how enjoyable and delectable!" Quoth she, "And where is this compared with that I would relate to you on the coming night an the Sovran suffer me to survive?" Now when it was the next night and that was

---

[1] By what physical process the author modestly leaves to the reader's imagination. Easterns do not often notice this feminine venereal paroxysm which takes the place of seminal emission in the male. I have seen it happen to a girl when hanging by the arms a trifle too long from a gymnastic cross-bar; and I need hardly say that at such moments (if men only knew them) every woman, even the most modest, is an easy conquest. She will repent it when too late, but the flesh has been too strong for her.

The Three Hundred and Seventy-eighth Night,

DUNYAZAD said to her, "Allah upon thee, O my sister, an thou be other than sleepy, finish for us thy tale that we may cut short the watching of this our latter night!" She replied, "With love and good will!" It hath reached me, O auspicious King, the director, the right-guiding, lord of the rede which is benefiting and of deeds fair-seeming and worthy celebrating, that when the Sultan entered and saw the youth sitting beside his daughter he commanded him to be arrested and they arrested him; they also seized the Princess and bound her forearms to her sides with straitest bonds. Then the King summoned the Linkman and bade him smite off both their heads: so he took them and went down with them to the place of execution. But when the tidings reached the Kunáfáni he shut up shop without stay and delay and fled. Presently the Sultan said in his mind, "Fain would I question the Youth touching his object in entering hither, and ask him who conducted him to my daughter and how he won access to her." Accordingly he sent to bring back the twain and imprisoned them till night-fall: then he went in to his Harem and caused his daughter's person to be examined, and when they inspected her she proved to be a pure maid. This made the King marvel, for he supposed that the Youth must have undone her maidenhead;[1] so he sent for him to the presence, and when he came he considered him and found him fairer even than his daughter; nay, far exceeding her in beauty and loveliness. So he cried, "By Allah this be a wondrous business! Verily my daughter hath excuse for loving this Youth nor to my judgment doth she even him in charms: not the less this affair is a shame to us, and the foulest of stains and needs must the twain be done to death to-morrow morning!" Herewith he commanded the jailer to take the Youth and to keep him beside him and he shut up the girl with her nurse. The jailer forthwith led his charge to the jail; but it so happened that its portal was low; and, when the Youth was ordered to pass through it, he bent his brow downwards for easier entrance, when his turband struck against the lintel and fell from his head. The jailer turned to look at him, and behold, his hair was braided and the plaits being loosed gleamed like an ingot of gold. He felt assured that the youth was a maiden so he returned to the King in all haste and hurry and

---

[1] A neat and suggestive touch of Eastern manners and morals.

cried, "Pardon, O our lord the Sultan!" "Allah pardon us and thee;" replied the King, and the man rejoined, "O King of the Age, yonder Youth is no boy; nay, he be a virgin girl." Quoth the Sultan, "What sayest thou?" and quoth the other, "By the truth of Him who made thee ruler of the necks of His worshippers, O King of the Age, verily this is a maiden." So he bade the prison-keeper bring her and set her in his presence and he returned with her right soon, but now she paced daintily as the gazelle and veiled her face, because she saw that the jailer had discovered her sex. The King then commanded them carry her to the Harem whither he followed her and presently, having summoned his daughter, he questioned her concerning the cause of her union with the so-seeming Youth. Herewith she related all that had happened with perfect truth: he also put questions to the Princess in man's habit, but she stood abashed before him and was dumb, unable to utter a single word. As soon as it was morning, the Sultan asked of the place where the Youth had dwelt and they told him that he lodged with a Kunáfah-baker, and the King bade fetch the man, when they reported that he had fled. However, the Sultan was instant in finding him, so they went forth and sought him for two days when they secured him and set him between the royal hands. He enquired into the Youth's case and the other replied, "By Allah, O King of the Age, between me and him were no questionings and I wot not whence may be his origin." The Monarch rejoined, "O man, thou hast my plighted word for safety, so continue thy business as before and now gang thy gait." Then he turned to the maiden and repeated his enquiries, when she made answer saying, "O my lord, my tale is wondrous and my adventures marvellous." "And what may they be?" he asked her.——And Shahrazad was surprised by the dawn of day and fell silent and ceased saying her permitted say. Then quoth her sister Dunyazad, "How sweet and tasteful is thy tale, O sister mine, and enjoyable and delectable!" Quoth she, "And where is this compared with that I would relate to you on the coming night an the Sovran suffer me to survive?" Now when it was the next night and that was

The Three Hundred and Seventy-ninth Night.

DUNYAZAD said to her, "Allah upon thee, O my sister, an thou be other than sleepy, finish for us thy tale that we may cut short the watching of this our latter night!" She replied, "With love and good will!" It hath reached me, O auspicious King, the director, the right-guiding, lord of the rede which is benefiting and of deeds fair-seeming and worthy celebrating, that the Princess said to the Sultan, "In very sooth my tale is passing strange," and he besought her to recount it. So she began to disclose the whole of her history and the adventures which had befallen her and her sisters and their mother; especially of the shipwreck in middle-most ocean and of her coming to land; after which she told the affair of the Wazir burnt by her sire, that traitor who had separated children from father and, brief, all that had betided them from first to last. Hearing her soft speech and her strange story the Sultan marvelled and his heart inclined herwards; then he gave her in charge to the Palace women and conferred upon her favours and benefits. But when he looked upon her beauty and loveliness, her brilliancy and perfect grace he fell deeply in love with her, and his daughter hearing the accidents which had happened to the Princess's father cried, "By Allah, the story of this damsel should be chronicled in a book, that it become the talk of posterity and be quoted as an instance of the omnipotence of Allah Almighty; for He it is who parteth and scattereth and re-uniteth." So saying she took her and carried her to her own apartment where she entreated her honourably; and the maiden, after she had spent a month in the Palace, showed charms grown two-fold and even more. At last one day of the days, as she sat beside the King's daughter in her chamber about eventide, when the sun was hot after a sultry summer day and her cheeks had flushed rosy red, behold, the Sultan entered passing through the room on his way to the Harem and his glance undesignedly[1] fell upon the Princess who was in home gear, and he looked a look of eyes that cost him a thousand sighs. So he was astounded and stood motionless knowing not whether to go or to come; and when his daughter sighted him in such plight she went up to him and said, "What hath betided thee and brought thee to this condition?" Quoth he, "By Allah, this girl hath stolen my senses from my soul: I am fondly enamoured of her and if thou aid me not by asking her in marriage and I fail to wed her 'twill make my wits go clean bewildered." Thereupon the King's daughter

---

[1] In text "Ghayr Wa'd," or "Min ghayr Wa'd." Lit. without previous agreement: much used in this text for suddenly, unexpectedly, without design.

returned to the damsel and drawing near her said, "O my lady and light of my eyes, indeed my father hath seen thee in thy deshabille and he hath hung[1] all his hopes upon thee, so do not thou contrary my words nor the counsel I am about to offer thee." "And what may that be, O my lady?" asked she, and the other answered, "My wish is to marry thee to my sire and thou be to him wife and he be to thee man." But when the maiden heard these words she wept with bitter weeping till she sobbed aloud and cried, "Time hath mastered us and decreed separation: I know nothing of my mother and sisters and father, an they be dead or on life, and whether they were drowned or came to ground; then how should I enjoy a bridal fête when they may be in mortal sadness and sorrow?" But the other ceased not to soothe her and array fair words against her and show her fondly friendship till her soul consented to wedlock. Presently the other brought out to her what habit befitted the occasion still comforting her heart with pleasant converse,[2] after which she carried the tidings to her sire. So he sent forthright to summon his Lords of the reign and Grandees of the realm and the knot was tied between them twain; and, going in unto her that night, he found her a hoard wherefrom the spell had freshly been dispelled; and of his longing for her and his desire to her he abode with her two se'nnights never going forth from her or by night or by day. Hereat the dignitaries of his empire were sore vexed for that their Sultan ceased to appear at the Divan and deal commandment between man and man, and his daughter went in and acquainted him therewith. He asked her how long he had absented himself and she answered saying, "Knowest thou how long thou hast tarried in the Palace?" whereto he replied, "Nay." "Fourteen whole days," cried she, whereupon he exclaimed, "By Allah, O my daughter, I thought to myself that I had spent with her two days and no more." And his daughter wondered to hear his words. Such was the case of the cadette Princess; but as regards the King, the father of the damsel, when he forgathered with the mother of his three daughters and she told him of the shipwreck and the loss of her children he determined to travel in search of the three damsels, he and the Wazir habited as Darwayshes.——

---

[1] The reader will have remarked the use of the Arabic " 'Alaka" = he hung, which with its branches greatly resembles the Lat. *pendere*.

[2] Arab. "Min al-Malábis," plur. of "Malbas" = anything pleasant or enjoyable; as the plural of "Milbas" = dress, garment, it cannot here apply.

And Shahrazad was surprised by the dawn of day and fell silent and ceased to say her permitted say. Then quoth her sister Dunyazad, "How sweet is thy story, O sister mine, and how enjoyable and delectable!" Quoth she, "And where is this compared with that I would relate to you on the coming night an the Sovran suffer me to survive?" Now when it was the next night and that was

The Three Hundred and Eightieth Night,

DUNYAZAD said to her, "Allah upon thee, O my sister, an thou be other than sleepy, finish for us thy tale that we may cut short the watching of this our latter night!" She replied, "With love and good will!" It hath reached me, O auspicious King, the director, the right-guiding, lord of the rede which is benefiting and of deeds fair-seeming and worthy celebrating, that the Sultan resolved to travel in search of his children (the three damsels) he and his Wazir habited as Darwayshes. So leaving the government in charge of his wife he went forth and the twain in their search first visited the cities on the seaboard beginning with the nearest; but they knew not what was concealed from them in the world of the future. They stinted not travelling for the space of a month till they came to a city whose Sultan had a place hight Al-Dijlah[1] whereupon he had built a Palace. The Darwayshes made for it and found the King sitting in his Kiosque[2] accompanied by two little lads, the elder eight years old and the second six. They drew near to him and saluting him offered their services and blessed him, wishing him length of life as is the fashion when addressing royalties; and he returned their greetings and made them draw near and showed them kindness; also, when it was eventide he bade his men serve them with somewhat of food. On the next day the King fared forth to Tigris-bank and sat in his Kiosque together with the two boys. Now the Darwayshes had hired them a cell in the Khan whence it was their daily wont to issue forth and wander about the city asking for what they sought; and this day they again came to the place

---

[1] *i.e.* "The Tigris" (Hid-dekel), with which the Egyptian writer seems to be imperfectly acquainted. See vols. i. 180; viii. 150.

[2] The word, as usual misapplied in the West, is to be traced through the Turk. Kúshk (pron. Kyúshk) to the Pers. "Kushk" = an upper chamber.

wherein sat the Sultan and they marvelled at the fair ordinance of
the Palace. They continued to visit it every day till one day of
the days the two went out, according to their custom, and when
entering the Palace one of the King's children, which was the
younger, came up to them and fell to considering them as if he
had forgotten his own existence. This continued till the Darwayshes retired to their cell in the caravanserai whither the boy
followed them to carry out the Secret Purpose existing in the
All-knowledge of Allah. And when the two sat down the Sultan's son went in to them and fell to gazing upon them and
solacing himself with the sight, when the elder Darwaysh clasped
him to his bosom and fell to kissing his cheeks, marvelling at his
semblance and at his beauty; and the boy in his turn forgot his
father and his mother and took to the old man. Now whenas
night fell the Sultan retired homewards fancying that his boy
had foregone him to his mother while the Sultánah fancied that
her child was with his father, and this endured till such time as
the King had entered the Harem. But only the elder child was
found there so the Sultan asked, "Where is the second boy?"
and the Queen answered, "Day by day thou takest them with
thee to Tigris-bank and thou bringest them back; but to-day
only the elder hath returned." Thereupon they sought him but
found him not and the mother buffeted her face in grief for her
child and the father lost his right senses. Then the high Officials
fared forth to search for their King's son and sought him from
early night to the dawn of day, but not finding him they deemed
that he had been drowned in Tigris-water. So they summoned
all the fishermen and divers and caused them to drag the river
for a space of four days. All this time and the boy abode with
the Darwayshes, who kept saying to him, "Go to thy father and
thy mother;" but he would not obey them and he would sit with
the Fakirs upon whom all his thoughts were fixed while theirs
were fixed upon him. This lasted till the fifth day when the
door-keeper unsummoned entered the cell and found the Sultan's
son sitting with the old men; so he went out hurriedly and repairing to the King cried, "O my Sovran, thy boy is with those
Darwayshes who were wont daily to visit thee." Now when
the Sultan heard the porter's words, he called aloud to his
Eunuchs and Chamberlains and gave them his orders; when they
ran a race, as it were, till they entered upon the holy men and
carried them from their cell together with the boy and set all

four[1] before the Sultan. The King exclaimed, "Verily these
Darwayshes must be spies and their object was to carry off my
boy;" so he took up his child and clasped him to his bosom and
kissed him again and again of his yearning fondness to him, and
presently he sent him to his mother who was well-nigh frantic.
Then he committed the two Fakirs (with commands to decapitate
them) to the Linkman who took them and bound their hands and
bared their heads and fell to crying, "This be his reward and the
least of awards who turneth traitor and kidnappeth the sons of
the Kings;" and as he cried all the citizens great and small flocked
to the spectacle. But when the boy heard the proclamation, he
went forth in haste till he stood before the elder Darwaysh who
was still kneeling upon the rug of blood and threw himself upon
him at full length till the Grandees of his father forcibly removed
him. Then the executioner stepped forward purposing to strike
the necks of the two old men and he raised his sword hand till
the dark hue of his arm-pit showed[2] and he would have dealt
the blow when the boy again made for the elder Fakir and threw
himself upon him not only once but twice and thrice, preventing
the Sworder's stroke and abode clinging to the old man. The
Sultan cried, "This Darwaysh is a Sorcerer:" but when the tidings reached the Sultanah, the boy's mother, she exclaimed,
"O King, needs must this Darwaysh have a strange tale to tell,
for the boy is wholly absorbed in him. So it is not possible to
slay him on this wise till thou summon him to the presence and
question him: I also will listen to him behind the curtain and
thus none shall hear him save our two selves." The King did
her bidding and commanded the old man to be brought: so they
took him from under the sword and set him before the King
——And Shahrazad was surprised by the dawn of day and fell
silent and ceased saying her permitted say. Then quoth her

---

[1] Four including the doorkeeper. The Darwayshes were suspected of kidnapping, a
practice common in the East, especially with holy men. I have noticed in my Pilgrimage
(vols. ii. 273; iii. 327), that both at Meccah and at Al-Medinah the cheeks of babes are
decorated with the locally called "Masháli" = three parallel gashes drawn by the barber
with the razor down the fleshy portion of each cheek, from the exterior angles of the eyes
almost to the corners of the mouth. According to the citizens, this "Tashrít" is a modern
practice distinctly opposed to the doctrine of Al-Islam; but, like the tattooing of girls, it
is intended to save the children from being carried off, for good luck, by kidnapping pil-
grims, especially Persians.
[2] The hair being shaven or plucked and showing the darker skin. In the case of the
axilla-pile, vellication is the popular process: see vol. ix. 139. Europeans who do not adopt
this essential part of cleanliness in hot countries are looked upon as impure by Moslems.

sister Dunyazad, "How sweet and tasteful is thy tale, O sister
mine, and enjoyable and delectable!" Quoth she, "And where
is this compared with that I would relate to you on the coming
night an the Sovran suffer me to survive?" Now when it was
the next night and that was

The Three Hundred and Eighty-first Night.

DUNYAZAD said to her, "Allah upon thee, O my sister, an thou
be other than sleepy, finish for us thy tale that we may cut short
the watching of this our latter night!" She replied, "With love
and good will!" It hath reached me, O auspicious King, the
director, the right-guiding, lord of the rede which is benefiting
and of deeds fair-seeming and worthy celebrating, that at the
King's bidding they took up the Fakir who was still kneeling
under the glaive and set him before the King who bade him be
seated. And when he sat him down the Sultan commanded all
who were in the presence of Eunuchs and Chamberlains to withdraw, and they withdrew leaving the Sovran with the old religious. But the second Darwaysh still knelt in his bonds under the
sword of the Sworder who, standing over against his head, kept
looking for the royal signal to strike. Then cried the King, "O
Mendicant, what drove thee to take my son, the core of my
heart?" He replied, "By Allah, O King, I took him not for mine
own pleasure; but he would not go from me and I threatened him,
withal he showed no fear till this destiny descended upon us."
Now when the Sultan heard these words his heart softened to the
old man and he pitied him while the Sultanah who sat behind the
curtain fell to weeping aloud. Presently the King said, "O Darwaysh, relate to us thy history, for needs must it be a singular;"
but the old man began to shed tears and said, "O King of the Age,
I have a marvellous adventure which were it graven with needle-
gravers upon the eye-corners were a warning to whoso would be
warned." The Sultan was surprised and replied, "What then
may be thy history, O Mendicant?" and the other rejoined, "O
King of the Age, I will recount it to thee."[1] Accordingly he told
him of his kingship and the Wazir tempting his wife and of her
slaying the nurse, the slave-girls, and the Eunuch; but when he

---

[1] Here a little abbreviation has been found necessary: "of no avail is a twice-told tale."

came to this point the Sultanah ran out in haste and hurry from
behind the curtain and rushing up to the Darwaysh threw herself
upon his bosom. The King seeing this marvelled and in a fury of
jealousy clapped hand to hilt crying to the Fakir, "This be most
unseemly behaviour!" But the Queen replied, "Hold thy hand,
by Allah, he is my father and I am his loving daughter;" and
she wept and laughed alternately[1] all of the excess of her joy.
Hereat the King wondered and bade release the second religious
and exclaimed, "Sooth he spake who said:—

Allah joineth the parted when think the twain * With firmest thought ne'er
    to meet again."

Then the Sultanah began recounting to him the history of her
sire and specially what befel him from his Wazir; and he, when he
heard her words, felt assured of their truth. Presently he bade
them change the habits of her father and of his Wazir and dress
them with the dress of Kings; and he set apart for them an apartment and allotted to them rations of meat and drink; so extolled
be He who disuniteth and reuniteth! Now the Sultanah in question was the youngest daughter of the old King who had been
met by the Knight when out hunting, the same that owed all his
fair fortunes to her auspicious coming. Accordingly the father
was assured of having found the lost one and was delighted to
note her high degree; but after tarrying with her for a time he
asked permission of his son-in-law to set out in quest of her two
sisters and he supplicated Almighty Allah to reunite him with
the other twain as with this first one. Thereupon quoth the
Sultan, "It may not be save that I accompany thee, for otherwise
haply some mishap of the world may happen to thee." Then the
three sat down in council debating what they should do and in
fine they agreed to travel, taking with them some of the Lords of
the land and Chamberlains and Nabobs. They made ready and
after three days they marched out of the city,——And Shahrazad was surprised by the dawn of day and fell silent and ceased
to say her permitted say. Then quoth her sister Dunyazad, "How
sweet is thy story, O sister mine, and how enjoyable and delectable!" Quoth she, "And where is this compared with that I
would relate to you on the coming night an the Sovran suffer me
to survive?" Now when it was the next night and that was

---

1 The nearest approach in Eastern tales to Western hysterics.

The Three Hundred and Eighty-second Night.

Dunyazad said to her, "Allah upon thee, O my sister, an thou be other than sleepy, finish for us thy tale that we may cut short the watching of this our latter night!" She replied, "With love and good will!" It hath reached me, O auspicious King, the director, the right-guiding, lord of the rede which is benefiting and of deeds fair-seeming and worthy celebrating, that the old King marched forth the city accompanied by his son-in-law and his Wazir after the Sultan had supplied his own place by a Vice-regent who would carry out his commandments. Then they turned to travelling in quest of the two lost daughters and stinted not their wayfare for a space of twenty days, when they drew near a city lofty of base, and, finding a spacious camping plain, thereon pitched their tents. The time was set of sun, so the cooks applied themselves to getting ready the evening meal and when supper was served up all ate what sufficed them, and it was but little because of the travails of travel, and they nighted in that site until morn was high. Now the ruler of that city was a Sultan mighty of might, potent of power and exceeding in energy; and he was surprised to hear a Chamberlain report to him saying, "O King of the Age, after an eventless night early this morning we found outside thy capital tents and pavilions with standards and banners planted overagainst them and all this after the fashion of the Kings." The Sovran replied, "There is no help but that to these creations of Allah some requirement is here: however, we will learn their tidings." So he took horse with his Grandees and made for the ensigns and colours, and drawing near he noted gravity and majesty in the array and eunuchs and followers and serving-men standing ready to do duty. Then he dismounted and walked till he approached the bystanders whom he greeted with the salam. They salam'd in return and received him with most honourable reception and highmost respect till they had introduced him into the royal Shahmiyánah; when the two Kings rose to him and welcomed him and he wished them long life in such language as is spoken by Royalties; and all sat down to converse one with other. Now the Lord of the city had warned his people before he fared forth that dinner must be prepared; so when it was mid-forenoon the Farrásh-folk[1] spread the

---

[1] A tent-pitcher, body servant, etc. See vol. vii. 4. The word is still popular in Persia.

tables with trays of food and the guests came forward, one and all, and enjoyed their meal and were gladdened. Then the dishes were carried away for the servants and talk went round till sun-set, at which time the King again ordered food to be brought and all supped till they had their sufficiency. But the Sultan kept wondering in his mind and saying, "Would Heaven I wot the cause of these two Kings coming to us!" and when night fell the strangers prayed him to return home and to revisit them next morning. So he farewelled them and fared forth. This lasted three days, during which time he honoured them with all honour, and on the fourth he got ready for them a banquet and invited them to his Palace. They mounted and repaired thither when he set before them food; and as soon as they had fed, the trays were removed and coffee and confections and sherbets were served up and they sat talking and enjoying themselves till supper-tide when they sought permission to hie campwards. But the Sultan of the city sware them to pass the night with him; so they re-turned to their session till the father of the damsels said, "Let each of us tell a tale that our waking hours may be the more pleasant." "Yes," they replied and all agreed in wishing that the Sultan of the city would begin. Now by the decree of the Decreer the lattice-window of the Queen opened upon the place of session and she could see them and hear every word they said. He began, "By Allah I have to relate an adventure which befel me and 'tis one of the wonders of our time." Quoth they, "And what may it be?"——And Shahrazad was surprised by the dawn of day and fell silent and ceased saying her permitted say. Then quoth her sister Dunyazad, "How sweet and tasteful is thy tale, O sister mine, and enjoyable and delectable!" Quoth she, "And where is this compared with that I would relate to you on the coming night an the Sovran suffer me to survive?" Now when it was the next night and that was

The Three Hundred and Eighty-third Night,

DUNYAZAD said to her, "Allah upon thee, O my sister, an thou be other than sleepy, finish for us thy tale that we may cut short the watching of this our latter night!" She replied, "With love and good will!" It hath reached me, O auspicious King, the director, the right-guiding, lord of the rede which is benefiting

and of deeds fair-seeming and worthy celebrating, that the Sultan
of the city said:— In such a year I had a malady which none
availed to medicine until at last an old woman came to me bearing
a tasse of broth which when I drank caused health return to me.
So I bade her bring me a cupful every day and I drank it till,
after a time, I chanced to ask her who made that broth and she
answered that it was her daughter. And one day I assumed a
disguise and went to the ancient dame's house and there saw the
girl who was a model of beauty and loveliness, brilliancy, symmetric stature and perfect grace, and seeing her I lost my heart to
her, and asked her to wife. She answered, "How can I wed; I
separated from my sisters and parents and all unknowing what
hath become of them?" Now when the father of the damsels
heard these words, tears rolled down his cheeks in rills and he
remembered his two lost girls and wept and moaned and complained, the Sultan looking on in astonishment the while; and
when he went to his Queen he found her lying in a fainting fit.
Hereupon he cried out her name and seated her and she on coming
to exclaimed, "By Allah, he who wept before you is my very
father: by Him who created me I have no doubt thereof!" So
the Sultan went down to his father-in-law and led him up to the
Harem and the daughter rose and met him and they threw their
arms round each other's necks, and fondly greeted each other.
After this the old King passed the night relating to her what had
befallen him while she recounted to him whatso hath betided her,
from first to last, whereupon their rejoicings increased and the
father thanked Almighty Allah for having found two of his three
children. The old King and his sons-in-law and his Wazir ceased
not to enjoy themselves in the city, eating and drinking[1] and
making merry for a space of two days when the father asked
aidance of his daughters' husbands to seek his third child that the
general joy might be perfected. This request they granted and
resolved to journey with him; so they made their preparations for
travel and issued forth the city together with sundry Lords of the
land and high Dignitaries, all taking with them what was required
of rations. Then travelling together in a body they faced the
march. This was their case; but as regards the third daughter
(she who in man's attire had served the Kunáfah-baker), after

---

[1] The amount of eating and drinking in this tale is phenomenal; but, I repeat, Arabs
enjoy reading of "meat and drink" almost as much as Englishmen.

being married to the Sultan his love for her and desire to her only
increased and she cohabited with him for a length of time. But
one day of the days she called to mind her parents and her kith
and kin and her native country, so she wept with sorest weeping
till she swooned away and when she recovered she rose without
stay or delay and taking two suits of Mameluke's habits patiently
awaited the fall of night. Presently she donned one of the dresses
and went down to the stables where, finding all the grooms
asleep, she saddled her a stallion of the noblest strain and clinging
to the near side mounted him. Then, having supplicated the veiling of the Veiler, she fared under cover of the glooms for her own
land, all unweeting the way, and when night gave place to day
she saw herself amidst mountains and sands; nor did she know
what she should do. However she found on a hill-flank some
remnants of the late rain which she drank; then, loosing the
girths of her horse she gave him also to drink and she was about
to take her rest in that place when, lo and behold! a lion big of
bulk and mighty of might drew near her and he was lashing his
tail[1] and roaring thunderously.——And Shahrazad was surprised
by the dawn of day and fell silent and ceased to say her permitted
say. Then quoth her sister Dunyazad, "How sweet is thy story,
O sister mine, and how enjoyable and delectable!" Quoth she,
"And where is this compared with that I would relate to you on
the coming night, an the Sovran suffer me to survive?" Now
when it was the next night and that was

The Three Hundred and Eighty-fourth Night,

DUNYAZAD said to her, "Allah upon thee, O my sister, an thou
be other than sleepy, finish for us thy tale that we may cut short
the watching of this our latter night!" She replied, "With love
and good will!" It hath reached me, O auspicious King, the
director, the right-guiding, lord of the rede which is benefiting
and of deeds fair-seeming and worthy celebrating, that when the
lion advanced to spring upon the Princess who was habited as a
Mameluke, and rushed to rend her in pieces, she, seeing her
imminent peril, sprang up in haste and bared her blade and met

---

[1] Arab writers always insist upon the symptom of rage which distinguishes the felines
from the canines; but they do not believe that the end of the tail has a sting.

him brand in hand saying, "Or he will slay me or I slay him."
But as she was hearty of heart she advanced till the two met and
fell to fight and struck each at other, but the lion waxed furious
and gnashed his tusks, now retreating and now circuiting around
her and then returning to front his foe purposing to claw her,
when she heartened her heart and without giving ground she
swayed her sabre with all the force of her forearm and struck the
beast between the eyes and the blade came out gleaming between
his thighs and he sank on earth life-forlore and weltering in his
gore. Presently she wiped her scymitar and returned it to its
sheath; then, drawing a whittle she came up to the carcass
intending to skin it for her own use, when behold, there towered
from afar two dust-clouds, one from the right and the other from
the left, whereat she withdrew from flaying the lion's fell and
applied herself to looking out. Now by the decree of the Decreer
the first dust-cloud approaching her was that raised by the host
of her father and his sons-in-law who, when they drew near all
stood to gaze upon her and consider her, saying in wonderment
one to other, "How can this white slave (and he a mere lad) have
slain this lion single-handed? Walláhi, had that beast charged
down upon us he had scattered us far and wide, and haply he
had torn one of us to pieces. By Allah, this matter is marvellous!"
But the Mameluke looked mainly at the old King whom he
knew to be his sire for his heart went forth to him. Meanwhile
the second dust-cloud approached until those beneath it met the
others who had foregone them, and behold, under it was the
husband of the disguised Princess and his many. Now the cause
of this King marching forth and coming thither was this. When
he entered the Palace intending for the Harem, he found not his
Queen, and he fared forth to seek her and presently by the decree
of the Decreer the two hosts met at the place where the lion had
been killed. The Sultan gazed upon the Mameluke and marvelled at his slaying the monster and said to himself, "Now were
this white slave mine I would share with him my good and stablish him in my kingdom." Herewith the Mameluke came forward
and flayed the lion of his fell and gutted him; then, lighting a fire
he roasted somewhat of his flesh until it was sufficiently cooked
all gazing upon him the while and marvelling at the heartiness of
his heart. And when the meat was ready, he carved it and set-

ting it upon a Sufrah[1] of leather said to all present, "Bismillah,
eat, in the name of Allah, what Fate hath given to you!" Thereupon all came forward and fell to eating of the lion's flesh except
the Princess's husband who was not pleased to join them and
said, "By Allah, I will not eat of this food until I learn the case of
this youth."[2] Now the Princess had recognised her spouse from
the moment of his coming, but she was concealed from him by her
Mameluke's clothing; and he disappeared time after time then
returned to gaze upon the white slave, eyeing now his eyes now
his sides and now the turn of his neck and saying privily in his
mind, "Laud to the Lord who created and fashioned him! By
Allah this Mameluke is the counterpart of my wife in eyes and
nose, and all his form and features are made likest-like unto hers.
So extolled be He who hath none similar and no equal!" He was
drowned in this thought but all the rest ate till they had eaten
enough; then they sat down to pass the rest of their day and their
night in that stead. When it was dawn each and every craved
leave to depart upon his own business; but the Princess's husband asked permission to wander in quest of her while the old
King, the father of the damsels, determined to go forth with his
two sons-in-law and find the third and last of his lost daughters.
Then the Mameluke said to them, "O my lords, sit we down, I
and you, for the rest of the day in this place and to-morrow I will
travel with you." Now the Princess for the length of her wanderings (which began too when she was a little one) had forgotten
the semblance of her sire; but when she looked upon the old King
her heart yearned unto him and she fell to talking with him,
while he on his part whenever he gazed at her felt a like longing
and sought speech of her. So the first who consented to the
Mameluke's proposal was the sire whose desire was naught save
to sit beside her; then the rest also agreed to pass the day repos-
ing in that place, for that it was a pleasant mead and a spacious,
garnished with green grass and bright with bourgeon and blossom. So they took seat there till sundown when each brought
out what victual he had and all ate their full and then fell to conversing; and presently said the Princess, "O my lords, let each
of you tell us a tale which he deemeth strange." Her father broke

---

[1] The circular leather which acts alternately provision bag and table-cloth. See vols.
i. 178; v. 8; viii. 269, and ix. 141.
[2] He refused because he suspected some trick and would not be on terms of bread and
salt with the stranger.

in saying, "Verily this rede be right and the first to recount will be I, for indeed mine is a rare adventure." Then he began his history telling them that he was born a King and that such-and-such things had befallen him and so forth until the end of his tale; and the Princess hearing his words was certified that he was her sire. So presently she said, "And I too have a strange history."——And Shahrazad was surprised by the dawn of day and fell silent and ceased saying her permitted say. Then quoth her sister Dunyazad, "How sweet and tasteful is thy tale, O sister mine, and enjoyable and delectable!" Quoth she, "And where is this compared with that I would relate to you on the coming night an the Sovran suffer me to survive?" Now when it was the next night and that was

The Three Hundred and Eighty-fifth Night,

Dunyazad said to her, "Allah upon thee, O my sister, an thou be other than sleepy, finish for us thy tale that we may cut short the watching of this our latter night!" She replied, "With love and good will!" It hath reached me, O auspicious King, the director, the right-guiding, lord of the rede which is benefiting and of deeds fair-seeming and worthy celebrating, that the Princess in Mameluke's habit said, "And I too have a strange history." Then she fell to relating all that had betided her from the very beginning to that which hath before been described; and when her father heard it he felt assured that she was his daughter. So he arose and threw himself upon her and embraced her and after he veiled her face with a kerchief was with him, and her husband exclaimed, "Would to Heaven that I also could forgather with my wife." Quoth she, "Inshallah, and that soon," and she inclined to him after kindly fashion and said to herself, "Indeed this be my true husband." Herewith all resolved to march from that stead and they departed, the Princess's spouse still unknowing that she was his wife; and they stinted not faring till they entered the Sultan's city and all made for the Palace. Then the Princess slipped privily into the Harem without the knowledge of her mate and changed her semblance, when her father said to her husband, "Hie thee to the women's apartment· haply Allah may show to thee thy wife." So he went in and found her sitting in her own apartment and he marvelled as he espied her and drew near her and threw his arms round her neck of his fond love to her and asked her concerning her absence. Thereupon she told him the truth saying, "I went forth seeking my sire and habited in a Mameluke's habit and 'twas I slew the lion and roasted his flesh over the fire, but thou wouldest not eat thereof." At these words the Sultan rejoiced and his rejoicings increased and all were in the highmost of joy and jolliment; he and her father with the two other sons-in-law, and this endured for a long while. But at last all deemed it suitable to revisit their countries and capitals and each farewelled his friends and the whole party returned safe and sound to their own homes.[1] Now when it was the next night and that was

The Three Hundred and Eighty-sixth Night,

Shahrazad began to relate

THE STORY OF THE KAZI WHO BARE A BABE.[2]

IT hath been related that in Tarábulus-town[3] of Syria was a Kází appointed under orders of the Caliph Hárún al-Rashíd to adjudge law-suits and dissolve contracts and cross-examine witnesses; and after taking seat in his Mahkamah[4] his rigour and severity became well known to all men. Now this judge kept a black hand-maiden likest unto a buffalo-bull and she cohabited with him for a lengthened while; for his nature was ever niggardly nor could anyone wrest from him half a Faddah or any alms-gift or aught else; and his diet was of biscuit[5] and onions. Moreover, he was

---

[1] The story contains excellent material, but the writer or the copier has "scamped" it in two crucial points, the meeting of the bereaved Sultan and his wife (Night ccclxxvii.) and the finale where we miss the pathetic conclusions of the Mac. and Bresl. Edits. Also a comparison of this hurried dénouement with the artistic tableau of "King Omar bin al-Nu'uman," where all the actors are mustered upon the stage before the curtain falls, measures the difference between this MS. and the printed texts, showing the superior polish and finish of the latter.

[2] Vol. iii. pp. 586-97, where it follows immediately the last story. Scott (Story of the Avaricious Cauzee and his Wife, vi. 112) has translated it after his own fashion, excising half and supplying it out of his own invention; and Gauttier has followed suit in the *Histoire du Cadi avare et de sa Femme*, vi. 254.

[3] Tarábulus and Atrábulus are Arabisations of Tripolis (hod. Tripoli) the well-known port-town north of Bayrút; founded by the Phœnicians, rose to fame under the Seleucidæ, and was made splendid by the Romans. See Socin's "Bædeker," p. 509.

[4] *I.e.* the Kazi's court-house.

[5] Arab. "Buksumah" = "hard bread" (Americanicè).

ostentatious as he was miserly: he had an eating-cloth bordered
with a fine bell-fringe,[1] and when any person entered about dinner-time or supper-tide he would cry out, "O handmaid, fetch the
fringed table-cloth;" and all who heard his words would say to
themselves, "By Allah, this must needs be a costly thing."
Presently one day of the days his assessors and officers said to
him, "O our lord the Kazi, take to thyself a wife, for yon negress
becometh not a dignitary of thy degree." Said he, "An this need
be, let any who hath a daughter give her to me in wedlock and I
will espouse her." Herewith quoth one present, "I have a fair
daughter and a marriageable," whereto quoth the Kazi, "An thou
wouldst do me a favour this is the time." So the bride was fitted
out and the espousals took place forthright and that same night
the Kazi's father-in-law came to him and led him in to his bride
saying in his heart, "I am now connected with the Kazi." And
he took pleasure in the thought for he knew naught of the judge's
stinginess and he could not suppose but that his daughter would
be comfortable with her mate and well-to-do in the matter of diet
and dress and furniture. Such were the fancies which occurred to
him; but as for the Kazi, he lay with the maid and abated her
maidenhead; and she in the morning awaited somewhat wherewith to break her fast and waited in vain. Presently the Kazi left
her and repaired to his court-house whither the city-folk came
and gave him joy of his marriage and wished him good morning,
saying in themselves, "Needs must he make a mighty fine bride-
feast." But they sat there to no purpose until past noon when
each went his own way privily damning the judge's penurious-
ness. As soon as they were gone he returned to his Harem and
cried out to his black wench, "O handmaiden, fetch the fringed
table-cloth;" and his bride hearing this rejoiced, saying to herself,
"By Allah, his calling for this cloth requireth a banquet which
befitteth it, food suitable for the Kings." The negress arose and
faring forth for a short time returned with the cloth richly fringed
and set upon it a Kursi-stool,[2] and a tray of brass whereon were

---

[1] Arab. "Sufrah umm jalájil." Lit. an eating-cloth with little bells, like those hung
to a camel, or metal plates as on the rim of a tambourine.

[2] The Kursi here = the stool upon which the "Siniyah" or tray of tinned copper is
placed, the former serving as a table. These stools, some 15 inches high and of wood
inlaid with bone, tortoise-shell or mother-of-pearl, are now common in England, where
one often sees children using them as seats. The two (Kursi and Siniyah) compose the
Sufrah, when the word is used in the sense of our "dinner-table." Lane (M.E. chapt. v.)
gives an illustration of both articles.

served three biscuits and three onions. When the bride saw this,
she prayed in her heart saying, "Now may my Lord wreak my
revenge upon my father!" but her husband cried to her, "Come
hither, my girl," and the three sat down to the tray wherefrom
each took a biscuit and an onion. The Kazi and the negress ate all
their portions, but the bride could not swallow even a third of the
hard bread apportioned to her; so she rose up, heartily cursing her
father's ambition in her heart. At supper-tide it was the same
till the state of things became longsome to her and this endured
continuously for three days, when she was ready to sink with
hunger. So she sent for her sire and cried aloud in his face. The
Kazi hearing the outcries of his bride asked, "What is to do?"
whereupon they informed him that the young woman was not in
love with this style of living.——And Shahrazad was surprised
by the dawn of day and fell silent and ceased to say her permitted
say. Then quoth her sister Dunyazad, "How sweet is thy story,
O sister mine, and how enjoyable and delectable!" Quoth she,
"And where is this compared with that I would relate to you on
the coming night an the Sovran suffer me to survive?" Now
when it was the next night and that was

The Three Hundred and Eighty-seventh Night,

DUNYAZAD said to her, "Allah upon thee, O my sister, an thou be
other than sleepy, finish for us thy tale that we may cut short the
watching of this our latter night!" She replied, "With love and
good will!" It hath reached me, O auspicious King, the director,
the right-guiding, lord of the rede which is benefiting and of
deeds fair-seeming and worthy celebrating, that the bride was
not in love with the Kazi's mode of living; so he took her and
cut off her nose and divorced her, falsely declaring that she had
behaved frowardly. On the next day he proposed for another
wife and married her and entreated her in like fashion as the first;
and when she demanded a divorce, he shredded off her nostrils
and put her away; and whatever woman he espoused he starved
by his stinginess and tortured with hunger, and when any demanded a divorce he would chop off her nose on false pretences
and put her away without paying aught either of her marriage
settlement or of the contingent dowry. At last the report of that
Kazi's avarice came to the ears of a damsel of Mosul-city, a model
of beauty and loveliness who had insight into things hidden and

just judgment and skilful contrivance. Thereupon, resolved to avenge her sex, she left her native place and journeyed till she made Tarábulus; and by the decree of the Decreer at that very time the judge, after a day spent in his garden, purposed to return home so he mounted his mule and met her half-way between the pleasance and the town. He chanced to glance at her and saw that she was wondrous beautiful and lovely, symmetrical and graceful and the spittle ran from his mouth wetting his mustachios; and he advanced and accosting her said, "O thou noble one, whence comest thou hither?" "From behind me!" "*Connu.* I knew that; but from what city?" "From Mosul." "Art thou single and secluded or femme couverte with a husband alive?" "Single I am still!" "Can it be that thou wilt take me and thou become to me mate and I become to thee man?" "If such be our fate 'twill take place and I will give thee an answer to-morrow;" and so saying the damsel went on to Tarábulus. Now the Kazi after hearing her speech felt his love for her increase; so next morning he sent to ask after her, and when they told him that she had alighted at a Khan, he despatched to her the negress his concubine with a party of friends to ask her in marriage, notifying that he was Kazi of the city. Thereupon she demanded a dower of fifty dinars and naming a deputy caused the knot be knotted and she came to him about evening time and he went in to her. But when it was the supper-hour he called as was his wont to his black handmaiden saying "Fetch the fringed table-cloth," and she fared forth and fetched it bringing also three biscuits and three onions, and as soon as the meal was served up all three sat down to it, the Kazi, the slave-girl, and the new bride. Each took a biscuit and an onion and ate them up and the bride exclaimed "Allah requite thee with wealth. By Allah, this be a wholesome supper." When the judge heard this he was delighted with her and cried out, "Extolled be the Almighty for that at last He hath vouchsafed to me a wife who thanketh the Lord for muchel or for little!" But he knew not what the Almighty had decreed to him through the wile and guile, the malice and mischief of women. Next morning the Kazi repaired to the Mahkamah and the bride arose and solaced herself with looking at the apartments, of which some lay open whilst others were closed. Presently she came to one which was made fast by a door with a wooden bolt and a padlock of iron: she considered it and found it strong but at the threshold was a fissure about the breadth of a finger; so she peeped through and espied gold and silver coins heaped up in trays of brass which stood upon Kursi-stools and the nearest about ten cubits from the door. She then arose and fetched a long wand, the mid-rib of a date-palm,[1] and arming the end with a lump of leaven she pushed it through the chink under the door and turned it round and round upon the money-trays as if sewing or writing. At last two dinars stuck to the dough and she drew them through the fissure and returned to her own chamber; then, calling the negress, she gave her the ducats saying, "Go thou to the Bazar and buy us some mutton and rice and clarified butter; and do thou also bring us some fresh bread and spices and return with them without delay." The negress took the gold and went to the market, where she bought all that her lady bade her buy and speedily came back, when the Kazi's wife arose and cooked a notable meal, after which she and the black chattel ate whatso they wanted. Presently the slave brought basin and ewer to her lady and washed her hands and then fell to kissing her feet, saying, "Allah feed thee, O my lady, even as thou hast fed me, for ever since I belonged to this Kazi I have lacked the necessaries of life." Replied the other, "Rejoice, O handmaiden, for henceforth thou shalt have every day naught but the bestest food of manifold kinds;" and the negress prayed Allah to preserve her and thanked her. At noon the Kazi entered and cried, "O handmaid fetch the fringed cloth," and when she brought it he sat down and his wife arose and served up somewhat of the food she had cooked and he ate and rejoiced and was filled and at last he asked, "Whence this provision?" She answered, "I have in this city many kinsfolk who hearing of my coming sent me these meats and quoth I to myself, When my lord the Kazi shall return home he shall make his dinner thereof." On the next day she did as before and drawing out three ducats called the slave-girl and gave her two of them bidding her go to the Bazar and buy a lamb ready skinned and a quantity of rice and clarified butter and greens and spices and whatso was required for dressing the dishes. So the handmaid went forth rejoicing, and bought all her lady had ordered and forthwith returned when her mistress fell to cooking meats of various kinds and lastly sent to invite all her neighbours, women and maidens. When they came

---

[1] Arab. "Jarídah," a palm-frond stripped of its leaves (Supplemental vol. i. 203); hence the "Jaríd" used as a javelin; see vol. vi. 263.

she had got ready the trays garnished with dainty food[1] and
served up to them all that was suitable and they ate and enjoyed
themselves and made merry. Now this was about mid-forenoon,
but as mid-day drew near they went home carrying with them
dishes full of dainties which they cleared and washed and sent
back till everything was returned to its place.——And Shahrazad perceived the dawn of day and fell silent and ceased saying
her permitted say. Then quoth her sister Dunyazad, "How sweet
and tasteful is thy tale, O sister mine, and enjoyable and delectable!" Quoth she, "And where is this compared with that I
would relate to you on the coming night an the Sovran suffer me
to survive?" Now when it was the next night and that was

The Three Hundred and Eighty-eighth Night,

Dunyazad said to her, "Allah upon thee, O my sister, an thou
be other than sleepy, finish for us thy tale that we may cut short
the watching of this our latter night!" She replied, "With love
and good will!" It hath reached me, O auspicious King, the
director, the right-guiding, lord of the rede which is benefiting
and of deeds fair-seeming and worthy celebrating, that the guests
of the Kazi's wife fared from her before turn of sun; and, when it
was noon, behold, the Kazi entered his Harem and said, "O handmaiden, fetch the fringed tablecloth," when the wife arose and
set before him viands of various sorts. He asked whence they
came and she answered saying, "This is from my maternal aunt
who sent it as a present to me." The judge ate and was delighted
and abode in the Harem till set of sun. But his wife ceased not
daily to draw money from his hoard and to expend it upon enter-
taining her friends and gossips, and this endured for a whole year.
Now beside her mansion dwelt a poor woman in a mean dwelling
and every day the wife would feed her and her husband and
babes; moreover she would give them all that sufficed them. The
woman was far gone with child and the other charged her saying,
"As soon as 'tis thy time to be delivered, do thou come to me for
I have a mind to play a prank upon this Kazi who feareth not
Allah and who, whenever he taketh to himself a wife, first de-
priveth her of food till she is well nigh famished, then shreddeth

---

[1] An Egyptian or a Syrian housewife will make twenty dishes out of roast lamb, wholly
unlike the "good plain cook" of Great or Greater Britain, who leaves the stomach to do
all the work of digestion in which she ought to but does not assist.

off her nose under false pretences and putteth her away taking all her belongings and giving naught of dower either the precedent or the contingent." And the poor woman replied, "To hear is to obey." Then the wife persisted in her lavish expenditure till her neighbour came to her already overtaken by birth-pains, and these lasted but a little while when she was brought to bed of a boy. Hereupon the Kazi's wife arose and prepared a savoury dish called a Baysárah,[1] the base of which is composed of beans and gravied mallows[2] seasoned with onions and garlic. It was noon when her husband came in and she served up the dish; and he being anhungered ate of it and ate greedily and at supper time he did likewise. But he was not accustomed to a Baysárah, so as soon as night came on his paunch began to swell; the wind bellowed in his bowels; his stress was such that he could not be more distressed and he roared out in his agony. Herewith his wife ran in and cried to him, "No harm shall befal thee, O my lord!" and so saying she passed her hand over his stomach and presently exclaimed "Extolled be He, O my lord; verily thou art pregnant and a babe is in thy belly."——And Shahrazad was surprised by the dawn of day and fell silent and ceased to say her permitted say. Then quoth her sister Dunyazad, "How sweet is thy story, O sister mine, and how enjoyable and delectable!" Quoth she, "And where is this compared with that I would relate to you on the coming night an the Sovran suffer me to survive?" Now when it was the next night and that was

The Three Hundred and Eighty-ninth Night,

DUNYAZAD said to her, "Allah upon thee, O my sister, an thou be other than sleepy, finish for us thy tale that we may cut short

---

[1] A plate of "Baysár" or "Faysár," a dish peculiar to Egypt; beans seasoned with milk and honey and generally eaten with meat. See Mr. Guy Lestrange's "Al-Mukaddasi," Description of Syria, p. 80; an author who wrote cir. A.H. 986. Scott (vi. 119) has "A savoury dish called byssarut, which is composed of parched beans and pounded salt meat, mixed up with various seeds, onions and garlic." Gauttier (vi. 261) carefully avoids giving the Arabic name, which occurs in a subsequent tale (Nights cdxliv.) when a laxative is required.

[2] Arab. "Mulúkhiyah náshiyah," lit. = flowing; i.e. soft like épinards au jus. Mulúkhíyá that favourite vegetable, the malva esculenta is derived from the Gr. μαλύχη, (also written μολύχη) from μαλάσσω = to soften, because somewhat relaxing. In ancient Athens it was the food of the poorer classes and in Egypt it is eaten by all, taking the place of our spinach and sorrel.

the watching of this our latter night!" She replied, "With love
and good will!" It hath reached me, O auspicious King, the
director, the right-guiding, lord of the rede which is benefiting
and of deeds fair-seeming and worthy celebrating, that the Kazi's
wife came up to him and passing her palm over his paunch
presently cried, "Extolled be He, O my lord: verily thou art
pregnant and a babe is in thy belly." Quoth the Kazi, "How
shall a man bear a child?" and quoth she, "Allah createth whatso
He willeth." And as they two sat at talk the flatulence and
belly-ache increased and violent colic[1] set in and the torments
waxed still more torturing. Then the wife rose up and disappeared but presently she returned with her pauper neighbour's
newly-born babe in her sleeve, its mother accompanying it: she
also brought a large basin of copper and she found her husband
rolling from right to left and crying aloud in his agony. At last
the qualms[2] in his stomach were ready to burst forth and the
rich food to issue from his body, and when this delivery was near
hand the wife privily set the basin under him like a close stool
and fell to calling upon the Holy Names and to shampooing and
rubbing down his skin while she ejaculated, "The name of Allah
be upon thee!"[3] But all this was of her malice. At last the prima
via opened and the Kazi let fly, whereat his wife came quickly
behind and setting the babe upon its back gently pinched it so
that it began to wail, and said, "O man, Alhamdolillah,—laud to
the Lord, who hath so utterly relieved thee of thy burthen,"
and she fell to muttering Names over the newborn. Then quoth
he, "Have a care of the little one and keep it from cold draughts;"
for the trick had taken completely with the Kazi and he said in his
mind, "Allah createth whatso He willeth: even men if so predestined can bring forth." And presently he added, "O woman,
look out for a wet nurse to suckle him;" and she replied, "O my
lord, the nurse is with me in the women's apartments." Then
having sent away the babe and its mother she came up to the

---

[1] Arab. "Kalak" = lit. "agitation," "disquietude" and here used as syn. with "Kúlanj,"
a true colic.

[2] Arab. "Mazarát," from "Mazr," = being addled (an egg).

[3] Here is an allusion to the "Massage," which in these days has assumed throughout
Europe all the pretensions of scientific medical treatment. The word has been needlessly
derived from the Arab. "Mas'h" = rubbing, kneading; but we have the Gr. synonym
μύσσω and the Lat. Massare. The text describes child-bed customs amongst Moslem
women; and the delivery of the Kazi has all the realism of M. Zola's accouchement in *La
Joie de Vivre*.

Kazi and washed him and removed the basin from under him
and made him lie at full length. Presently after taking thought
he said, "O woman, be careful to keep this matter private for fear
of the folk who otherwise might say, 'Our Kazi hath borne a
babe.'" She replied, "O my lord, as the affair is known to other
than our two selves how can we manage to conceal it?" and
after she resumed, "O my husband, this business can on no wise
be hidden from the people for more than a week or at most till
next month." Herewith he cried out, "O my calamity; if it
reach the ears of folk and they say, 'Our Kazi hath borne a babe,'
then what shall we do?" He pondered the matter until morning when he rose before daylight and, taking some provaunt
secretly, made ready to depart the city, saying, "O Allah, suffer
none to see me!" Then, after giving his wife charge of the house
and bidding her take care of his effects and farewelling her, he
went forth secretly from her and journeyed that day and a
second and a third until the seventh, when he entered Damascus
of Syria where none knew him. But he had no spending money
for he could not persuade himself to take even a single dinar from
his hoard and he had provided himself with naught save the
meagrest provision. So his condition was straitened and he was
compelled to sell somewhat of his clothes and lay out the price
upon his urgent needs; and when the coin was finished he was
forced to part with other portions of his dress till little or nothing of it remained to him. Then, in his sorest strait, he went to
the Shaykh of the Masons and said to him, "O master, my wish is
to serve in this industry;"[1] and said he, "Welcome to thee." So
the Kazi worked through every day for a wage of five Faddahs.
Such was his case; but as regards his wife,——And Shahrazad
was surprised by the dawn of day and fell silent and ceased saying
her permitted say. Then quoth her sister Dunyazad, "How sweet
and tasteful is thy tale, O sister mine, and enjoyable and delectable!" Quoth she, "And where is this compared with that I
would relate to you on this coming night an the Sovran suffer me
to survive?" Now when it was the next night and that was

The Three Hundred and Ninetieth Night,

Dunyazad said to her, "Allah upon thee, O my sister, an thou be
other than sleepy, finish for us thy tale that we may cut short the

---

[1] Arab. "Fa'álah" = the building craft, builders' trade.

watching of this our latter night!" She replied, "With love and
good will!" It hath reached me, O auspicious King, the director,
the right-guiding, lord of the rede which is benefiting and of
deeds fair-seeming and worthy celebrating, that when the Kazi
went forth from his wife she threw a sherd[1] behind him and
muttered, "Allah never bring thee back from thy journey." Then
she arose and threw open the rooms and noted all that was in
them of moneys and moveables and *vaiselle* and rarities, and she
fell to feeding the hungry and clothing the naked and doling
alms to Fakírs saying, "This be the reward of him who mortifieth
the daughters of folk and devoureth their substance and shreddeth off their nostrils." She also sent to the women he had married and divorced, and gave them of his good the equivalent of
their dowers and a solatium for losing their noses. And every
day she assembled the goodwives of the quarter and cooked for
them manifold kinds of food because her spouse the Kazi was
possessed of property approaching two Khaznahs[2] of money, he
being ever loath to expend what his hand could hend and unpre-
pared to part with aught on any wise, for the excess of his niggardness and his greed of gain. Nor did she cease from so doing
for a length of time until suddenly she overheard folk saying,
"Our Kazi hath borne a babe." And such bruit spread abroad
and was reported in sundry cities, nor ceased the rumour ere it
reached the ears of the Caliph Harun al-Rashid in Baghdad city.
Now hearing it he marvelled and cried, "Extolled be Allah! this
hap, by the Lord, never can have happened save at the hand of
some woman, a wise and a clever at contrivance; nor would she
have wrought after such fashion save to make public somewhat
erst proceeding from the Kazi, either his covetous intent or his
high-handedness in commandment. But needs must this goodwife be summoned before me and recount the cunning practice
she hath practised; — Allah grant her success in the prank she
hath played upon the Judge." Such was her case; but as con-
cerns the Kazi, he abode working at builders' craft till his bodily
force was enfeebled and his frame became frail; so presently
quoth he to himself, "Do thou return to thy native land, for a

---

[1] In text "Kawwárah," which is not found in the dictionaries. "Kuwáray" = that
which is cut off from the side of a thing, etc. My translation is wholly tentative: perhaps
Kawwára may be a copyist's error for "Kazizah" = vulg. a (flask of) glass.

[2] The "Khaznah," = treasury, is a thousand "Kis" = 500 piastres, or £5 at par; and
thus represents £5,000, a large sum for Tripoli in those days.

long time hath now passed and this affair is clean forgotten."
Thereupon he returned to Tarábulus, but as he drew near
thereto he was met outside the city by a bevy of small boys who
were playing at forfeits, and lo and behold! cried one to his
comrades, "O lads, do ye remember such and such a year when
our Kazi was brought to bed?"[1] But the Judge hearing these
words returned forthright to Damascus by the way he came,
saying to himself, "Hie thee not save to Baghdad city for 'tis
further away than Damascus!" and set out at once for the House
of Peace. However he entered it privily, because he was still in
the employ of the Prince of True Believers, Harun al-Rashid;
and, changing semblance and superficials, he donned the dress of
a Persian Darwaysh and fell to walking about the streets of the
capital. Here met he sundry men of high degree who showed him
favour, but he could not venture himself before the Caliph albe
sundry of the subjects said to him, "O Darwaysh, why dost
thou not appear in the presence of the Commander of the Faithful? Assuredly he would bestow upon thee many a boon, for
he is a true Sultan; and, specially, an thou panegyrise him in
poetry, he will largely add to his largesse." Now by the decree
of Destiny the viceregent of Allah upon His Earth had commanded the Kazi's wife be brought from Tarabulus: so they led
her into the presence and when she had kissed ground before him
and salam'd to him and prayed for the perpetuity of his glory
and his existence, he asked her anent her husband and how he
had borne a child and what was the prank she had played him
and in what manner she had gotten the better of him. She hung
her head groundwards awhile for shame nor could she return
aught of reply for a time, when the Commander of the Faithful
said to her, "Thou hast my promise of safety and again safety,
the safety of one who betrayeth not his word." So she raised
her head and cried, "By Allah, O King of the Age, the story of
this Kazi is a strange"——— And Shahrazad was surprised by the
dawn of day and fell silent and ceased to say her permitted say.
Then quoth her sister Dunyazad, "How sweet is thy story, O
sister mine, and how enjoyable and delectable!" Quoth she,
"And where is this compared with that I would relate to you
on the coming night an the Sovran suffer me to survive?" Now
when it was the next night and that was

---

[1] The same incident occurs in that pathetic tale with an ill name = "How Abu al-Hasan
brake Wind," vol. v. 135.

DUNYAZAD said to her, "Allah upon thee, O my sister, an thou be other than sleepy, finish for us thy tale that we may cut short the watching of this our latter night!" She replied, "With love and good will!" It hath reached me, O auspicious King, the director, the right-guiding, lord of the rede which is benefiting and of deeds fair-seeming and worthy celebrating, that quoth the Kazi's wife, "By Allah, O King of the Age, the story of this Kazi is a strange and of the wonders of the world and 'tis as follows. My spouse is so niggardly of nature and greedy of gain that whatso wife he weddeth he starveth her with hunger and, whenas she loseth patience, he shreddeth her nostrils and putteth her away, taking all her good and what not. Now this case continued for a while of time. Also he had a black slave-wench and a fine eating-cloth and when dinner-time came he would cry, O handmaid, fetch the fringed table-cloth! whereupon she would bring it and garnish it with three biscuits and three onions, one to each mouth. Presently accounts of this conduct came to me at Mosul, whereupon I removed me to Tarábulus, and there played him many a prank amongst which was the dish of Baysár by me seasoned with an over quantity of onions and garlic and such spices as gather wind in the maw and distend it like a tom-tom and breed borborygms.[1] This I gave him to eat and then befel that which befel. So I said to him, Thou art in the family way and tricked him, privily bringing into the house a new-born babe. When his belly began to drain off I set under him a large metal basin and after pinching the little one I placed it in the utensil and recited Names over it. Presently quoth he, Guard my little stranger from the draught and bring hither a wet-nurse; and I did accordingly. But he waxed ashamed of the birth and in the morning he fared forth the city nor knew we what Allah had done with him. But as he went I bespake him with the words which the poet sang when the Ass of Umm Amr[2] went off: —

---

[1] Arab. "Karkabah," clerical error (?) for "Karkarah" = driving (as wind the clouds); rumbling of wind in bowels. Dr. Steingass holds that it is formed by addition of a second "K," from the root "Karb," one of whose meanings is: "to inflate the stomach."

[2] For Ummu 'Amrin = mother of 'Amru, so written and pronounced "'Amr," a fancy name, see vol. v. 118, for the Tale of the Schoolmaster, a well-known "Joe Miller." [Ummu

Ass and Umm Amr bewent their way;   *   Nor Ass nor Umm Amr returned
    for aye;

and then I cited the saying of another: —

When I forced him to fare I bade him hie,   *   Where Umm Kash'am[1] caused
    her selle to fly."

Now as the Caliph Harun al-Rashid heard these words he
laughed so hearty a laugh that he fell backwards and bade the
goodwife repeat her history till he waxed distraught for excess of
merriment, when lo and behold! a Darwaysh suddenly entered
the presence. The wife looked at her husband and recognised
him; but the Caliph knew not his Kazi, so much had time and
trouble changed the Judge's cheer. However, she signalled to
the Commander of the Faithful that the beggar was her mate and
he taking the hint cried out, "Welcome to thee, O Darwaysh, and
where be the babe thou bearest at Tarabulus?" The unfortunate
replied, "O King of the Age, do men go with child?" and the
Prince of True Believers rejoined, "We heard that the Kazi bare
a babe and thou art that same Kazi now habited in Fakir's habit.
But who may be this woman thou seest?" He made answer
"I wot not;" but the dame exclaimed, "Why this denial, O thou
who fearest Allah so little? I conjure thee by the life of the King
to recount in his presence all that betided thee." He could deny
it no longer so he told his tale before the Caliph, who laughed at
him aloud; and at each adventure the King cried out, "Allah
spare thee and thy child, O Kazi!" Thereupon the Judge
explained saying, "Pardon, O King of the Age, I merit even

'Amrin, like Ummu 'Ámirin, is a slang term for "hyena." Hence, if Ass and Umm Amr
went off together, it is more than likely that neither came back.— St.]

[1] A slang name for Death. "Kash'am" has various sigs. esp. the lion, hence Rabí'at
al-Faras (of the horses), one of the four sons of Nizár was surnamed Al-Kash'am from his
cœur de lion (Al-Mas'údi iii. 238). Another pleasant term for departing life is Abú Yáhyá
= Father of *John*, which also means "The Living" from Hayy — Death being the lord of
all: hence "Yamút" lit. = he dies, is an ill-omened name amongst Arabs. Kash'am is
also a hyena, and Umm Kash'am is syn. with Umm 'Ámir (vol. i. 43). It was considered
a point of good breeding to use these "Kunyah" for the purpose of varying speech (see
al-Hariri Ass. xix.). The phrase in the text = meaning went to hell, as a proverb was first
used by Zuhayr, one of the "Suspended Poets." Umm Kash'am was the P.N. of a runaway
camel which, passing by a large fire, shied and flung its riding saddle into the flames. So
in Al-Siyúti's "History of the Caliphs" (p. 447), the text has "And Malak Shah went to
where her saddle was thrown by Umm Kash'am," which Major Jarrett renders "departed
to hell-fire."

more than what hath betided me." —— And Shahrazad was
surprised by the dawn of day and fell silent and ceased saying
her permitted say. Then quoth her sister Dunyazad, "How
sweet and tasteful is thy tale, O sister mine, and enjoyable and
delectable!" Quoth she, "And where is this compared with that
I would relate to you on the coming night an the Sovran suffer
me to survive?" Now when it was the next night and that was

The Three Hundred and Ninety-second Night.

DUNYAZAD said to her, "Allah upon thee, O my sister, an thou be
other than sleepy, finish for us thy tale that we may cut short the
watching of this our latter night!" She replied, "With love
and good will!" It hath reached me, O auspicious King, the
director, the right-guiding, lord of the rede which is benefiting
and of deeds fair-seeming and worthy celebrating, that quoth the
Kazi to the King, "I deserve even more than what hath betided
me for my deeds were unrighteous, O Ruler of the Time. But
now the twain of us be present between thy hands; so do thou,
of thy generous grace and the perfection of thy beneficence,
deign reconcile me unto my wife and from this moment forwards
I repent before the face of Allah nor will I ever return to the condition I was in of niggardise and greed of gain. But 'tis for her
to decide and on whatever wise she direct me to act, therein will
I not gainsay her; and do thou vouchsafe to me the further
favour of restoring me to the office I whilome held." When the
Prince of True Believers, Harun al-Rashid, heard the Kazi's words
he turned to the Judge's wife and said, "Thou also hast heard
what thy mate hath averred: so do thou become to him what
thou wast before and thou hast command over all which thy
husband requireth." She replied, "O King of the Age, even as
thou hast the advantage of knowing, verily the Heavens and the
son of Adam change not; for that man's nature is never altered
except with his existence nor doth it depart from him save when
his life departeth. However, an he speak the truth let him bind
himself by a deed documented under thy personal inspection
and thine own seal; so that if he break his covenant the case
may be committed to thee." The Caliph rejoined," Sooth thou
sayest that the nature of Adam's son is allied to his existence;"
but the Kazi exclaimed, "O our lord the Sultan, bid write for

me the writ even as thou hast heard from her mouth and do thou deign witness it between us twain." Thereupon the King reconciled their differences and allotted to them a livelihood which would suffice and sent them both back to Tarabulus-town. This is all that hath come down to us concerning the Kazi who bare a babe: yet 'tis as naught compared with the tale of the Bhang-eaters, for their story is wondrous and their adventures delectable and marvellous. "What may it be?" asked Shahryar; so Shahrazad began to recount

THE TALE OF THE KAZI AND THE BHANG-EATER.[1]

THERE was a certain eater of Bhang —— And Shahrazad was surprised by the dawn of day and fell silent and ceased to say her permitted say. Then quoth her sister Dunyazad, "How sweet is thy story, O sister mine, and how enjoyable and delectable!" Quoth she, "And where is this compared with that I would re-late to you on the coming night an the King suffer me to survive?" Now when it was the next night and that was

The Three Hundred and Ninety-third Night,

DUNYAZAD said to her, "Allah upon thee, O my sister, an thou be other than sleepy, finish for us thy tale that we may cut short the watching of this our latter night!" She replied, "With love and good will!" It hath reached me, O auspicious King, the director, the right-guiding, lord of the rede which is benefiting and of deeds fair-seeming and worthy celebrating, that there was a certain eater of Bhang whose wont it was every day to buy three Faddahs' worth of hemp and he would eat one third thereof in the morning and a second at noon and the rest about sundown. He was by calling a fisherman; and regularly as dawn appeared he would take hook and line and go down to the river a-fishing; then he would sell of his catch a portion, expending half a Faddah on bread and eat this with the remaining part of the fish broiled. He would also provide himself day by day with a waxen taper

---

[1] Scott's "Story of the Bhang-eater and Cauzee," vi. 126: Gauttier, *Histoire du Preneur d'Opium et du Cadi*, vi. 268.

and light it in his cell and sit before it, taking his pleasure and
talking to himself after his large dose of Bhang. In such condition he abode a while of time until one fine spring-night, about
the middle of the month when the moon was shining sheeniest,
he sat down to bespeak himself and said, "Ho, Such-an-one! hie
thee forth and solace thy soul with looking at the world, for this
be a time when none will espy thee and the winds are still." Herewith he went forth intending for the river; but as soon as he
issued from his cell-door and trod upon the square, he beheld the
moonbeams bestrown upon the surface and, for the excess of his
Bhang, his Fancy said to him, "By Allah, soothly the stream
floweth strong and therein needs must be much store of fish.
Return, Such-an-one, to thy cell, bring hook and line and cast
them into these waters; haply Allah our Lord shall vouchsafe
thee somewhat of fish, for men say that by night the fisherwight
on mighty fine work shall alight." He presently brought out his
gear and, having baited the hook, made a cast into the moonlit
square, taking station in the shadow of the walls where he believed the river bank to be. Then he bobbed[1] with his hook and
line and kept gazing at the waters, when behold! a big dog sniffed
the bait and coming up to it swallowed the hook till it stuck in his
gullet.[2] The beast feeling it prick his throttle yelped with pain
and made more noise every minute, rushing about to the right
and the left: so the line was shaken in the man's hand and he
drew it in, but by so doing the hook pierced deeper and the
brute howled all the louder; and it was pull Bhang-eater and
pull cur. But the man dared not draw near the moonlight, holding it to be the river, so he tucked up his gown to his hip-bones,
and as the dog pulled more lustily he said in his mind, "By Allah
this must be a mighty big fish and I believe it to be a ravenous."[3]
Then he gripped the line firmly and haled it in but the dog had
the better of him and dragged him to the very marge of the moonlight; so the fisherman waxed afraid and began to cry, "Alack!
Alack! Alack!"[4] To my rescue ye braves![5] Help me for a monster of the deep would drown me! Yállah, hurry ye, my fine

---

[1] Arab. "Lawwaha" = lit. pointing out, making clear.
[2] Text "in his belly," but afterwards in his "Halkah" = throat, throttle, which gives
better sense.
[3] In text "Háyishah" from "Haysh" = spoiling, etc.
[4] Arab. "Yauh!" See vols. ii. 321; vi. 235.
[5] Arab. "Yá Jad'án" (pron. "Gád'án") more gen. "Yá Jad'a" = mon brave!

fellows, hasten to my aid!" Now at that hour people were
enjoying the sweets of sleep and when they heard these unsea-
sonable outcries they flocked about him from every side and
accosting him asked, "What is it? What maketh thee cry aloud
at such an hour? What hath befallen thee?" He answered,
"Save me, otherwise a river-monster will cause me fall into
the stream and be drowned." Then, finding him tucked up to
the hips, the folk approached him and enquired, "Where is the
stream of which thou speakest?" and he replied, "Yonder's the
river; be ye all blind?" Thereat they understood that he spoke
of the moonbeams, whose sheen was dispread upon earth, deeming it a river-surface, and they told him this; but he would not
credit them and cried, "So ye also desire to drown me; be off
from me! our Lord will send me other than you to lend me good
aid at this hour of need." They replied, "O well-born one, this
be moonshine;" but he rejoined, "Away from me, ye low fellows,[1]
ye dogs!" They derided him and the angrier he grew the more
they laughed, till at last they said one to other, "Let us leave
him and wend our ways," and they quitted him in such condition —— And Shahrazad was surprised by the dawn of day and
fell silent and ceased saying her permitted say. Then quoth her
Sister Dunyazad, "How sweet and tasteful is thy tale, O sister mine, and enjoyable and delectable!" Quoth she, "And
where is this compared with that I would relate to you on the
coming night an the Sovran suffer me to survive?" Now when
it was the next night and that was

The Three Hundred and Ninety-fourth Night.

DUNYAZAD said to her, "Allah upon thee, O my sister, an thou be
other than sleepy, finish for us thy tale that we may cut short the
watching of this our latter night!" She replied, "With love
and good will!" It hath reached me, O auspicious King, the
director, the right-guiding, lord of the rede which is benefiting
and of deeds fair-seeming and worthy celebrating, that the folk
who flocked to the assistance of the Bhang-eater left him in such
condition, he crying aloud in affright, the dog being now before

---

[1] In text "Yá 'Arzád": prob. a clerical slip for "Urzát," plur. of "Urzah" == a companion, a (low) fellow, a man evil spoken of.

him in a phrenzy of pain for the hook sticking in his gullet and
being unable to rid himself of it, while the man dreaded to draw
near the moonshine, still deeming (albeit he stood upon terra
firma) that he was about to step into the stream. So he hugged
the wall shadow which to him represented the river-bank. In
this case he continued until day brake and light shone and the
to-ing and fro-ing of the folk increased; withal he remained as he
was, crying out for affright lest he be drowned. Suddenly a Kazi
rode by him and seeing him with gown kilted up and the hound
hanging on to the hook, asked, "What may be the matter with
thee, O man?" He answered saying, "O my lord, I dread lest I
be drowned in this stream, whither a monster of the deep is a-
dragging me." The judge looked at him and knew him for a
Bhang-eater, so he dismounted from his monture and cried to one
of his attendants, "Catch hold of yon dog and unhook him!"
Now this Kazi was also one who was wont to use Hashish; so
quoth he to himself, "By Allah, take this fellow with thee and
feed him in thy house and make a mocking-stock of him; and, as
each night cometh on do thou and he eat together a portion of
the drug and enjoy each other's company." Accordingly he
took him and carrying him to his quarters seated him in a private
stead until nightfall when the twain met and supped together;
then they swallowed a large dose of Bhang and they lit candles
and sat in their light to enjoy themselves.[1] Presently from excess
of the drug they became as men Jinn-mad, uttering words which
befit not to intend or to indite,[2] amongst which were a saying
of the Bhang-eater to the Kazi, "By Allah, at this season I'm as
great as the King;" and the Judge's reply, "And I also at such
time am as great as the Basha, the Governor." Thereupon quoth
to him the Bhang-eater, "I'm high above thee and if the King
would cut off the Governor's head what would happen to hinder
him?" And quoth the Kazi, "Yea, verily; naught would hinder
him; but 'tis the custom of Kings to appoint unto Governors a
place wherein they may deal commandment." Then they fell to
debating the affairs of the Government and the Sultanate, when
by decree of the Decreer the Sultan of the city went forth his
palace that very night, accompanied by the Wazir (and the twain

---

[1] Easterns love drinking in a bright light: see vol. ii. 59.
[2] Arab. "'Akl" (= comprehension, understanding) and "Nakl" (= copying, de-
scribing, transcribing), a favourite phrase in this MS.

in disguise); and they ceased not traversing the town till they
reached the house wherein sat the Bhang-eater and the Kazi. So
they stood at the door and heard their talk from first to last,
when the King turned to the Minister and asked, "What shall
we do with these two fellows?" "Be patient, O King of the
Age," answered the Wazir, "until they make an end of their
talk, after which whatso thou wilt do with them that will they
deserve." "True indeed,"[1] quoth the ruler, "nevertheless, instead of standing here let us go in to them." Now that night
the boon-companions had left the door open forgetting to padlock it; so the visitors entered and salam'd to them and they returned the greeting and rose to them and bade them be seated.
Accordingly they sat down and the Sultan said to the Bhang-
eater, "O man, fearest thou not aught from the Sovran, thou
and thy friend; and are ye sitting up until this hour?" He replied, "The Sultan himself often fareth forth at such untimely
time, and as he is a King even so am I, and yonder man is my
Basha: moreover, if the ruler think to make japery of us, we
are his equals and more." Thereupon the Sultan turned to his
Wazir and said by signals, "I purpose to strike off the heads of
these fellows;" and said the Minister in the same way, "O King,
needs must they have a story, for no man with his wits in his
head would have uttered such utterance. But patience were our
bestest plan." Then cried the Bhang-eater to the Sultan, "O
man, whenever we say a syllable, thou signallest to thine associate. What is it thou wouldst notify to him and we not understanding it? By Allah, unless thou sit respectfully in our presence we will bid our Basha strike off thy pate!" —— And Shahrazad was surprised by the dawn of day and fell silent and ceased
to say her permitted say. Then quoth her sister Dunyazad,
"How sweet is thy story, O sister mine, and how enjoyable and
delectable!" Quoth she, "And where is this compared with
that I would relate to you on the coming night an the Sovran
suffer me to survive?" Now when it was the next night and
that war

The Three Hundred and Ninety-fifth Night,

DUNYAZAD said to her, "Allah upon thee, O my sister, an thou
be other than sleepy, finish for us thy tale that we may cut short

---

[1] Arab. "Ummálí"; gen. L'mmál, an affirmation; Certes, I believe you!

the watching of this our latter night!" She replied, "With love
and good will!" It hath reached me, O auspicious King, the
director, the right-guiding, lord of the rede which is benefiting
and of deeds fair-seeming and worthy celebrating, that when
the Sultan heard the Bhang-eater's words he waxed the more
furious and would have arisen and struck off his head; but the
Wazir winked at him and whispered, "O King of the Age, I
and thou are in disguise and these men imagine that we are of
the commons: so be thou pitiful even as Almighty Allah is
pitiful and willeth not the punishment of the sinner. Furthermore, I conceive that the twain are eaters of Hashish, which
drug when swallowed by man, garreth him prattle of whatso he
pleaseth and chooseth, making him now a Sultan then a Wazir
and then a merchant, the while it seemeth to him that the world
is in the hollow of his hand." Quoth the Sultan, "And what
may be thy description of Hashish?" and quoth the Wazir,
" 'Tis composed of hemp leaflets, whereto they add aromatic
roots and somewhat of sugar: then they cook it and prepare a
kind of confection which they eat;[1] but whoso eateth it (especially an he eat more than enough), talketh of matters which
reason may on no wise represent. If thou wouldst know its
secret properties, on the coming night (Inshallah!) we will
bring some with us and administer it to these two men; and
when they eat it the dose will be in addition to their ordinary."
After this the Sultan left them and went forth, when the Bhang-
eater said to the Kazi, "By Allah, this night we have enjoyed
ourselves and next night (if Allah please!) we will enjoy ourselves yet more." The other replied, "Yes, but I fear from the
Sultan, lest he learn our practice and cut off our heads." "Who
shall bring the Sovran to us?" asked the other: "he is in his
palace and we are in our own place; and, granting he come, I
will divert him by recounting an adventure which befel me."
The Kazi answered, "Have no dread of the Sultan; for he may
not fare forth a-nights single-handed; nay, what while he issueth
forth he must be escorted by his high officials." Now when the
next night fell, the Kazi brought the Hashish which he divided

---

[1] For the many preparations of this drug, see Herklots, Appendix, pp. lxviii. ciii. It
is impossible to say how "Indian hemp," like opium, datura, ether and chloroform, will
affect the nervous system of an untried man. I have read a dozen descriptions of the
results, from the highly imaginative Monte Cristo to the prose of prosaic travellers;
and do not recognise that they are speaking of the same thing.

into two halves, eating one himself and giving the other to his
companion; and both swallowed their portions after supper and
then lit the waxen tapers and sat down to take their pleasure.[1]
Suddenly the Sultan and his Wazir came in upon them during
the height of their enjoyment, and the visitors were habited in
dress other than before, and they brought with them a quantity
of Bhang-confection and also some conserve of roses: so they
handed a portion of the first to the revellers, which these accepted and ate, while they themselves swallowed the conserve,
the others supposing it to be Hashísh like what they had eaten.
Now when they had taken an overdose, they got into a hurly-
burly of words and fell to saying things which can neither be
intended nor indited, and amongst these they exclaimed, "By
Allah, the Sultan is deposed and we will rule in his stead and
deal commandment to his reign." The other enquired, "And
if the Sultan summon us what wilt thou say to him?" "By
Allah, I will tell him a tale which befel myself and crave of him
ten Faddahs wherewithal to buy Bhang!" "And hast thou any
skill in tale-telling?" "In good sooth I have!" "But how wilt
thou depose the Sultan and reign in his stead?" "I will say to
him 'Be off!' and he will go." "He will strike thy neck." "Nay,
the Sultan is pitiful and will not punish me for my words." So
saying the Bhang-eater arose and loosed the inkle of his bag-
trowsers, then approaching the Sultan he drew forth his prickle
and proceeded to bepiss him;[2] but the King took flight as the
other faced him, and fled before him, he pursuing. —— And
Shahrazad was surprised by the dawn of day and fell silent and
ceased saying her permitted say. Then quoth her sister Dunyazad, "How sweet and tasteful is thy tale, O sister mine, and
enjoyable and delectable!" Quoth she, "And where is this compared with that I would relate to you on the coming night an
the Sovran suffer me to survive?" Now when it was the next
night and that was

---

[1] This tranquil enjoyment is popularly called "Kayf." See my Pilgrimage i. 13. In
a coarser sense it is applied to all manners of intoxication; and the French traveller Sonnini
says, "The Arabs (by which he means the Egyptians) give the name of Kayf to the volup-
tuous relaxation, the delicious stupor, produced by the smoking of hemp." I have smoked
it and eaten it for months without other effect than a greatly increased appetite and a
little drowsiness.

[2] These childish indecencies are often attributed to Bhang-eaters. See "Bákún's Tale
of the Hashísh-eater," vol. ii. 91. Modest Scott (vi. 129) turns the joke into "tweaking
the nose." Respectable Moslems dislike the subject, but the vulgar relish it as much
as the sober Italian enjoys the description of a drinking bout—in novels.

The Three Hundred and Ninety-sixth Night,

DUNYAZAD said to her, "Allah upon thee, O my sister, an thou be other than sleepy, finish for us thy tale that we may cut short the watching of this our latter night!" She replied, "With love and good will!" It hath reached me, O auspicious King, the director, the right-guiding, lord of the rede which is benefiting and of deeds fair-seeming and worthy celebrating, that the Bhang-eater holding up his bag-trowsers ran after the Sultan purposing to bepiss him and caught up the fugitive at the doorway when he fell over the threshold and began a-piddling upon his own clothes. In like manner the Kazi attempted to bepiss the Wazir and ran after him to the entrance, where he also fell upon the Bhang-eater and took to making water over him. So the Bhang-eater and the Kazi lay each bewraying other, and the Sultan and the Wazir stood laughing at them and saying, "By Allah, too much Hashísh injureth man's wits;" and presently they left and went their ways returning to their palaces. But the two drunkards ceased not lying in their own water till day broke; and when the fumes of the drug had left their brains, they arose and found themselves dripping and befouled with their own filth. Thereupon each said to other, "What be this cross hath betided us?" Presently they arose and washed themselves and their clothes; then sitting down together they said, "None did this deed by us save and except the two fellows who were with us; and who knoweth what they were, or citizens of this city or strangers; for 'twas they brought the intoxicant which we ate and it bred a madness in our brains. Verily 'twas they did the mischief; but, an they come to us a third time, needs must we be instant with them and learn from them an they be foreigners or folk of this city: we will force them to confess, but if they hide them from us we will turn them out." On the next night they met again and the two sat down and ate a quantity of Hashísh after they had supped: and they lit the waxen tapers and each of them drank a cup of coffee.[1] Presently their heads

---

[1] In the text "Finjál," a vulgarism for "Finján": so the converse "Isma'ín" for "Ism'aíl" = Ishmael. Mr. J. W Redhouse (The Academy No. 764) proposes a new date for coffee in Al-Yaman. Colonel Playfair (History of Yemen, Bombay 1859) had carelessly noted that its "first use at Aden was by a judge of the place who had seen it drunk at Zayla', on the African coast opposite Aden," and he made the judge die in A.H. 875 = A.D. 1470.

whirled round under the drug and they sat down to talk and
enjoy themselves when their drunkenness said to them, "Up
with you and dance." Accordingly they arose and danced, when
behold, the Sultan and his Wazir suddenly came in upon them and
salam'd to them: so they returned the salutation but continued
the saltation. The new comers considered them in this condition
and forthwith the King turned to the Minister and said, "What
shall we do with them?" Said the other, "Patience until their
case come to end in somewhat whereof we can lay hold." Then
they chose seats for themselves and solaced them with the
spectacle, and the dancers kept on dancing until they were tired
and were compelled to sit down and take their rest. Presently
the Bhang-eater looked at the Sultan and exclaimed, "You,
whence are you?" and he replied, "We be foreigner folk and
never visited this city before that night when we met you; and
as we heard you making merry we entered to partake of your
merriment." On this wise the device recoiled upon the Bhang-
eater and presently the King asked them, saying, "Fear ye not
lest the Sultan hear of you, and ye in this condition which would
cause your disgrace at his hands?" The Bhang-eater answered,
"The Sultan! What tidings of us can he have? He is in the
royal Palace and we in our place of Bhang-eating." The Sovran
rejoined, "Why not go to him! Belike he will gift you and
largesse you;" but the Bhang-eater retorted, "We fear his people
lest they drive us away." Whereto quoth the King, "They will
not do on such wise and if thou require it we will write thee a
note to his address, for we know him of old inasmuch as both of
us learned to read in the same school." "Write thy writ," quoth
the other to the Sultan who after inditing it and sealing it placed
it in their hands and presently the two visitors departed. Then

---

This is about the date of the Shaykh al-Sházalí's tomb at Mocha, and he was the first
who brought the plant from about African Harar to the Arabian seaboard. But Mr.
Redhouse finds in a Turkish work written only two centuries ago, and printed at Con-
stantinople, in A.D. 1732, that the "ripe fruit was discovered growing wild in the mountains of Yemen (?) by a company of dervishes banished thither." Finding the berry
relieve their hunger and support their vigils the prior, "Shaykh 'Umar advised their
stewing it (?) and the use became established. They dried a store of the fruit: and its
use spread to other dervish communities, who perhaps (?) sowed the seed wherever it
would thrive throughout Africa (N.B. where it is indigenous) and India (N.B. where
both use and growth are quite modern). From Africa, two centuries later, its use was
reimported to Arabia at Aden (?) by the judge above mentioned, who in a season of
scarcity of the dried fruit (?) tried the seed" (N.B. which is the fruit). This is passing
strange and utterly unknown to the learned De Sacy (Chrest. Arab. i. 412–481).

the Bhang-eater and the Kazi sat together through the night
until daylight did appear when the fumes of the Hashísh had fled
their brains and the weather waxed fine and clear. So they said,
each to other, "Let us go to the Sultan," and the twain set out
together and walked till they reached the square facing the Palace.
Here, finding a crowd of folk, they went up to the door and the
Bhang-eater drew forth his letter and handed it to one of the
Sultan's suite, who on reading it fell to the ground and presently
rising placed it upon his head. —— And Shahrazad was surprised by the dawn of day and fell silent and ceased to say her
permitted say. Then quoth her sister Dunyazad, "How sweet
is thy story, O sister mine, and how enjoyable and delectable!"
Quoth she, "And where is this compared with that I would
relate to you on the coming night an the Sovran suffer me to
survive?" Now when it was the next night and that was

The Three Hundred and Ninety-seventh Night,

DUNYAZAD said to her, "Allah upon thee, O my sister, an thou
be other than sleepy, finish for us thy tale that we may cut short
the watching of this our latter night!" She replied, "With
love and good will!" It hath reached me, O auspicious King, the
director, the right-guiding, lord of the rede which is benefiting
and of deeds fair-seeming and worthy celebrating, that the officer
who took the letter caused the Bhang-eater and his comrade enter
the presence, and the Sultan catching sight of them commanded
them to be seated in a private stead where none other man was.
His bidding was obeyed; and at noon-tide he sent them a tray of
food for dinner and also coffee; and the same was done at sundown. But as soon as supper-tide came the Sultan prayed and
recited sections of Holy Writ, as was his wont, until two hours
had passed when he ordered the twain be summoned; and when
they stood in the presence and salam'd to him and blessed him
the King returned their salute and directed them to be seated.
Accordingly they sat down and quoth the Sultan to the Bhang-
eater, "Where be the man who gave you the writ?" Quoth the
other, "O King of the Age, there were two men who came to us
and said, 'Why go ye not to the King? Belike he will gift you
and largesse you.' Our reply was, 'We know him not and we
fear lest his folk drive us away.' So one of them said to us, 'I

will write thee a note to his address for we know him of old, inasmuch as both of us learned to read in the same school.' Accordingly he indited it and sealed it and gave it to us; and coming hither we found his words true and now we are between his hands." The Sultan enquired, "Was there any lack of civility to the strangers on your part?" and they replied, "None, save our questioning them and saying, 'Whence come ye?' whereto they rejoined, 'We be strangers.' Beyond this there was nothing unpleasant; nothing at all." "Whither went they?" asked the King and the other answered, "I wot not." The Sultan continued, "Needs must thou bring them to me for 'tis long since I saw them;" and the other remarked, "O King of the Age, if again they come to our place we will seize them and carry them before thee even perforce, but in case they come not, we have no means to hand." Quoth the King, "An thou know them well, when thou catchest sight of them they cannot escape thee," and quoth the other, "Yea, verily." Then the Sultan pursued, "What did ye with the twain who came before them and ye wanted to bepiss them?" Now when the Bhang-eater heard these words his colour paled and his case changed, his limbs trembled and he suspected that the person which he had insulted was the Sultan; whereupon the King turned towards him and seeing in him signs of discomfiture asked, "What is in thy mind, O Bhang-eater? What hath befallen thee?" The other arose forthright and kissing ground cried, "Pardon, O King of the Age, before whom I have sinned." The Sovran asked, "How didst thou know this?" and he answered, "Because none other was with us and news of us goeth not out of doors; so needs must thou have been one of the twain and he who wrote the writ was thyself; for well we know that the kings read not in schools. Thou and thy friend did come in disguise to make merry at our expense; therefore pardon us, O King of the Age, for mercy is a quality of the noble, and Almighty Allah said, 'Whoso pardoneth and benefitteth his reward is with Allah,' and eke He said, 'And the stiflers of wrath and the pardoners of mankind and Allah loveth the doers of good'."[1] Herewith the

---

[1] Koran iii. 128. D'Herbelot and Sale (Koran, chap. iii. note) relate on this text a noble story of Hasan Ali-son and his erring slave which The Forty Vezirs (Lady's eighth story, p. 113) ignorantly attributes to Harun al-Rashid:—Forthwith the Caliph rose in wrath and was about to hew the girl to pieces, when she said, "O Caliph, Almighty Allah saith in His glorious Word (the Koran), 'And the stiflers of Wrath'" (iii. 128). Straight-

Sultan smiled and said, "No harm shall befal thee, O Bhang-
eater! Thine excuse is accepted and thy default pardoned, but,
O thou clever fellow, hast thou no tale to tell us?" He replied,
"O King of the Age, I have a story touching myself and my wife
which, were it graven with needle-gravers upon the eye-corners
were a warning to whoso would be warned. But I strave
against her on my own behalf, withal she overcame me and
tyrannised over me by her contrivance." "What is it?" asked
the King; so the man began to relate the

History of the Bhang-Eater and his Wife.

IN the beginning of my career I owned only a single bull and
poverty confused my wits. —— And Shahrazad was surprised
by the dawn of day and fell silent and ceased saying her permitted say. Then quoth her sister Dunyazad, "How sweet and
tasteful is thy tale, O sister mine, and enjoyable and delectable!"
Quoth she, "And where is this compared with that I would
relate to you on the coming night an the Sovran suffer me to
survive?" Now when it was the next night and that was

The Three Hundred and Ninety-eighth Night,

DUNYAZAD said to her, "Allah upon thee, O my sister, an thou
be other than sleepy, finish for us thy tale that we may cut short
the watching of this our latter night!" She replied, "With
love and good-will!" It hath reached me, O auspicious King, the
director, the right-guiding, lord of the rede which is benefiting
and of deeds fair-seeming and worthy celebrating, that the Bhang-

---

way the Caliph's wrath was calmed. Again said the girl, "'And the pardoners of men.'"
(*ibid.*) Quoth the Caliph, "I have forgiven the crimes of all the criminals who may be
in prison." Again said the slave-girl, "'And Allah loveth the beneficent.'" (*ibid.*) Quoth
the Caliph, "God be witness that I have with my own wealth freed thee and as many
male and female slaves as I have, and that this day I have for the love of Allah given
the half of all my good in alms to the poor." This is no improvement upon the simple
and unexaggerated story in Sale. "It is related of Hasan, the son of Ali, that a slave
having once thrown a dish on him boiling hot, as he sat at table, and fearing his master's
resentment, fell on his knees and repeated these words, Paradise is for those who bridle
their anger. Hasan answered, I am not angry. The slave proceeded, And for those who
forgive men. I forgive you, said Hasan. The slave, however, finished the verse, For
Allah loveth the beneficent. Since it is so, replied Hasan, I give you your liberty and
four hundred pieces of silver."

eater said to the Sultan:——I had no property save a single bull and poverty confused my wits. So I resolved to sell Roger[1] and going to the Bazar stood therein expecting someone to buy it, but none came to me until the last of the day. At that time I drove it forth and dragged it off till we reached half-way to my home, where I came upon a tree and sat down to rest in the cool shade. Now I had somewhat of Bhang with me, also a trifle of bread which I brought out and ate, and after I drank a draught of water from the spring. Presently the Bhang began to wobble in my brains and behold a bird in the tree-top which men call a Magpie[2] fell a-cawing, so I said to her, "Thou, O Mother of Solomon, hast thou a mind to buy the bull?" and she cawed again. I continued, "Whatso price ever thou settest upon the bull, at that will I cede it to thee." Again a croak, and I, "Haply thou hast brought no money?" Another croak and cried I, "Say the word and I will leave the bull with thee till next Friday when thou wilt come and pay me its price." But she still cawed, and I, whenever she opened beak, O King of the Age, fancied that she bespake me and wanted the bull. But all this was of the excess of my Bhang which kept working in my brains and I mistook the croaking for her conversing. Accordingly I left with her the bull bound to the tree and turned towards my village; and, when I went in to my wife, she asked me anent the bull and I told her of my selling it to the Mother of Solomon. "Who may she be?" asked my rib, and I replied, "She dwelleth in yonder tree;" whereat my spouse rejoined "Allah compensate thee with welfare." So I awaited patiently the appointed term; then, after swallowing somewhat of Bhang, I repaired to the tree and sat beneath it when, lo and behold! the pie cawed and I cried to her, "Hast thou brought the coin?" A second caw! Then said I, "Come hither and bring me the money." A third caw! Hereat I waxed wroth and arose and taking up a bittock of brick I threw it at her as she sat perched upon the tree, whereupon she flew off and alit upon an 'old man'[3] of clay hard by. So it oc-

---

[1] The old name of the parish bull in rural England.

[2] Arab. "Kawik:" see The Nights, vol. vi. 182, where the bird is called "Ak'ak." Our dicts. do not give the word, but there is a "Kauk" (Káka, yakúku) to cluck, and "Kauk" = an aquatic bird with a long neck. I assume "Kawik" to be an intensive form of the same root. The "Mother of Solomon" is a fanciful "Kunyah," or bye name given to the bird by the Bhang-eater, suggesting his high opinion of her wisdom.

[3] Arab. "Nátúr," prop. a watchman: also a land-mark, a bench-mark of tamped clay.

curred to my mind, "By Allah, the Mother of Solomon biddeth me follow her and recover the value of the bull from yonder 'old man.'" Presently I went up to it and digging therein suddenly came upon a crock[1] full of gold wherefrom I took ten ashrafis, the value of the bull, and returned it to its place, saying, "Allah ensure thy weal, O Mother of Solomon." Then I walked back to my village and went in to my wife and said, "By Allah, verily the Mother of Solomon is of the righteous! Lookye, she gave me these ten golden ducats to the price of our Roger." Said my wife, "And who may be the Mother of Solomon?" and I told her all that had befallen me especially in the matter of the crock of gold buried in the 'old man.' But after she heard my words she tarried until sundown; then, going to the land-mark she dug into it and carrying off the crock brought it home privily. But I suspected her of so doing and said to her, "O woman, hast thou taken the good of the Mother of Solomon (and she of the righteous) after we have received from her the price of our Roger out of her own moneys? And hast thou gone and appropriated her property? By Allah, an thou restore it not to its stead even as it was, I will report to the Wálí that my wife hath happened upon treasure-trove." And so saying I went forth from her. Then she arose and got ready somewhat of dough for cooking with flesh-meat and, sending for a fisherman, bade him bring her a few fishes fresh-caught and all alive, and taking these inside the house she drew sweet water and sprinkled them therewith, and lastly she placed the dough and meat outside the house ready for nightfall. Presently I returned and we supped, I and she; but 'twas my firm resolve to report my wife's find to the Chief of Police. We slept together till midnight when she awoke me saying, "O man, I have dreamed a dream, and this it is, that the sky hath rained down drink and meat and that the fishes have entered our house."

---

[1] In text "Bartamán" for "Martaban" = a pot, jar, or barrel-shaped vessel: others apply the term to fine porcelain which poison cannot affect. See Col. Yule's *Glossary*, s. v. Martabán, where the quotation from Ibn Batutah shows that the term was current in the xivth century. Linschoten (i. 101) writes, "In this town (Martaban of Pegu) many of the great earthen pots are made, which in India are called *Martananas*, and many of them are carried throughout all India of all sorts both small and great: and some are so great that they will fill two pipes of water." Pyrard (i. 259) applies the name to "certain handsome jars, of finer shape and larger than I have seen elsewhere" (Transl. by Albert Gray for the Hakluyt Soc. 1887). Mr. Hill adds that at Málé the larger barrel-shaped jars of earthenware are still called "Mátabán," and Mr. P. Brown (Zillah Dictionary, 1852) finds the word preserved upon the Madras coast = a black jar in which rice is imported from Pegu.

I replied to her of my folly and the overmuch Bhang which disported in my head, "Let us get up and look." So we searched the inside of the house and we found the fishes, and the outside where we came upon the doughboy and flesh-meat; so we fell to picking it up, I and she, and broiling it and eating thereof till morning. Then said I, "Do thou go and return the moneys of Solomon's Mother to their own place." But she would not and flatly refused. —— And Shahrazad was surprised by the dawn of day and fell silent and ceased to say her permitted say. Then quoth her sister Dunyazad, "How sweet is thy story, O sister mine, and how enjoyable and delectable!" Quoth she, "And where is this compared with that I would relate to you on the coming night an the Sovran suffer me to survive?" Now when it was the next night and that was

The Three Hundred and Ninety-ninth Night,

DUNYAZAD said to her, "Allah upon thee, O my sister, an thou be other than sleepy, finish for us thy tale that we may cut short the watching of this our latter night!" She replied, "With love and good will!" It hath reached me, O auspicious King, the director, the right-guiding, lord of the rede which is benefiting and of deeds fair-seeming and worthy celebrating, that the Bhang-eater continued: —— I said to my wife, "Do thou go and return the moneys of Solomon's Mother to their own place;" but she would not and flatly refused. Then I repeated[1] my words but without avail, so I flew into a fury and leaving her ceased not trudging till I found the Wali and said to him, "O my lord, my wife Such-an-one hath hit upon a hoard and 'tis now with her."[2] The Chief of Police asked, "O man, hast thou seen it?" and I answered, "Yes." So he sent a body of his followers to bring her before him and when she came said to her, "O woman, where is the treasure trove?" Said she, "O my lord, this report is a baseless;" whereupon the Chief of Police bade her be led to jail. They did his bidding and she abode in the prison a whole day, after which the Wali summoned her and repeated

---

[1] The Arabic here changes person, "he repeated" after Eastern fashion, and confuses the tale to European readers.

[2] Such treasure trove belonging to the State, *i.e.* the King.

his words to her adding, "An thou bring not the hoard I will
slay thee and cast thy corpse into the bogshop[1] of the Hammam." The woman (my wife) rejoined, "O my lord, I never
found aught;" and when he persisted threatening her with
death she cried, "O my lord, wherefore oppress me on this wise
and charge such load of sin upon thine own neck? I never came
upon treasure at all, at all!" The Chief of Police retorted, "My
first word and my last are these:——Except thou bring the
treasure trove I will slay thee and cast thee into the jakes."
Herewith quoth she, "O my lord, ask my husband where it was
I hit upon the hoard and at what time, by day or by night," and
the Wali's men cried, "By Allah, these her words are just and
right, nor is therein aught of harm." So he sent to summon me
and asked me, "O man, when did thy wife hit upon the hoard?"
I answered, "O my lord, she found it on the night when the
skies rained drink and food and fishes." Now when the Wali
heard my words he said to me, "O man, the skies are not wont to
shed aught save rainwater; and a man in his right wits speaketh
not such speech as this." Said I, "By the life of thy head, O my
lord, they did rain all three of them;" but the officers cried, "O
my lord, verily this man be Jinn-mad and his wife who telleth
plain truth is wronged by him: the fellow deserveth confining
in the Máristán."[2] Accordingly the Chief of Police bade the
men set the woman free and let her wend her ways and seize me
and throw me into the madhouse. They did his bidding and I
remained there the first day and the second till the third when
my wife said to herself, "There is no Majesty and there is no
Might save in Allah, the Glorious, the Great! By the Lord, needs
must I go and relieve my husband from Bedlam and charge him
never again to speak of that treasure trove." So she came to the
Maristan and entering said to me, "Ho, Such-an-one, if any ask
of thee saying, 'What do the skies rain?[3] do thou make answer,

---

[1] Arab. "Húrí" for "Húr" = a pool, marsh, or quagmire, in fact corresponding with
our vulgar "bogshop." Dr. Steingass would read "Haurí," a "mansúb" of "Haur" =
pond, quagmire, which, in connection with a Hammam, may = sink, sewer, etc.

[2] The Bedlam: see vol. i. 288.

[3] Arab. "Tamtar aysh?" (i.e. Ayyu shayyin, see vol. i. 79). I may note that the vulgar
abbreviation is of ancient date. Also the Egyptian dialect has borrowed, from its ancestor
the Coptic, the practice of putting the interrogatory pronoun or adverb after (not before)
the verb, e.g. "Rá'ih fayn?" = Wending (art thou) whither? It is regretable that Egyptian
scholars do not see the absolute necessity of studying Coptic, and this default is the sole
imperfection of the late Dr. Spitta Bey's admirable Grammar of Egyptian.

'They rain water!' Furthermore if they inquire of thee, 'Do
they ever rain drink and food and fishes?' reply thou, 'This is
clean impossible, nor can such thing ever take place!' Then
haply they will say to thee, 'How many days are in the week?'
and do thou say, 'Seven days and this day be such a day!' Lastly
have a guard on thyself when speaking." I rejoined, " 'Tis
well, and now hie thee forth and buy me half a faddah's worth
of Bhang, for during these days I have not eaten aught thereof."
So she went and bought me somewhat of food and of Hashísh:
—— And Shahrazad was surprised by the dawn of day and fell
silent and ceased saying her permitted say. Then quoth her
sister Dunyazad, "How sweet and tasteful is thy tale, O sister
mine, and enjoyable and delectable!" Quoth she, "And where is
this compared with that I would relate to you on the coming
night an the Sovran suffer me to survive?" Now when it was
the next night and that was

The Four Hundredth Night,

DUNYAZAD said to her, "Allah upon thee, O my sister, an thou
be other than sleepy, finish for us thy tale that we may cut short
the watching of this our latter night!" She replied, "With
love and good will!" It hath reached me, O auspicious King, the
director, the right-guiding, lord of the rede which is benefiting
and of deeds fair-seeming and worthy celebrating, that the Bhang-
eater's wife fared forth and brought back somewhat of food and
of Hashísh: then returning to the Maristan (he continued) she
gave both to me and I ate of them, after which I said to her,
"Let us up and be off!" whereto she, "And when we go to the
Wali what wilt thou say?" Then the Bhang wrought in my
brains and I cried, "O bawd,[1] O my nice young lady, well
thou wottest that the skies did rain flesh and drink and fishes!
Why then didst thou not tell the truth before the Chief of
Police?" Thereupon the Manager of the Madhouse cried to
me, "O fellow, this is the babble of madmen!" and I, "By Allah,
I ate of them boiled; and doubtless the same kind of rain fell
in your house." The other exclaimed, "There be nor doubt nor

---

[1] Arab. " 'Arsah," akin to "Mu'arris" (masc.) = a pimp, a pander. See vol. i. 338;
and Supp. vol. i. 138; and for its use Pilgrimage i. 276.

hesitation anent the insanity of one who sayeth such say!"
Now all this was related by the Bhang-eater to the Sultan who
marvelled and asked him, "What could have made thee go to
the Manager and recount to him such absurdities?"   But the
Bhang-eater resumed, saying, "I dwelt in the Maristan twenty
days until at last having no Bhang to eat I came to my senses
and confessed that the skies shed only rain-water, that the
week containeth seven days and that this day be such-and-such;
in fact I discoursed like a man in his right mind.   So they dis-
charged me and I went my ways."   But when the Kazi heard this
tale he cried out to the Sultan, "O King of the Age, my story is
still more wondrous than this, which is only a prank played by
a wife.   My name was originally Abú Kásim al-Tambúri[1] and I
was appointed Kazi after a neat thing I did, and if thou, O our
lord the Sultan, desire to be told of the adventures which befel
me and of the clever trick wherefor they made me a judge, deign
give thy commandment and I will commence it."   Quoth the
Sultan, "Recount to us why and where they entitled thee Kazi,"
and the judge began to relate

How Drummer Abu Kasim Became a Kazi.

THERE was once, O King of the Age, a merchant and a man of
Bassorah who went about trading with eunuchs and slave-boys
and who bore his goods in bales[2] from Bassorah to Ajam-land
there to sell them and to buy him other merchandise for vending
in Syria.   On this wise he tarried a long while until one year of
the years he packed up his property, as was his wont, and fared
forth with it to Persia.   But at that time there fortuned to be a
famine and when he arrived at one of the cities of Ajam-land,
where formerly the traders bought his goods, on this occasion
none of them would come near him.   In such case he continued a
long while till at last a Khwájah appeared before him, a man who

---

[1] _i.e._ Abú Kásim the Drummer. The word "Tambúr" is probably derived from "Tabl"
= a drum, which became by the common change of liquids "Tabur" in O. French and
"Tabour" in English. Hence the mod. form "Tambour," which has been adopted by
Turkey, _e.g._ Tambúrji = a drummer. In Egypt, however, "Tambúr" is applied to a
manner of mandoline or guitar, mostly used by Greeks and other foreigners. See Lane,
M.E. chap. xviii.

[2] Arab. "Bál" (sing. Bálah) = a bale, from the Span. Bala and Italian Balla, a small
parcel made up in the shape of a bale, Lat. Palla.

owned abundant riches in Persia, but his home was distant three days from the place. The visitor asked saying, "O Bassorite, wilt thou sell me thy stock-in-trade?" whereto the other answered, "And how? Of course I'll sell it!" So the buyer opened the gate of bidding and offered such-and-such; but the Bassorah man cried, "Allah openeth." Then the purchaser added somewhat and the seller rejoined, "Give me yet more?" At last the buyer exclaimed, "I will give nothing more than 'Anaught';"[1] and the seller accepted the offer saying, "May Allah grant us gain!" Thereupon the Persian Khwajah took over all the goods from the vendor and next day the twain met to settle money-matters. Now I, O King of the Age, happened to be abiding in that city. The seller received from the buyer payment in full nor did anything remain; but after, the Bassorah man said to his customer, "Thou still owest me the 'Anaught,' which thou must hand over to me." The other replied jeeringly, "And the 'Anaught' is a naught; to wit, no thing;" but the Bassorite rejoined, "Here with that 'Anaught'!" Upon this a violent ruffle befel between them, the cause was carried before the King and payment was required in the Divan, for the Bassorite still demanded from the purchaser his "Anaught." The Sultan asked, "And what be this 'Anaught'?" and the Bassorah man answered, "I wot not, O King of the Age;" whereat the Sultan marvelled.——And Shahrazad was surprised by the dawn of day and fell silent and ceased to say her permitted say. Then quoth her sister Dunyazad, "How sweet is thy story, O sister mine, and how enjoyable and delectable!" Quoth she, "And where is this compared with that I would relate to you on the coming night, an the Sovran suffer me to survive?" Now when it was the next night and that was

The Four Hundred and First Night,

DUNYAZAD said to her, "Allah upon thee, O my sister, an thou be other than sleepy, finish for us thy tale that we may cut short the watching of this our latter night!" She replied, "With love and good will!" It hath reached me, O auspicious King, the director, the right-guiding, lord of the rede which is benefiting and deeds fair-seeming and worthy celebrating, that the Sultan

---

[1] Arab. "Walásh," i.e. "Was lá shayya" = "And nihil" (nil, non ens, naught).

marvelled at the action of this Bassorite and his saying, "Give me my 'Anaught!'" Presently the tidings of that cause reached me, O King; so I went to the Divan which was thronged with folk and all present kept saying, "How would it be if this 'Anaught' were a fraud or a resiliation of the contract?" Thereupon the Sultan exclaimed, "Whoso shall settle this case, to him verily will I be bountiful." So I came forward, O King of the Age, thinking of a conceit and kissed ground and said to him, "I will conclude this cause," and he rejoined, "An thou determine it and dispose of it I will give thee largesse; but if not, I will strike off thy head." I rejoined, "To hear is to obey." Then I bade them bring a large basin which could hold a skinful of water and ordered them fill it; after which I called out to the Bassorite, "Draw near," and he drew near. All this and the King looked on and kept his eyes fixed upon us. Then I cried to the claimant, "Close thy fist!" and he did accordingly, and again I commanded him to close it and to keep it tight closed. He obeyed my bidding and I continued "Dip thy neave into the basin," and he dipped it. Presently I asked, "Is thy hand in the water and thy fist closed?" and he replied, "It is." Then said I, "Withdraw it," and he withdrew it, and I cried, "Open thy neave," and he opened it. Then I asked, "What thing hast thou found therein?" and he answered, "Anaught;" whereupon I cried to him, "Take thine 'Anaught' and wend thy ways." Hereupon the Sultan said to the Bassorite, "Hast thou taken thine 'Anaught,' O man?" and said he "Yes." Accordingly the King bade him gang his gait. Then the Sultan gifted me with costly gifts and named me Kazi; and hence, O King of the Age, is the cause of the title in the case of one who erst was Abu Kasim the Drummer. Hereat quoth the Sultan, "Relate to us what rare accident befel thee in thy proper person." So the judge began to recount

The Story of the Kazi and his Slipper.

ONCE upon a time, O King of the Age, I had a slipper which hardly belonged to its kind nor ever was there seen a bigger. Now one day of the days I waxed aweary of it and sware to myself that I would never wear it any more; so in mine anger I flung it away and it fortuned to fall upon the flat roof of a Khwájah's house where the stucco was weakest. Thence it

dropped through, striking a shelf that held a number of phials
full of the purest rose-water and the boarding yielded breaking
all the bottles and spilling their contents. The house-folk heard
the breakage ringing and rattling; so they crowded one after
other to discover what had done the damage and at last they
found my papoosh sprawling amiddlemost the room. Then they
made sure that the shelf had not been broken except by the
violence of that slipper, and they examined it when, behold, the
house-master cried, saying, "This be the papoosh of Abu Kasim
the Drummer." Hereupon he took it and carried it to the Governor who summoned me and set me before him; then he made
me responsible for the phials and whatso was therein and for the
repairing of the terrace-roof and upraising it again. And lastly
he handed to me the slipper which was exceedingly long and
broad and heavy and, being cruel old it showed upwards of an
hundred and thirty patches nor was it unknown to any of the
villagers. So I took it and fared forth and, being anangered with
the article, I resolved to throw it into some dark hole or out-of-
the-way place;——And Shahrazad was surprised by the dawn
of day and fell silent and ceased saying her permitted say. Then
quoth her sister Dunyazad, "How sweet and tasteful is thy tale,
O sister mine, and enjoyable and delectable!" Quoth she, "And
where is this compared with that I would relate to you on the
coming night an the Sovran suffer me to survive?" Now when
it was the next night and that was

The Four Hundred and Second Night,

DUNYAZAD said to her, "Allah upon thee, O my sister, an thou
be other than sleepy, finish for us thy tale that we may cut short
the watching of this our latter night!" She replied, "With love
and good will!" It hath reached me, O auspicious King, the
director, the right-guiding, lord of the rede which is benefiting
and of deeds fair-seeming and worthy celebrating, that Abu
Kasim the Drummer continued to the Sultan; I resolved to
throw it into some dark hole or out-of-the-way place; and presently I came to the watercloset of the Hammam and cast it into
the conduit saying, "Now shall none ever see it again; nor shall
I be troubled with its foul aspect for the rest of my life." Then I
returned home and abode there the first day and the second, but

about noon on the third a party of the Governor's men came and
seized me and bore me before him; and no sooner did he see me
than he cried out, "Throw him!" Accordingly they laid me out
at fullest length and gave me an hundred cuts with a scourge[1]
which I bore stoutly and presently said, "O my Sultan,[2] what be
the cause of this fustigation and wherefor do they oppress me?"
Said he, "O man, the conduit[3] of the jakes attached to the Mosque
was choked by thy slipper and the flow, unable to pass off,
brimmed over, whereby sundry houses belonging to the folk were
wrecked."[4] I replied, "O my lord, can a slipper estopp the flowing of a water that feedeth a Hammam?" Thereupon the Governor said to me, "Take it away and if any find it in his place and
again bring me a complaint thereanent, I will cut off thy head."
So they haled me away after tossing my slipper to me, and I
repaired to the Efendi[5] of the town and said to him, "O our lord,
I have a complaint against this Papoosh which is not my property
nor am I its owner: prithee do thou write me a deed to such purport between me and the Slipper and all who pass down this
road." The Efendi replied, "O man, how shall I write thee a
deed between thee and thy Papoosh, which is a senseless thing?
Nay, take it thyself and cut it up and cast it into some place
avoided of the folk." Accordingly I seized it and hacked it with
a hatchet into four pieces which I threw down in the four
corners of the city, saying to myself the while, "By Allah, I
shall nevermore in my life hear any further of its adventures;"
and walked away barefoot. But I had thrown one bit under a
bridge that crossed a certain of the small canals; and the season
was the dries, wherefore it collected a heap of sand which rose
thereupon, and the wind whenever it blew brought somewhat
of dust and raised the pile higher until the archway was blocked
up by a mound. Now when the Níl[6] flooded and reached that

---

[1] Arab. "Kurbáj" = cravache: vol. viii. 17. The best are made of hippopotamus-hide
(imported from East Africa), boiled and hammered into a round form and tapering to the
point. Plied by a strong arm they cut like a knout.

[2] The text "Yá Sultán-am," a Persian or Turkish form for the Arab. "Yá Sultán-i."

[3] In text "Kalb" for "Kulbat" = a cave, a cavern.

[4] The houses were of unbaked brick or cob, which readily melts away in rain and requires annual repairing at the base of the walls where affected by rain and dew. In Sind
the damp of the earth with its nitrous humour eats away the foundations and soon crumbles
them to dust.

[5] Here meaning the under-Governor or head Clerk.

[6] "Níl" (= the Nile), in vulgar Egyptian parlance the word is = "high Nile," or
the Nile in flood.

archway the water was dammed up and ceased running so the townsfolk said, "What may be the matter? The Nile-inundation hath reached the bridge but cannot pass under it. Come let us inspect the archway." They did so and presently discovered the obstacle; to wit, the mound before the arch which obstructed the waterway; whereupon a party kilted their clothes and waded into the channel that they might clear it. But when they came to the mound-base they found my quarter-slipper, and they exclaimed with one cry, "This be the Papoosh of Abu Kasim the Drummer!" But as soon as the tidings reached me, I fared away, flying from that town, and while so doing was met by my comrade, yonder Bhang-eater; so we agreed that we would travel together and he companied me till we came to this city, e'en as thou seest us, O our lord the Sultan. Thereupon the King said to them, "Do ye twain abide with me amongst my servants; but I have a condition with you which is that ye be righteous in your service and that ye be ready to join my séance every night after supper-tide." Then he cautioned them against disobedience and quoth he, "Be ye not deluded by becoming my companions nor say to yourselves, We be the assessors of the King; for that the byword declareth: Whenas the King sitteth beware of his severity, and be not refractory whenever he shall say to thee 'Do.'" They agreed to this condition and each whispered his mate, "Do thou have a care to act righteously!" Then they left the King nor did they see him again till one day of the days when behold, a Khwajah appeared before the Sultan.——And Shahrazad was surprised by the dawn of day and fell silent and ceased to say her permitted say. Then quoth her sister Dunyazad, "How sweet is thy story, O sister mine, and how enjoyable and delectable!" Quoth she, "And where is this compared with that I would relate to you on the coming night an the Sovran suffer me to survive?" Now when it was the next night and that was

The Four Hundred and Third Night,

Dunyazad said to her, "Allah upon thee, O my sister, an thou be other than sleepy, finish for us thy tale that we may cut short the watching of this our latter night!" She replied, "With love and good will!" It hath reached me, O auspicious King, the director, the right-guiding, lord of the rede which is benefiting and of deeds fair-seeming and worthy celebrating, that one day of the days, behold a Khwajah appeared before the Sultan and said, " 'Tis not lawful in Allah's sight, O King of the Age, that a Bhang-eater should propose to dishonour me in the person of my daughter and load me with infamy amongst His worshippers saying the while, 'I am of the King's suite.' " Now the cause of the merchant's complaint was as follows. One day of the days the Bhang-eater was passing by under the latticed window of the Khwajah's home when by decree of the Decreer, the daughter of the house was looking out at the casement and was solacing herself by observing all who walked the street. Perchance the Bhang-eater's glance fell upon the maiden and that sight of eyes entailed a thousand sighs, so he said to himself, "By Allah, if I meet not this maiden, although it be only once, I shall die of a broken heart nor shall any one know of my death." He then took to passing under the window every day and to gazing upwards and to tarrying there from morning-tide to set of sun; but the more he looked the less he saw of her because Fortune which was fair to him the first time had now turned foul. So he continued in this condition for a while, coming every day to look at the lattice and seeing naught. Presently his case became strait and ill health entered his frame for love to the merchant's daughter; and by reason of its excess he betook himself to his pillow turning and tossing right and left and crying, "O her eyes! O her loveliness! O her stature! O her symmetrical grace!" But as he was repeating these words behold, an old woman came in to him and, seeing his concern and chagrin, accosted him and said, "No harm to thee!" Quoth he, "Ah, my reverend mother, unless thou come to my aid I perish," and quoth she, "What is upon thy mind?" So he disclosed to her all he felt of fondness and affection for the Khwajah's daughter and she rejoined, "Thou wilt never win to thy wish in this matter except through me." Then she left him and repaired to her own place, pondering the wiles of women, till she entered her house and there she donned a woolen robe and hung three rosaries around her neck, after which she hent a palm-staff in hand and set out for the merchant's quarters. She ceased not walking till she reached the place and entered in her garb of a religious mendicant[1] crying out, "Allah, there is no

---

[1] Arab. "Darwayshah" = a she-Fakír, which in Europe would be represented by that prime pest a begging nun.

god but the God! extolled be Allah! Allah be with you all!"
When the girl, whose name was Sitt al-Husn—the Lady of
Beauty—heard these words she met her, hoping for a blessing,
and saying, "O my mother, pray for me!" and the old woman
responded, "The name of Allah be upon thee! Allah be thy safeguard!"[1] Then she sat down and the damsel came and took seat
beside her; so likewise did the girl's mother and both sought a
blessing from her and conversed together till about noon when
she arose and made the Wuzú-ablution and span out her prayers,
whilst those present exclaimed, "By Allah this be a pious
woman!" When her orisons were ended they served up dinner
to her; but she said, "I'm fasting;" whereat they increased in love
and belief herwards and insisted upon her abiding with them
until sunset that she might break her fast within their walls. On
such wise she acted but it was all a fraud. Then they persisted
in keeping her for the night; so she nighted with them, and when
it was morn she arose and prayed and mumbled words, some intelligible and others not to be understood of any, while the
household gazed upon her and, whenever she would move from
place to place, supported her with their hands under her armpits.
At last, when it was mid-forenoon she fared forth from them
albeit their intent was not to let her depart. But early on the
next day she came in to them and all met her with greetings and
friendly reception, kissing her hands and bussing her feet; so she
did as she had done on the first day and in like guise on the third
while they showed her increased honour and worship. On the
fourth day she came to them, as was her wont, and they prayed
her be seated; however she refused and said, "I have a daughter
whom I am about to marry and the bridal festivities will be in my
house; but I come to you at this hour to let you know my desire
that Sitt al-Husn may accompany me and be present at my girl's
wedding-feast and thus she will gain a blessing." Her mother
replied, "We dread lest somewhat befal her," but the ancient
woman rejoined, "Fear not for her as the Hallows[2] are with her!"
Thereupon cried the girl, "There is no help but that I accompany
her and be present at her daughter's wedding ceremony and enjoy
the spectacle and take my pleasure." The mother said, " 'Tis
well;" and the old trot added, "I will go and return within this

---

[1] Arab. "Allah háfiz-ik" == the popular Persian expression, "Khudá Háfiz!"
[2] Arab. "Sálihin" == the Saints, the Holy Ones.

moment." So saying, she went off as one aweary to the house of
the Bhang-eater and told him what she had done; then she
returned to the maiden whom she found drest and decorated and
looking her best. So she took the girl and fared forth with her.
——And Shahrazad was surprised by the dawn of day and fell
silent and ceased saying her permitted say. Then quoth her
sister Dunyazad, "How sweet and tasteful is thy tale, O sister
mine, and enjoyable and delectable!" Quoth she, "And where is
this compared with that I would relate to you on the coming
night an the Sovran suffer me to survive?" Now when it was the
next night and that was

The Four Hundred and Fourth Night,

DUNYAZAD said to her, "Allah upon thee, O my sister, an thou be
other than sleepy, finish for us thy tale that we may cut short the
watching of this our latter night!" She replied, "With love and
good will!" It hath reached me, O auspicious King, the director,
the right-guiding, lord of the rede which is benefiting and of deeds
fair-seeming and worthy celebrating, that the ancient woman
took the girl and fared forth with her and led her to the Bhang-
eater's house and brought her in to him who, seeing her in all her
beauty and loveliness, arose forthright and his wits fled him and
he drew near to her of his excessive love herwards. Therewith
the "Lady of Beauty" understood that the old woman was an
accursed procuress who had beguiled her in order to bring her
and the man together. So of her cleverness and clear intelligence
she said to her lover, "O my brave, whoso expecteth a visit of his
beloved getteth ready somewhat of meat and somewhat of fruit
and somewhat of wine, that their pleasure may be perfected; and,
if thou purpose love-liesse we will pass the night in this place."
Quoth the Bhang-eater, "By Allah, O my lady, thou speakest
sooth but what shall we do at such hour as this?" and quoth she,
"Hie thee to the market-street and bring all whereof I spoke."
Said he, "Hearkening and obedience," and said she, "I will sit
down, I and this my mother in this place, the while thou goest
and comest." He rejoined, "A sensible saying!" and forthright
fared from her intending for the Bazar to bring the requisites; and
he was right gladsome nor knew what was prepared for him in
the hidden future. Now as soon as he went the damsel arose and

without making aught of noise locked the door closely upon herself and the old trot: then she wandered about the rooms and
presently came upon a butcher's chopper[1] which she seized. Hereupon tucking up her sleeves above her elbows, in the firmness of
her heart she drew near the old crone until she was hard by her
right and so clove her skull asunder that she fell weltering in her
blood and her ghost fled her flesh. After this the damsel again
went about the house and all worth the taking she took, leaving
whatso was unworthy, till she had collected a number of fine
robes which the man had brought together after he had become a
cup-companion of the Sultan; and, lastly, she packed the whole
in a sheet[2] and went forth therewith. Now the season was morning but The Veiler veiled her and none met her on the way until
she reached her home and went in to her mother whom she
found awaiting her and saying, "By Allah, to-day my girl hath
tarried long at the bridal festivities of the Ascetic's daughter."
And behold Sitt al-Husn came in to her carrying a large sheet
stuffed with raiment, and as her mother saw her agitated and in
disorder she questioned her of her case and of what was packed
in the bundle. But the girl, who returned no reply and could not
speak one syllable for the emotion caused by the slaughter of the
ancient woman, fell to the ground in a fit. Her swoon endured
from noon until eventide, her mother sitting at her head the
while and sorrowing for her condition. But about set of sun
behold, in came her father who found his daughter aswoon; so he
questioned his wife who began by recounting to him what they
had noted in the old woman of prayer and display of devotion
and how she had told them, "I have a daughter whom I am about
to marry and the bridal festivities will be in my house." "And,"
pursued the mother, "she invited us to visit her; so at undurn-
tide I sent with her the girl; who at noontide came back bringing somewhat wrapped up and bundled, which be this. But
when she entered the house she fell to the floor in a fainting fit

---

[1] Arab. "Sharkh" = in dicts. the unpolished blade of a hiltless sword.

[2] In the text "Miláyah," a cotton stuff some 6 feet long, woven in small chequers of
white and indigo-blue with an ending of red at either extremity. Men wrap it round the
body or throw it over the shoulder like our plaid, whose colours I believe are a survival
of the old body-paintings, Pictish and others. The woman's "Miláyah" worn only out
of doors may be of silk or cotton: it is made of two pieces which are sewed together
lengthwise and these cover head and body like a hooded cloak. Lane figures it in M. E.
chapt. i. When a woman is too poor to own a "Miláyah" or a "Habarah" (a similar article)
she will use a bed-sheet for out-of-doors work.

and she is even **as thou** seest; nor do I know what befel her."
Then the father rose up and besprinkled somewhat of water upon
her face which revived her and she said, "Where am I?" whereto
said he, "Thou art with us." And when she had recovered and
returned to her senses, and her condition was as before the
swoon, she told them of the old woman and her ill designs and
of her death and lastly how **the** clothes had been brought by
herself from the house of the **Bhang-eater.** As soon as her sire
had heard her words, he set out from his home and sought the
Sultan.——And Shahrazad was surprised by the dawn of day
and fell silent and ceased to say her permitted say. Then quoth
her sister Dunyazad, "How sweet is thy story, O sister mine, and
how enjoyable and delectable!" Quoth she, "And where is this
compared with that I would relate to you on the coming night
an the Sovran suffer me to survive?" Now when it was the next
night and that was

The Four Hundred and Fifth Night,

DUNYAZAD said to her "Allah upon thee, O my sister, an thou
be other than sleepy, finish for us thy tale that we may cut short
the watching of this our latter night!" She replied, "With love
and good will!" It hath reached me, O auspicious King, the
director, the right-guiding, lord of the rede which is benefiting
and of deeds fair-seeming and worthy celebrating, that whilst the
Sultan was sitting behold, the Khwajah came in and complained
to him of the **Bhang-eater,** whereupon he ordered a company to go
fetch the accused and they went off and found him not. So they
returned and reported accordingly. Such was the cause of the
Khwajah coming to the King and such was the case with them;
but as regards the Bhang-eater, when he went off rejoicing to the
Bazar in order to buy whatso the merchant's daughter had asked
him, he brought many a thing wherewith he returned to his lodging. However as he returned he beheld the old woman slaughtered and weltering in her blood and he found nothing at all of
the choice articles wherewith his house was fulfilled, so he fell to
quoting this couplet:[1]——

---

[1] The pun here is "Khaliyát" = bee-hive and empty: See vols. vi. 246· ix. 291. It
will occur again in Supplementary vol. v. Night DCXLVI.

" 'Twas as a hive of bees that greatly thrived;   *   But, when the bee-swarm
     fled, 'twas clean unhived."

And when he beheld that condition of things he turned from his
home in haste and without stay or delay left it about the hour of
mid-afternoon and fared forth from the city. There he found a
caravan bound to some bourne or other, so he proceeded therewith hardly believing in his own safety and he ceased not accompanying the Cafilah[1] for the space of five days till it made the city
the travellers sought, albeit he was fatigued and footsore from
the stress of hardships and weariness he had endured. So he
entered the place and wandered about until he found a Khan
wherein he hired him a cell by way of nighting-stead and every
day he would go forth to seek service for wages whereby he
might make a livelihood. Now one day of the days a woman met
him face to face on the highway and said to him, "Dost thou do
service?" and said he, "Indeed I do, O my lady." She continued,
"There is a wall about my place which I desire to level and build
another in lieu thereof for that 'tis old and very old." He replied
to her, " 'Tis well," and she took him and repaired with him to
her house and showing him the wall in question handed to him a
pickaxe and said, "Break it down as much as thou art able be it for
two or three days, and heap up the stones in one place and the
dried mud in another." He replied, "Hearkening and obedience;"
after which she brought to him somewhat of food and of water
and he ate and drank and praised Almighty Allah. After this he
rose and began breaking down the wall and he ceased not working and piling up the stones and the dried mud until it was sunset
time when the woman paid him to his wage ten faddahs and
added a something of food which he took and turned towards his
own cell. As soon as it was the second day he repaired to the
house of the woman who again gave him somewhat to break his
fast and he fell to felling the wall even as he had done on the first
day and he worked till noon; but when it was midday and all
the household was asleep, lo and behold! he found in the middle
of the foundation a crock[2] full of gold. So he opened it and considered its contents whereat he was rejoiced and he went forth
without leisure or loss of time seeking his own cell and when he

---

[1] i.e. Caravan, the common Eastern term. In India it was used for a fleet of merchant-
men under convoy: see Col. Yule, *Glossary*, s. v.
[2] Again "Bartamán" for "Martabán."

reached it he locked himself within for fear lest any look upon
him. Then he opened the crock and counted therein one hundred
dinars which he pouched in his purse and stowed away in his
breast-pocket. Presently he returned, as he was, to break down
the rest of the wall and whilst he was trudging along the highway
suddenly he sighted a box surrounded by a crowd of whom none
knew what might be its contents and its owner was crying out,
"For an hundred gold pieces!" Thereupon the Bhang-eater
went forwards saying to himself, "Buy thee yonder box for the
hundred dinars and thy luck be thy lot, for if there be inside of it
aught of wonderful 'tis well, and if otherwise thou shalt stand by
thy bad bargain." So he drew near the broker[1] and said to him,
"This box for how much?"[2] and the other answered, "For an
hundred gold dinars!" But when he questioned him as to its
contents the man replied, "I know not; whoso taketh it his luck
be his lot." Thereupon he brought out to him the hundred
ducats and the broker made over to him the box which he charged
upon his shoulders and carried off to his cell. There arrived he
bolted himself in and opened the coffer wherein he found a white
slave-girl which was a model of beauty and loveliness and stature
and perfect grace: but she was like one drunken with wine. So
he shook her but she was not aroused when he said to himself,
"What may be the story of this handmaiden?" and he was never
tired of looking upon her while she was in that condition and he
kept saying to himself, "Would Heaven I wot an she be on life or
in death; withal I see her breath coming and going." Now when
it was about midnight, the handmaiden revived and looking
around and about her, cried, "Where am I?" and said the Bhang-
eater, "Thou, O my lady, art in my home;" whereby she understood what had befallen her.——And Shahrazad was surprised
by the dawn of day and fell silent and ceased saying her permitted say. Then quoth her sister Dunyazad, "How sweet and
tasteful is thy tale, O sister mine, and enjoyable and delectable!"
Quoth she, "And where is this compared with that I would
relate to you on the coming night, an the Sovran suffer me to
survive?" Now when it was the next night and that was

---

[1] The "Sáhib" = owner, and the "Dallál" = broker, are evidently the same person.
[2] "Alà kám" for "kam" (how much?)—peasants' speech.

The Four Hundred and Sixth Night,

DUNYAZAD said to her, "Allah upon thee, O my sister, an thou
be other than sleepy, finish for us thy tale that we may cut short
the watching of this our latter night!" She replied, "With love
and good will!" It hath reached me, O auspicious King, the
director, the right-guiding, lord of the rede which is benefiting
and of deeds fair-seeming and worthy celebrating, that the handmaiden understood what had befallen her at the hands of her
enemies. Now the cause thereof was that the Sultan of that city
had bought him for concubine one Kút al-Kulúb,[1] or Heart's-food
hight, and she became to him the liefest of all the women he
before had, amongst whom his wife, the daughter of his uncle,
had been preferred; but all fell into the rank of the common and
from the time he bought the new handmaid he was wholly
occupied with her love and he never went near the other inmates
of his Harem, not even his cousin. So they were filled with
exceeding jealousy against Heart's-food the new comer. Now
one day of the days the Sultan went forth to hunt and bird and
enjoy the occasion and solace himself in the gardens together
with the Lords of his land, and they rode on till they found themselves amiddlemost of the waste pursuing their quarry. But
when two days had passed, his wife together with the women
which were concubines arose and invited all the neighbourhood
whereamong was Kut al-Kulub, and she spread for them a
sumptuous banquet and lavished upon the new comers all manner
of attentions and the wife began to play with her rival and to
disport with her until it was thought that she loved none in the
assembly save Heart's-food; and on such wise she continued to
cheer her and solace her and gambol with her and make her
laugh until the trays were laid and the meats were dispread and
all the guests came forward and fell to eating and drinking.
Thereupon the King's cousin-wife brought a plate seasoned with
Bhang and set it before the concubine who had no sooner eaten
it and it had settled in her stomach than she trembled as with

---

[1] She has appeared already twice in The Nights, esp. in The Tale of Ghánim bin 'Ayyúb
(vol. ii. 45) and in Khalífah the Fisherman of Baghdad (vol. viii. 145). I must again
warn my readers not to confound "Kút" = food with "Kuwwat" = force, as in Scott's
"Kooout al Koolloob" (vi. 146). See Terminal Essay p. 101.

sudden palsy and fell to the ground without power of motion.
Then the Queen bade place her in a box and having locked her
therein sent for one who was Shaykh of the Brokers and committed to him the coffer saying, "Do thou sell it for an hundred
gold pieces whilst it is locked and fast locked and suffer not any
open it, otherwise we will work for the cutting off of thy hands."
He replied, "To hear is to obey;" and took up the box and went
with it to the market-street where he said to the brokers, "Cry
for sale this coffer at an hundred dinars and if any attempt to
open it, open it not to any by any manner of means." So they
took their station and made auction of it for an hundred gold
pieces, when by the decree of Destiny the Bhang-eater passed
down the street exulting in his hundred dinars which he had found
in the crock while levelling the wall belonging to the woman.
Thereupon he came up and having paid the price required carried
off his coffer saying in his mind, "My luck is my livelihood."
After this he went to his own cell and opened it and found there
the handmaid in condition as though drunken with wine. Such
is the history of that concubine Kut al-Kulub and she fell not
into the hand of the Bhang-eater save by the wile and guile of
the Sultan's cousin-wife. But when she recovered from her
fainting fit and gazed around and understood what had befallen
her she concealed her secret and said to the man, "Verily this
thy cell becometh us not;" and, as she had somewhat of gold
pieces with her and a collar of jewels around her neck worth a
thousand dinars, she brought out for him some money and sent
him forth to hire for them a house in the middle of the quarter
befitting great folk and when this was done she had herself transported thither. Then she would give him every day spending-
money to buy whatso she ever required and she would cook the
delicatest dishes fit for the eating of the Kings wherewith she fed
herself and her owner. This continued for twenty days when
suddenly the Sultan returned from his hunting party and as soon
as he entered his palace he asked for Kut al-Kulub.——And
Shahrazad was surprised by the dawn of day and fell silent and
ceased to say her permitted say. Then quoth her sister Dunyazad,
"How sweet is thy story, O sister mine, and how enjoyable and
delectable!" Quoth she, "And where is this compared with that
I should relate to you on the coming night, an the Sovran suffer
me to survive?" Now when it was the next night and that was

The Four Hundred and Seventh Night,

DUNYAZAD said to her, "Allah upon thee, O my sister, an thou be other than sleepy, finish for us thy tale that we may cut short the watching of this our latter night!" She replied, "With love and good will!" It hath reached me, O auspicious King, the director, the right-guiding, lord of the rede which is benefiting and of deeds fair-seeming and worthy celebrating, that as soon as the Sultan returned from the chase he asked after Kut al-Kulub from his exceeding desire to her, and the daughter of his uncle told him the tidings saying, "By Allah, O King of the Age, three days after the time thou faredst forth there came upon her malaise and malady wherein she abode six days and then she deceased to the mercy of Almighty Allah." He exclaimed, "There is no Majesty and there is no Might save in Allah, the Glorious, the Great! Verily we are the Almighty's and unto Him shall we return." Then befel him the extreme of grief and straitness of breast and he passed that night in exceeding cark and care for Kut al-Kulub. And when it was morning he sent after the Wazir and summoned him between his hands and bade him go forth to the Tigris-bank and there approve some place whereon he might build a palace which should command all the roads. The Minister replied, "Hearkening and obeying;" and hied to do his lord's bidding taking with him architects[1] and others, and having found a piece of level ground he ordered them to measure an hundred ells of length for the building by a breadth of seventy cubits. Presently he sent for surveyors and master-masons whom he commanded to make ready every requisite for the work, of ashlar and lime and lead; also to dig trenches for the base of the walls. Then they fell to laying the foundations, and the builders and handicraftsmen began to pile the stones and prepare the loads while the Wazir stood by them bidding and forbidding. Now when it was the third day, the Sultan went forth the Palace to look at the masons and artizans who were working at the foundations of his new edifice. And as soon as he had inspected it, it pleased him,

---

[1] In text "Mu'ammarjiyah" (master-masons), a vulgar Egyptianism for "Mu'ammarin." See "Jáwashiyah," vols. ii. 49; viii. 330. In the third line below we find "Muhandizín" = geometricians, architects, for "Muhandisín." [Perhaps a reminiscence of the Persian origin of the word "Handasah" = geometry, which is derived from "Andázah" = measurement, etc.— ST.]

so he said to the Wazir, "Walláhi! none would befit this palace save and except Kut al-Kulub, when 'twould have been full of significance;" and so saying he wept with sore weeping at the remembrance of her. Quoth the Wazir to him, "O King of the Age, have patience when calamity afflicteth thee, even as said one of them with much meaning, anent long-suffering:—

'Be patient under weight of wrath and blow of sore calamities: * The Nights compressed by Time's embrace *gravidæ miras gerunt res*.'"[1]

Then quoth the Sultan, " 'Tis well, O Wazir, I know that patience is praiseworthy and fretfulness is blameworthy, for indeed quoth the poet:—

'When Time shall turn on thee, have patience for 'tis best of plight: * Ease shall pursue unease and naught but suffrance make it light;'

and by Allah, O Wazir, human nature is never free from sad thought and remembrance. Verily that damsel pleased me and I delighted in her; nor can I ever think to find one like her in beauty and loveliness." Thereupon the Wazir fell to guiding the Sultan with fair words until his breast was broadened and the two began to solace themselves by inspecting the masons. After this the Sultan would go forth every morning for solace to Tigris-bank and tidings reached the ears of Kut al-Kulub that her lord was engaged on building a riverine palace, whereupon she said to the Bhang-eater, "Day by day we expend money upon our condition, and our outgoing is without incoming, so 'twere but right that each morning thou fare and work with the workmen who are edifying a mansion for the Sultan, inasmuch as the folk declare that he is of temper mild and merciful and haply thou shalt gain from him profit and provision." "O my lady," he replied, "by Allah, I have no patience to part with thee or to be far from thee;" and he said so because he loved her and she loved him, for that since the time he had found her locked in the box and had looked upon her he had never required of her her person and this was indeed from his remembrance, for he bore in mind but too well what had befallen him from the Khwajah's daughter. And she on her side used to say, " 'Tis a wondrous thing that yon Bhang-eater never asketh me aught nor draweth nigh me seeing

---

[1] The text ends this line in Arabic.

that I be a captive of his right hand." So she said to him, "Assuredly thou dost love me?" and said he, "How can it be otherwise when thou art the blood of my life and the light of mine eyes?" "O light of mine eyes," she replied, "take this necklace and set it in thy breast-pocket and go work at the Sultan's palace, and as often as thou shalt think of me, do thou take it out and consider it and smell it and it shall be as if thou wert to see me." Hearing this he obeyed her and went forth till he reached the palace where he found the builders at work and the Sultan and the Wazir sitting in a Kiosk hard by overseeing the masons and the workmen; ——And Shahrazad was surprised by the dawn of day and fell silent and ceased saying her permitted say. Then quoth her sister Dunyazad, "How sweet and tasteful is thy tale, O sister mine, and enjoyable and delectable!" Quoth she, "And where is this compared with that I would relate to you on the coming night an the Sovran suffer me to survive?" Now when it was the next night and that was

The Four Hundred and Eighth Night,

DUNYAZAD said to her, "Allah upon thee, O my sister, an thou be other than sleepy, finish for us thy tale that we may cut short the watching of this our latter night!" She replied, "With love and good will!" It hath reached me, O auspicious King, the director, the right-guiding, lord of the rede which is benefiting and of deeds fair-seeming and worthy celebrating, that when the Bhang-eater joined the masons he saw the Sultan and Wazir overseeing them; and, as soon as the King sighted him, he opened his breast to him and said, "O man, wilt thou also do work?" and said the other, "Yes." So he bade him labour with the builders and he continued toiling till hard upon noon-tide, at which time he remembered his slave-girl and forthright he bowed his head upon his bosom-pocket and he sniffed thereat. The Wazir saw him so doing and asked him, "What is the meaning of thy sniffing at what is in thy poke?" and he answered him, "No matter." However the Minister espied him a second time occupied in like guise and quoth he to the Sultan, "Look, O King of the Age, at yon labourer who is hiding something in his pocket and smelling thereat." "Haply," responded the Sovran, "there is in his pouch something he would look at." However when the Sultan's glance happened to fall that way he beheld the Bhang-eater sniffing and smelling at his poke, so he said to the Wazir, "Walláhi! Verily this workman's case is a strange." Hereupon both fixed their eyes upon him and they saw him again hiding somewhat in his pouch and smelling at it. The Wazir cried, "Verily this fellow is a-fizzling and he boweth his head toward his breast in order that he may savour his own farts."[1] The Sultan laughed and said, "By Allah, if he do on this wise 'tis a somewhat curious matter, or perhaps, O Wazir, he have some cause to account for it; at any rate do thou call out to him and ask him." So the Wazir arose and drawing near to him asked him saying, "Ho, this one![2] every time thou fizzlest thou smellest and sniffest at thy fizzlings;" whereto answered the workman, "Wag not thy tongue with these words seeing thou art in the presence of a King glorious of degree." Quoth the Minister, "What is the matter with thee in this case that thou art sniffing at thy pocket?" and quoth the labourer, "Verily my beloved is in my pouch." The Wazir wondered hereat and reported the same to the Sultan who cried, "Return to him and say, 'Is it possible that thou display to us thy beloved who is in thy breast-pocket?'" So he returned to him and said, "Show us what there is in thy pouch." Now the origin of this necklace was that the King had bought it for Kut al-Kulub at the price of a thousand dinars and the damsel had given it to the Bhang-eater with the sole object that the Sultan might look upon it and thereby be directed unto her and might learn the reason of her disappearance and her severance from him. Hereupon the man brought out to them the necklace from his breast-pocket and the Sultan on seeing it at once recognised it and wondered how it had fallen into the hands of that workman; accordingly he asked who was its owner and the other answered, "It belongeth to the handmaid whom I bought with an hundred

---

[1] Alluding to the curious phenomenon pithily expressed in the Latin proverb, "Suus cuique crepitus benè olet," I know of no exception to the rule, except amongst travellers in Tibet, where the wild onion, the only procurable green-stuff, produces an odour so rank and fetid that men run away from their own crepitations. The subject is not savoury, yet it has been copiously illustrated: I once dined at a London house whose nameless owner, a noted bibliophile, especially of "facetiæ," had placed upon the drawing-room table a dozen books treating of the "Crepitus ventris." When the guests came up and drew near the table, and opened the volumes, their faces were a study. For the Arab. "Faswah" = a silent break-wind, see vol. ix. 11 and 291. It is opposed to "Zirt" = a loud fart and the vulgar term, see vol. ii. 88.

[2] Arab. "Yá Házá," see vol. i. 290.

dinars." Quoth the Sultan to him, "Is it possible[1] thou invite us
to thy quarters that we may look upon this damsel;" and quoth
the other, "Would you look upon my slave-girl and not be
ashamed of yourselves? However I will consult her, and if she
be satisfied therewith we will invite you." They said to him,
"This be a rede that is right and an affair which no blame can
excite." When the day had reached its term the masons and
workmen were dismissed after they had taken their wage; but as
for the Bhang-eater the Sultan gave him two gold pieces and set
him free about sunset tide; so he fared to his handmaid and informed her of what had befallen him from the King, adding, "He
hath indeed looked upon the necklace and hath asked me to invite
him hither as well as the Wazir." Quoth she, "No harm in that;
but to-morrow (Inshallah!) do thou bring all we require for a
state occasion of meats and drinks, and let me have them here by
noon-tide, so they may eat the early meal. But when he shall ask
to buy me of thee compose thy mind and say thou, 'No,' when he
will reply to thee, 'Give me this damsel in free gift.' Hereat do
thou say, 'She is a present from me to thee'; because indeed I am
his slave and bought with his money for one thousand and five
hundred dinars; and thou hadst never become my lord save
through my foes who devised a device against me and who sold
me when thou boughtest me. However the hour of thy prosperity hath now come." And when morning morrowed she gave
him five gold pieces and said to him, "Bring for me things that be
such and such," and said he, "Hearing and obedience." So he
went to the market-street where he purchased all the supplies
wherewith she had charged him and returned to her forthright.
Hereupon she arose and tucking up her sleeves prepared meats
that befitted the King and likewise she got ready comfits and the
daintiest of dainties and sherbets and she tempered the pastilles
and she besprinkled the room with rosewater and looked to the
furniture of the place. About midday she sent to the Sultan and the
Wazir with notice that she was ready; so the Bhang-eater repaired
to the Palace and having gone in to the presence said, "Have the
kindness!"[2] The twain arose without more ado and hied with
him privily till they reached his house and entered therein.———
And Shahrazad was surprised by the dawn of day and fell silent

---

[1] In text "Yumkinshayy," written in a single word, a favourite expression, Fellah-
like withal, throughout this MS.
[2] In text "Tafazzalú," see vol. ii. 103.

and ceased to say her permitted say. Then quoth her sister Dunyazad, "How sweet is thy story, O sister mine, and how enjoyable and delectable!" Quoth she, "And where is this compared
with that I should relate to you on the coming night, an the
Sovran suffer me to survive?" Now when it was the next night
and that was

The Four Hundred and Ninth Night,

DUNYAZAD said to her, "Allah upon thee, O my sister, an thou
be other than sleepy, finish for us thy tale that we may cut short
the watching of this our latter night!" She replied, "With love
and good will!" It hath reached me, O auspicious King, the
director, the right-guiding, lord of the rede which is benefiting
and of deeds fair-seeming and worthy celebrating, that the Sultan and the Wazir entered the place wherein were the Bhang-
eater and the damsel, and took their seats. Now the meats were
ready and they served up to them the trays and the dishes, when
they fell to and were cheered by the sumptuous viands until they
had eaten after the measure of their sufficiency. And when their
hands were washed, the confections and sherbet and coffee were
set before them, so they ate and were satisfied and gladdened and
made merry. After this quoth the Sultan to the Bhang-eater,
"Where is the damsel?" and quoth the man, "She is here,"
whereat he was commanded to bring her. Accordingly he went
off and led her in and as soon as the King sighted her he recognised
her and ordered her owner to make her over to him and said when
he did so, "O man, wilt thou sell to me this damsel?" But the
other kissed ground before him and replied, "O King of the Age,
she is from me a free gift to thee;" and quoth the Sultan, "She is
accepted from thee, O Shaykh, and do thou come and bring her
thyself to the Palace about sundown-time." He replied, "To hear
is to obey." And at the hour named he took the damsel and
ceased not faring with her till he brought her to the Serai,[1] where
the Eunuchry met her and took her and carried her in to the

---

[1] The word (Saráy) is Pers. but naturalised throughout Egypt and Syria; in places
like Damascus where there is no king it is applied to the official head-quarters of the Wali
(provincial governor), and contains the prison like the Maroccan "Kasbah." It must
not be confounded with "Serraglio"= the Harem, Gynecium or women's rooms, which
appears to be a bastard neo-Latin word "Serrare," through the French *Serrer*. I therefore
always write it with the double "canine letter."

Sultan. But as soon as she entered she nestled in his bosom and
he threw his arms round her neck and kissed her of his excessive
desire to her. Then he asked her saying, "This man who purchased thee, hath he any time approached thee?" whereto she
answered, "By Allah, O King, from the time he bought me in the
box which he opened and found me alive therein until this present
never hath he looked upon my face, and as often as I addressed
him he would bow his brow earthwards." Quoth the Sultan,
"By Allah, this wight deserveth an aidance for that he paid down
for thee an hundred dinars and he hath presented thee in free
gift to me." Now when morrowed the morning the King sent
after the Bhang-eater and summoned him between his hands and
bestowed upon him one thousand five hundred dinars with a suit
of royal raiment, after which he presented to him, by way of
honourable robe,[1] a white slave-girl. He also set apart for him an
apartment and made him one of his boon companions. So look
thou, O hearer,[2] how it happened to this Bhang-eater from the
Khwajah's daughter and his love herwards; how he failed to win
her and how he gained of blows whatso he gained; and after
what prosperity befel him from the part of Kut al-Kulub. And
ever afterwards when the Sultan would ride out for disport or for
the hunt and chase he would take the man with him. Presently
of the perfection of his prosperity this Bhang-eater fully mastered
the affairs of the kingdom, both its income and its outgo, and his
knowledge embraced all the regions and cities which were under
the rule of his lord. Furthermore, whenever he would counsel
the King, his advice was found to be in place and he was con-
sulted upon all State affairs, and whenever he heard of any business he understood its inner as well as its outer meaning until the
Sultan and the Wazir both sought rede of him, and he would
point out to them the right and unright, and that which entaileth
trouble and no trouble, when they could fend it off and over-
throw it or by word or by deed of hand. Now one day of the
many days the King was in a certain of his gardens a-solacing
himself with the sights when his heart and stomach became full
of pain and he fell ill and his illness grew upon him, nor did he
last four days ere he departed to the mercy of Allah Almighty.
As he had no issue, either son or daughter, the country remained

---

[1] I have noted (vol. i. 95) that the "Khil'ah" = robe of honour, consists of many articles,
such as a horse, a gold-hilted sword, a fine turban, etc., etc.

[2] This again shows the "Nakkál" or coffee-house tale-teller. See vol. x. 144.

without a King for three days, when the Lords of the land forgathered and agreed upon a decision, all and some, that they
would have no King or Sultan save the Wazir and that the man
the Bhang-eater should be made Chief Councillor. So they
agreed upon this matter and their words went forth to the
Minister who at once took office. After this he gave general
satisfaction and lavished alms on the mean and miserable, also on
the widows and orphans, when his fame was bruited abroad and
it dispread far and wide till men entitled him the "Just Wazir"
and in such case he governed for a while of time.——And Shahrazad was surprised by dawn of day and fell silent and ceased
saying her permitted say. Then quoth her sister Dunyazad,
"How sweet and tasteful is thy tale, O sister mine, and enjoyable
and delectable!" Quoth she, "And where is this compared with
that I would relate to you on the coming night an the Sovran
suffer me to survive?" Now when it was the next night and
that was

The Four Hundred and Tenth Night,

DUNYAZAD said to her, "Allah upon thee, O my sister, an thou
be other than sleepy, finish for us thy tale that we may cut short
the watching of this our latter night!" She replied, "With love
and good will!" It hath reached me, O auspicious King, the
director, the right-guiding, lord of the rede which is benefiting
and of deeds fair-seeming and worthy celebrating, that the Wazir
governed for a while of time with all justice of rule so that the
caravans spread abroad the name and fame of him throughout
every city and all the countries. Presently there befel him an
affair between two women which were sister-wives to one man.[1]
Now these had conceived by him in the same month and when
the time of their pregnancy had passed, the twain were delivered
in the same place at the same hour and the midwife was one and
the same. One brought forth a babe but it was a daughter which
incontinently died and the other a man-child who lived. The
women quarrelled and fought about the boy-babe and both of
them said, "This is my child;" and there befel between them

---

[1] This is the Moslem version of "Solomon's Judgment" (1 Kings iii. 16–20). The Hebrew
legend is more detailed but I prefer its rival for sundry reasons. Here the women are not
"harlots" but the co-wives of one man and therefore hostile; moreover poetical justice is
done to the constructive murderess.

exceeding contention and excessive hostility. So they carried
their cause before the divines and the Olema and the head men of
the place, yet did none of them know how to decide between the
twain and not a few of the folk said, "Let each woman take the
child to her for a month," whilst others declared that they might
keep it between them at all times, whilst of the women one said,
" 'Tis well: this be my boy!" and the other declared, " 'Tis well,
this be my son!" nor could any point out to which of the women
the boy belonged. So the town's people were gathered together
and said, "None can determine this dispute except the Just
Wazir;" and they agreed upon this, so that the husband of the
two women and sundry of his associates arose and took the twain
of them and travelled with them to hear the Minister's judgment.
Also the Olema and the great men of the place declared "By
Allah, we also needs must travel with the party and produce the
two women and be present at the Just Wazir's judgment." So
they all assembled and followed after the two adversaries, nor
did they cease travelling until they entered the city where the
Minister abode. There they delayed for rest during one day and
on the second they all joined one another and went in to the
Wazir and recounted to him the case of the two women. Hearing
this he bowed his brow groundwards and presently raising it he
cried, "Bring me two eggs and void them of their contents and
see that the shells be clean empty." Then he commanded that
each of the women drain somewhat of milk from her nipple into
the egg-shell till she had filled it. They did accordingly and set
before him the egg-shells brimful when he said, "Bring me a pair
of scales."[1] After this he placed both eggs in the balance-pan
and raising it aloft from its rounded stead perceived that one was
weighty and the other was light. Quoth he, "The milk of the
woman in this egg is the heavier and she is the mother of the
boy-babe whereas the other bare the girl-child and we know not
an it be alive or dead." Hereat the true mother of the boy held
her peace but the other wailed aloud and said, " 'Tis well: still
this be my babe!" Thereupon quoth the Wazir, "I am about to
take the boy and hew him in halves whereof I will give one to
each of you twain." But the true mother arose and cried out,
"No! O my lord, do not on this wise: I will forfeit my claim for

---

[1] I am not aware that the specific gravity of the milks has ever been determined by
modern science; and perhaps the experiment is worthy a trial.

Allah's sake;" while the other one exclaimed, "All this is right good!" Now all the folk of the city who were then standing by heard these words and looked on; but when this order was pronounced and the woman was satisfied and declared, "I will take half the boy," the Wazir gave orders forthright that they seize her and hang her; so they hanged her and he gave the babe to the right mother. Then said they to him, "O our lord, how was it proved to thee that the boy was the child of this one?" and he said, "It became evident to me from two sides; in the first place because her milk was the heavier, so that I knew that the boy was her boy, and secondly when I commanded, 'Let us cut the boy in half,' the real mother consented not to this and the matter was hard upon her because the child was a slice of her liver, and she said to herself, 'His life is better than his death, even though my sister-wife take him, at any rate I shall be able to look upon him.' But the second woman designed only to gratify her spite whether the boy died or not and to harm her sister-wife; so when I saw that she was contented to have the babe killed, I knew that it was right to do her die." Then all who were present of the Lords of the land and the Olema and divines and notables wondered at the judgment and exclaimed, "By Allah, well done,[1] O Wazir of the realm." Now this history of the Minister's perspicacity and penetration was spread abroad and all folk went from his presence and everyone who had wives that had borne girls took somewhat of milk from the women and went to each and every of those who had borne boys and took from them milk in the same quantity as the Wazir had taken, and weighed it in the scales, when they found that the mothers of males produced milk that was not equal to, nay it weighed two-fold that of those who bare girls. Hereupon they said, "It is not right that we call this Minister only the Just Wazir;" and all were agreed that he should be titled "The Wazir-wise-in-Allah-Almighty;"[2] and the reason whereof was the judgment which he passed in the cause between the two women. Now after this it befel him to deliver a decision more wondrous than the former.——And Shahrazad was surprised by the dawn of day and fell silent and ceased to say her permitted say. Then quoth her sister Dunya-

---

[1] Arab. "Dúna-k." See vol. iv. p. 20.

[2] "Al-Wazíru'l-'Arif bi-lláhi Ta'álà," a title intended to mimic those of the Abbaside Caliphs; such as "Mu'tasim bi'llah" (servant of Allah), the first of the long line whose names begin with an epithet (the Truster, the Implorer, etc.), and end with "bi'llah."

zad, "How sweet is thy story, O sister mine, and enjoyable and delectable!" Quoth she, "And where is this compared with that I should relate to you on the coming night an the Sovran suffer me to survive?" Now when it was the next night and that was

The Four Hundred and Eleventh Night,

DUNYAZAD said to her, "Allah upon thee, O my sister, an thou be other than sleepy, finish for us thy tale that we may cut short the watching of this our latter night!" She replied, "With love and good will!" It hath reached me, O auspicious King, the director, the right-guiding, lord of the rede which is benefiting and of deeds fair-seeming and worthy celebrating, that to the Wazir-wise-in-Almighty-Allah there befel between his hands a strange matter which was as follows. As he was sitting one day of the days there came in to him unexpectedly two men, of whom one led a cow and a little colt whilst the second had with him a mare and a little calf. Now the first who came forward was the owner of the mare and quoth he, "O my lord, I have a claim upon this man." Quoth the Minister, "What be thy claim?" And the plaintiff continued, "I was going a-morn to the meadow for pasture and with me was my mare followed by her young one, her little colt, when yonder man met me upon the road and the colt began to play and to throw up gravel with its hoofs as is the wont of horse-flesh and draw near to the cow. Hereupon this man came up and seized it and said, 'This colt is the offspring of my cow,' and so saying he took it away and he gave me his calf, crying, 'Take this which be the issue of thy mare.'" So the Wazir turning to the master of the cow asked, "O man, what sayest thou concerning what thy comrade hath spoken?" and the other answered, "O my lord, in very deed this colt is the produce of my cow and I brought it up by hand." Quoth the Wazir, "Is it right that black cattle should bring forth horses and that horses should bear cows? indeed the intelligence of an intelligent man may not compass this;" and quoth the other, "O my lord, Allah createth whatso He willeth and maketh kine to produce horses and horses to produce kine." Hereupon the Minister said to him, "O Shaykh, when thou seest a thing before thee and lookest thereon canst thou speak of it in the way of truth?" And the other assented. Then the Wazir continued addressing the

two men, "Wend your ways at this time and on the morrow be
present here at early morn and let it be at a vacant hour." Accordingly they forthright went forth, and the next day early the
two men came to the divan of the Wazir who set before them a
she-mouse he had provided and called for a sack which he filled
with earth. And as the men stood between his hands he said,
"Wait ye patiently without speaking a word;" so they held their
peace and presently he bade them set the sack and the mouse
before him and he ordered the men to load the sack upon the
mouse. Both cried, "O our lord, 'tis impossible that a mouse can
carry a sack full of earth," when he answered, "How then can a
cow bear a colt? and when a mouse shall be able to bear a sack
then shall a cow bear a colt." All this and the Sultan was looking
out at the latticed window listening and gazing. Hereupon the
Wazir gave an order that the master of the mare take her colt
and the master of the cow carry off her calf; after which he bade
them go about their business.——And Shahrazad was surprised
by the dawn of day and fell silent and ceased saying her permitted say. Then quoth her sister Dunyazad, "How sweet and
tasteful is thy tale, O sister mine, and enjoyable and delectable!"
Quoth she, "And where is this compared with that I would relate
to you on the coming night an the Sovran suffer me to survive?"
Now when it was the next night and that was

The Four Hundred and Twelfth Night,

DUNYAZAD said to her, "Allah upon thee, O my sister, an thou
be other than sleepy, finish for us thy tale that we may cut short
the watching of this our latter night!" She replied, "With love
and good will!" It hath reached me, O auspicious King, the
director, the right-guiding, lord of the rede which is benefiting
and of deeds fair-seeming and worthy celebrating, that the Sultan,
whose Minister was the Wazir-wise-in-Allah-Almighty, on a
certain day summoned his Chief Councillor and when he came
said to him, "Verily my breast is straitened and I am beset by
unease, so I desire to hear something which may broaden my
bosom;" and said the other, "O King of the age, by Allah, I
have a friend who is named Mahmúd the 'Ajamí and that man
is a choice spirit and he hath all kind of rare tales and strange
anecdotes and wondrous histories and marvellous adventures."
Said the Sultan, "There is no help but that thou summon him to

us hither and let us hear from him somewhat." So the Wazir
sent after the Persian and when the man stood in the presence
said to him, "Verily the Sultan hath summoned thee." He replied, "Hearing and obeying," when he was taken and set before
the Sovran and as he entered he saluted him with the salams of
the Caliphs and blessed him and prayed for him.[1] The King
returned his greeting and after seating him said to him, "O Mah-
mud, at this moment my breast is indeed straitened and I have
heard of thee that thou hast a store of rare stories which I would
that thou cause me hear[2] and let it be somewhat sweet of speech
which shall banish my cark and my care and the straitness of my
breast." Hereto the other replied, "Hearing and obeying;" and
began to relate the

Tale of Mahmud the Persian and the Kurd Sharper.[3]

*   *   *   *   *   *   *   *   *

THE SULTAN was delighted with the 'Ajami's relation and largessed him two thousand pieces of gold; after which he returned
to his palace and took seat upon his Divan when suddenly a poor
man appeared before him carrying a load of fruit and greens and
greeted him and prayed for him and expressed a blessing which
the Sultan returned and bade him fair welcome. After which he
asked, "What hast thou with thee, O Shaykh?" and the other
answered, "O King of the Age, I have an offering to thee of fresh
greens and firstfruits;" and the King rejoined, "It is accepted."
Thereupon the man placed them between his royal hands and
stood up, and the King having removed the cover[4] found under it

---

[1] [Tarajjama, which is too frequently used in this MS. to be merely considered as a
clerical error, I suppose to mean: he pronounced for him the formula: "A'uzzu bi llâhi
mina 'l-Shaytâni 'l-*Rajimi*" = I take refuge with Allah against Satan the Stoned. See
Koran xvi. 100. It would be thus equivalent with the usual ta'awwaza. — Sr.]

[2] The MS. here ends Night cdxii. and begins the next. Up to this point I have followed
the numeration but from this forwards as the Nights become unconscionably short compared with the intervening dialogues, I have thrown two and sometimes three into one.
The Arabic numbers are, however, preserved for easier reference.

[3] This is a poor and scamped version of "Ali the Persian and the Kurd Sharper," in
vol. v. 149. It is therefore omitted.

[4] The dish-cover, usually made of neatly plaited straw variously coloured, is always
used, not only for cleanliness but to prevent the Evil Eye falling upon and infecting the
food.

a portion of ordinary cucumbers and sundry curling cucumbers
and bundles of rose-mallows[1] which had been placed before him.
So he took thereof some little matter and ate it and was much
pleased and bade the Eunuchry bear the rest into the Harem.
They carried out his commands and the women also were delighted and having eaten somewhat they distributed the remainder
to the slave-girls. Then said they, "By Allah, this man, the fruit-
owner, deserveth Bakhshísh;"[2] so they sent to him by the Eunuch
one hundred gold pieces whereto the Sultan added twain, so the
whole of his gain was three hundred dinars. But the Sultan was
much pleased with the man and a part of the care which he felt
was lightened to him, whereupon asked he, "O Shaykh, knowest
thou aught of boon-companionship with the Kings?" to which the
other answered, "Yes;" for he was trim of tongue and ready of
reply and sweet of speech. Presently the Sultan continued, "O
Shaykh, for this present go back to thy village and give to thy
wife and family that which Allah hath made thy lot." Accordingly the man went forth and did as the King bade him; after
which he returned in a short time and went into the presence
about set of sun when he found his liege lord at supper. The
King bade him sit to the trays which he did and he ate after the
measure of his sufficiency, and again when the Sultan looked upon
him he was pleased with him. And when the hour of night-
prayers came all prayed together;[3] then the King invited him to
sit down as a cup-companion and commanded him to relate one
of his tales.——And Shahrazad was surprised by the dawn of
day and fell silent and ceased to say her permitted say. Then
quoth her sister Dunyazad, "How sweet is thy story, O sister
mine, and how enjoyable and delectable!" Quoth she, "And

---

[1] The "Bámiyah," which = the Gumbo, Occra (Okrá) or Bhendi of Brit. India which
names the celebrated bazar of Bombay, is the esculent hibiscus, the polygonal pod (some
three inches long and thick as a man's finger) full of seeds and mucilage making it an
excellent material for soups and stews. It is a favourite dish in Egypt and usually eaten
with a squeeze of lime-juice. See Lane, Mod. Egypt. chapt. v., and Herklots (App. p.
xlii.) who notices the curry of "Bandaki" or *Hibiscus esculentus*.

[2] Written "Bakshísh," after Fellah-fashion.

[3] [In the MS.: Wa'l-Sultánu karaa Wirduh (Wirda-hu) wa jalasa li Munádamah = And
the Sovran recited his appointed portion of the Koran, and then sat down to convivial converse. This reminds of the various passages of the present Shah of Persia's Diary, in which
he mentions the performance of his evening devotions, before setting out for some social
gathering, say a supper in the Guildhall, which he neatly explains as a dinner after midnight
(Shám ba'd az nisf-i-shab). — Sr.]

where is this compared with that I should relate to you on the coming night an the Sovran suffer me to survive?" Now when it was the next night and that was

The Four Hundred and Seventeenth Night,

DUNYAZAD said to her, "Allah upon thee, O my sister, an thou be other than sleepy, finish for us thy tale that we may cut short the watching of this our latter night!" She replied, "With love and good will!" It hath reached me, O auspicious King, the director, the right-guiding, lord of the rede which is benefiting and of deeds fair-seeming and worthy celebrating, that the man took seat as a boon-companion of the King, and began to relate

The Tale of the Sultan and His Sons and the Enchanting Bird.[1]

IT is told anent a man, one of the Kings of Orient-land, that he had three sons, of whom the eldest one day of the days heard the folk saying, "In such a place there is a bird hight the shrilling Philomelet,[2] which transmews everyone who comes to it into a form of stone." Now when the heir apparent heard this report he went to his father and said, " 'Tis my desire to fare forth and to get that marvellous bird;" and said the father, "O my son, thou wouldst work only to waste thy life-blood and to deprive us of thee; for that same bird hath ruined Kings and Sultans, not to speak of Bashas and Sanjáks,[3] men in whose claws[4] thou wouldst be as nothing." But the son replied, "Needs must I go and if thou forbid my going I will kill myself." So quoth his father, "There is no Majesty and no Might save in Allah, the Glorious, the Great;" and saith the son, "Affects are affected and

---

[1] This is Scott's "Story of the Three Princes and Enchanting Bird," vol. vi. 160. On the margin of the W. M. MS. he has written, "Story of the King and his Three Sons and the Enchanting Bird" (vol. i., Night cdxvii.). Gauttier, vi. 292, names it *Histoire des Trois Princes et de l'Oiseau Magicien*. Galland may have used parts of it in the "Two Sisters who envied their Cadette": see Supp. vol. iii. pp. 313–361.

[2] In text "Al-Bulaybul" (the little Nightingale, Philomelet) "Al Sayyáh" (the Shrieker). The latter epithet suggests to me the German novel which begins, "We are in Italy where roses bestink the day and Nightingales howl through the live-long night," &c.

[3] "Sanjak," Turk. = flag, banner, and here used (as in vulg. Arab.) for Sanják-dár, the banner-bearer, ensign. In mod. parlance, Sanják = minor province, of which sundry are included in an "Iyálah" = government-general, under the rule of a Wáli (Wiláyah).

[4] In the MS. "Zifr" = nail, claw, talon.

steps are sped towards a world that is vile and distributed daily bread."[1] Then he said to him, "O my child, set out upon thy journey and mayest thou win to thy wish." Hereupon they prepared for him somewhat of victual and he went forth on his wayfare. But before departing he took off his seal-ring from his finger and gave it to his second brother saying, "O my brother, an this signet press hard upon thy little finger do thou know and make certain that mishap hath happened to me." So the second Prince took it and put it upon his minim finger, after which the eldest youth farewelled his father and his mother and his brothers and the Lords of the land and departed seeking the city wherein the Bird woned. He ceased not travelling by nights and days, the whole of them, until he reached the place wherein was the bird Philomelet whose habit it was to take station upon his cage between mid-afternoon and sunset, when he would enter it to pass the night. And if any approached him with intent of capturing him, he would sit afar from the same and at set of sun he would take station upon the cage and would cry aloud speaking in a plaintive voice, "Ho thou who sayest to the mean and mesquin, 'Lodge!'[2] Ho thou who sayest to the sad and severed, 'Lodge!' Ho thou who sayest to the woeful and doleful, 'Lodge!'" Then if these words were grievous to the man standing before him and he make reply "Lodge!" ere the words could leave his lips the Bird would take a pinch of dust from beside the cage and hovering over the wight's head would scatter it upon him and turn him into stone. At length arrived the youth who had resolved to seize the Bird and sat afar from him till set of sun: then

---

[1] "Al-Rizk maksúm," an old and sage byword pregnant with significance: compare "Al-Khauf (fear) maksúm" = cowardice is equally divided. Vol. iii. 173. [I read: "Yas'à 'l-Kadamu li-'Umrin danà au li-Rizkin qusima," taking "Rizk" as an equivalent for "al-Rizku 'l-hasanu" = any good thing which a man obtains without exerting himself in seeking for it, and the passive "qusima" in the sense of Kismah, vulgo "Kismet." Hence I would translate: The foot speeds to a life that is mean, or to a boon that is pre-ordained. — St.]

[2] In the text "Bát" (for Bit), in Fellah-speech "Pass the night here!" The Bird thus makes appeal to the honour and hospitality of his would-be captor, and punishes him if he consent. I have translated after Scott (v. 161). [I cannot persuade myself to take "bát" for an imperative, which would rather be "bit" for "bit," as we shall find "kúm" for "kum," "rúh" for "ruh." It seems to me that the preterite "bát" means here "the night has passed," and rendering "man" by the interrogative, I would translate: "O! who will say to the sad, the separated, night is over?" Complaints of the length of night are frequent with the parted in Arab poetry. This accords also better with the following 'Atús al-Shams, the sneezing of the sun, which to my knowledge, applies only to daybreak, as in Hariri's 15th Assembly (al-Farzíyah), where "the nose of the morning" sneezes. — St.]

Philomelet came and stood upon his cage and cried, "Ho thou who sayest to the mean and mesquin, 'Lodge!' Ho thou who sayest to the sad and severed, 'Lodge!' Ho thou who sayest to the woeful and doleful, 'Lodge!'" Now the cry was hard upon the young Prince and his heart was softened and he said, "Lodge!" This was at the time when the sun was disappearing, and as soon as he spake the word the Bird took a somewhat of dust and scattered it upon the head of the youth, who forthright became a stone. At that time his brother was sitting at home in thought concerning the wanderer, when behold, the signet squeezed his finger and he cried, "Verily my brother hath been despoiled of life and done to death!"——And Shahrazad was surprised by the dawn of day and fell silent and ceased saying her permitted say. Then quoth her sister Dunyazad, "How sweet and tasteful is thy tale, O sister mine, and enjoyable and delectable!" Quoth she, "And where is this compared with that I would relate to you on the coming night an the Sovran suffer me to survive?" Now when it was the next night and that was

The Four Hundred and Eighteenth Night,

Dunyazad said to her, "Allah upon thee, O my sister, an thou be other than sleepy, finish for us thy tale that we may cut short the watching of this our latter night!" She replied, "With love and good will!" It hath reached me, O auspicious King, the director, the right-guiding, lord of the rede which is benefiting and of deeds fair-seeming and worthy celebrating, that the second Prince, when the signet squeezed his little finger, cried out saying, "My brother, by Allah, is ruined and lost; but needs must I also set forth and look for him and find what hath befallen him." Accordingly he said to his sire, "O my father, 'tis my desire to seek my brother;" and the old King answered, "Why, O my son, shouldst thou become like thy brother, both bereaving us of your company?" But the other rejoined, "There is no help for that nor will I sit at rest till I go after my lost one and espy what hath betided him." Thereupon his sire gave orders for his journey and got ready what would suffice him of victual, and he departed, but before he went he said to his youngest brother, "Take thou this ring and set it upon thy little finger, and if it press hard thereupon do thou understand and be certified that my

life's blood is shed and that I have perished." After this he farewelled them and travelled to the place of the Enchanting Bird,
and he ceased not wayfaring for whole days and nights and
nights and days until he arrived at that stead. Then he found
the bird Philomelet and sat afar from him till about sundown
when he took station upon his cage and began to cry, "Ho thou
who sayest to the mean and mesquin, 'Lodge!' Ho thou who
sayest to the sad and severed, 'Lodge!' Ho thou who sayest to
the woeful and doleful, 'Lodge!'" Now this cry of the Bird was
hard upon the young Prince and he had no sooner pronounced the
word "Lodge!" than the Philomelet took up somewhat of dust
beside his cage and scattered it upon him, when forthright he
became a stone lying beside his brother. Now the youngest of
the three Princes was sitting at meat with his sire when suddenly
the signet shrank till it was like to cut off his finger; so he rose
forthright to his feet and said, "There is no Majesty and there is
no Might save in Allah, the Glorious, the Great." Quoth his
father, "What is to do with thee, O my son?" and quoth he,
"By Allah, my brother is ruined and wasted, so needs must I also
fare forth and look after the twain of them." Exclaimed his sire,
"Why, O my son, should you three be cut off?" but the other
answered, "Needs must I do this, nor can I remain after them
without going to see what hath betided them, and either we
three shall return in safety and security or I also shall become
one of them." So the father bade them prepare for his journey
and after they had got ready for him a sufficiency of provision
he farewelled him and the youth set out. But when he departed
from his sire the old man and his wife filleted their brows with
the fillets of sorrow[1] and they fell to weeping by night and by
day. Meanwhile the youth left not wayfaring till he reached the
stead of the Bird and the hour was mid-afternoon, when he
found his brothers ensorcelled to stones, and about sunset he sat
down at a distance from Philomelet who took station upon his
cage and began to cry, "Ho thou who sayest to the mean and
mesquin, 'Lodge!' Ho thou who sayest to the sad and severed,
'Lodge!'" together with many words and instances of the same
kind. But the Prince hardened his heart nor would speak the

---

[1] i.e., they bound kerchiefs stained blue or almost black round their brows. In modern days Fellah women stain their veils (face and head), kerchiefs and shirts with indigo; and some colour their forearms to the elbow.

word, and albeit the Bird continued his cry none was found to
answer him. Now when the sun evanished and he had kept up
his appeal in vain he went into the cage, whereupon the youngest
of the Princes arose and running up shut the door upon him.
Quoth the Bird, "Thou hast done the deed, O son of the Sultan,"
and the youth replied, "Relate to me whatso thou hast wrought
in magic to these creations of God." Replied Philomelet, "Beside
thee lie two heaps of clay whereof one is white and the other
blue: this is used in sorcery and that to loose the spells."———
And Shahrazad was surprised by the dawn of day and fell silent
and ceased to say her permitted say. Then quoth her sister
Dunyazad, "How sweet is thy story, O sister mine, and how
enjoyable and delectable!" Quoth she, "And where is this compared with that I should relate to you on the coming night an
the Sovran suffer me to survive?" Now when it was the next
night and that was

The Four Hundred and Twentieth Night,

Dunyazad said to her, "Allah upon thee, O my sister, an thou
be other than sleepy, finish for us thy tale that we may cut short
the watching of this our latter night!" She replied, "With love
and good will!" It hath reached me, O auspicious King, the
director, the right-guiding, lord of the rede which is benefiting
and of deeds fair-seeming and worthy celebrating, that the Bird
said to the youngest son of the Sultan, "By the side of my cage
are two heaps of clay, this blue and that white; and the first is
the material for sorcery whilst the second looseth the spell."
Hereupon the youth approached them and finding the mounds
took somewhat of the white and scattered it upon the stones and
cried, "Be ye returned unto your olden shapes;" and, as he did so,
each and every of the stones became men as they had been. Now
amongst them were sundry sons of the Sultans, also the children
of Kings and Wazirs and Bashas and Lords of the land, and of the
number two were the elder brothers of the young Prince: so they
salamed to him and all congratulated one another on their safety.
After this one came forward to the youth and said to him, "Verily
this place is a city, all and some of whose folk are ensorcelled."
So he took a somewhat of clay from the white and entered the
streets, where, finding the case as described to him, he fell to sift-

ing the clay upon them and they **were** transmewed from statues
of stone into the shapes of Adam's sons. Then, at last, the sons
of that city rose one and all and began offering to the Prince gifts
and rarities until he had of them a mighty matter But when his
brothers saw that he had become master of the bird Philomelet
and his cage, and all these presents and choice treasures, they
were filled with envy of him[1] and said each to other, "How shall
our brother win him all this and we abide with him **in servile**
condition, especially when we hie us homewards and return to
our own land? And will not folk say that the salvation of the
two elder brothers was by the hand of the **youngest?** But we
cannot endure such disgrace as this!" So envy entered them and
in their jealousy they planned and plotted the death of their
cadet, who knew not that was in their minds **or whatso was**
hidden from him in the Limbo of Secrets. And when they had
wrought their work the youngest Prince arose and **bade** his pages
and eunuchs lade the loads upon the camels and mules and, when
they had done his bidding, they all set forth on the homewards
march. They travelled for whole days and nights till **they** drew
near their destination and the youngest Prince bade his attendants seek an open place wherein they might **take repose,** and **they**
said, "Hearkening and obedience." But **when they came upon**
it they found a well builded of stone, and **the brothers said to the**
cadet, "This be a place befitting rest by reason of this well being
here; for the water thereof is sweet and good for our drink and
therewith we can supply our folk and our beasts." Replied the
youth, "This is what we desire." So they set up their tents
hard by that well, and when the camp was pitched they let
prepare the evening meal, and as soon as it was sunset-tide
they spread the trays and supped their sufficiency until presently
night came down upon them. Now the youngest Prince had a
bezel'd signet-ring which he had taken from the bird Philomelet,
and he was so careful thereof that he never slept without it.
But his brothers awaited until he was drowned in sleep, when
coming softly upon him they pinioned him and carried him off and
cast him into the well without anyone knowing aught thereof.
Then as soon as morning morrowed the two eldest Princes arose
and commanded the attendants to load, but these said to them,

---

[1] Here again and in the following adventure we have "Khudadad and his Brothers."
Suppl. vol. iii. 145-174.

"Where be our lord?" and said the others, "He is sleeping in the Takhtrawán." So the camel men arose and loaded the loads and the litter and the two Princes sent forwards to the King their sire a messenger of glad tidings who when he found him informed him of the fair news. Accordingly he and all his Lords took horse and rode forth to meet his sons upon the road that he might salam to them and give them joy of their safe return. Now he chanced in their train to catch sight of the caged bird which is called "the shrilling Philomelet," and he rejoiced thereat and asked them, "How did ye become masters of him?" Then he enquired anent their brother.——And Shahrazad was surprised by the dawn of day and fell silent and ceased saying her permitted say. Then quoth her sister Dunyazad, "How sweet and tasteful is thy tale, O sister mine, and enjoyable and delectable!" Quoth she, "And where is this compared with that I would relate to you on the coming night an the Sovran suffer me to survive?" Now when it was the next night and that was

The Four Hundred and Twenty-second Night,

DUNYAZAD said to her, "Allah upon thee, O my sister, an thou be other than sleepy, finish for us thy tale that we may cut short the watching of this our latter night." She replied, "With love and good will!" It hath reached me, O auspicious King, the director, the right-guiding, lord of the rede which is benefiting and of deeds fair-seeming and worthy celebrating, that the Sultan enquired of the two elder sons concerning their younger brother and they said, "We made ourselves masters of the Bird and we have brought him hither and we know nothing about our cadet." However, the King who loved his youngest with exceeding love put the question, "Have ye not looked after him and have ye not been in his company?" whereto they answered saying, "A certain wayfarer declared to have seen him on some path or other." When the father heard this from them he cried, "There is no Majesty and there is no Might save in Allah, the Glorious, the Great;" and he fell to striking palm upon palm.[1] On this wise it befel these, but as regards the case of their brother, when they cast him into the well he awoke from his sleep and he felt himself falling into the depths, so he cried, "I take refuge with the All-

---

[1] In sign of despair. See vol. i. 298.

sufficient Words of Allah[1] from the mischief He hath created."
And by the blessing of these Holy Names he reached the sole
of the well without aught of harm or hurt. Here finding himself
pinioned, he strained upon his bonds and loosed them; but the
well was deep of bottom and he came upon an arched recess, so
he sat in it and exclaimed, "Verily we are Allah's and to Him we
are returning and I who wrought for them such work[2] am re-
warded with the contrary thereof; withal the power is unto
Allah." And suddenly he heard the sound of speaking at some
little distance beside him, and the voice was saying, "O Black of
Head, who hath come amongst us?" and his comrade responded,
"By Allah, this youth is the son of the Sultan and his best beloved, and the same hath released his brothers from sorcery and
was carrying them to their homes when they played him false
and cast him into this well. However, he hath a signet-ring
with a bezel which if he rub 'twill bespeak him with whatso he
desireth, and will do what he may wish." So the Prince said in
his mind, "I bid the Servant of this Ring to take me out;" after
which he rubbed it and the Jinni appeared and cried, "Yea verily,
O son of the Sultan, what is it thou requirest of me?"——And
Shahrazad was surprised by the dawn of day and fell silent and
ceased to say her permitted say. Then quoth her sister Dunyazad, "How sweet is thy story, O sister mine, and how enjoyable
and delectable!" Quoth she, "And where is this compared with
that I should relate to you on the coming night an the Sovran
suffer me to survive?" Now when it was the next night and
that was

The Four Hundred and Twenty-third Night,

DUNYAZAD said to her, "Allah upon thee, O my sister, an thou be
other than sleepy, finish for us thy tale that we may cut short
the watching of this our latter night!" She replied, "With
love and good will!" It hath reached me, O auspicious King, the

---

[1] In text "Kalamátu 'llah" = the Koran: and the quotation is from chapt. cxiii. 5.
For the "Two Refuge-takings" (Al-Mu'awizzatáni), see vol. iii. 222.

[2] *i.e.*, caused his brothers to recover life.

[I read: Allazí 'amaltu fí-him natíjah yujázúní bi-Ziddi-há = Those to whom I did a
good turn, requite me with the contrary thereof. Allazí, originally the masc. sing. is in
this MS. vulgarly, like its still more vulgar later contraction, "illí," used for both genders
and the three numbers. — ST.]

director, the right-guiding, lord of the rede which is benefiting
and of deeds fair-seeming and worthy celebrating, that the Ring-
bezel said to him, "What dost thou require of me?" and said the
Prince, "I demand that thou hoist me out of the well: and this
done that thou summon for me an host with Pages and Eunuchs
and tents and pavilions and ensigns and banners." Whereto the
other replied, "Present."[1] Then he brought him forth the well
and the youth found hard by it all he needed, so he bade them
load their belongings upon the beasts and when this was done
he set out seeking the city of his sire. And as he drew so near
it that it was within shot of eye, he alighted there upon a broad
plain and ordered them to pitch the camp. Accordingly they set
up the tents and the sitting pavilions while the Farráshes fell to
sprinkling water upon the ground afront the abodes and to setting
up the ensigns and colours whilst the band of kettledrums went
dub-a-dub and the trumpets blared tantaras. The cooks also
began at once to prepare the evening meal. Now when the city-
folk saw this pomp and circumstance, they held in their minds
that the new comer was some Sultan approaching to take their
town; so they gathered together and went in to their own King
and informed him thereof. But he, having heard their words, felt
his heart melt and his vitals throb and a certain joy penetrate
into his heart, so he said, "Praise to the Lord, there hath entered
into my heart a certain manner of pleasure, albeit I know not what
may be the case and Allah hath said in his Holy Book, 'We have
heard good news.' "[2] Hereupon he and the Lords of his land
took horse and rode till they reached the front of the pavilions
where the King dismounted from his steed. Now the Prince
his younger son was dressed in a habit that might have belonged
to a hidden Hoard, and when he saw his father he recognised
him, so he rose and met him and kissed his hands, but his sire
knew him not by reason of the case the youth was in, so he supposed him to be a strange Sultan. Presently, the Prince asked
him, "Where be thy youngest son?" and the King hearing this
fell down a-fainting, but, soon recovering from his swoon, he
said, "Verily my son hath wasted the blood of his life and hath
become food for wild beasts." Hereupon the youth laughed

---

1 Arab. "Házir!" I have noted that this word, in Egypt and Syria, corresponds with the
English waiter's "Yes sir!"

2 Koran, Chapter of Joseph, xii. 19.

aloud and cried, "By Allah, thy son hath not suffered aught from the shifts and changes of the World, and he is still in the bonds of life, safe and sound; nor hath there befallen him anything of harm whatever." "Where is he?" quoth the father: "He standeth between thy hands," quoth the son. So the Sultan looked at him and straightly considering him found that it was his very son who was bespeaking him, and of his delight he threw his arms around his neck and fell with him aswoon to the ground. This lasted for a full-told hour; but when he recovered from his fainting he asked his son what had betided him, so he told all that had befallen, to wit how he had become master of the Enchanting Bird Philomelet, and also of the magical clay wherewith he had besprinkled his brethren and others of the city-folk who had been turned to stone, all and some, and how they had returned to the shapes whilome they wore. Moreover he recounted to him the presents and offerings which had been made to him and also how, when they arrived at a certain place, his brothers had pinioned him and cast him into the well. And ere he finished speaking, lo and behold! the two other Princes came in and when they looked upon his condition and noted the state of prosperity he was in, surrounded as he was by all manner of weal, they felt only increase of envy and malice. But as soon as their sire espied them he cried, "Ye have betrayed me in my son and have lied to me and, by Allah, there is no retribution for you on my part save death;" and hereupon the Sultan bade do them die. Then the youngest Prince made intercession for his brethren and said, "O my sire, whoso doeth a deed shall meet its deserts," and thus he obtained their pardon. So they passed that night one and all in camp and when morning morrowed they loaded and returned to the city and all were in the most pleasurable condition. Now when the King heard this tale from the owner of the fruit it pleased him and he rejoiced therein and said, "By Allah, O Shaykh, indeed that hath gone from us which we had of cark and care; and in good sooth this history deserveth that it be written with water of gold upon the pages of men's hearts." Replied the other, "By Allah, O King of the Age, this adventure is marvellous, but I have another more wondrous and pleasurable and delectable than any thou hast yet heard." Quoth the Sultan, "Needs must thou repeat it to us," and quoth the fruit-seller, "Inshallah—God willing—I will recite it to thee on the coming night." Hereupon the Sultan called for a handmaiden who was a model of beauty and loveliness and stature and perfect grace and from the time of his buying her he never had connection with her nor had he once slept with her, and he gave her in honourable gift to the reciter. Then he set apart for them both an apartment with its furniture and appurtenances and the slave-girl rejoiced greatly thereat. Now when she went in to her new lord she donned her best of dresses so he lay down beside her and sought carnal copulation, but his prickle would not stand erect, as was its wont, although he knew not the cause thereof.——And Shahrazad was surprised by the dawn of day and fell silent and ceased saying her permitted say. Then quoth her sister Dunyazad, "How sweet and tasteful is thy tale, O sister mine, and enjoyable and delectable!" Quoth she, "And where is this compared with that I would relate to you on the coming night an the Sovran suffer me to survive?" Now when it was the next night and that was

The Four Hundred and Twenty-Fifth Night,

DUNYAZAD said to her, "Allah upon thee, O my sister, an thou be other than sleepy, finish for us thy tale that we may cut short the watching of this our latter night!" She replied, "With love and good will!" It hath reached me, O auspicious King, the director, the right-guiding, lord of the rede which is benefiting and of deeds fair-seeming and worthy celebrating, that the prickle of the Fruiterer would not stand to the handmaid as was the wont thereof, so he cried, "Verily this is a wondrous business." Then the girl fell to rubbing it up and to toying therewith, her object being to stablish an erection. But the article in question grew not and remained limp, whereupon she said, "O my lord, Allah increase the progress of thy pego!" Thereupon she arose and opened a bag wherefrom she drew out kerchiefs and dried aromatic herbs[1] such as are scattered upon corpses; and she also brought a gugglet of water. Presently she fell to washing the prickle as it were a dead body, and after bathing it she shrouded it with a kerchief: then she cried upon her women and they all bewept the untimely fate of his yard which was still clothed in

---

[1] Arab. "Hanút:" this custom has become almost obsolete: the corpse is now sprinkled with a mixture of water, camphor diluted and the dried and pounded leaves of various trees, especially the "Nabk" (lote-tree or *Zizyphus lotus*). — Lane M. E. chapt. xxviii.

the kerchief.[1]   And when morning morrowed the Sultan sent after the man and summoned him and said to him, "How passed thy night?"   So he told him all that had betided him, and concealed from him naught; and when the Sultan heard this account from him he laughed at him on such wise that from excess of merriment he well nigh fell upon his back and cried, "By Allah, if there be such cleverness in that girl, she becometh not any save myself."   Accordingly he sent to fetch her as she stood and left the furniture of the place wholly and entirely to the owner of the fruit.   And when this was done the Sultan made of him a booncompanion for that day from morning to evening and whenever he thought of the handmaid's doings he ordered the man to repeat the tale and he laughed at him and admired the action of the slave-girl with the Limpo.   When darkness came on they prayed the night-prayer and they supped and sat down to converse and to tell anecdotes.[2]   Thereupon the King said to the Fruiterer, "Relate us somewhat of that thou hast heard anent the Kings of old;" and said the other, "Hearing and obeying," and forthwith began the

Story of the King of Al-Yaman and his Three Sons.

IT IS related that there was a Sultan in the land of Al-Yaman who had three male children, two of them by one mother and a third

---

[1] These comical measures were taken by "Miss Lucy" in order to charm away the Evil Eye which had fascinated the article in question. Such temporary impotence in a vigorous man, which results from an exceptional action of the brain and the nervous system, was called in old French *Nouement des aiguilettes* (*i.e.* point-tying, the points which fastened the *haut-de-chausses* or hose to the jerkin, and its modern equivalent would be to "button up the flap"). For its cure, the "*Deliement des aiguilettes*" see Davenport "Aphrodisiacs" p. 36, and the French translation of the Shaykh al-Nafzáwi (Jardin Parfumé, chapt. xvii. pp. 251–53). The Moslem heals such impotence by the usual simples, but the girl in the text adopts a moral course which buries the dead parts in order to resurrect them. A friend of mine, a young and vigorous officer, was healed by a similar process. He had carried off a sergeant's wife, and the husband lurked about the bungalow to shoot him, a copper cap being found under the window hence a state of nervousness which induced perfect impotence. He applied to the regimental surgeon, happily a practised hand, and was gravely supplied with pills and a draught; his diet was carefully regulated and he was ordered to sleep by the woman but by no means to touch her for ten days. On the fifth he came to his adviser with a sheepish face and told him that he had not wholly followed the course prescribed, as last night he had suddenly — by the blessing of the draught and the pills — recovered and had given palpable evidence of his pristine vigour. The surgeon deprecated such proceeding until the patient should have had full benefit of his drugs — bread pills and cinnamon-water.

[2] Here ends vol. iii. of the W. M. MS. and begins Night cdxxvi.

by another. Now that King used to dislike this second wife and
her son, so he sent her from him and made her, together with her
child, consort with the handmaids of the kitchen, never asking
after them for a while of time. One day the two brothers-german
went in to their sire and said to him, " 'Tis the desire of us to
go forth a-hunting and a-chasing," whereto their father replied,
"And have ye force enough for such sport?" They said, "Yea,
verily, we have!" when he gave to each of them a horse with its
furniture of saddle and bridle, and the twain rode off together.
But as soon as the third son (who together with his mother had
been banished to the kitchen) heard that the other two had gone
forth to hunt, he went to his mother and cried, "I also would
fain mount and away to the chase like my brethren." His mother
responded, saying, "O my son, indeed I am unable to buy thee a
horse or aught of the kind;" so he wept before her and she
brought him a silvern article, which he took and fared forth
with it to the bazar, and there, having sold it for a gold piece,
he repaired to a neighbouring mill and bought him a lame garron.
After this he took a bittock of bread; and, backing the beast
without saddle or bridle, he followed upon the footsteps of his
brothers through the first day and the second, but on the third
he took the opposite route. Presently he reached a Wady, when
behold, he came across a string[1] of pearls and emeralds which

---

[1] In the next "Rísah," copyist's error for "Ríshah" = a thread, a line: it afterwards
proves to be an ornament for a falcon's neck. [I cannot bring myself to adopt here the explanation of "Ríshah" as a string instead of its usual meaning of "feather," "plume." **My**
reasons are the following: 1. The youth sets it upon his head; that is, I suppose, his cap,
or whatever his head-gear may be, which seems a more appropriate place for a feather
than for a necklace. 2. Further on, Night cdxxx., it is said that the Prince left the residence
of his second spouse *in search* (tálib) of the city of the bird. If the word "Ríshah," which,
in the signification of thread, is Persian, had been sufficiently familiar to an Arab to suggest, as a matter of course, a bird's necklace, and hence the bird itself, we would probably
find a trace of this particular meaning, if not in other Arabic books, at least in Persian
writers or dictionaries; but here the word "Ríshah," by some pronounced "Reshah" with
the Yá majhúl, never occurs in connection with jewels; it means fringe, filament, fibre.
On the other hand, the suggestion of the bird presents itself quite naturally at the sight
of the feather. 3. Ib. p. 210 the youth requests the old man to tell him concerning the
"Tayrah allazí Rísh-há (not Rishat-há) min Ma'ádin," which, I believe, can only be rendered by: the bird whose plumage is of precious stones. The "Ríshah" itself was said to be
"*min* Zumurrud wa Lúlú," of emeralds and pearls; and the cage will be "min Ma'ádin wa
Lúlú," of precious stones and pearls, in all which cases the use of the preposition "min"
points more particularly to the material of which the objects are wrought than the mere
Izáfah. The wonderfulness of the bird seems therefore rather to consist in his jewelled
plumage than the gift of speech or other enchanting qualities, and I would take it for one
of those costly toys, in imitation of trees and animals, in which Eastern princes rejoice,

glittered in the sunlight, so he picked it up and set it upon his
head and he fared onwards singing for very joy. But when he
drew near the town he was met by his two brothers who seized
him and beat him and, having taken away his necklace, drove
him afar from them. Now he was much stronger and more beautiful than they were, but as he and his mother had been cast off by
the King, he durst not offer aught of resistance.[1] Now the two
brothers having taken the necklace from him went away joyful,
and repairing to their father, showed him the ornament and he
rejoiced in them and hending it in his hand marvelled thereat.
But the youngest son went to his mother with his heart well
nigh broken. Then the Sultan said to his two sons, "Ye have
shown no cleverness herein until ye bring me the wearer of this
necklace." They answered, "Hearkening and obedience, and
we will set out to find her."——And Shahrazad was surprised
by the dawn of day and fell silent and ceased to say her permitted
say. Then quoth her sister Dunyazad, "How sweet is thy story,
O sister mine, and how enjoyable and delectable!" Quoth she
"And where is this compared with that I should relate to you
on the coming night an the King suffer me to survive?" Now
when it was the next night and that was

The Four Hundred and Twenty-seventh Night,

DUNYAZAD said to her, "Allah upon thee, O my sister, an thou be
other than sleepy, finish for us thy tale that we may cut short the
watching of this our latter night!" She replied, "With love and
good will!" It hath reached me, O auspicious King, the director,
the right-guiding, lord of the rede which is benefiting and of deeds
fair-seeming and worthy celebrating, that the sons of the Sultan
made them ready for the march whereby they might bring back
the bird to whom the necklace belonged. So they took them a
sufficiency of provision and, farewelling their father, set out for

---

and of which we read so many descriptions, not only in books of fiction, but even in his-
torical works. If it were a live-bird of the other kind, he would probably have put in his
word to expose the false brothers of the Prince. — Sr.]

[1] This is conjectural: the text has a correction which is hardly legible. [I read: "Wa
lákin hú ajmalu min-hum bi-jamálin mufritin, lakinnahu matrúdun hú wa ummu-hu" =
"and yet he was more beautiful than they with surpassing beauty, but he was an outcast,
he and his mother," as an explanation, by way of parenthesis, for their daring to treat him
so shamefully. — Sr.]

the city wherein they judged the bird might be. Such was their
case; but as regards their unhappy brother, when he heard the
news of their going he took with him a bittock of bread and having bidden adieu to his mother mounted his lame garron and
followed upon the traces of his brethren for three days. Presently he found himself in the midst of the wild and the wold,
and he ceased not faring therethrough till he came to a city
whose folk were all weeping and wailing and crying and keening.
So he accosted an aged man and said to him, "The Peace be upon
thee!" and when the other returned his salam and welcomed him
he asked saying, "O my uncle, tell me what causeth these groans
and this grief?" The other replied, "O my son, verily our city
is domineered over by a monstrous Lion who every year cometh
about this time and he hath already done on such wise for forty
and three years. Now he expecteth every twelvemonth as he
appeareth to be provided with a damsel arrayed and adorned in
all her finery, and if he chance to come as is his wont and find her
not he would assault the city and destroy it. So before the
season of his visit they cast lots upon the maidens of the place
and whomso these befal, her they decorate and lead forth to a
place without the walls that the monster may take her. And
this year the sort hath fallen upon the King's daughter."[1] When
the youth heard these words he held his peace and, having taken
seat by the old man for an hour or so, he arose and went forth to
the place where the Lion was wont to appear and he took his
station there, when behold, the daughter of the King came to
him and right heavy was she of heart. But as she found the
youth sitting there, she salam'd to him and made friendship with
him and asked, "What brought thee to this stead?" Answered
he, "That which brought *thee* brought me also." Whereto
quoth she, "Verily at this hour the Lion shall come to seize me,
but as soon as he shall see me he will devour thee before me, and
thus both of us shall lose our lives; so rise up and depart and
save thyself, otherwise thou wilt become mere wasted matter
in the belly of the beast." "By Allah, O my lady," quoth he,
"I am thy sacrifice at such a moment as this!" And as they were

---

[1] The venerable myth of Andromeda and Perseus (who is Horus in disguise) brought
down to Saint George (his latest descendant), the Dragon (Typhon) and the fair Saba
in the "Seven Champions of Christendom." See my friend M. Clermont Ganneau's *Horus
et Saint-Georges*; Mr. J. R. Anderson's "Saint Mark's Rest; the Place of Dragons;" and
my "Book of the Sword," chapt. ix.

speaking, suddenly the world was turned topsy-turvy,[1] and dust-clouds and sand-devils[2] flew around and whirlwinds began to play about them, and lo and behold! the monster made his appearance; and as he approached he was lashing his flanks with his tail like the sound of a kettle-drum. Now when the Princess espied him, the tears poured down her cheeks, whereat the youth sprang to his feet in haste, and unsheathing his sword, went forth to meet the foe, who at the sight of him gnashed his tusks at him. But the King's son met him bravely, springing nimbly from right to left, whereat the Lion raged furiously, and with the design to tear him limb from limb, made a rush at the youth, who smote him with all the force of his forearm and planted between his eyes a sway of scymitar so sore that the blade came out flashing between his thighs, and he fell to the ground slain and bleeding amain. When the Princess saw this derring-do of her defender, she rejoiced greatly and fell to wiping with her kerchief the sweat from his brow; and the youth said to her, "Arise and do thou fare to thy family." "O my lord, and O light of mine eyes!" said she, "we twain together will wend together as though we were one flesh;" but he rejoined, "This is on no wise possible." Then he arose from beside her and ceased not faring until he had entered the city, where he rested himself beside a shop. She also sprang up, and faring homewards, went in to her father and mother, showing signs of sore sorrow. When they saw her, their hearts fluttered with fear lest the monster should attack the town and destroy it, whereupon she said to them, "By Allah, the Lion hath been slain and lieth there dead." They asked her saying, "What was it killed him?" and she answered, "A handsome youth fair of favour," but they hardly believed her words and both went to visit the place, where they found the monster stone-dead. The folk of the city, one and all, presently heard this fair news, and their joy grew great, when the Sultan said to his daughter, "Thou! knowest thou the man who slew him?" to which she answered, "I know him." But as all tidings of the youth were cut off, the King let proclaim about the city——And Shahrazad was surprised by the dawn of day and fell silent and ceased saying her permitted say. Then quoth

---

[1] *i.e.* there was a great movement and confusion.
[2] [In the text 'Afár, a word frequently joined with "Ghubár," dust, for the sake of emphasis; hence we will find in Night cccxxix. the verb "yu'affiru," he was raising a dust-cloud. — St.]

her sister Dunyazad, "How sweet and tasteful is thy tale, O sister mine, and enjoyable and delectable!" Quoth she, "And where is this compared with that I would relate to you on the coming night an the King suffer me to survive?" Now when it was the next night and that was

The Four Hundred and Twenty-ninth Night,

DUNYAZAD said to her, "Allah upon thee, O my sister, an thou be other than sleepy, finish for us thy tale that we may cut short the watching of this our latter night." She replied, "With love and good will!" It hath reached me, O auspicious King, the director, the right-guiding, lord of the rede which is benefiting and of deeds fair-seeming and worthy celebrating, that the King let proclaim through the city how none should oppose him or delay to obey his bidding; nay, that each and every, great and small, should come forth and pass before the windows of his daughter's palace. Accordingly the Crier went abroad and cried about the city to that purport, bidding all the lieges muster and defile in front of the Princess's windows; and they continued so doing for three full-told days, while she sat continually expecting to sight the youth who had slain the Lion, but to no purpose. At last never a soul remained who had not passed in the review, so the Sultan asked, "Is there anyone who hath absented himself?" and they answered, "There is none save a stranger youth who dwelleth in such and such a place." "Bring him hither!" cried the King, "and command him to pass muster," when the others hastened to fetch him; and as soon as he drew near to the window, behold, a kerchief was thrown upon him.[1] Then the Sultan summoned him, and he, when standing in the presence, saluted and made obeisance and blessed the Sovran with the blessings fit for the Caliphs. The Sultan was pleased thereat and said, "Art thou he who slew the Lion?" and said the other, "I did." Hereupon quoth the King, "Ask a favour of me, that I grant it to thee;" and quoth the Youth, "I pray of Allah and then of our lord the Sultan that he marry me to his daughter." But the King continued, "Ask of me somewhat of wealth,"

---

[1] Upon the subject of "throwing the kerchief" see vol. vi. 285. Here it is done simply as a previously concerted signal of recognition.

and all the Lords of the land exclaimed, "By Allah, he deserveth the Princess who saved her from the Lion and slew the beast." Accordingly the King bade the marriage-knot be tied, and let the bridegroom be led in procession to the bride, who rejoiced in him with extreme joy, and he abated her maidenhead and the two lay that night together. But the Prince arose about the latter hours without awaking his bride, and withdrawing her seal-ring from her finger, passed his own thereupon and wrote in the palm of her hand, "I am Aláeddín,[1] son of King Such-and-such, who ruleth in the capital of Al-Hind, and, given thou love me truly, do thou come to me, otherwise stay in thy father's house." Then he went forth without awaking her and fared through wilds and wolds for a term of ten days, travelling by light and by night, till he drew near a certain city which was domineered over by an Elephant. Now this beast would come every year and take from the town a damsel; and on this occasion it was the turn of the Princess, daughter to the King who governed that country. But as the youth entered the streets he was met by groans and moans and crying and keening; so he asked thereanent and was answered that the Elephant was presently approaching to seize the maiden and devour her.[2] He asked, "To what stead cometh he?" and they pointed out to him a place without the city whereto he repaired and took his seat. Suddenly the Princess presented herself before him a-weeping and with tears down her cheeks a-creeping, when he said to her, "O my lady, there is no harm for thee." Said she, "O youth, by Allah! thou wastest thy life to no purpose and seekest thy death without cause, so rise up and save thyself, for the Elephant will be here this very hour." And behold, the beast came up to the heart of the waste and he was raising a dust-cloud and trumpeting with rage[3] and lashing flanks with tail. But when he arrived at the wonted place he was confronted by the youth

---

[1] In text " 'Alá Yadín;" for which vulgarism see vol. iii. 51.

[2] Elephants are usually, as Cuvier said of the (Christian) "Devil" after a look at his horns and hoofs, vegetarians.

[3] [The MS. has "yughaffiru wa yuzaghdimu." The former stands probably for "yu'-affiru," for which see supra p. 205, note 2. The writing is, however, so indistinct that possibly "yufaghghiru" is intended, which means he opened his mouth wide. "Yuzagh-dimu" is one of those quadriliterals which are formed by blending two triliterals in one verb, in order to intensify the idea. "Zaghada" and "Zaghama" mean both "he roared," more especially applied to a camel, and by joining the "d" of the one with the "m" of the other, we obtain "Zaghdama," he roared fiercely. — St.]

who, with heart stronger than granite, hastened to fall upon him[1]
and fatigued him and dealt blows without cease; and, when the
Elephant charged down upon him, he met the monster with a
stroke between the eyes dealt with all the force of his forearm,
and the blade came flashing out from between his thighs, when
the beast fell to the ground slain and weltering in his blood
amain. Thereupon, in the stress of her joy, the Princess arose
hurriedly and walked towards the youth——And Shahrazad
was surprised by the dawn of day and fell silent and ceased to
say her permitted say. Then quoth her sister Dunyazad, "How
sweet is thy story, O sister mine, and how enjoyable and delectable!" Quoth she, "And where is this compared with that I
should relate to you on the coming night an the King suffer me
to survive?" Now when it was the next night and that was

The Four Hundred and Thirtieth Night,

DUNYAZAD said to her, "Allah upon thee, O my sister, an thou
be other than sleepy, finish for us thy tale that we may cut short
the watching of this our latter night!" She replied, "With
love and good will!" It hath reached me, O auspicious King, the
director, the right-guiding, lord of the rede which is benefiting
and of deeds fair-seeming and worthy celebrating, that the Princess walked hurriedly towards the youth and in the stress of her
joy she threw her arms around his neck and kissed him between
the eyes and cried, "O my lord, may thy hands never palsied
grow nor exult over thee any foe!" Said he to her, "Return to
thy people!" and said she, "There is no help but that I and thou
fare together." But he replied, "This matter is not the right
rede," and he went from her at a double quick pace, saying, "O
Allah, may none see me!" until he entered the city and presently
seating him beside a tailor's shop fell to conversing with its owner.
Presently the man said, "There is no Majesty and there is no
Might save in Allah, the Glorious, the Great: by this time the
daughter of the King will have been seized by the Elephant and
torn to pieces and devoured, and she the mainstay of her mother

---

[1] [Sára'a-hu wa láwa'a-hu = he rushed upon him and worried him. The root law'
means to enfeeble, render sick, especially applied to love-sickness (Lau'ah). The present
3rd form is rarely used, but here and in a later passage, Night cdxlv., the context bears
out the sense of harassing. — ST.]

and her father." And behold loud lullilooing[1] flew about the
city and one began exclaiming, "Verily the Elephant which is
wont to come hither year by year hath been slaughtered by a
man quite young in years, and the Sultan hath sent a Crier to
cry amongst the crowds, 'Let the slayer of the beast come into
the presence and crave a boon and marry the maiden.'" So
quoth the Youth to the tailor, "What is to do?" and the other
informed him of the truth of the report, whereupon he asked, "If
I go to the King will he give her to me?" Answered the tailor,
"Who art thou that thou shouldest intermarry with the daughter
of the King?" and the Prince rejoined, "We will go and bespeak
him and lie to him saying, I am he who slew the monster."
But the other retorted, "O Youth, thou art willingly and wilfully
going to thy death, for an thou lie to him he will assuredly cut off
thy head." Presently the Prince, who was listening to the Crier,
said to his companion, "Up with thee and come with us that
thou mayest look upon my execution;" and cried the other,
"Why so, O thou true-born son?"[2] whereto the Youth replied,
"Needs must I do this!" Hereupon he and the man arose and
went till they came to the palace of the Sultan, where they craved
leave to enter, but were forbidden by the Chamberlain, when lo
and behold! the Princess looked out from the lattice and saw the
Prince together with the tailor. So she threw the kerchief upon
his head and cried aloud, "By Allah, here he be, and 'tis none but
he who slew the Elephant and who saved me from him." Hereat
the tailor fell to wondering at the youth, but when the King saw
that his daughter had thrown the kerchief upon him, he presently sent to summon him between his hands and asked him how
it happened, and heard from him the truth of the tale. Then said
he, "By Allah, verily my daughter was lost, so that this youth
well deserveth her." Thereupon he tied the marriage tie between the twain and the youth after wedding her went to her in
procession and did away her pucelage, and lay the night with
her. And presently when day was nigh, the young Prince arose
and seeing her slumbering wrote in the palm of her hand, "I am
Such-and-such, the son of such a King in Such-and-such a capital;
and if thou love me truly, come to find me, or otherwise stay in

---

[1] In text "Zaghárit" plur. of Zaghrútah: see vol. ii. p. 80.
[2] [Yá walad al-Halál. I would translate: "O! son of a lawful wedlock," simply meaning
that he takes him to be a decent fellow, not a scamp or Walad al-Harám. — St.]

thy father's house." Then without awaking her he fared forth
to the city of the Enchanting Bird and ceased not cutting athwart
the wilds and the wolds throughout the nights and the days till he
arrived at the place wherein dwelt the Bird Philomelet whereto
the necklace belonged. And she was the property of the Princess
the daughter to the Sovran whose seat was in that capital, and it
was the greatest of cities and its King was the grandest of the
Kings. When he entered the highways he leant against the shop
of an Oilman to whom he said, "The Peace be upon you," and the
other returned his salutation and seated him beside himself, and
the two fell to conversing. Presently the Prince asked him, "O
my lord, what canst thou tell me concerning a certain Bird and
her owner?" and the other made answer, "I know nothing but of
oil and of honey and of clarified butter, whereof whatever thou
requirest I will give to thee." Quoth the youth, "This is no
reply to my question," and quoth the oilman, "I know not nor
regard aught save what is by me in my shop." So the Prince
rising from beside him left him and went forth to continue his
search; but whenever he asked concerning the Bird and its
owner, the folk changed the subject and returned him no reply
save, "We know not." This lasted until he accosted a man
well stricken in years, whose age was nigh to an hundred; and
he was sitting alone at one side of the city; so the Youth walked
up to him and salam'd; and, after the other returned his greeting
and kindly welcomed him and seated him near him, the two fell
a-talking together, and the Prince asked him, "O my uncle,
what canst thou tell me concerning the Bird whose necklet is of
precious stones, and what concerning the owner thereof?" The
aged man held his peace for awhile and presently exclaimed, "O
my son, why ask me of this? O my child,[1] verily the Kings and
sons of the Kings have sought her in marriage but could not
avail; indeed and the lives of folks manifold have been wasted
upon her. How, then, canst thou hope to win her? Nevertheless, O my son, go and buy thee seven lambs and slaughter them
and skin them, after which do thou roast them and cut them all
in halves; for she hath seven doors at each whereof standeth as
warder a rending Lion; and at the eighth which guardeth the
maiden and the Bird are posted forty slaves who at all times
are there lying. And now I leave thee to thy luck, O my son."

---

[1] The repetition is a sign of kindness and friendliness; see vol. vi. 370.

But when the Prince heard these words he asked his aidance of the Shaykh and went forth from him——And Shahrazad was surprised by the dawn of day and fell silent and ceased saying her permitted say. Then quoth her sister Dunyazad, "How sweet and tasteful is thy tale, O sister mine, and how enjoyable and delectable!" Quoth she, "And where is this compared with that I would relate to you on the coming night an the King suffer me to survive?" Now when it was the next night and that was

The Four Hundred and Thirty-second Night,

Dunyazad said to her, "Allah upon thee, O my sister, an thou be other than sleepy, finish for us thy tale that we may cut short the watching of this our latter night." She replied, "With love and good will!" It hath reached me, O auspicious King, the director, the right-guiding, lord of the rede which is benefiting and of deeds fair-seeming and worthy celebrating, that the Prince craved for the prayers of the Shaykh, who blessed him. Then he went forth from him and bought of the lambs what he had been charged to buy, and these he slaughtered and skinned and roasted and he cut each and every into two halves. He waited until night descended with its darkness and ceased the to-ing and fro-ing of folk, when he arose and walked to the place pointed out and there he found the Lion whose shape and size equalled the stature of a full-grown bull. He threw to him half a lamb and the beast allowed him to pass through that door, and it was the same with the other entrances, all seven of them, until he reached the eighth. Here he found the forty slaves who were bestrewn on the ground bedrowned in sleep; so he went in with soft tread and presently he came upon the Bird Philomelet in a cage encrusted with pearls and precious stones and he saw the Princess who owned him lying asleep upon a couch. Hereat he wrote upon the palm of her hand, "I am Such-and-such, son to the King Such-and-such, of such a city; and I have come in upon thee and beheld thee bared whilst thou wast sleeping, and I have also taken away the Bird. However, an thou love me and long for me, do thou come to me in mine own city." Then he seized the Bird to his prize and fared forth and what he did with the Lions coming that he did when going out. The Veiler[1] veiled

---

[1] This Arabian "Sattár" corresponds passing well with "Jupiter Servator."

him, and he went forth the city and met not a single soul, and he
ceased not faring the livelong night till next morning did appear,
when he hid in a place seeking repose and ate somewhat of victual.
But as soon as the daylight shone bright, he arose and continued
his journey, praying Allah for protection on his wayfare, till it
was mid-afternoon: then he found, like an oasis in the middle
of the waste, certain pastures of the wild Arabs and as he drew
near the owner met him and salam'd to him and greeted him and
blessed him. So he lay that night with them till dawn when the
Shaykh of the encampment who had heard of the stranger came
to him and welcomed him and found him a youth fair of form
and favour and saw by his side the Enchanting Bird in its cage.
He recognised it and wondered at the young man's derring-do
and cried, "Subhana 'lah—praise be to God—who hath committed his secret unto the weakliest of His creation![1] Verily
this Bird hath caused on its account to be slain many of the
Wazirs and the Kings and the Sultans, yet hath yonder lad
mastered it and carried it away. This however is by virtue of his
good fortune." Then the old man had compassion on him and
gave him a horse that he had by him together with somewhat of
provaunt. The Prince took them from him and returning to his
march traversed the wilds and the wolds for days and nights,
all of them; and he continued in that case when he drew near
his father's capital which rose within eye-shot. And as he
walked on without heed, behold, his brethren met him and
confronted him and fell upon him and, having taken away the
Enchanting Bird, reviled him and beat him and shook him off
and drove him away. Then they entered the city and sought
their sire who received them with fair reception and greeted
them and rejoiced in them; after which they presented him with
the Bird Philomelet, and said, "Here we bring him to thee and
there befel us through his account much toil and trouble." But
their brother who had really won the prize went to his mother in
sadness of heart——And Shahrazad was surprised by the dawn
of day and fell silent and ceased to say her permitted say. Then
quoth her sister Dunyazad, "How sweet is thy story, O sister
mine, and how enjoyable and delectable!" Quoth she, "And

---

[1] "Out of the mouth of babes and sucklings thou hast perfected praise." Matt. xxi. 16.
The idea is not less Moslem than Christian.

where is this compared with that I should relate to you on the coming night an the King suffer me to survive?" Now when it was the next night and that was

The Four Hundred and Thirty-third Night,

DUNYAZAD said to her, "Allah upon thee, O my sister, an thou be other than sleepy, finish for us thy tale that we may cut short the watching of this our latter night!" She replied, "With love and good will!" It hath reached me, O auspicious King, the director, the right-guiding, lord of the rede which is benefiting and of deeds fair-seeming and worthy celebrating, that the young Prince who had brought the Bird and whom his brothers had beaten and robbed of his prize, went to his mother in sadness of heart and shedding tears. Quoth she, "What is thy case and what hath befallen thee?" So he told her what had betided him and she said, "Sorrow not, O my son; the course of the right shall be made manifest." Then she quieted him and soothed his heart. This is what happened to these persons; but as regards the Princess, the owner of the Bird, when she awoke at dawn of day and opened her eyes, she found her favourite gone and as her glance fell upon the things about her, suddenly she saw something written in the palm of her hand. But as soon as she had read it and comprehended its purport, she cried aloud with a mighty grievous cry which caused the palace-women to flock around,[1] and her father to ask what was to do but none could explain it because no one knew. So the Sultan arose forthright and, going in to his daughter, found her buffeting her face for the sake of her Bird and asked her, "What is to do with thee?" So she informed him of what had befallen her, adding, "Verily he who came into my bower and discovered me bare and looked upon me and wrote upon the palm of my hand, him I am determined to have and none other save that one." Quoth her father, "O my daughter, many sons of the Wazirs and the Kings have sought the bird and have failed; and now do thou suppose that

---

[1] [I read "Sarkhah adwat la-há al-Saráyah" == a cry to which the palace-women raised an echo, a cry re-echoed by the palace-women. "Adwá" is the fourth form of "Dawiya," to hum or buzz, to produce an indistinct noise, and it is vulgarly used in the above sense, like the substantive "Dawi," an echo. Al-Saráyah is perhaps only an Arabised form of the Persian Saráy, and the sentence might be, to which the palace resounded.—ST.]

he hath died;" but quoth the Princess, "I desire none save the man who found me in sleep and looked upon me, and he is the son of King So-and-so, reigning in such a capital." Said her father, "Then how standeth the case?" and said she, "Needs must I thank him and seek his city and marry him, for assuredly amongst the sons of the Kings, all of them, none can be fairer or more delightsome than he who hath craftily devised this entrance to me in so guarded a stead as this. How then can anyone be his peer?"[1] Hereupon her father bade muster the forces without the city and he brought out for his daughter rarities and presents and mule-litters, and they pitched the tents and after three days they loaded the loads for travel. Then they fared for whole days and nights until they drew near the city wherein the youth had slain the Elephant and had saved the daughter of the King. So the Sultan set up his encampment with its tents and pavilions hard by the walls, to the end that all might take their rest, but when the King of the City saw this he rode forth to visit the stranger, and after greeting asked him the cause of his coming with such a host. The Sultan apprised him of what had happened to his daughter, how she had lost the Enchanting Bird, also how the youth had come into her bower and had written a writ upon the palm of her hand. But when the King heard from him this account he knew and was certified that it was the same Prince who had also slain the Elephant and who had on such wise saved his daughter's life; so he said to the Sultan, "Verily he who took the Bird belonging to thy Princess hath also married my daughter, for he hath done such-and-such deeds." After which he related to him the slaughter of the Elephant and all that had happened from beginning to end. Now as soon as the Sultan heard these words he cried, "By Allah, my daughter is excusable and she hath shown her insight and her contrivance;" and presently he arose and going in to her related what he had heard from the King of the City, and she wondered at the tale of the youth's adventures and the killing of the Elephant. They nighted in that stead and the tidings soon reached the ears of the youth's wife, the Princess who had been saved from the Elephant, and she said to her sire, "I also needs must go to him and forgather with him." Hereupon the King her father bade muster his troops together with the Lords of the land without the city beside the

---

[1] The Princess is not logical: on the other hand she may plead that she is right.

host of the chief Sultan, and on the second day both Sovrans bade the loads be loaded for the march. When their bidding was obeyed the twain set out together and travelled for days and nights until they drew near to the capital of the King where the youth had slain the Lion, and they pitched their tents in its neighbourhood. Presently the Sovran of that capital came out and greeted them and asked them the cause of their coming; so they informed him of their adventures from commencement to conclusion; and he, when certified of the truth of this tale, returned to inform his daughter thereof.——And Shahrazad was surprised by the dawn of day and fell silent and ceased saying her permitted say. Then quoth her sister Dunyazad, "How sweet and tasteful is thy tale, O sister mine, and enjoyable and delectable!" Quoth she, "And where is this compared with that I would relate to you on the coming night an the King suffer me to survive?" Now when it was the next night and that was

The Four Hundred and Thirty-fifth Night,

DUNYAZAD said to her, "Allah upon thee, O my sister, an thou be other than sleepy, finish for us thy tale that we may cut short the watching of this our latter night!" She replied, "With love and good will!" It hath reached me, O auspicious King, the director, the right-guiding, lord of the rede which is benefiting and of deeds fair-seeming and worthy celebrating, that the third King informed his daughter of the certainty of the tidings, and she also exclaimed, "Needs must I as well as they set out to seek him and forgather with him." So her father returned to the Sultan and the King and told them of the adventures of the youth, and how he was the cause of his daughter's salvation from the Lion which he had slain; and when the twain heard his words they marvelled and cried, "By Allah, verily this youth is fortunate in all his doings: would Heaven we knew how be his condition with his father and whether he is loved or he is loathed." Then the three fell to talking of the Prince's qualities, and presently the third King arose and gave orders for gathering together the Lords of his land and his army, and he brought out for his daughter mule-litters, and gat ready all she might require of rarities and offerings. Then the three Kings gave orders to load the beasts and fared together, taking with them their three daughters who, whenever they conversed together used to praise the high gifts of the Prince, and she who was the mistress of the Bird would say, "Ye twain have forgathered with him;" and the others would answer, "We passed with him no more than a single night;" after which they would relate to her the slaughter of the Lion and the Elephant. So she wondered and cried, "By Allah! verily he is auspicious of fortune." And they ceased not to be in such case for whole days and nights, and nights and days, throughout the length of the journey till they drew near the far-famed[1] city which was the bourne of their wayfare and the object of their wishes. Now this happened about sunset-tide, so the three Kings who had alighted together bade their tents and pavilions be set up, and when their behest was obeyed, each and every of the three commanded that the firemen and the linkmen light up their torches and cressets, and they did so, one and all, until that Wady was illumined as by the sheen of day. But when the city folk saw what was done by the three Kings, their hearts quaked and their flesh quivered, and they cried, "Verily for the mighty hosts of these Kings there needs must be a cause of coming." However the strangers nighted in sight until morn grew light, when the three Sovrans forgathered, and sent a messenger with an invite to the Lord of the city, who on receiving him, exclaimed, "Hearkening and obedience!" Then mounting without stay or delay he rode forth till he reached the strangers' camp, where he alighted and went in and greeted them; and they, on similar guise, arose to him and wished him long life, and seated him and fell to conversing with him for a full-told hour. But he was whelmed in the ocean of thought, and he kept saying to himself, "Would Heaven I knew what be the cause of the Kings coming to this my country." However, the four Sovrans continued to converse until the noon-tide hour, when the trays were dispread for them, and the tables were laid with sumptuous meats in platters and chargers of pre-cious metal, the very basins and ewers being of virgin gold. But when the King of that city beheld this he marvelled, and said in his mind, "By Allah, there is not with me aught of rarities like these." As soon as they had ended eating what sufficed them, water was brought to them and they washed their hands, after which they were served with confections and coffee and sher-

---

[1] Arab. "Ma'lúmah," which may also mean the "made known," or "aforementioned."

bets. Anon the three Kings said to their guest, "Thou, hast thou any children?" and said he, "Yes, I have two sons." Quoth they, "Summon them before us that we may look upon them;" so he sent and bade them make act of presence. The Princes donned their finest dresses and perfumed themselves; then they took horse and rode until they had reached their father's palace. But the three Princesses stood to look at them, and she who was owner of the Bird Philomelet asked of the two others, saying, "Is he amongst these twain?" and they answered, "Nay, he is not." She exclaimed, "By Allah, both of them be fine men," and the others cried, "Indeed, our husband is far fairer and finer than they." But when the Kings saw the two brothers they said to their sire, "Verily our need is not with them."——And Shahrazad was surprised by the dawn of day and fell silent and ceased to say her permitted say. Then quoth her sister Dunya-zad, "How sweet is thy story, O sister mine, and how enjoyable and delectable!" Quoth she, "And where is this compared with that I would relate to you on the coming night an the King suffer me to survive?" Now when it was the next night and that was

The Four Hundred and Thirty-seventh Night,

DUNYAZAD said to her, "Allah upon thee, O my sister, an thou be other than sleepy, finish for us thy tale that we may cut short the watching of this our latter night!" She replied, "With love and good will!" It hath reached me, O auspicious King, the director, the right-guiding, lord of the rede which is benefiting and of deeds fair-seeming and worthy celebrating, that the two Kings said to the lord of the city, "Verily our need is not in this pair of youths," and the third King added, "By Allah, indeed these two young men be fair of favour," for that he had not seen the Prince who had taken his daughter's Bird Philomelet. Presently the two asked the father saying, "Thou, is there by thee no issue other than these two?" and said he, "Yes, I have a son, but I have cast him out and I have placed his mother amongst the handmaids of the kitchen." "Send to fetch him," quoth they; so he despatched a messenger to bring him into the presence. And he came, withal he was without any finery of dress; but as soon as the two damsels saw him they communed

concerning him and he inclined to them and went into their
pavilion, when they rose to him and threw their arms round his
neck and kissed him between his eyes. Hereupon the mistress of
the Bird said to the two others, "Be this he?" and said they,
"Yes;" so she also arose and kissed his hand. But when he had
finished greeting them he at once went forth to the assembled
Kings, who stood up in honour to him and welcomed him and
greeted him; and when his father saw that case he wondered
with great wonderment. Then the youth took seat afar from his
brothers and addressed them, saying, "Which of the twain was
first to take the necklace?" And they held their peace. He
resumed speech and said to them, "Which of you killed the Lion
and which of you slew the Elephant and which of you embraved
his heart and going into the bower of the august damsel, daughter
to this Sultan, carried off her Bird Philomelet?" But they
answered him never a syllable and were far from offering a reply.
So he resumed, "Wherefore did you fall upon me and beat me
and take away the Enchanting Bird, when I was able to slay you
both? Yet to everything is its own time and this my father had
banished me and banished my mother nor did he give her aught
of what became her." Saying these words the youth fell upon
his two brethren with his sword and striking a single stroke he
slew the twain, after which he would have assaulted his sire, and
put him to death. However the three Kings forbade him and
presently he whose daughter owned the Bird put an end to this by
insisting upon the marriage-tie with him being tied. So he went
in unto her that very night and the three damsels became his
acknowledged spouses. After this his father gave command that
his mother be admitted into the Palace and he honoured her and
banished the parents of his two elder sons for he was assured
that their cadet had done such derring-do by slaying the Lion
and the Elephant and by bringing into the presence Philomelet
the Enchanting Bird and he was certified that the deed had been
done by none other. So he set apart a palace for the young Prince
and his three Princesses and he gave him a commandment and
their joys ever increased. And lastly the three Kings ceased not
abiding in that place for forty days after which they devised their
departure.——And Shahrazad was surprised by the dawn of
day and fell silent and ceased saying her permitted say. Then
quoth her sister Dunyazad, "How sweet and tasteful is thy tale,
O sister mine, and enjoyable and delectable!" Quoth she, "And

where is this compared with that I would relate to you on the coming night an the King suffer me to survive?" Now when it was the next night and that was

The Four Hundred and Thirty-eighth Night,

DUNYAZAD said to her, "Allah upon thee, O my sister, an thou be other than sleepy, finish for us thy tale that we may cut short the watching of this our latter night!" She replied, "With love and good will!" It hath reached me, O auspicious King, the director, the right-guiding, lord of the rede which is benefiting and of deeds fair-seeming and worthy celebrating, that the three Kings desired, one and all of them, to depart and return to their countries and their capitals; and their son-in-law presented them with gifts and rarities, whereupon they blessed him and went their ways. After this the young Prince, who had become Sovran and Sultan, took seat upon the throne of his realm and by the reign he was obeyed and the servants of Allah for him prayed. Presently on a day of the days he inclined to the hunt and the chase, so he went off with his suite till they found themselves in the middle of the wildest of wolds where the ruler came upon an underground cavern. He proposed to enter therein, when his followers prevented him and behold, a man came to him from the desert showing the signs of wayfare and carrying a somewhat of water and victual and his garments were all threadbare. The King enquired of him saying, "Whence hast thou come and whither art thou going?" and the other replied, "We be three in this antre who have fled our country; and whenever we require aught of meat and drink, one of us fareth forth to fetch what will suffice us of provision for ten days." "And what is the cause of your flying your native land?" asked the King, and the other answered, "Verily our tale is wondrous and our adventures are joyous and marvellous." Hereupon quoth the King, "Walláhi, we will not quit this spot till such time as we shall have heard your histories; and let each one of you three recount to us what befel him, so that we hear it from his own mouth." Hereupon the King commanded sundry of his suite to set forth home and the rest to abide beside him; and he sent a Chamberlain of the Chamberlains that he might go bring from the city somewhat of victual and water and wax candles and all the case required, saying the while to himself, "Verily the hearing of histories is better than hunting and birding, for haply they may solace and gladden the hearts of men."[1] So the Chamberlain went forth and, after an absence of an hour or so he returned bringing all the King had commanded; upon which he and the suite brought in the Larrikin[2] together with his two companions until they led them to the presence and seated the three together. All this while none of the vagabonds knew that the personage before them was King of the city. So they fell to conversing until the next night came on when the Sovran bade them tell their tales of themselves and what had befallen each and every of them. They replied, "Hearkening and obedience;" and the foremost of them began to recite the

History of the First Larrikin.

VERILY, O King, my tale is a rare and it is e'en as follows:—I had a mother of whose flocks the World had left her but a single kid, and we owned ne'er another. Presently we determined to sell it; and, having so done, we bought with its price a young calf, which we brought up for a whole year till it grew fat and full-sized. Then my mother said to me, "Take yon calf and go sell it;" so I went forth with it to the Bazar, and I saw that not one was like it, when behold, a body of vagabonds,[3] who numbered some forty, looked at the beast, and it pleased them; so they said one to other, "Let us carry this away and cut its throat and flay it." Then one of them, as all were standing afar off, came near me and said, "O youth, wilt thou sell this kid?" and quoth I, "O my uncle, verily this is a calf and not a kid;" and the other rejoined, "Art thou blind? This is a kid." Cried I, "A calf!" So he asked, "Wilt thou take from me a dollar?"[4] and I answered, "Nay, O my uncle!" Thereupon he went away

---

[1] A sensible remark which shows that the King did not belong to the order called by Mr. Matthew Arnold "Barbarians."

[2] In text: "Rajul Ja'idi," for which see supra p. 9.

[3] Arab. "Fidawiyah," sing. "Fidáwi" = lit. one who gives his life to a noble cause, a forlorn hope, esp. applied to the Ismai'liyah race, disciples of the "Assassin" Hasan-i-Sabáh. See De Sacy, "Mémoire sur les Assassins Mém. de l'Institut," etc. iv. 7 et seqq. Hence perhaps a castaway, a "perdido," one careless of his life. I suspect, however, that it is an Egyptianised form of the Pers. "Fidá'i" = a robber, a murderer. The Lat. catalogue prefers "Sicarius" which here cannot be the meaning.

[4] Arab. "Kirsh," pop. "Girsh."

from me, and another came after him and said, "O youth, wilt
thou sell this kid?" and said I, "This is a calf," and quoth he
"This is a kid," and reviled me the while I held my peace. Again
quoth he, "Wilt thou take for this a dollar?" but I was not
satisfied therewith, and they ceased not to wrangle with me,
one after other, each coming up and saying, "O youth, wilt thou
sell this kid?" At last their Shaykh[1] accosted me and cried,
"Wilt thou sell it?" and I rejoined, "There is no Majesty save in
Allah! I will sell it on one condition, to wit, that I take from
thee its tail." Replied to me[2] the Shaykh of the Vagabonds,
"Thou shalt take the tail when we have slaughtered it;" then,
paying me a dollar, he led off the beast, and returned to his own
folk. Presently they killed it and flayed it, when I took the tail
and hastened back to my mother. She said to me, "Hast thou
sold the calf?" and said I, "Yes, I have sold it, and have taken a
dollar and the calf's tail." "And what wilt thou do for the tail?"
asked she; and I answered, "I will do him brown[3] who took it
from me saying, This is a kid, and I will serve him a sleight which
shall get out of him to its price ten times one hundred."[4] With
these words I arose and, taking the tail, I flayed it and studded it
with nails and bits of glass, and I asked of my mother a maiden's
dress, which she brought me; and presently I covered my face
with a Burka'-veil,[5] and I adorned me and perfumed myself and I
girded my loins underneath my clothes with the tail of that calf.
Then went I forth like a virgin girl till I reached the barrack of
those blackguards, when I found that they had cooked the whole
calf and naught of it remained undressed, and they had prepared
to spread the table and were about sitting down to supper.
Then I went[6] in to them and said, "The Peace be upon you,"

---

[1] I have noticed that there is a Shaykh or head of the Guild, even for thieves, in most
Moslem capitals. See vol. vi. 204.

[2] Here is the normal enallage of persons, "luh" = to him for "li" = to me.

[3] In text "Na'mil ma'allazí, etc. . . . makídah." I have attempted to preserve
the idiom.

[4] [In the MS. "al-'Ashrah Miah," which, I think, can scarcely be translated by "ten
times one hundred." If Miah were dependent on al-'Ashrah, the latter could not have
the article. I propose therefore to render "one hundred for the (i.e. every) ten" = ten-
fold. — ST.]

[5] For this "nosebag," see vols. ii. 52, and vi. 151, 192.

[6] [Until here the change from the first person into the third, as pointed out in note 2, has
been kept up in the MS. — "He reached the barracks," "he found," etc. Now suddenly
the gender changes as well, and the tale continues: "And lo, the girl went to them and
said," etc. etc. This looseness of style may, in the mouth of an Eastern Ráwí, have an

and they rose to me in a body of their joy, and returned my
greetings and said, "By Allah, our night is a white one." So I
entered to them and supped with them, and they all inclined to
me, and their mustachios wagged in token that they would disport with me. But when darkness came on they said, "This
night is for our Shaykh, but after this each one of us shall take
her for his own night."——And Shahrazad was surprised by the
dawn of day, and fell silent and ceased to say her permitted say.
Then quoth her sister Dunyazad, "How sweet is thy story, O
sister mine, and how enjoyable and delectable!" Quoth she,
"And where is this compared with that I should relate to you on
the coming night an the King suffer me to survive?" Now when
it was the next night and that was

The Four Hundred and Forty-first Night,

DUNYAZAD said to her, "Allah upon thee, O my sister, an thou be
other than sleepy, finish for us thy tale that we may cut short the
watching of this our latter night!" She replied, "With love
and good will!" It hath reached me, O auspicious King, the
director, the right-guiding, lord of the rede which is benefiting and
of deeds fair-seeming and worthy celebrating, that the vagabonds
said, "Each one of us shall take her to him for a night after the
Shaykh," and so saying they left me and went their ways. Then
the Chief fell to chatting with me and he was in high spirits,
when suddenly my glance fell upon a rope hanging from the
ceiling of that barrack and I cried, "O Shaykh!" whereto he
replied, "Yes, O my lady and light of mine eyes." Said I to him,
"What may be this cord thus suspended?" and said he, "This is
called 'hanging-gear'; and, when any of ours requireth chastise-
ment from my associates, we hoist him up by this rope and we
bash him." Quoth I, "Hang me up and let me see how 'tis done,"
but quoth he, "Heaven forfend, O my lady! I will hang myself
in thy stead and thou shalt look upon me." Hereat he arose and
tied himself tight and cried, "Haul up this rope and make it fast
in such a place!" I did his bidding and bound it right firmly and
left him hanging in the air. Presently he cried, "Let go the

---

additional dramatic charm for his more eager than critical audience; but it would be
intolerable to European readers. Sir Richard has, therefore, very properly substituted
the first person all through. — ST.]

cord," and replied I, "O Shaykh, first let me enjoy the spectacle."
Then I stripped him of all his clothing and drawing forth the
calf's tail which was studded with nails and glass splinters, I
said to him, "O Shaykh, is this the tail of a kid or of a calf?"
"What woman art thou?" asked he, and I answered, "I am the
owner of the calf;" and then, tucking up my two sleeves to the
elbows, I beat him till I stripped him of his skin and he lost his
senses and he had no breath wherewith to speak. Thereupon I
arose and fell to searching the hall, where I found sundry valuables
amongst which was a box, so I opened it and came upon three
hundred gold pieces and a store of reals[1] and silverlings and
jadids.[2] I laid hands on the whole of it and then bore off somewhat of the most sumptuous dresses; and, having wrapped them
all up in a sheet, I carried them away; and about dawn I went in
to my mother and cried, "Take these to the price of the calf,
which I have received from the purchaser." But when the day
was high and the sun waxed hot the whole troop of the Shaykh
collected and said, "Verily our Elder hath slept till the undurn
hour;" and one of them declared, " 'Tis from enjoying so much
pleasure and luxury, he and the girl; and doubtless their night
hath been a white[3] night." So they ceased not talking together
and each of them had his word until the noon was high, when
certain of them said, "Come with us and let us rouse him from
sleep:" and, saying thus, all went to the door of the hall and
opened it. Hereupon they found their Shaykh hanging up and
his body bleeding profusely;[4] so they asked him, "What hath

---

[1] "Riyál" is from the Span. "Real" = royal (coin): in Egypt it was so named by order of
Ali Bey, the Mameluke, in A.H. 1185 (A.D. 1771–72) and it was worth ninety Faddahs =
5½d. The word, however, is still applied to the dollar proper (Maria Theresa), to the
Riyál Fransá or five-franc piece and to the Span. pillar dollar: the latter is also nicknamed
'Abu Madfa' " Father of a Cannon (the columns being mistaken for cannons); also
the Abú Tákah (Father of a Window), whence we obtain the Europeanised "Pataceo"
(see Lane, Appendix ii.) and "Pataca," which Littré confounds with the "Patard" and of
which he ignores the origin.

[2] See The Nights, vol. x. 12.

[3] i.e. "pleasant," "enjoyable"; see "White as milk" opposed to "black as mud," etc.,
vol. iv. 140. Here it is after a fashion synonymous with the French nuit blanche.

[4] [The MS. seems here to read "wa jasad-hu yuhazdimu," (thus at least the word, would
have to be vocalised if it were a quadriliteral verbal form), and of this I cannot make out
any sense. I suspect the final syllable is meant for "Dam," blood, of which a few lines
lower down the plural "Dimá" occurs. Remains to account for the characters immediately
preceding it. I think that either the upper dot of the Arabic belongs to the first radical
instead of the second, reading "yukhirru," as the fourth or causative form of "kharra
yakhurru," to flow, to ripple, to purl; or that the two dots beneath are to be divided
between the first two characters, reading "bajaza." The latter, it is true, is no dictionary

befallen thee?" and he answered in a weak voice, "Verily that
girl is no girl at all, but she is the youth who owned the calf."
They replied, "By Allah, there is no help but that we seize him
and slay him;" whereto the Elder said, "Loose me and lead me
to the Hammam that I may wash clean my skin of all this blood."
Then they let him down and after mounting him upon a donkey
they bore him to the baths. Hereat I went to the slaughter-
house and covered my body with bullocks' blood and stuck to it
pledgets of cotton so that I became like one sorely diseased and I
repaired to the same Hammam propped upon a staff and required
admittance. They refused me saying, "The Shaykh of the
Vagabonds is now in the baths nor may anyone go in to him."
Quoth I to them, "I am a man with a malady," whereto quoth
one of them, "This is a poor wight, so let him come within."
Accordingly I entered and found the Chief alone, whereupon I
drew forth the tail and asked him, "O Shaykh, is this the tail
of a calf or a kid?" "Who art thou?" said he, and I said, "I am
the owner of the calf;" after which I fell to beating him with
the tail until his breath was clean gone. Then I left him and
went forth from the Hammam by another door so as to avoid his
followers.——And Shahrazad was surprised by the dawn of day
and fell silent and ceased saying her permitted say. Then quoth
her sister Dunyazad, "How sweet and tasteful is thy tale, O
sister mine, and how enjoyable and delectable!" Quoth she,
"And where is this compared with that I should relate to you on
the coming night an the King suffer me to survive?" Now when
it was the next night and that was

The Four Hundred and Forty-second Night,

DUNYAZAD said to her, "Allah upon thee, O my sister, an thou be
other than sleepy, finish for us thy tale that we may cut short the
watching of this our latter night!" She replied, "With love and
good will!" It hath reached me, O auspicious King, the director,
the right-guiding, lord of the rede which is benefiting and of
deeds fair-seeming and worthy celebrating, that the youth, the
owner of the calf, after beating the Shaykh of the Vagabonds

---

word, but we have found supra p. 176, "muhandiz" for "muhandis," so here "bajaza"
may stand for "bajasa" = gushed forth, used intransitively and transitively. In either
case the translation would be "his body was emitting blood freely." — St.]

with a sore bashing within the Bath went forth by the back door. Whereupon (continued the Larrikin) the followers of the Chief went in and they found him at his last breath and moaning from the excess of blows. Quoth they, "What is the matter with thee?" and quoth he, "That man with a malady who came into the Hammam is none other but the owner of the calf and he hath killed me." So they took him up and carried him from the place and he said to them, "Do ye bear me outside the city and set up for me a tent and lay me therein, after which do ye gather round about me and never leave me at all." Hereat they mounted him upon an ass and bore him to the place he described and, pitching a tent, set him therein and all sat around him. Presently the tidings reached me, whereupon I changed my clothes for a disguise and drew near the tent whereabouts I found a Badawi-man feeding his sheep. So I said to him, "O Badawi, take this ducat and draw near yonder tent and call aloud, saying, 'I am the owner of the calf;' after which make off with thy life for an they catch thee they will slay thee." "By Allah," quoth the Arab, "even if they rode their best mares none of them could come up with me!" So I took charge of the sheep while the Badawi approaching the tent cried in his loudest voice, "By Allah, I am the owner of the calf." Hearing this the vagabonds sprang to their feet as one body and drew their weapons and rushed after the Badawi; but, when he had run some distance from the tent with all the men behind him, I went in and drawing from below my clothes the tail of the calf said, "O Shaykh, is this the tail of a calf or a kid?" The Elder asked, "Art thou not he who cried out, I am the owner of the calf?" and I answered, "No, I am not," and came down upon him with the tail and beat him until he could no longer breathe. Then I took the properties belonging to his party and wrapping them in a sheet carried them off and quitting the place I went in to my mother and said to her, "Take them to the worth of the calf." Now those who had run after the Badawi ceased not pursuing him, yet could none of them come up with him and when they were tired they returned from the chase and stinted not walking until they entered the tent. There they found the Shaykh breathless nor could he move save to make signs; so they sprinkled a little water upon his face; and the life returned to him and he said to them, "Verily the owner of the calf came to me and beat me till he killed me and the wight who cried, 'I am the owner of the calf' is an accomplice of his."

Thereupon all waxed furious and the Elder said to them, "Bear me home and give out that your Shakyh is deceased; after which do you bathe my body and carry me to the cemetery and bury me by night and next morning disinter me so that the owner of this calf may hear that I am dead and leave me in peace. Indeed as long as I continue in this condition he will devise for me device after device and some day will come in to me and kill me down-right." They did what their Shaykh bade them and began crying and keening and saying, "Verily our Chief is deceased," so that the report was bruited abroad that the Shaykh of the Vagabonds had died. But I, the owner of the calf, said to myself, "By Allah, an he be dead, they will assuredly make for him some mourning ceremony." Now when they had washed him and shrouded him and carried him out upon the bier, and were proceeding to the graveyard that they might bury him, and had reached half way to it, lo and behold! I joined the funeral train and suddenly walk-ing under the coffin with a sharp packing-needle[1] in hand,——— And Shahrazad was surprised by the dawn of day and fell silent and ceased saying her permitted say. Then quoth her sister Dunyazad, "How sweet is thy story, O sister mine, and how enjoyable and delectable." Quoth she, "And where is this com-

---

[1] The MS. here is hardly intelligible but the sense shows the word to be "Misallah" (plur. "Misáll") = a large needle for sewing canvas, &c. In Egypt the usual pronuncia-tion is "Musallah," hence the vulgar name of Cleopatra's needle "Musallat Far'aun" (of Pharaoh) the two terms contending for which shall be the more absurd. I may note that Commander Gorridge, the distinguished officer of the U. S. Navy who safely and easily carried the "Needle" to New York after the English had made a prodigious mess with their obelisk, showed me upon the freshly uncovered base of the pillar the most dis-tinct intaglio representations of masonic implements, the plumb-line, the square, the compass, and so forth. These, however, I attributed to masonry as the craft, to the guild; he to Freemasonry, which in my belief was unknown to the Greeks and Romans, and is never mentioned in history before the eight Crusades (A.D. 1096–1270). The practices and procedure were evidently borrowed from the various Vehms and secret societies which then influenced the Moslem world, and our modern lodges have strictly preserved in the "Architect of the Universe," Arian and Moslem Unitarianism as opposed to Athanasian and Christian Tritheism; they admit the Jew and the Mussulman as apprentices, but they refuse the Hindú and the Pagan. It seems now the fashion to run down the mystic craft, to describe it as a "goose-club" and no more; it is, however, sleeping, not dead; the charities of the brethren are still active, and the society still takes an active part in politics throughout the East. As the late Pope Pius IX. (fitly nicknamed "Pio no-no"), a free mason himself, forbade Freemasonry to his church because a secret society is incompatible with oral confession (and priestcraft tolerates only its own mysteries), and made excom-munication the penalty, the French lodges have dwindled away and the English have thriven upon their decay, thus enlisting a host of neophytes who, when the struggle shall come on, may lend excellent aid.

pared with that I should relate to you on the coming night an the King suffer me to survive?" Now when it was the next night and that was

The Four Hundred and Forty-third Night,

DUNYAZAD said to her, "Allah upon thee, O my sister, an thou be other than sleepy, finish for us thy tale that we may cut short the watching of this our latter night!" She replied, "With love and good will!" It hath reached me, O auspicious King, the director, the right-guiding, lord of the rede which is benefiting and of deeds fair-seeming and worthy celebrating, that I walked under the bier packing-needle in hand, and thrust it into the Shaykh of the Vagabonds, whereat he cried out and sprang up and sat upright upon his shell.[1] Now when the King heard this tale he laughed and was cheered and the Larrikin resumed:—By Allah, when I thrust the needle into him and he sat upright in his coffin all the folk fell to wondering and cried, "Verily the dead hath come to life." Hereupon, O my lord, my fear waxed great and I said to myself, "All adventures are not like one another: haply the crowd[2] will recognise me and slay me." So I went forth the city and came hither. Cried the King, "Of a truth, this tale is marvellous;" when the second Larrikin ex-claimed, "By Allah, O my lord, my tale is rarer and stranger than this, for indeed therein I did deeds worthy of the Jinn-mad and amongst the many tricks that came from my hand I died and was buried and I devised a device whereby they drew me from my tomb." Quoth the King, "Walláhi, if thy tale be more wondrous than that which forewent it I needs must reward thee with somewhat. But now tell us of what betided thee." So the man began to relate the

History of the Second Larrikin.

I WAS living, O my lord, under the same roof with my father's wife and I had with me some bundles of sesame cobs, but no

---

[1] The "Janázah" or bier, is often made of planks loosely nailed or pegged together into a stretcher or platform, and it would be easy to thrust a skewer between the joints. I may remind the reader that "Janázah" = a bier with a corpse thereon (vol. ii. 46), whereas the "Sarír" is the same when unburdened, and the "Na'ash" is a box like our coffin, but open at the tip.

[2] [In the Arab. text "they will recognise me," which I would rather refer to the Vagabonds

great quantity, which I stored in a little basket hanging up in
the great ceiling-vault of our house. Now one day of the days
a party of merchants, numbering five or so, together with their
head man, came to our village and began asking for sesame; and
they happened to meet me on the road hard by our place, so
they put me the same question. I asked them, "Do you want
much of it?" and they answered, "We require[1] about an hundred
ardabbs."[2] Quoth I, "By me is a large quantity thereof;" and
quoth they, "Have the kindness to show us the muster;"[3] whereto
I rejoined, "Upon the head and the eye!" Hereat I led them
into the room wherein the basket was suspended with a few cobs
of sesame (there being none other) and I went up by an outside
staircase to the top of the vault, which I pierced, and putting
forth my hand, took up a palm-full and therewith returned to
them and showed the specimen. They saw that the sesame was
clean grain, and said one to other, "This house is naught but full
to the vault,[4] for had there been a small quantity there he would
have opened the door and shown us the heaps." Hereupon I conversed with them and settled the price and they paid me as
earnest money for an hundred ardabbs of sesame six hundred
reals. I took the coin and gave it to the wife of my father, saying
to her, "Cook for us a supper that shall be toothsome." Then I
slaughtered for her five chickens and charged her that, after she
should have cooked the supper, she must prepare for us a pot of
Baysárah[5] which must be slab and thick. She did as I bade her
and I returned to the merchants and invited them to sup with us
and night in our house. Now when sunset time came I brought
them in for the evening meal and they supped and were cheered,
and as soon as the hour for night-prayer had passed I spread for

---

than to the crowd, as the latter merely cries wonder at the resuscitation, without apparently troubling much about the wonder-worker. — St.]

[1] [Ar. "na'tázu," viii. form of 'áza = it escaped, was missing, lacked, hence the meaning
of this form, "we are in want of," "we need." — St.]

[2] For the "Ardabb" (prop. "Irdabb") = five bushels: see vol. i. 263.

[3] [In the MS. "'Ayyinah," probably a mis-reading for "'Ayniyyah" = a sample,
pattern. — St.]

[4] In text "Kubbah" = vault, cupola, the dome of unbaked brick upon peasants' houses
in parts of Egypt and Syria, where wood for the "Sat'h" or flat roof is scarce. The household granary is in the garret, from which the base of the dome springs, and the "expense-
magazines" consist of huge standing coffers of wattle and dab propped against the outside
walls of the house.

[5] Gen. "Baysár" or "Faysár," = beans cooked in honey and milk. See retro, Night
ccclxxxviii., for its laxative properties.

them sleeping-gear and said to them, "O our guests, be careful of yourselves lest the wind come forth from your bellies, for with me dwelleth the wife of my father, who disgusteth fizzles and who dieth if she hear a fart." After this they slept soundly from the stress of their fatigue and were overwhelmed with slumber; but when it was midnight, I took the pot of Baysarah and approached them as they still slumbered and I besmeared[1] their backsides with the Baysarah and returned and slept until dawn of day in my own stead hard beside them. At this time all five were awake, and as each one arose before his companions he sensed a somewhat soft below him and putting forth his hand felt his bum bewrayed[2] with the stuff, and said to his neighbour, "Ho, such an one, I have skited!" and the other said, "I also have conskited myself;" and then all said together, "We have skited." But when I heard this, O my lord, I arose forthwith and cried out saying, "Haste ye to my help, O ye folk, for these guests have killed my father's wife."——And Shahrazad was surprised by the dawn of day and fell silent and ceased saying her permitted say. Then quoth her sister Dunyazad, "How sweet and tasteful is thy tale, O sister mine, and how enjoyable and delectable!" Quoth she, "And where is this compared with that I should relate to you on the coming night an the King suffer me to survive?" Now when it was the next night and that was

The Four Hundred and Forty-fifth Night,

DUNYAZAD said to her, "Allah upon thee, O my sister, an thou be other than sleepy, finish for us thy tale, that we may cut short the watching of this our latter night!" She replied, "With love and good will!" It hath reached me, O auspicious King, the director, the right-guiding, lord of the rede which is benefiting and of deeds fair-seeming and worthy celebrating, that quoth the second Larrikin to the King:—O my lord, I cried out saying,

---

[1] [In the MS. "barbastu," with the dental instead of the palatal sibilant (Sín instead of Sád). Spelled in the former way the verb "barbasa" means, he sought, looked for, and is therefore out of place here. Spelled in the second manner, it signifies literally, he watered the ground abundantly. Presently we shall find the passive participle "mubarbasah" in the feminine, because referring to the noun "Tíz" = anus, which, like its synonym "Ist," professes the female gender. — ST.]

[2] [In Ar. "Mubarbasah," for which see the preceding note. — ST.]

"The guests have slain the wife of my father." But when they heard me the merchants arose and ran away, each following other, so I rushed after them, shouting aloud, "Ye have killed my father's wife," till such time as they had disappeared from sight. Then said I to myself, "Inshallah! they will never more come back." But after they had disappeared for a whole year they returned and demanded their coin, to wit, six hundred reals; and I, when the tidings reached me, feigned myself dead and ordered my father's wife to bury me in the cemetery and I took to my grave a portion of charcoal and a branding-iron. Now when the five merchants came and asked after me the folk said, "He hath deceased and they have graved him in his grave;" whereupon the creditors cried, "By Allah, there is no help but that we go and piss upon his fosse." Now I had made a crevice in the tomb[1] and I had lighted the charcoal and I had placed the branding-iron ready till it became red hot and, when they came to piddle upon my grave, I took the iron and branded their hinder cheeks with sore branding, and this I did to one and all till the five had suffered in the flesh. Presently they departed to their own country, when my father's wife came and opened the tomb and drew me forth and we returned together to our home. After a time, however, the news reached these merchants in their towns that I was living and hearty, so they came once more to our village and demanded of the Governor that I be given up to them. So the rulers sent for and summoned me, but when the creditors made a claim upon me for six hundred reals, I said to the Governor, "O my lord, verily these five fellows were slaves to my sire in bygone-times." Quoth the ruler, "Were ye then in sooth chattels to his sire?" and said they to me, "Thou liest!" Upon this I rejoined, "Bare their bodies; and, if thou find a mark thereupon, they be my father's serviles, and if thou find no sign then are my words false." So they examined them and they found upon the rumps of the five, marks of the branding-iron, and the Governor said, "By Allah, in good sooth he hath told the truth and you five are

---

[1] The Moslem's tomb is an arched vault of plastered brick, large enough for a man to sit up at ease and answer the Questioning Angels; and the earth must not touch the corpse as it is supposed to cause torture. In the graves of the poorer classes a niche (*lahad*) offsets from the fosse and is rudely roofed with palm-fronds and thatch. The trick played in the text is therefore easy; see Lane's illustration M.E. chapt. xviii. The reader will not forget that all Moslems make water squatting upon their hunkers in a position hardly possible to an untrained European: see vol. i. 259.

the chattels of his father." Hereupon began dispute and debate
between us, nor could they contrive aught to escape from me
until they paid me three hundred reals in addition to what I had
before of them. When the Sultan heard these words from the
Larrikin he fell to wondering and laughing at what the wight had
done and he said, "By Allah, verily thy deed is the deed of a
vagabond who is a past-master in fraud." Then the third Larrikin
spoke and said, "By Allah, in good sooth my story is more marvellous and wondrous than the tales of this twain, for that none
(methinketh) save I could have done aught of the kind." The
King asked him, "And what may be thy story?" so he began
to relate

The History of the Third Larrikin.

O MY LORD, I was once an owner of herds whereof naught remained to me but a single bull well advanced in years and un-
healthy of flesh and of hide; and when I sought to sell him to the
butchers none was willing to buy him of me, nor even to accept
him as a gift. So I was disgusted with the beast and with the
idea of eating him; and, as he could not be used either to grind[1]
or to plough, I led him into a great courtyard, where I slaughtered
him and stripped off his hide. Then I cut the flesh into bittocks
——And Shahrazad was surprised by the dawn of day and fell
silent and ceased to say her permitted say. Then quoth her
sister Dunyazad, "How sweet is thy story, O sister mine, and
how enjoyable and delectable!" Quoth she, "And where is this
compared with that I should relate to you on the coming night
an the King suffer me to survive?" Now when it was the next
night and that was

The Four Hundred and Forty-seventh Night,

DUNYAZAD said to her, "Allah upon thee, O my sister, an thou be
other than sleepy, finish for us thy tale that we may cut short the
watching of this our latter night!" She replied, "With love and
good will!" It hath reached me, O auspicious King, the director,
the right-guiding, lord of the rede which is benefiting and of
deeds fair-seeming and worthy celebrating, that the whilome
owner of the bull said to the King: — O my lord, I cut his flesh

---

[1] The bull being used in the East to turn the mill and the water-wheel; vol. i. 16.

into bittocks and went forth and cried aloud upon the dogs of the quarter, when they all gathered together nor did one remain behind. Then I caused them to enter the court and having bolted the door gave to each dog a bit of the meat weighing half a pound.[1] So all ate and were filled, after which I shut them up in the house which was large, for a space of three days when, behold, the folk came seeking their tykes and crying, "Whither can the curs have gone?" So I related how I had locked them up within the house and hereupon each man who had a hound came and took it away. Then quoth I, "Thy dog hath eaten a full pound of flesh," and I took from each owner six faddahs and let him have his beast until I had recovered for the meat of that bull a sum of two thousand faddahs.[2] At last of these dogs there remained to me but one unclaimed and he had only a single eye and no owner. So I took up a staff and beat him and he ran away and I ran after him to catch him until he came upon a house with the door open and rushed within. Now by the decree of the Decreer it so happened that the mistress of the house had a man living with her who was one-eyed and I ran in and said to her, "Bring out the one-eyed that is with thee," meaning the dog. But when the house mistress heard me say, "Bring out the one-eyed," she fancied that I spoke of her mate, so knowing naught about the matter of the tyke she came up to me and cried, "Allah upon thee, O my lord, do thou veil what Allah hath veiled and rend not our reputation and deal not disgrace to us;"[3] presently adding, "Take this bangle from me and betray us not." So I took it and left her and went my ways, after which she returned to the house and her heart was heaving and she found that her man had been in like case ever since he heard me say, "Bring out the one-eyed." So I went away carrying off the bracelet and fared homeward. But when she looked about the room, lo and behold! she espied the one-eyed dog lying in a corner and, as soon as she caught sight of him, she was certified that I had alluded to the beast. So she buffeted her face and regretted the loss of her bangle and following me she came up and said to me, "O my lord, I have found the one-eyed dog, so do thou return with me and

---

[1] In text "Ratl." See vol. iv. 124.   [2] About 1s. 2d.

[3] The man was therefore in hiding for some crime. [The MS. has "lá tafzah-ní" = Do not rend *my* reputation, etc. I would, therefore, translate "Sáhib-há" by "her lover," and suggest that the crime in question is simply what the French call "conversation criminelle." — ST.]

take him;" whereat I had pity upon the woman and restored to her the ornament. However, when this had befallen me, fear possessed my heart lest she denounce me, and I went away from my village and came to this place where the three of us forgathered and have lived ever since. When the King had given ear to this story he was cheered and said, "By Allah, verily the adventures of you three are wondrous, but my desire of you is to know if any of you have heard aught of the histories of bygone Sultans; and, if so, let him relate them to me. First, however, I must take you into the city that you may enjoy your rest." "O my lord," quoth they, "who art thou of the citizens?" and quoth he, "I am the King of this country, and the cause of my coming hither was my design to hunt and chase and the finding you here hath diverted me therefrom." But when they heard his words, they forthwith rose to their feet and did him obeisance saying, "Hearing and obeying," after which the three repaired with him to the city. Here the King commanded that they set apart for them an apartment and appointed to them rations of meat and drink and invested them with robes of honour; and they remained in company one with other till a certain night of the nights when the Sultan summoned them and they made act of presence between his hands and the season was after the King had prayed the Ishá[1] prayers. So he said to them, "I require that each and every of you who knoweth an history of the Kings of yore shall relate it to me," whereat said one of the four, "I have by me such a tale." Quoth the King, "Then tell it to us;" when the first Larrikin began to relate the

Story of a Sultan of Al-Hind and his Son Mohammed.[2]

THERE was in days of yore a King in the land of Al-Hind, who reigned over wide dominions (and praise be to Him who ruleth

---

[1] The " 'Ishá"-prayer (called in Egypt " 'Eshè") consists of ten "Ruka'át" = bows or inclinations of the body (not "of the head" as Lane has it, M. E. chapt. iii.): of these four are "Sunnah" = traditional or customary (of the Prophet), four are Farz (divinely appointed *i.e.* by the Koran) and two again Sunnah. The hour is nightfall when the evening has closed in with some minor distinctions, *e.g.* the Hanafi waits till the whiteness and the red gleam in the west ("Al-Shafak al-ahmar") have wholly disappeared, and the other three orthodox only till the ruddy light has waned. The object of avoiding sundown-tide (and sunrise equally) was to distinguish these hours of orisons from those of the Guebres and other faiths which venerate, or are supposed to venerate, the sun.

[2] Scott. "History of the Sultan of Hind," vol. vi. 194–209.

the worlds material and spiritual!), but this Sultan had nor daughter nor son. So once upon a time he took thought and said, "Glory to Thee! no god is there save Thyself, O Lord; withal Thou hast not vouchsafed to me a child either boy or girl." On the next day he arose a-morn wholly clad in clothes of crimson hue,[1]——And Shahrazad was surprised by the dawn of day and fell silent and ceased saying her permitted say. Then quoth her sister Dunyazad, "How sweet and tasteful is thy tale, O sister mine, and how enjoyable and delectable!" Quoth she, "And where is this compared with that I should relate to you on the coming night an the King suffer me to survive?" Now when it was the next night and that was

The Four Hundred and Forty-ninth Night,

DUNYAZAD said to her, "Allah upon thee, O my sister, an thou be. other than sleepy, finish for us thy tale that we may cut short the watching of this our latter night!" She replied, "With love and good will!" It hath reached me, O auspicious King, the director, the right-guiding, lord of the rede which is benefiting and of deeds fair-seeming and worthy celebrating, that the King of Al-Hind arose a-morn wholly clad in clothes of crimson hue, and the Wazir, coming into the Divan, found him in such case. So he salam'd to him and blessed him with the blessing due to Caliphs, and said to him, "O King of the Age, doth aught irk thee that thou art robed in red?" whereto he replied, "O Wazir, I have risen with my heart gript hard." Said the other, "Go into thy treasury of moneys and jewels and turn over thy precious ores, that thy sorrow be dispersed." But said the Sultan, "O Wazir, verily all this world is a transitory, and naught remaineth to any save to seek the face of Allah the Beneficent: withal the like of me may never more escape from cark and care, seeing that I have lived for this length of time and that I have not been blessed with or son or daughter, for verily children are the ornament of the world." Hereupon a wight dark of hue, which was a Takrúri[2] by birth, suddenly appeared before the Sultan and standing

---

[1] Red robes being a sign of displeasure: see vol. iv. 72; Scott (p. 294) wrongly makes them "robes of mourning."

[2] A Moslem negroid from Central and Western North Africa. See vol. ii. 15. They share in popular opinion the reputation of the Maghrabi or Maroccan for magical powers.

between his hands said to him, "O King of the Age, I have by me certain medicinal roots the bequeathal of my forbears and I have heard that thou hast no issue; so an thou eat somewhat thereof haply shall they gladden thy heart." "Where be these simples?" cried the King, whereat the Takruri man drew forth a bag and brought out from it somewhat that resembled a confection and gave it to him with due injunctions. So when it was night-time the Sultan ate somewhat of it and then slept with his wife who, by the Omnipotence of Allah Almighty, conceived of him that very time. Finding her pregnant the King was rejoiced thereat and fell to distributing alms to the Fakirs and the mesquin and the widows and the orphans, and this continued till the days of his Queen's pregnancy were completed. Then she bare a man-child fair of face and form, which event caused the King perfect joy and complete; and on that day when the boy was named Mohammed, Son of the Sultan,[1] he scattered full half his treasury amongst the lieges. Then he bade bring for the babe wet-nurses who suckled him until milktime ended, when they weaned him, after which he grew every day in strength and stature till his age reached his sixth year. Hereupon his father appointed for him a Divine to teach him reading and writing and the Koran and all the sciences, which he mastered when his years numbered twelve. And after this he took to mounting horses and learning to shoot with shafts and to hit the mark, up to the time when he became a knight who surpassed all other knights. Now one day of the days Prince Mohammed rode off a-hunting, as was his wont, when lo and behold! he beheld a fowl with green plumage wheeling around him in circles and rocketing in the air and seeing this he was desirous to bring it down with an arrow. But he found this impossible so he ceased not following the quarry with intent to catch it but again he failed and it flew away from his ken; whereat he was sore vexed and he said to himself, "Needs must I seize this bird," and he kept swerving to the right and the left in order to catch sight of it but he saw it not. This endured until the end of day when he returned to the city and sought his father and his mother, and when they looked upon him they found his case changed and they asked him concerning his condition, so he related to them all about the bird and they said to him, "O our son,

---

[1] This is introduced by the translator; as usual with such unedited tales, the name does not occur till much after the proper place for specifying it.

O Mohammed, verily the creations of Allah be curious and how many fowls are like unto this, nay even more wondrous." Cried he, "Unless I catch her[1] I will wholly give up eating." Now when morning dawned he mounted according to his custom and again went forth to the chase; and presently he pushed into the middle of the desert when suddenly he saw the bird flying in air and he pushed his horse to speed beneath her and shot at her a shaft with the intent to make her his prey, but again was unable to kill the bird. He persisted in the chase from sunrise until sundown when he was tired and his horse was aweary, so he turned him round purposing a return city-wards, when behold, he was met in the middle of the road by an elderly man who said to him, "O son of the Sultan, in very sooth thou art fatigued and on like wise is thy steed." The Prince replied, "Yes," and the Elder asked him, "What is the cause thereof?" Accordingly he told him all anent the bird and the Shaykh replied to him, "O my son, an thou absent thyself and ride for a whole year in pursuit of yonder fowl thou wilt never be able to take her; and, O my child, where is this bird![2] I will now inform thee that in a City of the Islands hight of Camphor there is a garden wide of sides wherein are many of such fowls and far fairer than this, and of them some can sing and others can speak with human speech; but, O my son, thou art unable to reach that city. However, if thou leave this bird and seek another of the same kind, haply I can show thee one and thou wilt not weary thyself any more." When Mohammed, Son of the Sultan, heard these words from the Elder he cried, "By Allah, 'tis not possible but that I travel to that city." Hereupon he left the Shaykh and returned to his own home, but his heart was engrossed with the Capital of the Camphor Islands, and when he went in to his sire, his case was troubled. The father asked him thereof and he related to him what the oldster had said. "O my son," quoth the sire, "cast out this accident from thy heart and weary not thy soul, inasmuch as whoso would seek an object he cannot obtain, shall destroy his own life for the sake thereof and furthermore he shall fail of his gain. Better therefore thou set thy heart at rest[3] and weary thyself no more." Quoth the Son, "Walláhi, O my sire, verily

---

[1] In text "Iz lam naakhaz-há, wa-illá," &c. A fair specimen of Arab. ellipsis. —— If I catch her not ('twill go hard with me), and unless (I catch her) I will, &c.

[2] *i.e.* "How far is the fowl from thee!"

[3] [In the MS. "turayyih," a modern form for "turawwih." — St.]

my heart is hung to yonder fowl and specially to the words of the Elder; nor is it possible to me to sit at home until I shall have reached the city of the Camphor Islands and I shall have gazed upon the gardens wherein such fowls do wone." Quoth his father, "But why, O my child, wouldst thou deprive us of look-ing upon thee?" And quoth the son, "There is no help but that I travel."——And Shahrazad was surprised by the dawn of day and fell silent and ceased to say her permitted say. Then quoth her sister Dunyazad, "How sweet is thy story, O sister mine, and how enjoyable and delectable!" Quoth she, "And where is this compared with that I should relate to you on the coming night an the King suffer me to survive?" Now when it was the next night and that was

The Four Hundred and Fifty-second Night.

Dunyazad said to her, "Allah upon thee, O my sister, an thou be other than sleepy, finish for us thy tale that we may cut short the watching of this our latter night!" She replied, "With love and good will!" It hath reached me, O auspicious King, the director, the right-guiding, lord of the rede which is benefiting and of deeds fair-seeming and worthy celebrating, that Mohammed the Son of the Sultan cried, "Needs must I travel, otherwise I will slay myself." "There is no Majesty and there is no Might," quoth the father, "save in Allah the Glorious, the Great; and saith the old saw, 'The chick is unsatisfied till the crow see it and carry it off.' "[1] Thereupon the King gave orders to get ready provisions and other matters required for the Prince's wayfare, and he sent with him an escort of friends and servants, after which the youth took leave of his father and mother and he with his many set forth seeking the Capital of the Camphor Islands. He ceased not travelling for the space of an entire month till he arrived at a place wherein three highways forked, and he saw at the junction a huge rock whereon were written three lines. Now the first read, "This is the road of safe chance," and the second,

---

[1] [The above translation pre-supposes the reading "Farkhah lá atammat," and would require, I believe, the conjunction "hattà" or "ilà an" to express "till." I read with the MS. "lá tammat," and would translate: "a chick not yet full grown, when the crow seized it and flew away with it," as a complaint of the father for the anticipated untimely end of his son. — St.]

"This is the way of repentance;" and the third, "This is the path whereon whoso paceth shall return nevermore." When the Prince perused these inscriptions he said to himself, "I will tread the path whereon whoso paceth shall nevermore return." Then he put his trust in Allah, and he travelled over that way for a space of days a score, when suddenly he came upon a city deserted and desolate, nor was there a single created thing therein and it was utterly in ruins. So he alighted beside it and, as a flock of sheep accompanied his suite, he bade slaughter five lambs and commanded the cooks to prepare of them delicate dishes and to roast one of them whole and entire. They did his bidding, and when the meats were cooked he ordered the trays be spread in that site and, as soon as all was done to his satisfaction, he purposed sitting down to food, he and his host, when suddenly an 'Aun[1] appeared coming from the ruined city. But when Prince Mohammed beheld him he rose to him in honour saying, "Welcome and fair welcome to him who of 'Auns is the head, and to the brethren friend true-bred,[2] and the Haunter of this stead;" and he satisfied him with the eloquence of his tongue and the elegance of his speech. Now this 'Aun had hair that overhung either eye and fell upon his shoulders, so the Prince brought out his scissors[3] and trimmed his locks clearing them away from his face, and he pared his nails which were like talons, and finally let bathe his body with warm water. Then he served up to him the barbecue of lamb which he caused to be roasted whole for the use of the Jinni and bade place it upon the tray, so the Haunter

---

[1] For " 'Aun," a high degree amongst the "Genies," see vol. iv. p. 83. Readers will be pleased with this description of a Jinni; and not a few will regret that they have not one at command. Yet the history of man's locomotion compels us to believe that we are progressing towards the time when humanity will become volatile. Pre-historic Adam was condemned to "Shanks his mare," or to "go on footback," as the Boers have it, and his earliest step was the chariot; for, curious to say, driving amongst most peoples preceded riding, as the row-boat forewent the sailer. But as men increased and the world became smaller and time shorter the eighteenth and the nineteenth centuries, after many abortive attempts, converted the chariot into a railway-car and the sailer into a steamer. Aerostatics are still in their infancy and will grow but little until human society shall find some form of flying an absolute necessity when, as is the history of all inventions, the winged woman (and her man) of Peter Wilkins will pass from fiction into fact. But long generations must come and go before "homo sapiens" can expect to perfect a practice which in the present state of mundane society would be fatal to all welfare.

[2] Scott (p. 200) "Welcome to the sovereign of the Aoon, friendly to his brethren," (sidlik al Akhwán) etc. Elsewhere he speaks of "the Oone."

[3] So he carried a portable "toilette," like a certain Crown Prince and Prince Bahman in Suppl.vol. iii. 329.

ate with the travellers and was cheered by the Prince's kindness and said to him, "By Allah, O my lord Mohammed, O thou Son of the Sultan, I was predestined to meet thee in this place but now let me know what may be thy need." Accordingly the youth informed him of the city of the Camphor Islands and of the garden containing the fowls which he fared to seek, and of his design in wayfaring thither to bring some of them away with him. But when the 'Aun heard from him these words, he said to him, "O thou Son of the Sultan, that site is a far cry for thee, nor canst thou ever arrive thereat unless assisted, seeing that its distance from this place be a march of two hundred years for a diligent traveller. How then canst thou reach it and return from it? However, the old saw saith, O my son, 'Good for good and the beginner is worthier, and ill for ill and the beginner is unworthier.'[1] Now thou hast done to me a kindly deed and I (Inshallah!) will requite thee with its match and will reward thee with its mate; but let whatso is with thee of companions and slaves and beasts and provisions abide in this site and we will go together, I and thou, and I will win for thee thy wish even as thou hast wrought by me a kindly work." Hereupon the Prince left all that was with him in that place and the 'Aun said to him, "O son of the Sultan, come mount upon my shoulders." The youth did accordingly, after he had filled his ears with cotton, and the 'Aun rose from earth and towered in air and after the space of an hour he descended again and the rider found himself in the grounds about the capital of the Camphor Islands. So he dismounted from the Jinni's shoulders and looked about that wady where he espied pleasant spots and he descried trees and blooms and rills and birds that trilled and shrilled with various notes. Then quoth the 'Aun to him, "Go forth to yonder garden and thence bring thy need;" so he walked thither and, finding the gates wide open, he passed in and fell to solacing himself with looking to the right and the left. Presently he saw bird-cages suspended and in them were fowls of every kind, to each two, so

---

[1] There is another form of the saw in verse.—

　　Good is good and he's best whoso worketh it first;　*　And ill is for me of provisions the worst.

The provision is = viaticum, provaunt for the way.

[The MS. has "akram" and "azlam" = "the more generous," "the more iniquitous," meaning that while good should be requited by good, and evil provokes further evil in retaliation, the beginner in either case deserves the greater praise or blame. — Sr.]

he walked up to them and whenever he noted a bird that pleased
him he took it and caged it till he had there six fowls and of all
sorts twain. Then he designed to leave the garden when suddenly a keeper met him face to face at the door crying aloud, "A
thief! a thief!" Hereat all the other gardeners rushed up and
seized him, together with the cage, and carried him before the
King, the owner of that garden and lord of that city. They set
him in the presence saying, "Verily we found this young man
stealing a cage wherein be fowls and in good sooth he must be a
thief." Quoth the Sultan, "Who misled thee, O Youth, to enter
my grounds and trespass thereon and take of my birds?" Whereto the Prince returned no reply. So the Sultan resumed, "By
Allah, thou hast wilfully wasted thy life, but, O Youngster, an
it be thy desire to take my birds and carry them away, do thou go
and bring me from the capital of the Isles of the Súdán[1] bunches of
grapes which are clusters of diamonds and emeralds, when I will
give thee over and above these six fowls six other beside." So
the Prince left him and going to the 'Aun informed him of what
had befallen him, and the other cried, " 'Tis easy, O Mohammed;" and mounting him upon his shoulders flew with him for
the space of two hours and presently alighted. The youth saw
himself in the lands surrounding the capital of the Sudan Islands
which he found more beautiful than the fair region he had left;
and he designed forthright to approach the garden containing
great clusters of diamonds and emeralds, when he was confronted
by a Lion in the middle way. Now it was the wont of this beast
yearly to visit that city and to pounce upon everything he met of
women as well as of men; so seeing the Prince he charged down
upon him, designing to rend him limb from limb——And Shahrazad was surprised by the dawn of day and fell silent and ceased
saying her permitted say. Then quoth her sister Dunyazad,
"How sweet and tasteful is thy tale, O sister mine, and how enjoyable and delectable!" Quoth she, "And where is this com-

---

[1] I have noted (vols. iii. 75, and viii. 266) that there are two "Soudans" as we write
the word, one Eastern upon the Upper Nile Valley and the other Western and drained
by the Niger water-shed. The former is here meant. It is or should be a word of shame
to English ears after the ungodly murder and massacre of the gallant "Soudanese" negroids
who had ever been most friendly to us and whom with scant reason to boast we attacked
and destroyed because they aspired to become free from Turkish task-masters and Egyptian tax-gatherers. That such horrors were perpetrated by order of one of the most humane
amongst our statesmen proves and decidedly proves one thing, an intense ignorance of
geography and ethnology.

pared with that I should relate to you on the coming night an the
King suffer me to survive?" Now when it was the next night,
and that was

The Four Hundred and Fifty-fifth Night,

Dunyazad said to her, "Allah upon thee, O my sister, an thou be
other than sleepy, finish for us thy tale, that we may cut short the
watching of this our latter night!" She replied, "With love and
good will!" It hath reached me, O auspicious King, the director,
the right-guiding, lord of the rede which is benefiting and of deeds
fair-seeming and worthy celebrating, that the Lion charged down
upon Mohammed, Son of the Sultan, designing to rend him in
pieces, but he confronted him and unsheathing his scymitar
made it glitter in the sunshine[1] and pressed him close and bashed
him with brand between his eyes so that the blade came forth
gleaming from between his thighs. Now by doom of Destiny the
daughter of the Sultan was sitting at the latticed window of her
belvedere and was looking at her glass and solacing herself, when
her glance fell upon the King's son as he was smiting the Lion.
So she said to herself, "May thy hand never palsied grow nor
exult over thee any foe!" But the Prince after slaying the Lion
left the body and walked into the garden whose door had been
left open and therein he found that all the trees were of precious
metal bearing clusters like grapes of diamonds and emeralds. So
he went forwards and plucked from those trees six bunches which
he placed within a cage, when suddenly he was met by the keeper
who cried out, "A thief! a thief!" and when joined by the other
gardeners seized him and bore him before the Sultan saying, "O
my lord, I have come upon this youth who was red-handed in
robbing yonder clusters." The King would have slain him forthright, but suddenly there came to him a gathering of the folk
who cried, "O King of the Age, a gift of good news!"[2] Quoth
he, "Wherefore?" and quoth they, "Verily the Lion which was
wont hither to come every year and to pounce upon all that met

---

[1] [In the MS. "lawá 'a-hu" for which Sir Richard conjectures the reading "lawwaha-
hu" taking the pronoun to refer to the sword. I believe, however, the word to be a clerical
error for our old acquaintance "láwa'a-hu" (see supra p. 203) and, referring the pronoun in
the three verbs to the Lion, would translate: "and he worried him," etc.— St.]

[2] Arab. "Al-bashárah," see vol. i. 30; Scott has (vi. 204) "Good tidings to our sovereign."

him of men and of women and of maidens and of children, we
have found him in such a place clean slain and split into twain."
Now the Sultan's daughter was standing by the lattice of the
belvedere which was hard by the Divan of her sire and was
looking at the youth who stood before the King and was awaiting
to see how it would fare with him. But when the folk came in
and reported the death of the Lion, the Sultan threw aside the
affair of the youth of his joy and delight and fell to asking, "Who
was it slew the beast?" and to saying, "Walláhi! By the rights
of my forbears in this kingdom,[1] let him who killed the monster
come before me and ask of me a boon which it shall be given to
him; nay, even if he demand of me a division of all my good he
shall receive that same." But when he had heard of all present
that the tidings were true then the city-folk followed one another
in a line and went in to the Sultan and one of them said, "I have
slain the Lion." Said the King, "And how hast thou slain him; and
in what manner hast thou been able to prevail over and master
him?" Then he spake with him softly[2] and proved him and at
last so frightened him that the man fell to the ground in his con-
sternation; when they carried him off and the King declared,
"This wight lieth!" All this and Mohammed, the Son of the
Sultan, was still standing and looking on and when he heard the
man's claim he smiled. Suddenly the King happening to glance
at him saw the smile and was astounded and said in his mind,
"By Allah, this Youth is a wondrous for he smileth he being in
such case as this." But behold, the King's daughter sent an
eunuch to her father and he delivered the message, when the
King arose and went into his Harem and asked her, "What is in
thy mind and what is it thou seekest?" She answered, "Is it thy
desire to know who slew the Lion that thou mayest largesse
him?" and he rejoined, saying, "By virtue of Him who created

---

[1] [The MS. is here rather indistinct; still, as far as I can make out, it runs: "wa Hakki
man auláni házá 'l-Mulk" ═ and by the right of (i.e. my duty towards) Him who made me
ruler over this kingdom. — St.]

[2] [The word in the MS. is difficult to decipher. In a later passage we find corresponding
with it the expression "yumázasa-hu fí 'l-Kalám," which is evidently a clerical error for
"yumárasa-hu" ═ he tested or tried him in his speech. Accordingly I would read here:
"yakhburu ma'ahu fí 'l-Kalám," lit. ═ he experimented with him, i.e. put him to his test.
The idea seems to be, that he first cross-examined him and then tried to intimidate him.
With this explanation "yusáhí-hu" and later on "yulhí-hu" would tally, which both have
about the same meaning: to divert the attention, to make forget one thing over another,
hence to confuse and lead one to contradict himself. — St.]

His servants and computeth their numbers,[1] when I know him and am certified of his truth my first gift to him shall be to wed thee with him and he shall become to me son-in-law were he in the farthest of lands." Retorted she, "By Allah, O my father, none slew the Lion save the young man who entered the garden and carried off the clusters of gems, the youth whom thou art minded to slay." When he heard these words from his daughter, the King returned to the Divan and bade summon Mohammed the Son of the Sultan, and when they set him between his hands he said to him, "O Youth, thou hast indemnity from me and say me, art thou he who slew the Lion?" The other answered, "O King, I am indeed young in years; how then shall I prevail over a Lion and slaughter him, when, by Allah, in all my born days I never met even with a hyena much less than a lion? However, O King of the Age, an thou largesse me with these clusters of gems and give them to me in free gift, I will wend my ways, and if not my luck will be with Allah!" Rejoined the King, "O Youth, speak thou sooth and fear not!" Here he fell to soothing him with words and solacing him and gentling him, after which he threatened him with his hand, but Mohammed the Son of the Sultan raised his neave swiftlier than the lightning and smote the King and caused him swoon. Now there was none present in the Divan save Mohammed and the Monarch, who after an hour came to himself and said, "By Allah, thou art he who slew the Lion!" Hereupon he robed him with a robe of honour and, summoning the Kazi, bade tie the marriage-tie with his daughter; but quoth the young man, "O King of the Age, I have a counsel to consult, after which I will return to thee." Quoth the King, "Right rede is this same and a matter not to blame." Accordingly the Prince repaired to the 'Aun in the place where he had left him and related to him all that had betided himself, and of his intended marriage with the King's daughter, whereupon said the Jinni, "Condition with him that if thou take her to wife thou shalt carry her along with thee to thine own country." The youth did his bidding and returned to the King who said, "There is no harm in that," and the marriage-knot was duly knotted. Then the bridegroom was led in procession to his bride with

---

[1] Here we find the old superstitious idea that no census or "numbering of the people" should take place save by direct command of the Creator. Compare the pestilence which arose in the latter days of David when Joab by command of the King undertook the work (2 Sam. xxiv. 1–9, etc.).

whom he remained a full month of thirty days, after which he
craved leave to fare for his own motherland.——And Shahrazad
was surprised by the dawn of day and fell silent and ceased to say
her permitted say. Then quoth her sister Dunyazad, "How sweet
is thy story, O sister mine, and how enjoyable and delectable!"
Quoth she, "And where is this compared with that I should
relate to you on the coming night an the King suffer me to survive?" Now when it was the next night and that was

The Four Hundred and Fifty-seventh Night,

DUNYAZAD said to her, "Allah upon thee, O my sister, an thou
be other than sleepy, finish for us thy tale that we may cut short
the watching of this our latter night!" She replied, "With love
and good will!" It hath reached me, O auspicious King, the
director, the right-guiding, lord of the rede which is benefiting
and of deeds fair-seeming and worthy celebrating, that Mohammed Son of the Sultan craved leave to return to his own motherland, when his father-in-law gave him an hundred clusters of the
diamantine and smaragdine grapes, after which he farewelled the
King and taking his bride fared without the city. Here he found
expecting him the 'Aun, who, after causing them to fill their ears
with cotton, shouldered him, together with his wife, and then
flew with them through the firmament for two hours or so and
alighted with them near the capital of the Camphor Islands.
Presently Mohammed the Son of the Sultan took four clusters of
the emeralds and diamonds, and going in to the King laid them
before him and drew him back. The Sultan gazed upon them and
marvelled and cried, "Wallàhi! doubtless this youth be a Magician for that he hath covered a space of three hundred years in
three[1] of coming and going, and this is amongst the greatest of
marvels." Presently he resumed, saying, "O Youth, hast thou
reached the city of the Sudan?" and the other replied, "I have."
The King continued, "What is its description and its foundation
and how are its gardens and its rills?" So he informed him of all
things required of him and the Sultan cried, "By Allah, O Youth,
thou deservest all thou askest of me." "I ask for nothing," said
the Prince, "save the birds," and the King, "O Youth, there is

---

[1] The text has "Salásín" = thirty, evidently a clerical error.

with us in our town a Vulture which cometh every year from
behind Mount Káf and pounceth upon the sons of this city and
beareth them away and eateth them on the heads of the hills.
Now an thou canst master this monster-fowl and slay that same
I have a daughter whom I will marry to thee." Quoth the
Prince, "I have need of taking counsel;" and returned to the
'Aun to inform him thereof when behold, the Vulture made its
appearance. But as soon as the Jinni espied it, he flew and made
for it, and caught it up; then, smiting it with a single stroke of his
hand, he cut it in two and presently he returned and settled down
upon the ground. Then, after a while, he went back to Mohammed, the Son of the Sultan, and said to him, "Hie thee to the
King and report to him the slaughter of the Vulture." So he went
and entering the presence reported what had taken place, whereupon the Sultan with his lords of the land mounted[1] their horses,
and, going to the place, found the monster killed, and cut into
two halves. Anon the King returned, and leading Prince Mohammed with him bade knit the marriage-knot with his daughter
and caused him to pay her the first visit. He tarried beside her
for a full-told month after which he asked leave to travel and to
seek the city of his first spouse, carrying with him the second.
Hereupon the King his father-in-law presented to him ten cages,
each containing four birds of vari-coloured coats and farewelled
him. After which he fared forth and left the city, and outside it
he found the 'Aun awaiting him and the Jinni salam'd to the
Prince and congratulated him in what he had won of gifts and
prizes. Then he arose high in air, bearing Mohammed and his
two brides and all that was with them, and he winged his way
for an hour or so until he alighted once more at the ruined city.
Here he found the Prince's suite of learned men, together with
the bât-beasts and their loads[2] and everything other even as he
had left it. So they sat down to take their rest when the 'Aun
said, "O Mohammed, O Son of the Sultan, I have been predestined to thee in this site whither thou wast fated to come; but I
have another and a further covenant to keep wherewith I would

---

[1] [In Ar. "yanjaaru," vii. form of "jaara" (med. Hamzah), in which the idea of "raising,"
"lifting up," seems to prevail, for it is used for raising the voice in prayer to God, and for
the growing high of plants. — Sr.]

[2] The text, which is wholly unedited, reads, "He found the beasts and their loads (? the
camels) and the learned men," &c. A new form of "Bos atque sacerdos" and of *place pour
les ânes et les savants*, as the French soldiers cried in Egypt when the scientists were admitted into the squares of infantry formed against the doughty Mameluke cavalry.

charge thee." "What is that?" quoth he, and quoth the 'Aun, "Verily thou shalt not depart this place until thou shalt have laved me and shrouded me and graved[1] me in the ground;" and so saying he shrieked a loud shriek and his soul fled his flesh. This was grievous to the son of the King and he and his men arose and washed him and shrouded him and having prayed over him buried him in the earth. After this the Prince turned him to travel, so they laded the loads and he and his set forth intending for their families and native land. They journeyed during the space of thirty days till they reached the fork of the highway whereat stood the great rock, and here they found tents and pavilions and a host nor did they know what this mighty many might mean. Now the father, when his son left him, suffered from straitness of breast and was sore perplexed as to his affair and he wot not what to do; so he bade make ready his army and commanded the lords of the land to prepare for the march and all set out seeking his son and determined to find tidings of him. Nor did they cease faring till they reached the place where the road forked into three and on the first rock they saw written the three lines—"This is the road of safe chance;" and "This is the way of repentance;" and "This is the path whereon whoso paceth shall return nevermore." But when the father read it he was posed and perplext as to the matter and he cried, "Would Heaven I knew by which road of these three my son Mohammed may have travelled;" and as he was brooding over this difficulty ——And Shahrazad was surprised by the dawn of day and fell silent and ceased saying her permitted say. Then quoth her sister Dunyazad, "How sweet and tasteful is thy tale, O sister mine, and how enjoyable and delectable!" Quoth she, "And where is this compared with that I should relate to you on the coming night an the King suffer me to survive?" Now when it was the next night and that was

The Four Hundred and Fifty-ninth Night,

DUNYAZAD said to her, "Allah upon thee, O my sister, an thou be other than sleepy, finish for us thy tale that we may cut short

---

[1] [In the MS. "wáraytaní ilà l-turáb" == thou hast given me over to the ground for concealment, iii. form of "wará," which takes the meaning of "hiding," "keeping secret." — ST.]

the watching of this our latter night!" She replied, "With love and good will!" It hath reached me, O auspicious King, the director, the right-guiding, lord of the rede which is benefiting and of deeds fair-seeming and worthy celebrating, that as the Sultan was brooding over this difficulty lo and behold! his son Mohammed appeared before him by the path which showed written, "This is the path whereon whoso passeth shall never-more return." But when the King saw him, and face confronted face, he arose and met him and salam'd to him giving him joy of his safety; and the Prince told him all that had befallen him from beginning to end—how he had not reached those places save by the All-might of Allah, and how he had succeeded in winning his wish by meeting with the 'Aun. So they nighted in that site and when it was morning they resumed their march, all in glad-ness and happiness for that the Sultan had recovered his son Mohammed. They ceased not faring a while until they drew near their native city when the bearers of good tidings ran for-ward announcing the arrival of the Sultan and his son and, here-upon the houses were decorated in honour of the Prince's safe return and crowds came out to meet them till such time as all had entered the city-walls, after which their joys increased and their annoy fell from them. And this is the whole of the tale told by the first Larrikin. Now when the Sultan heard it he mar-velled at what had befallen the chief adventurer therein, when the second Larrikin spoke saying "I have by me a tale, a marvel of marvels, and which is a delight to the hearer and a diversion to the reader and to the reciter." Quoth the Sovran, "What may that be, O Shaykh?" and the man fell to relating the

Tale of the Fisherman and his Son.

THEY tell that whilome there was a Fisherman, a poor man with a wife and family, who every day was wont to take his net and go down to the river a-fishing for his daily bread which is distributed. Then he would sell a portion of his catch and buy victual and the rest he would carry to his wife and children that they might eat. One day of the many days he said to his son who was growing up to a biggish lad, "O my child, come forth with me this morning, haply All-Mighty Allah may send us somewhat of livelihood by thy footsteps;" and the other answered, " 'Tis well, O my

father." Hereupon the Fisherman took his son and his net and
they twain went off together till they arrived at the river-bank,
when quoth the father, "O my boy I will throw the net upon the
luck of thee." Then he went forward to the water and standing
thereby took his net and unfolded it so that it spread when entering the stream, and after waiting an hour or so he drew it in
and found it heavyofweight: so he cried, "O my son, bear a hand"
and the youth came up and lent him aidance in drawing it in.
And when they had haled it to shore they opened it and found
a fish of large size and glittering with all manner of colours.
Quoth the father, "O my son, by Allah, this fish befitteth not
any but the Caliph; do thou therefore abide with it till I go and
fetch a charger wherein to carry it as an offering for the Prince
of True Believers." The youth took his seat by the fish and when
his father was afar off he went up to her and said, "Doubtless
thou hast children and the byword saith, Do good and cast it
upon the waters." Then he took up the fish and setting her near
the river besprinkled[1] her and said, "Go thou to thy children,
this is even better than being eaten by the Caliph." But having
thrown the fish into the stream, his fear of his father grew strong
upon him, so he arose and without stay or delay fled his village;
and he ceased not flying till he reached the Land of Al-Irák whose
capital was under a King wide of dominions (and praise be to the
King of all kingdoms!). So he entered the streets and presently
he met a baker-man who said to him, "O my son, wilt thou
serve?" whereto he replied, "I will serve, O uncle." The man
settled with him for a wage of two silver nusfs a day together
with his meat and his drink, and he remained working with him
for a while of time. Now one day of the days behold, he saw
a lad of the sons of that city carrying about a cock with the
intention of vending it, when he was met by a Jew who said to
him, "O my child, wilt thou sell this fowl?" and the other said,

---

1 [The MS. has "wa dazz-há," which is an evident corruption. The translator, placing
the diacritical point over the first radical instead of the second, reads "wa zarr-há," and
renders accordingly. But if in the MS. the dot is misplaced, the Tashdíd over it would
probably also belong to the Dál, resp. Zál, and as it is very feasible that a careless writer
should have dropped one Wáw before another, I am inclined to read "wa wazzar-ha" =
"and he left her," "let her go," "set her free." In classical Arabic only the imperative
"Zar," and the aorist "yazaru" of the verb "wazara" occur in this sense, while the preterite
is replaced by "taraka," or some other synonym. But the language of the common people
would not hesitate to use a form scorned by the grammarians, and even to improve upon it
by deriving from it one of their favourite intensives. — St.]

"I will." Quoth the Jew, "For ten faddahs?" and quoth the
youth, "Allah openeth!" Said the other, "For twenty faddahs?"
and the lad, "Allah veileth!"[1] Then the Jew fell to increasing
his offer for the cock until he reached a full dinar.——And Shahrazad was surprised by the dawn of day and fell silent and ceased
to say her permitted say. Then quoth her sister Dunyazad,
"How sweet is thy story, O sister mine, and how enjoyable and
delectable!" Quoth she, "And where is this compared with that
I should relate to you on the coming night an the King suffer me
to survive?" Now when it was the next night and that was

The Four Hundred and Sixty=first Night.

DUNYAZAD said to her, "Allah upon thee, O my sister, an thou be
other than sleepy, finish for us thy tale that we may cut short the
watching of this our latter night!" She replied, "With love
and good will!" It hath reached me, O auspicious King, the
director, the right-guiding, lord of the rede which is benefiting
and of deeds fair-seeming and worthy celebrating, that the Jew
raised his bid for the cock till he reached a gold piece when the
lad said, "Here with it." So the man gave him the dinar and took
from him the fowl and slaughtered it forthright. Then he turned
to a boy, one of his servants, and said to him, "Take this cock and
carry it home and say to thy mistress, 'Pluck it, but open it
not until such time as I shall return.'" And the servant did his
bidding. But when the Fisherman's son who was standing hard
by heard these words and saw the bargain, he waited for a while
and as soon as the servant had carried off the fowl, he arose and
buying two cocks at four faddahs he slaughtered them and repaired with them to the house of the Jew. Then he rapped at
the door and when the mistress came out to him he bespoke her
saying, "The house master saith to thee, 'Take these two silvers
and send me the bird which was brought to thee by the servant
boy.'"[2] Quoth she, "'Tis well," so he gave her the two fowls
and took from her the cock which her husband had slaughtered.
Then he returned to the bakery, and when he was private he
opened the belly of the cock and found therein a signet-ring with

---

[1] Both are civil forms of refusal: for the first see vols. i. 32; vi. 216; and for the second
ix. 309.
[2] Everything being fair in love and war and dealing with a "Káfir," i.e. a non-Moslem.

a bezel-gem which in the sun showed one colour and in the shade another. So he took it up and hid it in his bosom, after which he gutted the bird and cooked it in the furnace and ate it. Presently the Jew having finished his business, returned home and said to his wife, "Bring me the cock." She brought him the two fowls and he seeing them asked her, "But where be the first cock?" And she answered him, "Thou thyself sentest the boy with these two birds and then orderedst him to bring thee the first cock." The Jew held his peace but was sore distressed at heart, so sore indeed that he came nigh to die and said to himself, "Indeed it hath slipped from my grasp!" Now the Fisherman's son after he had mastered the ring waited until the evening evened when he said, "By Allah, needs must this bezel have some mystery;" so he withdrew into the privacy of the furnace and brought it out from his bosom and fell a-rubbing it. Thereupon the Slave of the Ring appeared and cried, "Here I stand[1] between thy hands." Then the Fisherman's son said to himself, "This indeed is the perfection of good fortune," and returned the gem to his breast-pocket as it was. Now when morning morrowed the owner of the bakery came in and the youth said to him, "O my master, I am longing for my people and my native land and 'tis my desire to fare and look upon them and presently I will return to thee." So the man paid him his wage, after which he left him and walked from the bakery till he came to the Palace of the Sultan where he found near the gate well nigh an hundred heads which had been cut off and there suspended; so he leaned for rest against the booth of a sherbet-seller and asked its owner, "O master, what is the cause of all these heads being hung up?" and the other answered, "O my son, inquire not, anent what hath been done." However when he repeated the question the man replied, "O my son, verily the Sultan hath a daughter, a model of beauty and loveliness, of symmetric stature and perfect grace, in fact likest a branch of the Rattan-palm;[2] and whoso cometh ever to seek her in marriage her father conditioneth with him a condition." Cried the Fisherman's son, "What may be that condition?" and the other replied, "There is a great mound of ashes under the latticed windows of the Sultan's palace, and

---

[1] In text "Labbayka" = here am I: see vol. i. 226.
[2] In text "'Úd Khayzarán" = wood of the rattan, which is orig. "Rota," from the Malay "Rotan." Vol. ii. 66, &c.

whoso wisheth to take his daughter to wife he maketh a covenant with him that he shall carry off that heap. So the other accepted the agreement with only the proviso that he should have forty days' grace and he consented that, an he fail within that time, his head be cut off." "And the heap is high?" quoth the Fisherman's son. "Like a hill," quoth the other. Now when the youth had thoroughly comprehended what the sherbet-seller had told him, he farewelled him and left him; then, going to a Khan, he hired him a cell and taking seat therein for a time he pondered how he should proceed, for he was indeed fearful yet was his heart hanging to the love of the Sultan's daughter. Presently he brought out his ring, and rubbed it, when the voice of the Slave cried to him, "Here I stand between thy hands and what mayst thou require of me?" Said the other, "I want a suit of kingly clothes;" whereat without delay a bundle was set before him and when he opened it he found therein princely gear. So he took it and rising without loss of time he went into the Hammam and caused himself to be soaped and gloved and thoroughly washed, after which he donned the dress and his case was changed into other case——And Shahrazad was surprised by the dawn of day and fell silent and ceased saying her permitted say. Then quoth her sister Dunyazad, "How sweet and tasteful is thy tale, O sister mine, and enjoyable and delectable!" Quoth she, "And where is this compared with that I would relate to you on the coming night an the King suffer me to survive?" Now when it was the next night and that was

The Four Hundred and Sixty-third Night,

DUNYAZAD said to her, "Allah upon thee, O my sister, an thou be other than sleepy, finish for us thy tale that we may cut short the watching of this our latter night!" She replied, "With love and good will!" It hath reached me, O auspicious King, the director, the right-guiding, lord of the rede which is benefiting and of deeds fair-seeming and worthy celebrating, that when the son of the Fisherman came forth the Bath-house and donned his fine dress, his was changed into other case and he appeared before the folk in semblance of the sons of Kings. Presently he went to the Sultan's palace and entering therein made his salam and, blushing for modesty, did his obeisance and blessed the Sultan with the blessing due to Caliphs. His greetings were returned and the King welcomed him and after that looked at him, and finding him after princely fashion, asked him, "What is thy need, O Youth, and what requirest thou?" Answered the other, "I seek connection with thy house, and I come desirous of betrothal with the lady concealed and the pearl unrevealed, which is thy daughter." "Art thou able to perform the condition, O Youth?" asked the King; "For I want neither means nor moneys nor precious stones nor other possession; brief, none other thing save that thou remove yon mound of ashes from beneath the windows of my palace." Upon this he bade the youth draw near him and when he obeyed threw open the lattice; and, showing him the hillock that stood underneath it, said, "O Youth, I will betroth to thee my daughter an thou be pleased to remove this heap; but if thou prove thee unable so to do I will strike off thy head." Quoth the Fisherman's son, "I am satisfied therewith," presently adding, "A delay![1] grant me the term of forty days." "I have allowed thy request to thee," said the King and wrote a document bearing the testimony of those present, when cried the youth, "O King, bid nail up thy windows and let them not be unfastened until the fortieth day shall have gone by." "These words be fair," quoth the Sultan, and accordingly he gave the order. Hereat the youth went forth from him whereupon all present in the palace cried, "O the pity of it, that this youngster should be done to die; indeed there were many stronger than he, yet none of them availed to remove the heap." In this way each and every said his say, but when the Fisherman's son returned to his cell (and he was thoughtful concerning his life and perplext as to his affair) he cried, "Would Heaven I knew whether the Ring hath power to carry it off." Then shutting himself up in his cell he brought out the signet from his breast-pocket and rubbed it, and a Voice was heard to cry, "Here I stand (and fair befal thy command) between thy hands. What requirest thou of me, O my lord?" The other replied, "I want thee to remove the ash-heap which standeth under the windows of the royal palace, and I demand that thou lay out in lieu thereof a garden wide of sides in whose middlemost must be a mansion tall and choice-builded of base, for the special domicile of the Sultan's daughter: further-

more, let all this be done within the space of forty days." "Aye
ready," quoth the Jinni, "to do all thou desirest." Hereupon the
youth felt his affright assuaged and his heart rightly directed; and
after this he would go every day to inspect the heap and would
find one quarter of it had disappeared, nor did aught of it remain
after the fourth morning for that the ring was graved with the
cabalistic signs of the Cohens[1] and they had set upon the work
an hundred Marids of the Jann that they might carry out the
wishes of any who required aught of them. And when the
mound was removed they dispread in its site a garden wide of
sides in whose midst they edified a palace choice-builded of base,
and all this was done within the space of fifteen days, whilst the
Fisherman's son ever repaired thither and inspected the work.
But when he had perfected his intent he entered to the Sultan
and kissing ground between his hands and having prayed for his
glory and permanence, said, "O King of the Age, deign open the
lattices of thy Palace!" So he went to them and threw them open
when lo and behold, he found in lieu of the mound a mighty fine
garden wherein were trees and rills and blooms and birds hymn-
ing the praises of their Creator; moreover he saw in that garden
a palace, an edifice choice-builded of base which is not to be
found with any King or Kaysar. Seeing this he wondered at the
circumstance and his wits were wildered and he was perplext as
to his affair; after which he sent for the Minister and summoned
him and said, "Counsel me, O Wazir, as to what I shall do in the
case of this youth and in what way shall I fend him from me."
Replied the Councillor, "How shall I advise thee, seeing that
thou madest condition with him that should he fail in his under-
taking thou wouldst strike off his head? Now there is no contrivance in this matter and there is naught to do save marrying
him with the girl." By these words the King was persuaded and
caused the knot to be knotted and bade them lead the bridegroom in procession to the bride, after which the youth set her
in the garden-palace and cohabited with her in all joy and enjoyment and pleasure and disport. On this wise fared it with them;
but as regards the case of the Jew, when he lost the cock he went

---

[1] Arab. "Al-Kuhná," plur. of "Káhin 't"=diviner, priest (non-Levitical): see "Cohen,"
ii. 221. [The form is rather curious. The Dictionaries quote "Kuhná" as a Syriac singular,
but here it seems to be taken as a plural of the measure "fu'alá" (Kuhaná), like Umará
of Amír or Shu'ará of Shá'ir. The usual plurals of Káhin are Kahanah and Kuhhán.—St.]

forth in sore disappointment like unto one Jinn-mad; and neither
was his sleep sound and good nor were meat and drink pleasant
food, and he ceased not wandering about till the Fates threw him
into that garden. Now he had noted in past time that a huge
heap of ashes stood under the palace-windows and when he
looked he cried, "Verily, the youth hath been here and all this
work is the work of the signet-ring, for that none other than the
Márids of the Jánn could remove such a hillock." So saying, the
Jew returned to his place, where he brought out a parcel of fine
pearls and some few emeralds and specimens of coral and other
precious minerals, and set them as for sale in a tray. Then he
approached the palace which was builded in the garden and cried
out saying, "The pearls! and the emeralds! and the corals! and
various kinds of fine jewels!" and he kept up this cry.——And
Shahrazad was surprised by the dawn of day and fell silent and
ceased to say her permitted say. Then quoth her sister Dunyazad, "How sweet is thy story, O sister mine, and how enjoyable
and delectable!" Quoth she, "And where is this compared with
that I should relate to you on the coming night an the King suffer
me to survive?" Now when it was the next night and that was

The Four Hundred and Sixty-fifth Night,

DUNYAZAD said to her, "Allah upon thee, O my sister, an thou
be other than sleepy, finish for us thy tale that we may cut short
the watching of this our latter night!" She replied, "With love
and good will!" It hath reached me, O auspicious King, the
director, the right-guiding, lord of the rede which is benefiting
and of deeds fair-seeming and worthy celebrating, that the Jew
fell to hawking about his minerals and crying them for sale beside
the garden-palace and the Sultan's daughter hearing him exclaimed, "O Handmaid, bring me that which is for sale with this
Jew." So the girl went down and said to the man, "What hast
thou by thee?" and said the other, "Precious stones." Quoth she,
"Wilt thou sell them for gold?" and quoth he, "No, O my lady,
I will sell them for nothing save for rings which must be old."[1]
Accordingly she returned and herewith acquainted her lady who

---

[1] This is the celebrated incident in "Alaeddin," "New lamps for old:" See Suppl.
vol. iii. 119.

said, "By Allah, my Lord hath in his pencase[1] an old worn-out ring, so do thou go and bring it to me while he sleepeth." But she knew not what was hidden for her in the Secret Purpose, nor that which was fated to be her Fate. So presently she brought out of the pencase the bezel-ring afore-mentioned and gave it to the handmaid who took it and faring outside the house handed it to the Jew, and he received it with extreme joy and in turn presented to her the tray with all thereon. Then he went forth the city and set out on a voyage to the Seven Islands which are not far from the earth-surrounding Ocean;[2] and when he arrived thither he landed upon a sea-holm and travelled to the middle-most thereof. Anon he took seat, and presently brought out the signet-ring and rubbed it, when the slave appeared and cried, "Here I stand and between thy hands, what is it thou needest of me?" "I require of thee," quoth the Jew, "to transport hither the bower of the Sultan's daughter and to restore the ash-heap to the stead it was in whilome under the lattice of the King's Palace." Now ere night had passed away both Princess and Palace were transported to the middlemost of the island; and when the Jew beheld her his heart flamed high for the excess of her beauty and loveliness. So he entered her bower and fell to conversing with her, but she would return to him no reply and, when he would have approached her, she started away in disgust. Hereupon, seeing no signs of conquest, the Jew said in his mind, "Let her wax accustomed to me and she will be satisfied," and on this wise he continued to solace her heart. Now as regards the son of the Fisherman his sleep had extended deep into the fore-noon and when the sun burnt upon his back he arose and found himself lying on the ash-heap below the Palace, so he said to himself, "Up and away, otherwise the Sultan will look out of the window and will behold this mound returned to its place as it was before, and he will order thy neck to be smitten." So he hurried him forth hardly believing in his escape, and he ceased not hastening his pace until he came to a coffee-house, which he entered; and there he took him a lodging and used to lie the night, and to rise amorn. Now one day of the days behold, he met

---

[1] In text "Jazdán" = a pencase (Pers.) more pop. called "Kalamdán" = reed-box, vol. iv. 167: Scott (p. 212) has a "writing-stand." It appears a queer place wherein to keep a ring, but Easterns often store in these highly ornamented boxes signets and other small matters.

[2] Arab. "Bahr al-Muhit" = Circumambient Ocean; see vol. i. 133.

a man who was leading about a dog and a cat and a mouse[1] and crying them for sale at the price of ten faddahs; so the youth said in his mind, "Let me buy these at their cheap price;" and he called aloud to the man and having given him the ten silverlings took away his purchase. After this he would fare every day to the slaughter-house and would buy for them a bit of tripe or liver and feed them therewith, but ever and anon he would sit down and ponder the loss of the Ring and bespeak himself and say, "Would Heaven I wot that which Allah Almighty hath done with my Ring and my Palace and my bride the Sultan's daughter!" Now the dog and the cat and the mouse heard him, and one day of the days as, according to his custom, he took them with him and led them to the slaughter-house and bought a meal of entrails and gave somewhat to each that it might eat thereof, he sat down in sad thought and groaned aloud and sorrow prevailed upon him till he was overcome by sleep. The season was the mid-forenoon[2] and the while he slumbered and was drowned in drowsiness, the Dog said to the Cat and the Mouse, "O brethren mine, in very deed this youth, who hath bought us for ten faddahs, leadeth us every day to this stead and giveth us our rations of food. But he hath lost his Ring and the Palace wherein was his bride, the daughter of the Sultan: so let us up and fare forth and seek therefor and do ye twain mount upon my back so that we can overwander the seas and the island-skirts." They did as he bade them and he walked down with them to the waters and swam with them until they found themselves amiddlemost the main; nor did he cease swimming with them for about a day and a night until the morning morrowed and they saw from afar a somewhat that glittered. So they made for it till they drew near, when they saw that it was the Palace in question, whereat the Dog continued swimming till such time as he came ashore and dismounted the Cat and the Mouse. Then he said to them, "Let us abide here."——And Shahrazad was surprised by the dawn of day and fell silent and ceased saying her permitted say. Then quoth her sister Dunyazad, "How sweet and tasteful is thy tale, O sister mine, and how enjoyable and delectable!" Quoth she,

---

[1] Arab. "Fár" (plur. "Firán") == mouse rather than rat.
[2] Sleep at this time is considered very unwholesome by Easterns. See under "Kaylúlah" == siesta, vols. i. 51; ii. 178, and viii. 191.

"And where is this compared with that I should relate to you on the coming night an the King suffer me to survive?" Now when it was the next night and that was

The Four Hundred and Sixty-seventh Night,

DUNYAZAD said to her, "Allah upon thee, O my sister, an thou be other than sleepy, finish for us thy tale that we may cut short the watching of this our latter night!" She replied, "With love and good will!" It hath reached me, O auspicious King, the director, the right-guiding, lord of the rede which is benefiting and of deeds fair-seeming and worthy celebrating, that the Dog said to the Cat and the Mouse, "I will abide and await you here, and do ye twain fare into the Palace, where the Cat shall take her station upon the crenelles over the lattice window and the Mouse shall enter the mansion and roam about and search through the rooms until she come upon the Ring required." So they did the Dog's bidding and sought the places he had appointed to them and the Mouse crept about but found naught until she approached the bedstead and beheld the Jew asleep and the Princess lying afar off. He had been longsome in requiring of her her person and had even threatened her with slaughter, yet he had no power to approach her nor indeed had he even looked upon the form of her face. Withal the Mouse ceased not faring about until she approached the Jew, whom she discovered sleeping upon his back and drowned in slumber for the excess of his drink that weighed him down. So she drew near and considered him and saw the Ring in his mouth below the tongue whereat she was perplext how to recover it; but presently she went forth to a vessel of oil and dipping her tail therein approached the sleeper and drew it over his nostrils, whereat he sneezed with a sneeze so violent that the Ring sprang from between his jaws and fell upon the side of the bedstead. Then she seized it in huge joy and returning to the Cat said to her, "Verily the prosperity of our lord hath returned to him." After this the twain went back to the Dog whom they found expecting them, so they marched down to the sea and mounted upon his back and he swam with them both, all three being in the highest spirits. But when they reached the middle of the main, quoth the Cat to the Mouse, "Pass the Ring to me that I may carry it awhile;" and the other did so, when she placed it in her chops for an hour of time. Then quoth the Dog to them, "Ye twain have taken to yourselves charge of the Ring, each of you for a little time, and I also would do likewise." They both said to him, "O our brother, haply 'twill fall from thy mouth:" but said he to them, "By Allah, an ye give it not to me for a while I will drown you both in this very place." Accordingly the two did in their fear as the Dog desired and when he had set it in his chops it dropped therefrom into the abyss of the ocean; seeing which all repented thereat and they said, "Wasted is our work we have wrought." But when they came to land they found their lord sleeping from the excess of his cark and his care, and so the trio stood on the shore and were sorrowing with sore sorrow, when behold, there appeared to them a Fish strange of semblance who said to them, "Take ye this Signet-ring and commit it to your lord, the son of the Fisherman, and when giving it to him say, 'Since thou diddest a good deed and threwest the Fish into the sea thy kindness shall not be for naught; and, if it fail with the Creature, it shall not fail with Allah the Creator.' Then do ye inform him that the Fish which his father the Fisher would have presented to the King and whereupon he had mercy and returned her to the waters, that Fish am I, and the old saw saith, 'This for that, and tit for tat is its reward!'" Hereupon the Dog took the Signet-ring and the other two went up with him to their lord and awaking him from sleep returned to him his Ring. But when he saw it he became like one Jinn-mad from the excess of his joy and the three related to him the affair of the Signet; how they had brought it away from the Jew and how it had dropped from the Dog's mouth into the abyss of the sea and lastly how the Fish who had found it brought it back to them declaring that it was she whom his sire had netted and whom the son had returned to the depths. Cried he, "Alham-dolillah"—Glory be to the Lord—"who caused us work this weal and requited us for our kindness;" after which he took the Signet and waited until night had nighted. Then he repaired to the mount which was under the Sultan's Palace and brought out the Ring and rubbed it, when the Slave appeared and cried to him, "Here I stand (and fair befal thy command!) between thy hands: what is it needest thou and requirest thou of me?" The other replied, "I demand that thou carry off for me this mound."——And Shahrazad was surprised by the dawn of day and fell silent and ceased to say her permitted say. Then quoth her sister Dunyazad, "How sweet is thy story, O sister mine, and how enjoyable and delectable!" Quoth she, "And where is this compared with that I should relate to you on the coming night an the King suffer me to survive?" Now when it was the next night and that was

The Four Hundred and Sixty-ninth Night,

DUNYAZAD said to her, "Allah upon thee, O my sister, an thou be other than sleepy, finish for us thy tale that we may cut short the watching of this our latter night!" She replied, "With love and good will!" It hath reached me, O auspicious King, the director, the right-guiding, lord of the rede which is benefiting and of deeds fair-seeming and worthy celebrating, that the Son of the Fisherman bade the Slave of the Ring remove the mound and return the garden as whilome it was and restore the Palace containing the Jew and the Sultan's daughter. Nor did that hour pass before everything was replaced in its proper stead. Then the Youth went up to the saloon where he found the Jew recovered from his drunkenness and he was threatening the Princess and saying, "Thou! for thee there is no escape from me." But cried she, "O dog, O accurst, joy from my lord is well nigh to me." Hearing these words the Youth fell upon the Jew and dragging him along by his neck, went down with him and bade them light a furious fire, and so they did till it flamed and flared; after which he pinioned his enemy and caused him to be cast therein when his bones were melted upon his flesh. Then returning to the Palace he fell to blaming the Sultan's daughter for the matter of the Ring, and asking her, "Why didst thou on this wise?" She answered, "From Fate there is no flight, and Alhamdolillah—praise to the Lord—who after all that befel us from the Jew hath brought us together once more." Now all that happened from the Jew and the return of the Sultan's daughter and the restoring of the Palace and the death of his deceiver remained unknown to the Sultan, and here is an end to my history. And when the second Larrikin held his peace quoth the King, "Allah quicken thee for this story; by the Almighty 'tis wondrous, and it delighteth the hearer and rejoiceth the teller." Then cried the third Larrikin, "I also have by me an history more marvellous than these two; and, were it written in water of gold upon the pages of men's hearts, it were worthy thereof." Quoth the King,

"O Larrikin, if it prove stranger and rarer than these I will surely largesse thee." Whereupon quoth he, "O King of the Age, listen to what I shall relate," and he fell to telling the

Tale of the Third Larrikin Concerning Himself.

IN my early years I had a cousin, the daughter of my paternal uncle, who loved me and I loved her whilst her father loathed me. So one day she sent to me saying, "Do thou fare forth and demand me in marriage from my sire;" and, as I was poor and her father was a wealthy merchant, she sent me to her dowry fifty gold pieces which I took; and, accompanied by four of my comrades, I went to the house of my father's brother and there arrived I went within. But when he looked upon me his face showed wrath and my friends said to him, "Verily, thy nephew seeketh in marriage the daughter of his uncle;" and as soon as he heard these words he cried aloud at them and reviled me and drave me from his doors. So I went from him well nigh broken-hearted and I wept till I returned to my mother who cried, "What is to do with thee, O my son!" I related to her all that had befallen me from my uncle and she said to me, "O my child, to a man who loveth thee not thou goest, forsooth, to ask his daughter in marriage!" Whereto I replied, "O mother mine, she sent a message bidding me so do and verily she loveth me." Quoth my mother, "Take patience, O my son!" I heartened my heart, and my parent promised me all welfare and favour from my cousin; moreover she was thinking of me at all times and presently she again sent to me and promised me that she never would love any other. Then behold, a party of folk repaired to her father and asked her to wife of him and prepared to take her away. But when the tidings reached her that her parent purposed marrying her to one of those people, she sent to me saying, "Get thee ready for this midnight and I will come to thee." When night was at its noon she appeared, carrying a pair of saddle-bags wherein was a somewhat of money and raiment, and she was leading a she-mule belonging to her father whereupon her saddle-bags were packed. "Up with us," she cried, so I arose with her in that outer darkness and we went forth the town forthright and the Veiler veiled us, nor did we stint faring till morning when we hid ourselves in fear lest we be overtaken. And when the next night fell we made ready

and set out again, but we knew not whither we were wending,
for the Predestinator existeth and what is decided for us is like
Destiny. At last we came to a wide and open place where the
heat smote us, and we sat down under a tree to smell the air.
Presently sleep came upon me and I was drowned in slumber
from the excess of my toil and travail, when suddenly a dog-faced
baboon came up to the daughter of my uncle——And Shahrazad
was surprised by the dawn of day and fell silent and ceased saying
her permitted say. Then quoth her sister Dunyazad, "How sweet
and tasteful is thy tale, O sister mine, and how enjoyable and
delectable!" Quoth she, "And where is this compared with that
I should relate to you on the coming night an the King suffer me
to survive?" Now when it was the next night and that was

The Four Hundred and Seventy-first Night,

DUNYAZAD said to her, "Allah upon thee, O my sister, an thou be
other than sleepy, finish for us thy tale that we may cut short the
watching of this our latter night!" She replied, "With love and
good will!" It hath reached me, O auspicious King, the director,
the right-guiding, lord of the rede which is benefiting and of deeds
fair-seeming and worthy celebrating, that the Larrikin continued
his tale saying to the King:——And as I was drowned in slumber
a dog-faced baboon came up to the daughter of my uncle and
assaulted her and knew her carnally; then, having taken her
pucelage he ran away,[1] but I knew nothing thereof from being

---

[1] Modern science which, out of the depths of its self-consciousness, has settled so many
disputed questions, speaking by the organs of Messieurs Woodman and Tidy ("Medical
Jurisprudence") has decided that none of the lower animals can bear issue to man. But
the voice of the world is against them and as Voltaire says one cannot be cleverer than
everybody. To begin with there is the will: the she-quadruman shows a distinct lust for
man by fondling him and displaying her parts as if to entice him. That carnal connection
has actually taken place cannot be doubted: my late friend Mirza Ali Akbar, of Bombay,
the famous Munshi to Sir Charles Napier during the conquest of Sind, a man perfectly
veracious and trustworthy, assured me that in the Gujarát province he had witnessed a
case with his own eyes. He had gone out "to the jungle," as the phrase is, with another
Moslem who, after keeping him waiting for an unconscionable time, was found carnally
united to a she-monkey. My friend, indignant as a good Moslem should be, reproved him
for his bestiality and then asked him how it had come to pass: the man answered that the
she-monkey came regularly to look at him on certain occasions, that he was in the habit
of throwing her something to eat and that her gratitude displayed such sexuality that he
was tempted and "fell." That the male monkey shows an equal desire for the woman is

fast asleep. Now when I awoke I found my cousin was changed
of case and her colour had waxed pale and she was in saddest
condition; so I asked her and she told me all that had betided
her and said to me, "O son of my uncle, from Fate there is no
flight, even as saith one of those who knoweth:—

'And when death shall claw with his firm-fixt nail   *   I saw that spells[1] were
    of scant avail.'

---

known to every frequenter of the "Zoo." I once led a party of English girls to see a collection of mandrils and other anthropoid apes in the Ménagerie of a well-known Russian
millionaire, near Florence, when the Priapism displayed was such that the girls turned
back and fled in fright. In the mother-lands of these anthropoids (the Gaboon, Malacca,
etc.) the belief is universal and women have the liveliest fear of them. In 1853 when the
Crimean war was brewing a dog-faced baboon in Cairo broke away from his "Kuraydati"
(ape-leader), threw a girl in the street and was about to ravish her when a sentinel drew his
bayonet and killed the beast. The event was looked upon as an evil omen by the older
men, who shook their heads and declared that these were bad times when apes attempted
to ravish the daughters of Moslems. But some will say that the grand test, the existence
of the mule between man and monkey, though generally believed in, is characteristically
absent, absent as the "missing link" which goes so far as to invalidate Darwinism in one
and perhaps the most important part of its contention. Of course the offspring of such
union would be destroyed, yet the fact of our never having found a trace of it except in
legend and idle story seems to militate against its existence. When, however, man shall
become "Homo Sapiens" he will cast off the prejudices of the cradle and the nursery and
will ascertain by actual experiment if human being and monkey can breed together. The
lowest order of bimana, and the highest order of quadrumana may, under most favourable
circumstances, bear issue and the "Mule," who would own half a soul, might prove most
serviceable as a hewer of wood and a drawer of water, in fact as an agricultural labourer.
All we can say is that such "miscegenation" stands in the category of things not proven
and we must object to science declaring them non-existing. A correspondent favours me
with the following note upon the subject:— Castanheda (Annals of Portugal) relates
that a woman was transported to an island inhabited by monkeys and took up her abode
in a cavern where she was visited by a huge baboon. He brought her apples and fruit and
at last had connection with her, the result being two children in two to three years; but
when she was being carried off by a ship the parent monkey kissed his progeny. The
woman was taken to Lisbon and imprisoned for life by the King. Langius, Virgilius Poly-
dorus and others quote many instances of monstruous births in Rome resulting from the
connection of women with dogs and bears, and cows with horses, &c. The following rela-
tive conditions are deduced on the authority of MM. Jean Polfya and Mauriceau:— 1. If
the sexual organism of man or woman be more powerful than that of the monkey, dog, etc.,
the result will be a monster in the semblance of man. 2. If vice-versâ the appearance will
be that of a beast. 3. If both are equal the result will be a distinct sub-species as of the
horse with the ass.

[1] Arab. "Tanim" (plur. of Tamimat) = spells, charms, amulets, as those hung to a
horse's neck, the African Greegree and the Heb. Thummim. As was the case with most of
these earliest superstitions, the Serpent, the Ark, the Cherubim, the Golden Calf (Apis)
and the Levitical Institution, the Children of Israel derived the now mysterious term
"Urim" (lights) and "Thummim" (amulets) from Egypt and the Semitic word (Tamimah)
still remains to explain the Hebrew. "Thummim," I may add, is by "general consensus"
derived from "Tôm" = completeness and is englished "Perfection," but we can find a
better origin near at hand in spoken Arabic.

And one of them also said:—

'When God would execute His will in anything On one endowed with sight,
    hearing and reasoning,
He stops his ears and blinds his eyes and draws his will From him, as one
    draws out the hairs to paste that cling;
Till, His decrees fulfilled, He gives him back his wit, That therewithal he may
    receive admonishing.'"[1]

Then she spake concerning the predestination of the Creator till she could say no more thereof. Presently we departed that stead and we travelled till we came to a town of the towns frequented by merchants, where we hired us a lodging and furnished it with mats and necessaries. Here I asked for a Kazi and they pointed out to me one of them amongst the judges of the place whom I summoned with two of his witnesses; then I made one of them deputy[2] for my cousin and was married to her and went in unto her and I said to myself, "All things depend upon Fate and Lot." After that I tarried with her for a full told year in that same town, a disease befel her and she drew nigh unto death. Hereat quoth she to me, "Allah upon thee, O son of my uncle, when I shall be dead and gone and the Destiny of Allah shall come upon thee and drive thee to marry again, take not to wife any but a virgin-girl or haply do thou wed one who hath known man but once;[3] for by Allah, O my cousin, I will say thee nothing but sooth when I tell thee that the delight of that dog-faced baboon who deflowered me hath remained with me ever since."[4] So saying she expired[5] and her soul fled forth her flesh. I brought to her a woman who washeth the dead and shrouded her and buried her; and after her decease I went forth from the town

---

[1] These verses have already occurred, see my vol. i. p. 275. I have therefore quoted Payne, i. p. 246.

[2] Arab. "Wakíl" who, in the case of a grown-up girl, declares her consent to the marriage in the presence of two witnesses and after part payment of the dowry.

[3] Such is the meaning of the Arab. "Thayyib."

[4] This appears to be the popular belief in Egypt. See vol. iv. 297, which assures us that "no thing poketh and stroketh more strenuously than the Girl" (or hideous Abyssinian cynocephalus). But it must be based upon popular ignorance: the private parts of the monkey although they erect stiffly, like the priapus of Osiris when swearing upon his Phallus, are not of the girth sufficient to produce that friction which is essential to a woman's pleasure. I may here allude to the general disappointment in England and America caused by the exhibition of my friend Paul de Chaillu's Gorillas: he had modestly removed penis and testicles, the latter being somewhat like a bull's, and his squeamishness caused not a little grumbling and sense of grievance — especially amongst the curious sex.

[5] [In the MS. "fahakat," *lit.* she flowed over like a brimful vessel. — St.]

until Time bore me along and I became a wanderer and my condition was changed and I fell into this case. And no one knew
me or aught of my affairs till I came and made friends with
yonder two men. Now the King hearing these words marvelled
at his adventure and what had betided him from the Shifts of
Time and his heart was softened to him and he largessed him and
his comrades and sent them about their business. Then quoth
one of the bystanders to the King, "O Sultan, I know a tale still
rarer than this;" and quoth the King, "Out with it;" whereat the
man began to relate

The History of Abu Niyyah and Abu Niyyatayn.[1]

It is recounted that in Mosul was a King and he was Lord of
moneys and means and troops and guards. Now in the beginning
of his career his adventures were strange for that he was not of
royal rank or race, nor was he of the sons of Kings but prosperity
met him because of the honesty of his manners and morals. His
name was Abu Niyyah, the single-minded—and he was so poor
that he had naught of worldly weal, so quoth he to himself,
"Remove thee from this town and haply Allah will widen thy
means of livelihood inasmuch as the byword said, 'Travel, for
indeed much of the joys of life are in travelling.'" So he fixed his
mind upon removal from the town; and, having very few articles
of his own, he sold them for a single dinar which he took and fared
forth from his place of birth seeking another stead. Now when
journeying he sighted following him a man who was also on the

---

[1] In 1821, Scott (p. 214) following Gilchrist's method of transliterating eastern tongues
wrote "Abou Neeut" and "Neeuteen" (the latter a bad blunder making a masc. plural
of a fem. dual). In 1822 Edouard Gauttier (vi. 320) gallicised the names to "Abou-Nyout"
and "Abou-Nyoutyn" with the same mistake and one superadded; there is no such Arabic
word as "Niyút." Mr. Kirby in 1822, "The New Arabian Nights" (p. 366) reduced the
words to "Abu Neut" and "Abu Neuteen," which is still less intelligible than Scott's; and,
lastly, the well-known Turkish scholar Dr. Redhouse converted the tortured names to
"Abú Niyyet" and "Abú Niyyeteyn," thus rightly giving a "tashdíd" (reduplication sign)
to the Yá (see Appendix p. 430 to Suppl. Vol. No. iii. and Turk. Dict. sub voce "Niyyat").
The Arab. is "Niyyah" = will, purpose, intent; "Abú Niyyah" (Grammat. "Abú Niy-
yatin") Father of one Intent = single-minded and "Abú Niyyatayn" = Father of two
Intents or double-minded; and Richardson is deficient when he writes only "Niyat" for
"Niyyat." I had some hesitation about translating this tale which begins with the "Envier
and the Envied" (vol. i. 123) and ends with the "Sisters who envied their Cadette" (Suppl.
vol. iii. 313). But the extant versions of it are so imperfect in English and French that I
made up my mind to include it in this collection.— [Richardson's "Niyat" is rather another,
although rarer form of the same word. — St.]

move and he made acquaintance with him and the two fell to communing together upon the road. Each of the twain wished to know the name of his comrade and Abu Niyyah asked his fellow, saying, "O my brother, what may be thy name?" whereto the other answered, "I am called Abu Niyyatayn—the two-minded." "And I am Abu Niyyah!" cried the other, and his fellow-traveller questioned him saying, "Hast thou with thee aught of money?" Whereto he replied, "I have with me a single Ashrafi and no more." Quoth the other, "But I have ten gold pieces, so do thou have a care of them and the same will be eleven." Abu Niyyah accepted the charge and they went upon the road together and as often as they entered a town they nighted therein for a single night or two and in the morning they departed therefrom. This continued for a while of time until they made a city which had two gates and Abu Niyyah forewent his fellow through one of the entrances and suddenly heard an asker which was a slave begging and saying, "O ye beneficent, O doers of good deeds, an alms shall bring ten-fold." And as the chattel drew near[1] and Abu Niyyah noted his words, his heart was softened and he gave him his single Ashrafi; whereupon his comrade looked upon him and asked, "What hast thou doled to him?" Answered he, "An Ashrafi;" and quoth the other, "Thou hast but a single gold piece whilst I have ten;" so he took the joint stock from him and left him and went his way.——And Shahrazad was surprised by the dawn of day and fell silent and ceased to say her permitted say. Then quoth her sister Dunyazad, "How sweet is thy story, O sister mine, and how enjoyable and delectable!" Quoth she, "And where is this compared with that I should relate to you on the coming night an the King suffer me to survive?" Now when it was the next night and that was

The Four Hundred and Seventy-third Night.

DUNYAZAD said to her, "Allah upon thee, O my sister, an thou be other than sleepy, finish for us thy tale that we may cut short the watching of this our latter night!" She replied, "With love and good will!" It hath reached me, O auspicious King, the

---

[1] [I read: "wa tukarribu 'l-'abda ilayya," referring the verb to "al-Sadakah" (the alms) and translating: "and it bringeth the servant near to me," the speaker, in Coranic fashion supposed to be Allah. — St.]

director, the right-guiding, lord of the rede which is benefiting
and of deeds fair-seeming and worthy celebrating, that the man
Abu Niyyatayn took from Abu Niyyah the ten Ashrafis[1] and
said to him, "The gold piece belonging to thee thou hast given
to the asker;" then, carrying away the other ten he left him and
went about his business. Now Abu Niyyah had with him not
a single copper neither aught of provaunt so he wandered about
the town to find a Cathedral-mosque and seeing one he went
into it and made the Wuzu-ablution and prayed that which was
incumbent on him of obligatory prayers. Then he seated himself
to rest until the hour of the sunset devotions and he said to himself "Ho, Such-an-one! this be a time when no one knoweth thee;
so go forth and fare round about the doors and have a heed, haply
Allah Almighty our Lord shall give thee somewhat of daily bread
thou shalt eat blessing the Creator." Hereupon he went forth
the Mosque and wandered through the nearest quarter, when
behold, he came upon a lofty gate and a well adorned; so he stood
before it and saw a slave lad coming out therefrom and bearing on
his head a platter wherein was a pile of broken bread and some
bones, and the boy stood there and shook the contents of the
platter upon the ground. Abu Niyyah seeing this came forward
and fell to picking up the orts of bread and ate them and gnawed
the flesh from sundry of the bones till he was satisfied and the
slave diverted himself by looking on. After that he cried, "Alhamdolillah—Glory be to God!"[2] and the chattel went upstairs
to his master and said, "O my lord, I have seen a marvel!" Quoth
the other, "And what may that be?" and quoth the servile, "I
found a man standing at our door and he was silent and spoke
not a word; but when he saw me throwing away the remnants[3]
of our eating-cloth he came up to them and fell to devouring
bittocks of the bread and to breaking the bones and sucking them,

---

[1] The text prefers the Egyptian form "Sheriff" pl. "Sheriffyah," which was adopted by
the Portuguese.

[2] The grace after meat, "Bismillah" being that which precedes it. Abu Niyyah was
more grateful than a youth of my acquaintance who absolutely declined asking the Lord
to "make him truly thankful" after a dinner of cold mutton.

[3] [The root "Kart" is given in the dictionaries merely to introduce the word "karit"
= complete, speaking of a year, &c., and "Takrit," the name of a town in Mesopotamia,
celebrated for its velvets and as the birth-place of Saladin. According to the first mentioned word I would take the signification of "Kart" to be "complement" which here
may fitly be rendered by "remainder," for that which with regard to the full contents of
the dinner tray is their complement would of course be their remainder with regard to
the viands that have been eaten. — ST.]

after which he cried, 'Alhamdolillah.'" Said the master, "O my
good slave, do thou take these ten Ashrafis and give them to the
man;" so the lad went down the stair and was half-way when he
filched one of the gold pieces and then having descended he gave
the nine. Hereupon Abu Niyyah counted them and finding only
nine, said, "There wanteth one Ashrafi, for the asker declared,
An almsdeed bringeth tenfold, and I gave him a single gold piece."
The house-master heard him saying, "There wanteth an Ashrafi,"
and he bade the slave call aloud to him and Abu Niyyah went
upstairs to the sitting room, where he found the owner, a merchant of repute, and salam'd to him. The other returned his
greeting and said, "Ho fellow!" and the other said "Yes," when
the first resumed, "The slave, what did he give thee?" "He gave
me," said Abu Niyyah, "nine Ashrafis;" and the house-master
rejoined, "Wherefore didst thou declare, There faileth me one
gold piece? Hast thou a legal claim of debt upon us for an Ashrafi,
O thou scanty of shame?" He answered, "No, by Allah, O my
lord; my intent was not that but there befel me with a man which
was a beggar such-and-such matter." Hereupon the merchant
understood his meaning and said to him, "Do thou sit thee down
here and pass the night with us." So Abu Niyyah seated himself by his side and nighted with the merchant until the morning.
Now this was the season for the payment of the poor-rates,[1] and
that merchant was wont to take the sum from his property by
weight of scales, so he summoned the official weigher who by
means of his balance computed the account and took out the
poor-rate and gave the whole proceeds to Abu Niyyah. Quoth
he, "O my lord, what shall I do with all this good, especially as
thou hast favoured me with thy regard?" "No matter for that,"
quoth the other; so Abu Niyyah went forth from the presence
of his patron and hiring himself a shop fell to buying what suited
him of all kinds of merchandise such as a portion of coffee-beans
and of pepper and of tin;[2] and stuffs of Al-Hind, together with
other matters, saying to himself, "Verily this shop is the property
of thy hand." So he sat there selling and buying and he was in
the easiest of life and in all comfort rife for a while of time when
behold, his quondam companion, Abu Niyyatayn was seen

---

[1] For the "Zakát" = legal alms, which must not be less than two-and-a-half per cent.,
see vol. i. 339.

[2] In text "Kazdír," for which see vols. iv. 274 and vi. 39. Here it may allude to the
canisters which make great show in the general store of a petty shopkeeper.

passing along the market-street. His eyes were deep[1] sunken and he was propped upon a staff as he begged and cried, "O good folk, O ye beneficent, give me an alms for the love of Allah!" But when his sometime associate, Abu Niyyah looked upon him, he knew him and said to the slave whom he had bought for his service, "Go thou and bring me yonder man." Hereat the chattel went and brought him and Abu Niyyah seated him upon the shop-board and sent his servile to buy somewhat of food and he set it before Abu Niyyatayn who ate till he was filled. After this the wanderer asked leave to depart but the other said to him, "Sit thou here, O Shaykh; for thou art my guest during the coming night." Accordingly he seated himself in the shop till the hour of sundown, when Abu Niyyah took him and led him to his lodging where the slave served up the supper-tray and they ate till they had eaten their sufficiency. Then they washed their hands and abode talking together till at last quoth Abu Niyyah, "O my brother, hast thou not recognised me?" to which the other responded, "No, by Allah, O my brother." Hereupon said the house-master, "I am thy whilome comrade Abu Niyyah, and we came together, I and thou, from such-and-such a place to this city. But I, O my brother, have never changed mine intent[2] and all thou seest with me of good, the half thereof belongeth to thee." When it was morning tide he presented him with the moiety of all he possessed of money and means and opened for him a shop in the Bazar by the side of his own and Abu Niyyatayn fell to selling and buying, and he and his friend Abu Niyyah led the most joyous of lives. This endured for a while of time until one day of the days when quoth Abu Niyyatayn to Abu Niyyah, "O my brother, we have exhausted our sitting in this city, so do thou travel with us unto another." Quoth Abu Niyyah, "Why, O my brother, should we cease abiding here in comfort when we have gained abundance of wealth and moveables and valuables and we seek naught save a restful life?" However Abu Niyyatayn ceased not to repeat his words to him and persist in his purpose and reiterate his demand, till Abu

---

[1] [The MS. reads "murafraf" (passive) from, "Rafraf" = a shelf, arch, anything over-hanging something else, therefore here applying either to the eyebrows as overhanging the eyes, or to the sockets, as forming a vault or cave for them. Perhaps it should be "murafrif" (active part), used of a bird, who spreads his wings and circles round his prey, ready to pounce upon it; hence with prying, hungry, greedy eyes. — Sr.]

[2] Arab. "Niyyah" with the normal pun upon the name.

Niyyah was pleased with the idea of travelling——And Shah-razad was surprised by the dawn of day and fell silent and ceased saying her permitted say. Then quoth her sister Dunyazad, "How sweet and tasteful is thy tale, O sister mine, and how enjoyable and delectable!" Quoth she, "And where is this compared with that I should relate to you on the coming night and the King suffer me to survive?" Now when it was the next night and that was

The Four Hundred and Seventy-fifth Night,

DUNYAZAD said to her, "Allah upon thee, O my sister, an thou be other than sleepy, finish for us thy tale that we may cut short the watching of this our latter night!" She replied, "With love and good will!" It hath reached me, O auspicious King, the director, the right-guiding, lord of the rede which is benefiting and of deeds fair-seeming and worthy celebrating, that Abu Niyyah was pleased with the idea of travelling companied by Abu Niyyatayn: so they got themselves ready and loaded a caravan of camels and mules and went off from that city and travelled for a space of twenty days. At last they came to a camping ground about sunset-hour and they alighted therein seeking rest and a nighting stead, and next morning when they arose they sought where they could fodder and water their cattle. Now the only place they found was a well and one said to other, "Who will descend therein and draw for us drink?" Cried Abu Niyyah, "I will go down" (but he knew not what was fated to him in the Eternal Purpose), and so saying he let himself down by the rope into the well and filled for them the water-buckets till the caravan had its sufficiency. Now Abu Niyyatayn for the excess of his envy and hatred was scheming in his heart and his secret soul to slay Abu Niyyah, and when all had drunk he cut the cord and loaded his beasts and fared away leaving his companion in the well, for the first day and the second until the coming of night. Suddenly two 'Ifrits forgathered in that well and sat down to converse each with other, when quoth the first, "What is to do with thee and how is thy case and what mayest thou be?" Quoth his fellow, "By Allah, O my brother, I am satisfied with extreme satisfaction and I never leave the Sultan's daughter at all at all." The second Ifrit asked, "And

what would forbid thee from her?" and he answered, "I should be
driven away by somewhat of wormwood-powder scattered beneath the soles of her feet during the congregational prayers of
Friday." Then quoth the other, "I also, by Allah, am joyful
and exulting in the possession of a Hoard of jewels buried without the town near the Azure Column which serveth as bench-
mark."[1] "And what," asked the other to his friend, "would
expel thee therefrom and expose the jewels to the gaze of man?"
whereto he answered, "A white cock in his tenth month[2]
slaughtered upon the Azure Column would drive me away from
the Hoard and would break the Talisman when the gems would
be visible to all." Now as soon as Abu Niyyah had heard the
words of the two Ifrits, they arose and departed from the well;
and it was the morning hour when, behold, a caravan was passing
by that place, so the travellers halted seeking a drink of water.
Presently they let down a bucket which was seized by Abu
Niyyah and as he was being drawn up they cried out and asked,
"What art thou, of Jinn-kind or of man-kind?" and he answered,
"I am of the Sons of Adam." Hereupon they drew him up from
the pit and questioned him of his case and he said, "I have fallen
into it and I am sore anhungered." Accordingly they gave him
somewhat to eat and he ate and travelled with them till they
entered a certain city and it was on First day.[3] So they passed
through the market streets which were crowded and found the
people in turmoil and trouble;[4] and as one enquired the cause
thereof he was answered, "Verily the Sultan hath a beautiful
daughter who is possessed and overridden by an 'Ifrit, and whoso
of the physicians would lay[5] the Spirit and is unable or ignorant

---

[1] Arab. "'Amil Rasad," lit. acting as an observatory: but the style is broken as usual,
and to judge from the third line below the sentence may signify "And I am acting as
Talisman (to the Hoard)".

[2] In the text "Ishári," which may have many meanings: I take "a shot" at the most
likely. In "The Tale of the Envier and the Envied" the counter-spell in a fumigation
by means of some white hair plucked from a white spot, the size of a dirham, at the tail-end
of a black tom-cat (vol. i. 124). According to the Welsh legend, "the Devil hates cocks"
— I suppose since that fowl warned Peter of his fall.

[3] In text "Yaum al-Ahad," which begins the Moslem week: see vols. iii. 249, and vi. 190.

[4] [In Ar. "Harj wa Laght." The former is generally joined with "Marj" (Harj wa Marj)
to express utter confusion, chaos, anarchy "Laght" (also pronounced Laghat and written
with the palatal "t") has been mentioned supra p. 11 as a synonym of "Jalabah" ==
clamour, tumult, etc. — ST.]

[5] [In Ar. "yahjubu," aor. of "hajaba" == he veiled, put out of sight, excluded, warded
off. Amongst other significations the word is technically used of a nearer degree of relationship excluding entirely or partially a more distant one from inheritance. — ST.]

so to do, the King taketh him and cutteth off his head and hangeth
it up before his palace. Indeed of late days a student came
hither, a youth who knew nothing of expelling the Evil One,
and he accepted the task and the Sultan designeth to smite his
neck at this very hour; so the people are flocking with design to
divert themselves at the decapitation." Now when Abu Niyyah
heard these words he rose without stay or delay and walked in
haste till he came into the presence of the Sultan whom he found
seated upon his throne and the Linkman standing with his scymitar
brandished over the head of the young student and expecting
only the royal order to strike his neck. So Abu Niyyah salam'd
to him and said, "O King of the Age, release yonder youth from
under the sword and send him to thy prison, for if I avail to laying the Spirit and driving him from thy daughter thou shalt have
mercy upon yonder wight, and if I fail thou wilt shorten by the
head me as well as him." Hereupon the King let unbind
the youth and sent him to jail; then he said to Abu Niyyah,
"Wouldst thou go at once to my daughter and unspell her from
the Jinni?" But the other replied, "No, O King, not until
Meeting-day[1] at what time the folk are engaged in congregational
prayers." Now when Abu Niyyah had appointed the Friday,
the King set apart for his guest an apartment and rationed him
with liberal rations.——And Shahrazad was surprised by the
dawn of day and fell silent and ceased to say her permitted say.
Then quoth her sister Dunyazad, "How sweet is thy story, O
sister mine, and how enjoyable and delectable!" Quoth she,
"And where is this compared with that I should relate to you
on the coming night an the King suffer me to survive?" Now
when it was the next night and that was

The Four Hundred and Seventy-seventh Night,

DUNYAZAD said to her, "Allah upon thee, O my sister, an thou
be other than sleepy, finish for us thy tale that we may cut short
the watching of this our latter night!" She replied, "With love
and good will!" It hath reached me, O auspicious King, the
director, the right-guiding, lord of the rede which is benefiting
and of deeds fair-seeming and worthy celebrating, that Abu
Niyyah having appointed the Sultan for Meeting-day, when he

---

[1] Arab. "Yaum al-Jum'ah" = Assembly-day, Friday: see vol. vi. 120.

would unsorcel the Princess, waited till the morning dawned. Then he went forth to the Bazar and brought him a somewhat of wormwood[1] for a silvern Nusf and brought it back, and, as soon as the time of congregational prayers came, the Sultan went forth to his devotions and gave orders that Abu Niyyah be admitted to his daughter whilst the folk were busy at their devotions. Abu Niyyah repaired to his patient, and scattered the Absinthium beneath the soles of her feet, when, lo, and behold! she was made whole, and she groaned and cried aloud, "Where am I?" Hereat the mother rejoiced and whoso were in the Palace; and, as the Sultan returned from the Mosque, he found his daughter sitting sane and sound, after they had dressed her and perfumed her and adorned her, and she met him with glee and gladness. So the two embraced and their joy increased, and the father fell to giving alms and scattering moneys amongst the Fakirs and the miserable and the widows and orphans, in gratitude for his daughter's recovery. Moreover he also released the student youth and largessed him, and bade him gang his gait. After this the King summoned Abu Niyyah into the presence and said to him, "O young man, ask a boon first of Allah and then of me and let it be everything thou wishest and wantest." Quoth the other, "I require of thee to wife the damsel from whom I drove away the Spirit," and the King turning to his Minister said, "Counsel me, O Wazir." Quoth the other, "Put him off until the morrow;" and quoth the Sultan, "O youth, come back to me hither on the morning of the next day." Hereupon Abu Niyyah was dismissed the presence, and betimes on the day appointed he came to the Sultan and found the Wazir beside him hending in hand a gem whose like was not to be found amongst the Kings. Then he set it before the Sultan and said to him, "Show it to the Youth and say to him, 'The dowry of the Princess, my daughter, is a jewel like unto this.'" But whilst Abu Niyyah was standing between his hands the King showed him the gem and repeated to him the words of the Wazir, thinking to himself that it was a pretext for refusing the youth, and saying in his mind, "He will never be able to produce aught like that which the Wazir hath brought." Hereupon Abu Niyyah asked,

---

[1] A regular Badawi remedy. This Artemisia (Arab. Shayh), which the Dicts. translate "wormwood of Pontus," is the sweetest herb of the Desert, and much relished by the wild men: see my "Pilgrimage," vol. i. 228. The Finnish Arabist Wallin, who died Professor of Arabic at Helsingfors, speaks of a "Faráshat al-Shayh" = a carpet of wormwood.

"An so be I bring thee ten equal to this, wilt thou give me the damsel?" and the King answered, "I will." The youth went from him when this was agreed upon and fared to the Market Street, where he bought him a white cock in its tenth month, such as had been described by the 'Ifrit, whose plume had not a trace of black or red feathers but was of the purest white. Then he fared without the town and in the direction of the setting sun until he came to the Azure Column, which he found exactly as he had heard it from the Jinni, and going to it, he cut the throat of the cock thereupon, when all of a sudden the earth gaped and therein appeared a chamber full of jewels sized as ostrich eggs. That being the Hoard, he went forth and brought with him ten camels, each bearing two large sacks, and returning to the treas-ure-room, he filled all of these bags with gems and loaded them upon the beasts. Presently he entered to the Sultan with his string of ten camels and, causing them kneel in the court-yard of the Divan, cried to him, "Come down, O King of the Age, and take the dowry of thy daughter." So the Sultan turned towards him and, looking at the ten camels, exclaimed, "By Allah, this Youth is Jinn-mad; yet will I go down to see him." Accordingly he descended the staircase to the place where the camels had been made kneel, and when the sacks had been unloaded and as the King came amongst them, the bags were opened and were found full of jewels greater and more glorious than the one was with him. Hereupon the Sultan was perplext and his wits were bewildered, and he cried to the Wazir, "Wallá-hi! I think that all the Kings of the Earth in its length and its breadth have not one single gem the like of these: but say me how shall I act, O Wazir?" The Minister replied, "Give him the girl."——And Shahrazad was surprised by the dawn of day and fell silent and ceased saying her permitted say. Then quoth her sister Dunyazad, "How sweet and tasteful is thy tale, O sister mine, and how enjoyable and delectable!" Quoth she, "And where is this compared with that I should relate to you on the coming night, an the King suffer me to survive?" Now when it was the next night and that was

The Four Hundred and Seventy-ninth Night.

DUNYAZAD said to her, "Allah upon thee, O my sister, an thou be other than sleepy, finish for us thy tale that we may cut short the watching of this our latter night!" She replied, "With love and good will!" It hath reached me, O auspicious King, the director, the right-guiding, lord of the rede which is benefiting and of deeds fair-seeming and worthy celebrating, that the Wazir said to the King, "Give him the girl." Hereupon the marriage-tie was tied and the bridegroom was led in to the bride, and either rejoiced mightily in his mate,[1] and was increased their joy and destroyed was all annoy. Now Abu Niyyah was a favourite of Fortune, so the Sultan appointed to him the government during three days of every week, and he continued ruling after that fashion for a while of time. But one day of the days, as he was sitting in his pleasaunce, suddenly the man Abu Niyyatayn passed before him leaning on a palm-stick, and crying, "O ye beneficent, O ye folk of good!" When Abu Niyyah beheld him he said to his Chamberlain, "Hither with yonder man;" and as soon as he was brought he bade them lead him to the Hammam and dress him in a new habit. They did his bidding and set the beggar before his whilome comrade who said to him, "Dost thou know me?" "No, O my lord," said the other; and he, "I am thy companion of old whom thou wouldst have left to die in the well; but I, by Allah, never changed my intent, and all that I own in this world I will give unto thee half thereof." And they sat in converse for a while of time, until at last the Double-minded one, "Whence camest thou by all this?" and quoth he, "From the well wherein thou threwest me." Hereupon from the excess of his envy and malice Abu Niyyatayn said to Abu Niyyah, "I also will go down that well and what to thee was given the same shall be given to me." Then he left him and went forth from him, and he ceased not faring until he made the place. Presently he descended, and having reached the bottom, there sat until the hour of nightfall, when behold! the two 'Ifrits came and, taking seat by the well-mouth, salam'd each to other. But they had no force nor contrivance and both were as weaklings; so said one of them, "What is thy case, O my brother, and how is thy health?" and said the other, "Ah me, O my brother, since the hour that I was with thee in this place on such a night, I have been cast out of the Sultan's daughter, and until this tide I have been unable to approach her or indeed at any other time."

---

1 "Sáhibi-h," the masculine; because, as the old grammar tells us, that gender is more worthy than the feminine.

Said his comrade, "I also am like thee, for the Hoard hath gone forth from me, and I have waxed feeble."[1] Then cried the twain, "By Allah, the origin of our losses is from this well, so let us block it up with stones." Hereupon the twain arose and brought with them crumbling earth and pebbles,[2] and threw it down the well when it fell upon Abu Niyyatayn, and his bones were crushed upon his flesh.[3] Now his comrade, Abu Niyyah sat expecting him to return, but he came not, so he cried, "Walláhi! needs must I go and look for him in yonder well and see what he is doing." So he took horse and fared thither and found the pit filled up; so he knew and was certified that his comrade's intent had been evil, and had cast him into the hands of death.——And Shahrazad was surprised by the dawn of day and fell silent and ceased to say her permitted say. Then quoth her sister Dunyazad, "How sweet is thy story, O sister mine, and how enjoyable and delectable!" Quoth she, "And where is this compared with that I should relate to you on the coming night, an the Sovran suffer me to survive?" Now when it was the next night and that was

The Four Hundred and Eightieth Night,

DUNYAZAD said to her, "Allah upon thee, O my sister, an thou be other than sleepy, finish for us thy tale that we may cut short the watching of this our latter night!" She replied, "With love and good will!" It hath reached me, O auspicious King, the director, the right-guiding, lord of the rede which is benefiting and of deeds fair-seeming and worthy celebrating, that Abu Niyyah knew and was certified of his comrade Abu Niyyatayn being dead, so he cried aloud, "There is no Majesty and there is no Might save in Allah the Glorious, the Great. O Allah mine, do thou deliver me from envy, for that it destroyeth the envier and haply jealousy may lead to frowardness against the Lord (glorified be His Glory!);" and so saying he returned to the seat

---

[1] *i.e.* his strength was in the gold: see vol. i. 340.

[2] Arab. "Haysumah" = smooth stones (water-rounded?).

[3] For "his flesh was crushed upon his bones," a fair specimen of Arab. "metonomy-cum-hyperbole." In the days when Mr. John Bull boasted of his realism *versus* Gallic idealism, he "got wet to the skin" when M. Jean Crapaud was *mouillé jusqu'aux os.*

For the Angels supposed to haunt a pure and holy well, and the trick played by Ibn Túmart, see Ibn Khaldun's Hist. of the Berbers, vol. ii. 575.

of his kingdom. Now the Sultan's daughter his spouse had two
sisters, both married,[1] and she after the delay of a year or so proved
with child, but when her tale of days was told and her delivery
was nearhand her father fell sick and his malady grew upon him.
So he summoned the Lords of his court and his kingdom one and
all and he said, "In very deed this my son-in-law shall after my
decease become my successor;" and he wrote a writ to that
purport and devised to him the realm and the reign before his
demise; nor was there long delay ere the old King departed to
the ruth of Allah and they buried him. Hereupon trouble arose
between his two other sons-in-law who had married the Princesses and said they, "We were connected with him ere this
man was and we are before him in our claim to the kingdom."
Thereupon said the Wazir, "This rede is other than right, for
that the old King before his decease devised his country to this
one and also wrote it in his will and testament: here therefore
ye are opposing him, and the result will be trouble and repentance." And when the Minister spoke on such wise they kept
to their houses. Presently the wife of Abu Niyyah bare him a
babe, her two sisters being present at her accouchement; and
they gave to the midwife an hundred gold pieces and agreed
upon what was to be done. So when the babe was born they
put in his place a pup and taking the infant away sent it by a
slave-girl who exposed it at the gateway of the royal garden.
Then they said and spread abroad, "Verily the Sultan's wife
hath been delivered of a doglet," and when the tidings came
to Abu Niyyah's ears he exclaimed, "Verily this also is a creation
of Allah Almighty's:" so they clothed the pup and tended it
with all care. Anon the wife became pregnant a second time
and when her days were fulfilled she bare a second babe which
was the fairest of its time and the sisters did with it as they had
done with the first and taking the infant they exposed him at the
door of the garden. Then they brought to the mother another
dog-pup in lieu of her babe, saying, "Verily the Queen hath been
delivered a second time of a doglet." Now on this wise it fared
with them: but as regards the two infants which were cast away
at the garden gate the first was taken up by the Gardener whose
wife, by the decree of the Decreer, had become a mother on that
very same night; so the man carried away the infant he found

---

[1] Here begins the second tale which is a weak replica of Galland's "Two Sisters," &c.

exposed and brought the foundling home and the woman fell to
suckling it.   After the third year the Gardener went forth one
day of the days and happening upon the second infant in similar
case he bore it also back to his wife who began to suckle it and
wash it and tend it and nurse it, till the twain grew up and entered into their third and fourth years.   The Sultan had in the
meantime been keeping the two pups which he deemed to have
been brought forth by his wife until the Queen became in the
family-way for the third time.   Hereupon the Sultan said, "By
Allah, 'tis not possible but that I be present at and witness her
accouchement;" and the while she was bringing forth he sat
beside her.   So she was delivered of a girl-child, in whom the
father rejoiced with great joy and bade bring for her wet-nurses
who suckled her for two years until the milk time was past.[1]
This girl grew up till she reached the age of four years and she
could distinguish between her mother and her father who,
whenever he went to the royal garden would take her with him.
But when she beheld the Gardener's two boys she became familiar
with them and would play with them; and, as each day ended,
her father would carry her away from the children and lead her
home, and this parting was grievous to her and she wept right
sore.   Hereat the Sultan would take also the boys with her until
sleep prevailed over her, after which he would send the twain
back to their sire the Gardener.   But Abu Niyyah the Sultan
would ever wonder at the boys and would exclaim, "Praise be
to Allah, how beautiful are these dark-skinned children!"   This
endured until one day of the days when the King entered the
garden and there found that the two beautiful[2] boys had taken
some clay and were working it into the figures of horses and
saddles and weapons of war and were opening the ground and
making a water-leat;[3] so the Sultan wondered thereat time after
time for that he ever found them in similar case.   And he mar-

---

[1] This is the usual term amongst savages and barbarians, and during that period the
father has no connection with the mother.   Civilisation has abolished this natural practice
which is observed by all the lower animals and has not improved human matters.   For an
excellent dissertation on the subject see the letter on Polygamy by Mrs. Belinda M. Pratt,
in "The City of the Saints," p. 525.

[2] In text "Kuwayyis," dim. of "Kayyis," and much used in Egypt as an adj. ="pretty,"
"nice" and an adv. "well," "nicely."   See s.v. Spitta Bey's Glossary to *Contes Arabes
Modernes.*   The word is familiar to the travellers in the Nile-valley.

[3] In Arab. a "Kanát;" see vol. iii. 141.   The first occupation came from nature; the
second from seeing the work of the adopted father.

velled the more because whenever he looked upon them his heart was opened to both and he yearned to the twain and he would give them some gold pieces although he knew not the cause of his affection. Now one day he entered the garden, as was his wont, and he came upon the two boys of whom one was saying, "I am the Sultan!" and the other declaring, "I am the Wazir!" He wondered at their words and forthwith summoned the Gardener and asked him concerning the lads, and lastly quoth he to him, "Say me sooth and fear naught from me." Quoth the other, "By Allah, O King of the Age, albe falsehood be saving, yet is soothfastness more saving and most saving; and indeed as regards these children the elder was found by me exposed at the gateway of the royal garden on such a night of such a year, and I came upon the second in the very same place; so I carried them to my wife who suckled them and tended them and they say to her, 'O mother,' and they say to me, 'O father.' " Hereupon Abu Niyyah the King returned home and summoning the midwife asked her, saying, "By the virtue of my predecessors in this kingdom, do thou tell me the truth concerning my spouse, whether or no she was delivered of two dog-pups," and she answered, "No, by Allah, O King of the Age, verily the Queen bare thee two babes like full moons, and the cause of their exposure before the garden gate was thy wife's two sisters who envied her and did with her these deeds whereof she was not aware."[1] Hereupon cried Abu Niyyah, "Alhamdolillah— Glory be to God who hath brought about this good to me and hath united me with my children, and soothfast is the say, 'Whoso doeth an action shall be requited of his Lord and the envious wight hath no delight and of his envy he shall win naught save despight.' "[2] Then the King of Mosul, being a man of good intent, did not put to death his wife's sisters and

---

[1] Abu Niyyah, like most house masters in the East, not to speak of Kings, was the last to be told a truth familiar to everyone but himself and his wife.

[2] The MS. breaks off abruptly at this sentence and evidently lacks finish. Scott (vi., 228) adds, "The young princes were acknowledged and the good Abou Neeut had the satisfaction of seeing them grow up to follow his example."

In the MS. this tale is followed by a "Story of his own Adventures related by a connection to an Emir of Egypt." I have omitted it because it is a somewhat fade replica of "The Lovers of the Banú Ozrah" (Vol. vii. 117; Lane iii. 247).

their husbands, but banished them his realm, and he lived happily with his Queen and children until such time as the Destroyer
of delights and the Severer of societies came to him and he deceased to the mercy of Almighty Allah.

END OF VOLUME XIV.

Appendix A.

INEPTIÆ BODLEIANÆ.

The reader will not understand this allusion (Foreword, p. ix.) without some *connaissance de cause.* I would apologise for deforming the beautiful serenity and restfulness of The Nights by personal matter of a tone so jarring and so discordant a sound, the chatter and squabble of European correspondence and contention; but the only course assigned to me perforce is that of perfect publicity. The first part of the following papers appeared by the editor's kindness in "The Academy" of November 13, 1886. How strange the contrast of "doings" with "sayings," if we compare the speech reported to have been delivered by Mr. Librarian Nicholson at the opening of the Birmingham Free Public Central Lending and Reference Libraries, on June 1, 1882:—

"As for the Bodleian, I claim your sympathies, not merely because we are trying to do as much for our readers as you are for yours, but because, if the building which you have opened to-day is the newest free public library in the world, the building which I left earlier in the morning is the oldest free public library in the world. (*No!*) I call it a free public library because any Birmingham artizan who came to us with a trustworthy recommendation might ask to have *the rarest gem* in our collection placed before him, and need have no fear of asking in vain; and because, if a trusty Birmingham worker wanted the *loan of a MS.* for three months, it would be lent to the Central Free Library for his use." See Twentieth and Twenty-first Annual Reports of the Free Libraries Committee (Borough of Birmingham), 1883.

And now to my story. The play opens with the following letter:—

No. I.

23, Dorset Street, Portman Square,
Sept. 13, 1886.

"Sir,

"I have the honour to solicit your assistance in the following matter:—

"Our friend Dr. Steingass has kindly consented to collaborate with me in re-translating from the Wortley Montague MS. of the Bodleian Library, Oxford, the tales originally translated in vol. vi. of Dr. Jonathan Scott's 'Arabian Nights.' Dr. Steingass cannot leave town, and I should find it very inconvenient to live at Oxford during the work, both of us having engagements in London. It would be a boon to us if the Curators of the Bodleian would allow the MS. to be transferred, volume by volume, to the India Office, and remain under the custody of the Chief Librarian — yourself. The whole consists of seven volumes, as we would begin with vols. iii. and iv. I may note that the translated tales (as may be seen by Scott's version) contain nothing indelicate or immoral; in fact the whole MS. is exceptionally pure. Moreover, the MS., as far as I can learn, is never used at Oxford I am the more anxious about this matter as the November fogs will presently drive me from England, and I want to end the extracts ere winter sets in, which can be done only by the co-operation of Dr. Steingass.

I have the honour to be, sir,

Yours obediently,

(Signed) RICHARD F. BURTON."

"DR. R. ROST,
Chief Librarian, India Office."

As nearly a month had elapsed without my receiving any reply, I directed the following to the Vice-Chancellor of the University, Rev. Dr. Bellamy: —

No. II.

ATHENÆUM CLUB, PALL MALL,
Oct. 13, 1886.

"SIR,

"I have the honour to submit to you the following details: —

"On September 13, 1886, I wrote to Dr. Rost, Chief Librarian, India Office, an official letter requesting him to apply to the Curators of the Bodleian Library, Oxford, for the temporary transfer of an Arabic Manuscript, No. 522 (the Wortley Montague text of the Arabian Nights) to the library of the India Office, there to be kept under special charge of the Chief Librarian. There being seven volumes, I wanted only one or two at a time. I undertook not to keep them long, and, further, I pledged myself not to translate tales that might be deemed offensive to propriety.

"Thus, I did not apply for a personal loan of the MS. which, indeed, I should refuse on account of the responsibility which it would involve. I applied for the safe and temporary transfer of a work, volume by volume, from one public library to another.

"My official letter was forwarded at once by Dr. Rost, but this was the only expeditious step. On Saturday, September 25, the Curators could form no quorum; the same thing took place on Saturday, October 9; and there is a prospect that the same will take place on Saturday, October 23.

"I am acquainted with many of the public libraries of Europe, but I know of none that would throw such obstacles in the way of students.

"The best authorities inform me that until June, 1886, the signatures of two Curators enabled a student to borrow a book or a manuscript; but that since June a meeting of three Curators has been required; and that a lesser number does not form a quorum.

"May I be permitted to suggest that the statute upon the subject of borrowing books and manuscripts urgently calls for revision?

I have the honour to be, sir,

Yours obediently,

(Signed) RICHARD F. BURTON."

"THE VICE-CHANCELLOR, OXFORD."

The Curators presently met and the following was the highly unsatisfactory result which speaks little for "Bodleian" kindness or courtesy: —

No. III.

Monday, Nov. 1, 1886.

"DEAR SIR RICHARD BURTON,

"The Curators considered your application on Saturday, Oct. 30, afternoon, and the majority of them were unwilling to lend the MS [1]

Yours very truly,

(Signed) EDWARD B. NICHOLSON."

---

[1] Mr. Chandler remarks (p. 25, "On Lending Bodleian Books, &c."): — "It is said that

Learning through a private source that my case had been made an unpleasant exception to a long-standing rule of precedent, and furthermore that it had been rendered peculiarly invidious by an act of special favour,[1] I again addressed the Vice-Chancellor, as follows: —

No. IV.

23, DORSET STREET, PORTMAN SQUARE,
November 3rd, 1886.

"SIR,

"I have the honour to remind you that, on October 13, I communicated with you officially requesting a temporary transfer of the Wortley Montague manuscript (Arabian Nights) from the Bodleian Library to the personal care of the Librarian, India Office.

"To this letter I received no reply. But on November 1, I was informed by Mr. Librarian Nicholson that the Curators had considered my application on Saturday, October 30, and that the majority of them were unwilling to lend the manuscript.

"The same Curators at the same meeting allowed sundry manuscripts for the use of an Indian subject to be sent to the India Office.

"I cannot but protest against this invidious proceeding, and I would willingly learn what cause underlies it.

"1. It cannot be the importance of the manuscript, which is one of the meanest known to me—written in a schoolmaster character, a most erroneous, uncorrected text, and valuable only for a few new tales.

"2. It cannot be any consideration of public morals, for I undertook (*if the loan were granted*) not to translate tales which might be considered offensive to strict propriety.

"3. It cannot be its requirement for local use. The manuscript stands on an upper shelf in the manuscript room, *and not one man in the whole so-called 'University' can read it.*

I have the honour to be, sir,

Yours obediently,

RICHARD F. BURTON."

"THE VICE-CHANCELLOR, OXFORD."

In due time came the reply:—

No. V.

ST. JOHN'S COLLEGE, OXFORD,
November 6th, 1886.

"DEAR SIR,

"I will remove from your mind the belief that I treated your former letter with discourtesy.

---

the Curators can refuse any application if they choose; of course they can, but as a matter of fact no application has ever been refused, and every name added will make it more and more difficult, more and more invidious to refuse anyone." I have, therefore, the singular honour of being the first chosen for rejection.

[1] Mr. Chandler's motion (see p. 28, "Booklending, &c.") was defeated by an amendment prepared by Professor Jowett and the former fought, with mixed success, the report of the Committee of Loans; the document being so hacked as to become useless, and, in this mangled condition, it was referred back to the Committee with a recommendation to consider the best way of carrying out the present statute. The manly and straightforward course of at once proposing a new statute was not adopted, nor was it even formally proposed. Lastly, the applications for loans, which numbered sixteen, were submitted to the magnates and were all refused! whilst the application of an Indian subject that MSS. be sent to the India Office for his private use was at once granted. In my case Professors B. Price and Max Müller, who had often voted for loans, and were willing enough to lend anything to anybody, declined to vote.

"I may say, that it did not appear to me to contain any question or request which I could answer. You informed me that you had made formal application in September for a loan of MSS., and your letter was to complain of the delay in considering this request. You told me that you had learned from the Librarian the cause of the delay (the want of a quorum), and that he had intimated that there would probably be no meeting formed before October 30th.

"You complained of this, and suggested that the statute regulating the lending of the Bodleian books should be speedily revised.

"As I had no power to make a quorum, nor to engage that your suggestion should be adopted; and as your letter made no demand for any further information, I thought it best to reserve it for the meeting of the 30th, when I communicated it to the Curators.

"I will lay the letter (dated November 3rd), with which you have favoured me, before the next meeting of the Curators.

I beg to remain,

Yours faithfully,

(Signed) J. BELLAMY."

"SIR R. F. BURTON."

To resume this part of the subject.

The following dates show that I was kept waiting six weeks before being finally favoured with the curtest of refusals:

Application made on September 13th, and sent on.

On Saturday, September 25th, Curators could not form quorum, and deferred next meeting till Saturday, October 9th.

Saturday, October 9th. Again no quorum; and yet it might easily have been formed, as three Curators were on or close to the spot.

Saturday, October 23rd. Six Curators met and did nothing.

Saturday, October 30th. Curators met and refused me the loan of MS.

My letter addressed to the Vice-Chancellor was read, and notice was given for Saturday (December 3rd, 1886) of a motion, "That the MS. required by Sir R. F. Burton be lent to him"—and I was not to be informed of the matter unless the move were successful. Of course it failed. One of the Curators (who are the delegates and servants of Convocation) was mortally offended by my letter to "The Academy," and showed the normal smallness of the official mind by opposing me simply because I told the truth concerning the *laches* of his "learned body."

Meanwhile I had addressed the following note to the Most Honourable the Chancellor of the University.[1]

23, DORSET STREET, PORTMAN SQUARE,
November 30th, 1886.

"MY LORD,

"I deeply regret that the peculiar proceedings of the Bodleian Library, Oxford, necessitate a reference to a higher authority with the view of eliciting some explanation.

"The correspondence which has passed between the Curators of the Bodleian Library and myself will be found in the accompanying printed paper.

"Here it may be noticed that the Committee of the Orientalist Congress, Vienna, is preparing to memorialise H.M.'s Secretary of State, praying that Parliament will empower the British Museum to lend out Oriental MSS. under proper guarantees. The same

---

[1] According to the statutes, "The Chancellor must be acquainted with the Business (of altering laws concerning the Library), and he must approve, and refer it to the Head of Houses, else no dispensation can be proposed."

measure had been proposed at the Leyden Congress of 1883; and thus an extension, rather than a contraction of the loan-system has found favour with European savants.[1]

"I believe, my Lord, that a new statute upon the subject of the Bodleian loans of books and MSS. is confessedly required, and that it awaits only the initiative of the **Chancellor** of the University, without whose approval it cannot be passed.

I have, &c.,
(Signed) RICHARD F. BURTON."

"THE RIGHT HONOURABLE THE CHANCELLOR."

My object being only publicity I was not disappointed by the following reply:—

HATFIELD HOUSE, HATFIELD, HERTS,
December 1st, 1886.

"DEAR SIR RICHARD,

"I beg to acknowledge your letter of the 30th of November with enclosure.

"I have, however, no power over the Bodleian Library, and, therefore, I am unable to assist you.

Yours, very truly,
(Signed) SALISBURY."

"SIR RICHARD F. BURTON, K.C.M.G."

On January 29, 1887, there was another "Bodleian Meeting," all the Curators save one being present and showing evident symptoms of business. The last application on the list of loans entered on the Agenda paper ran thus:—

> V MS. Bodl. Vols. 550–556 to the British Museum (the 7 vols. successively) for the use of Mr. F. F. Arbuthnot's Agent.
>> [The MS. lately refused to Sir R. Burton. Mr. Arbuthnot wishes to have it copied.]

It was at once removed by the Regius Professor of Divinity (Dr. Ince) and carried *nem. con.* that, until the whole question of lending Bodleian books and MSS. then before

---

[1] The following telegram from the Vienna correspondent of "The Times" (November 16, 1886), is worth quotation:—

"The Committee of the Vienna Congress (of Orientalists) is now preparing a memorial, which will be signed by Archduke Renier, and will be forwarded in a few days to the trustees of the British Museum and to the Secretary of State, praying that a Bill may be introduced into Parliament empowering the British Museum to lend out its Oriental MSS. to foreign savants under proper guarantees. A resolution pledging the members of the Oriental Congress to this course was passed at the Congress of Leyden, in 1883, on the motion of Professor D. H. Müller, of Vienna; but it has not yet been acted upon so thoroughly as will be the case now.

"The British Museum is the only great library in Europe which does not lend out its MSS. to foreigners. The university and court libraries of Vienna, the royal and state libraries of Berlin and Munich, those of Copenhagen and Leyden, and Bibliothèque Nationale in Paris all are very liberal in their loans to well-recommended foreigners. In Paris a diplomatic introduction is required. In Munich the library does not lend directly to the foreign borrower; but sends to the library of the capital whence the borrower may have made his application, and leaves all responsibility to that library. In the other libraries, the discretion is left to the librarian, who generally lends without any formalities beyond ascertaining the *bona fides* and trustworthiness of the applicant. In Vienna, however, there has occasionally been some little excess of formality, so a petition is about to be presented to the Emperor by the University professors, begging that the privilege of borrowing may be considered as general, and not as depending on the favour of an official.

"As regards Oriental MSS., it is remarked that the guarantees need not be so minute as in the case of old European MSS., which are often unique copies. According to the learned Professor of Sanskrit in this city, Herr George Bühler, there are very few unique Oriental MSS. in existence of Sanskrit — perhaps not a dozen."

Council, be definitely settled, no applications be entertained; and thus Professor Van Helton, Bernard Kolbach and Mr. Arbuthnot were doomed, like myself, to be disappointed.

On January 31, 1887, a hebdomadal Council was called to deliberate about a new lending statute for submission to Convocation; and an amendment was printed in the "Oxford University Gazette." It proposed that the Curators by a vote of two-thirds of their body, and at least six forming a quorum, might lend books or MSS. to students, whether graduates or not; subject, when the loans were of special value, to the consent of Convocation. Presently the matter was discussed in "The Times" (January 25th; April 28th; and May 31st), which simply re-echoed the contention of Mr. Chandler's vigorous pamphlets.[1] Despite the letters of its correspondent "F. M. M." (May 6th, 1887), a "host in himself," who ought to have added the authority of his name to the sensible measures which he propounded, the leading journal took a sentimental view of "Bodley's incomparable library" and strongly advocated its being relegated to comparative inutility.

On May 31, 1887, an amendment practically forbidding all loans came before the House. In vain Professor Freeman declared that a book is not an idol but a tool which must wear out sooner or later. To no purpose Bodley's Librarian proved that of 460,000 printed volumes in the collection only 460 had been lent out, and of these only one had been lost. THE AMENDMENT FORBIDDING THE PRACTICE OF LENDING WAS CARRIED BY 106 VOTES TO 60.

Personally I am not dissatisfied with this proceeding. It is retrograde legislation befitting the days when books were chained to the desks. It suffers from a fatal symptom— the weakness of extreme measures. And the inevitable result in the near future will be a strong reaction: Convocation will presently be compelled to adopt some palliation for the evil created by its own folly.

The next move added meanness to inertness. I do not blame Mr. E. B. Nicholson, Bodley's Librarian, because he probably had orders to write the following choice specimen:

30/3/1887.

"DEAR SIR RICHARD BURTON,

"I have received two vols. of four (read *six*) 'Supplemental Nights' with a subscription form. If a Bodleian MS. is to be copied for any volume, I must stipulate that that volume be supplied to us gratis. Either my leave or that of the Curators is required for the purpose of copying for publication, and I have no doubt that they would make the same stipulation. I feel sure you would in any case not propose to charge us for such a volume, but until I hear from you I am in a difficulty as to how to reply to the subscription form I have received.

Yours faithfully,

(Signed)   E. B. NICHOLSON,

Librarian."

The able and energetic papers, two printed and one published by Mr. H. W. Chandler, of Pembroke College, Oxford, clearly prove the following facts:—

---

[1] (1.) "On Lending Bodleian Books and Manuscripts" (not published). June 10, 1866; (2) Appendix. Barlow's Argument. June, 1866; (3) On Book-lending as practised at the Bodleian Library. July 27, 1886: Baxter, Printer, Oxford. The three papers abound in earnestness and energy; but they have the "defects of their qualities," as the phrase is; and the subject often runs away with the writer. A single instance will suffice. No. i. p. 23 says, "In a library like the Bodleian, where the practice of lending prevails as it now does, a man may put himself to great inconvenience in order to visit it; he may even travel from Berlin, and when he arrives he may find that all his trouble has been in vain, the very book he wants is out." This must have been written during the infancy of Sir Rowland Hill, and when telegrams were unknown to mankind; all that the Herr has to do in our times is to ask per wire if the volume be at home or not.

1. That on June 20, 1610, a Bodleian Statute peremptorily forbade any books or manuscripts being taken out of the Library.

2. That, despite the peremptory and categorical forbiddance by Bodley, Selden, and others, of lending Bodleian books and MSS., loans of both have for upwards of two centuries formed a precedent.

3. That Bodley's Statute (June 20th, An. 1610) was formally and officially abrogated by Convocation on May 22nd, 1856; Convocation retaining the right to lend.

4. That a "privileged list" of (113) borrowers presently arose and is spoken of as a normal practice:—*sicut mos fuit*, says the Statute (Tit. xx. iii. § 11) of 1873; and, lastly,

5. That loans of MSS. and printed books have for years been authorised to approved public libraries.

After these premises I proceed to notice other points bearing upon the subject which, curious to say, are utterly neglected or rather ignored by Mr. Chandler and "The Times." Sir Thomas Bodley never would have condemned students to study in the Bodleian had he known the *peines fortes et dures* to which in these days they are thereby doomed. "So picturesque and so peculiar is its construction," says a writer, "that it ensures the maximum of inefficiency and discomfort." The whole building is a model of what a library ought *not* to be. It is at once over solid and ricketty: room for the storage of books is wanted, and its wooden staircases, like touchwood or tinder, give one the shudders to think of fire. True, matches and naked lights are forbidden in the building; but all know how these prohibitions are regarded by the public, and it is dreadful to think of what might result from a lucifer dropped at dark upon the time-rotten planks. The reading public in the XIXth century must content itself with boxes or stalls, like those of an old-fashioned tavern or coffee-house of the humbler sort wherein two readers can hardly find room for sitting back to back. The atmosphere is unpleasant and these mean little cribs, often unduly crowded, are so dark that after the 1st October the reading-room must be closed at 3 p.m. What a contrast are the treasures in the Bodleian with their mean and miserable surroundings and the way in which the public is allowed to enjoy them. The whole establishment calls urgently for reform. Accommodation for the books is wanted; floor and walls will hardly bear the weight which grows every year at an alarming ratio— witness the Novel-room. The model Bodleian would be a building detached and isolated, the better to guard its priceless contents, and containing at least double the area of the present old and obsolete Bibliotheca. An establishment of the kind was proposed in 1857; but unfortunately, the united wisdom of the University preferred new "Examination Schools" for which the old half-ruinous pile would have been sufficiently well fitted. The "Schools," however, were for the benefit of the examiners; *ergo* the scandalous sum of £100,000 (some double the amount) was wasted upon the well-nigh useless Gothic humbug in High Street, and thus no money was left for the prime want of the city. After some experience of public libraries and reading-rooms on the Continent of Europe I feel justified in asserting that the Bodleian in its present condition is a disgrace to Oxford; indeed a dishonour to letters in England.

The Bodleian has a *succursale*, the Radcliffe, which represents simply a step from bad to worse. The building was intended for an especial purpose, the storage of books, not for a *salle de lecture*. Hence the so-called "Camera" is a most odious institution, a Purgatory to readers. It is damp in the wet season from October to May; stuffy during the summer heats and a cave of Eolus in windy weather: few students except the youngest and strongest, can support its changeable and nerve-depressing atmosphere. Consequently the Camera is frequented mainly by the townsfolk, a motley crew who there study their novels and almanacs and shamefully misuse the books.[1] In this building lights, forbidden by the Bodleian, are allowed; it opens at 10 a.m. and closes at 10 p.m.. and the sooner it reverts to its original office of a book-depôt the better.

---

[1] Chandler, "On Lending Bodleian Books," etc., p. 18.

But the Bodleian-Radcliffe concern is typical of the town· and, if that call for reform, so emphatically does

> "Oxford, that scarce deserves the name of land."

From my childhood I had heard endless tirades and much of what is now called "blowing" about this ancient city, and my youth (1840–42) suffered not a little disappointment. The old place, still mostly resembling an overgrown monastery-village, lies in the valley of the Upper Thames, a meadowland drained by two ditches; the bigger or Ise, classically called the Isis, and the lesser the Charwell. This bottom is surrounded by high and healthy uplands, not as the guide-books say "low scarce-swelling hills that softly gird the old town;" and these keep off the winds and make the riverine valley, with its swamped meads and water-meadows, more fenny and feverish even than Cambridge. The heights and woods bring on a mild deluge between October 1st and May 1st; the climate is rainy as that of Shap in Westmoreland (our old home) and, as at Fernando Po and Singapore, the rain it raineth more or less every day during one half of the year. The place was chosen by the ancient Britons for facility of water transport, but men no longer travel by the Thames and they have naturally neglected the older road. Throughout England, indeed a great national work remains to be done. Not a river, not a rivulet, but what requires cleaning out and systematic excavation by *élévateurs* and other appliances of the Suez Canal. The channels filled up by alluvium and choked by the American weed, are now raised so high that the beds can no longer act as drains: at Oxford for instance the beautiful meadows of Christ Church are little better than swamps and marshes, the fittest homes for Tergiana, Quartana and all the fell sisterhood: a blue fog broods over the pleasant site almost every evening, and a thrust with the umbrella opens up water. This is the more inexcusable as the remedy would be easy and by no means costly: the river-mud, if the ignorant peasants only knew the fact, forms the best of manures; and this, instead of being deposited in spoil-heaps on the banks for the rain to wash back at the first opportunity, should be carried by tram-rails temporarily laid down and be spread over the distant fields, thus almost paying for the dredge works. Of course difficulties will arise: the management of the Thames is under various local "Boards," and each wooden head is able and aye ready to show its independence and ill temper at the sacrifice of public interests to private fads.

Hence the climate of Oxford is detestable. Strong undergraduates cannot withstand its nervous depression and the sleeplessness arising from damp air charged with marsh gases and bacteria. All students take time to become acclimatized here, and some are never acclimatized at all. And no wonder, when the place is drained by a fetid sewer of greenish yellow hue containing per 10,000, 245 parts of sewage. The only tolerable portion of the year is the Long Vacation, when the youths in mortar-boards all vanish from the view, while many of the oldsters congregate in the reformed convents called Colleges.

Climate and the resolute neglect of sanitation are probably the chief causes why Oxford never yet produced a world-famous and epoch-making man, while Cambridge can boast of Newton and Darwin. The harlequin city of domes and spires, cribs and slums shows that curious concurrence of opposites so common in England. The boasted High Street is emblematical of the place, where moral as well as material extremes meet and are fain to dwell side by side. It is a fine thoroughfare branching off into mere lanes, neither these nor that apparently ever cleaned. The huge buildings of scaling, mouldering stone are venerable-looking piles which contrast sadly with the gabled cottages of crepi, hurlin, or wattle and dab; and the brand-new store with its plate-glass windows hustles the old-fashioned lollipop-shop. As regards minor matters there are new market passages but no Public Baths; and on Sundays, the stands are destitute of cabs, although with that queer concession to democracy which essentially belongs to the meaner spirited sort of Conservatism, " 'busses" are allowed to ply after 2 p.m., when the thunder of bells somewhat abates.

Old "Alma Mater," who to me has ever been a "durissima noverca," dubs herself "University;" and not a few of her hopefuls *entre faiblesse et folie*, still entitle themselves "University men." The title once belonged to Oxford but now appertains to it no more. Compare with it the model universities of Berlin, Paris and Vienna, where the lists of lecturers bear the weightiest names in the land. Oxford is but a congeries of twenty-one colleges and five halls or hostels, each educating its pupils (more or less) with an especial eye to tutors' fees and other benefices, the vested rights of the "Dons." Thus all do their best to prevent the scholars availing themselves of University, as opposed to Collegiate, lectures; and thus they can stultify a list of some sixty-six professors. This boarding-school system is simply a dishonest obstacle to students learning anything which may be of use to them in after-life, such as modern and Oriental languages, chemistry, anthropology and the other -ologies. Here in fact men rarely progress beyond the Trivium and the Quadrivium of the Dark Ages, and tuition is a fine study of the Res scibilis as understood by the Admirable Crichton and other worthies, circa A.D. 1500. The students of Queen Elizabeth's day would here—and here only—find themselves in congenial company. Worse still, Oxford is no longer a "Seat of learning" or a "House of the Muses," nor can learned men be produced under the present system. The place has become a collection of finishing schools, in fact little better than a huge board for the examination of big boys and girls.

Oxford and her education are thoroughly disappointing; but the sorest point therein is that this sham University satisfies the hapless Public, which knows nothing about its *fainéance*. It is a mere stumbling-block in the way of Progress especially barring the road to one of the main wants of English Education, a great London University which should not be ashamed to stand by Berlin, Paris and Vienna.

Had the good knight and "Pious Founder," Sir Thomas Bodley, who established his library upon the ruins of the University Bibliotheca wrecked by the "Reformation," been able to foresee the condition of Oxford and her libraries—Bodleian and Radcliffean—in this latter section of the XIXth century, he would hardly, I should hope, have condemned English students and Continental scholars to compulsory residence and labour in places so akin to the purgatorial.

Appendix B.

❖

THE THREE UNTRANSLATED TALES IN Mr. E. J. W. GIBB'S "FORTY VEZIRS."

THE THIRTY-EIGHTH VEZIR'S STORY.
(Page 353 of Mr. Gibb's translation.)

There was in the city of Cairo a merchant, and one day he bought a slave-girl, and took her to his house. There was in his house an ape; this the merchant fetched and dragged up to the slave-girl. He said, "Yield thyself over to this, and I will set thee free." The slave-girl did so of necessity, and she conceived by him. When her time was come she bare a son all of whose members were shaped like those of a man, save that he had a tail like an ape. The merchant and the slave-girl occupied themselves bringing up this son. One day, when the son was five or six months old, the merchant filled a large cauldron with milk, and lighted a great fire under it. When it was boiling, he seized the son and cast him into the cauldron; and the girl began to lament. The merchant said, "Be silent, make no lamentation; go and be free;" and he gave her some sequins. Then he turned, and the cauldron had boiled so that not even any bones were left. The merchant took down the cauldron, and placed seven strainers, one above the other; and he took the scum that had gathered on the liquid in the cauldron and filtered it through the seven strainers, and he took that which was in the last and put it into a bottle. And the slave-girl bare in her heart bitter hatred against the merchant, and she said in herself, "Even as thou hast burned my liver will I burn thee;" and she began to watch her opportunity. (One day) the merchant said to her, "Make ready some food," and went out. So the girl cooked the food, and she mixed some of that poison in the dish. When the merchant returned she brought the tray and laid it down, and then withdrew into a corner. The merchant took a spoonful of that food, and as soon as he put it into his mouth, he knew it to be the poison, and he cast the spoon that was in his hand at the girl. A piece, of the bigness of a pea, of that poisoned food fell from the spoon on the girl's hand, and it made the place where it fell black. As for the merchant, he turned all black, and swelled till he became like a blown-out skin, and he died. But the slave-girl medicined herself and became well; and she kept what remained of the poison and sold it to those who asked for it.

THE FORTIETH VEZIR'S STORY.
(Page 366 in Mr. Gibb's translation.)

There was of old time a tailor, and he had a fair wife. One day this woman sent her slave-girl to the carder's to get some cotton teased. The slave-girl went to the carder's shop and gave him cotton for a gown to get teased. The carder while teasing the cotton displayed his yard to the slave-girl. She blushed and passed to his other side. As she thus turned round the carder displayed his yard on that side also. Thus the slave-girl saw it on that side too. And she went and said to her mistress, "Yon carder, to whom I went, has two yards." The lady said to her, "Go and say to yon carder, 'My mistress wishes thee; come at night.'" So the slave-girl went and said this to the carder. As soon as it was night the carder went to that place and waited. The woman went out and met the carder and said, "Come and have to do with me while I am lying by my husband." When it was midnight the carder came and waked the woman. The woman lay conveniently and the carder fell to work. She felt that the yard which entered her was but one, and said, "Ah my soul, carder, at it with both of them." While she was softly speaking her husband awaked and asked, "What means thy saying, 'At it with both of them?'" He stretched out his hand to his wife's kaze and the carder's yard came into it. The carder drew himself back and his yard slipped out of the fellow's hand, and he made shift to get away. The fellow said, "Out on thee, wife, what meant that saying of thine, 'At it with both of them?'" The woman said, "O husband, I saw in my dream that thou wast fallen into the sea and wast swimming with one hand and crying out, 'Help! I am drowning!' I shouted to thee from the shore, 'At it with both of them,' and thou begannest to swim with both thy hands." Then the husband said, "Wife, I too know that I was in the sea, from this that a wet fish came into my hand and then slipped out and escaped; thou speakest truly." And he loved his wife more than before.

THE LADY'S THIRTY-FOURTH STORY.

(From the India Office MS.)

(Page 399 in Mr. Gibb's translation.)

They tell that there was a Khoja and he had an exceeding fair son, who was so beautiful that he who looked upon him was confounded. This Khoja watched over his son right carefully; he let him not come forth from a certain private chamber, and he left not the ribbon of his trousers unsealed. When the call to prayer was chanted from the minaret, the boy would ask his father saying, "Why do they cry out thus?" and the Khoja would answer, "Someone has been undone and has died, and they are calling out to bury him." And the boy believed these words. The beauty of this boy was spoken of in Persia; and a Khoja came from Persia to Baghdad with his goods and chattels for the love of this boy. And he struck up a friendship with the boy's father, and ever gave to him his merchandise at an easy price, and he sought to find out where his son abode. When the Khoja had discovered that the boy was kept safe in that private chamber, he one day said to his father, "I am about to go to a certain place; and I have a chest whereinto I have put whatsoever I possess of valuables; this I shall send to thee, and do thou take it and shut it up in that chamber where thy son is." And the father answered, "Right gladly." So the Khoja let build a chest so large that he himself might lie in it, and he put therein wine and all things needful for a carouse. Then he said to his servant, "Go, fetch a porter and take this chest to the house of Khoja Such-an-one, and say, 'My master has sent this to remain in your charge,' and leave it and come away. And again on the morrow go and fetch it, saying, 'My master wishes the chest.'" So the servant went for a porter, and the Khoja hid himself in the chest. Then the boy laded the porter with the chest and took it to the other Khoja's house, where he left it and went away. When it was night the Khoja came forth from the chest, and he saw a moon-face sleeping in the bed-clothes, and a candle was burning in a candlestick at his head; and when the Khoja beheld this he was confounded and exclaimed, "And blessed be God, the fairest of Creators!"[1] Then the Khoja laid out the

---

[1] Koran, xxiii. 14.

wine and so forth; and he went up softly and waked the boy. And the boy arose from his place and addressed himself to speak, saying, "Wherefore hast thou come here?" Straightway the Khoja filled a cup and gave it to him, saying, "Drink this, and then I shall tell thee what manner of man I am." And he besought the boy and spread out sequins before him. So the boy took the cup and drank what was in it. When the Khoja had given him to drink three or four cups the face of the boy grew tulip-hued, and he became heated with the wine and began to sport with the Khoja. So all that night till morning did the Khoja make merry with the boy; and whatsoever his desire was, he attained thereto. When it was morning, the Khoja again went into the chest; and the servant came and laded the porter with the same and took it back to his house. And on the morrow, when the boy and his father were sitting together, the mu'ezzin chanted the call to prayer, whereupon the boy exclaimed, "Out on thee, father; and the boy who is undone dies, and so this fellow goes up there and bawls out; last night they undid me; how is it that I am not dead?" Then the father smote the boy on the mouth and said, "Speak not such words; they are a shame." And then he knew why the chest had come.

INDEX.

Ghayr Wá'd or "Min ghayr Wa'd" =
lit. without previous agreement (tr.
"undesignedly"), 116.

Gháziyah (Arab.) = a gypsy (pl. Ghawázi), 18.

Ghiovendé (Turk.), a race of singers and
dancers, professional Nautch-girls, 53.

Ghubár = dust (joined to 'Afár = "sand-
devils"), 205.

HALF-MAN, an old Plinian fable (Pers.
Ním-Chihreh, and Arab. Shikk), 57.

Hálik (Arab.) = intensely black, 14.

Halkah = throat, throttle, 145.

"Halwá" = sweetmeat, 3.

Hámiz = pop. term for pickles (i.e. "Sour
meat" as opposed to "sweetmeats"),
3.

Hamlat al-jamal = according to Scott, a
"Camel's load of Treasure," 43.

Hanút (Arab.) = aromatic herbs, 200.

Haráj (in Egypt. "Harág") = the cry
with which the Dallál (broker) announces each sum bidden at an auction, 25.

Harj, gen. joined with Marj (Harj wa
Marj) = utter confusion, chaos (ST.),
270.

Harj wa Laght (Arab.) = turmoil and
trouble (ST.), 270.

Hashísh = Bhang in general, 10; confection of, 150.

Háyishah from "Haysh" = spoiling, 145.

Haysumah (Arab.) = smooth stones (tr.
"pebbles"), 275.

Házir (Arab.) corresponds with English
"Yes sir!" (tr. "Present"), 198.

He for she, 18.

"He found the beasts and their loads and
the learned men," etc., a new form of
"bos atque sacerdos," 245.

Head cut off and set upon the middle of
the corpse (in case of a Jew), or under
the armpit (in case of a Moslem), 47.

Hemp, Indian, 149.

Her desire was quenched, 113.

Hidyah (Arab.) in Egypt = a falcon (tr.
"a Kite"), 77.

Hikáyah (= literal production of a discourse, etc.), 27.

Hilm (vision), "au 'Ilm" (knowledge)
Arab. (tr. dreaming or awake) a phrase
peculiar to this M.S., 26.

"His bones were crushed upon his flesh"
for "His flesh . . . bones," 275.

House masters (also Kings) in the East
are the last to be told a truth familiar
to all but themselves and their wives,
278.

Houses made of cob or unbaked brick,
which readily melts in rain, 165.

Housewife, Egyptian or Syrian, will make
twenty dishes out of roast lamb, 135.

Hubban li-raasi-k (Arab.) lit. = out of love
for thy head, i.e., from affection for
thee, 36.

Hummus (or Himmis) = vetches, 3.

Húrí (Arab.) for Húr = pool, marsh or
quagmire (vulg. "bogshop"), 159.

"Huwa inná lam na'rifu-h" (Arab.) lit.
= He, verily we wot him not (suggesting "I am he"), 104.

"I AM as one who hath fallen from the
heavens to the earth," i.e. an orphan
and had seen better days, 56.

"I changed the pasture" = I pass from
grave to gay, etc., 3.

'Ilm al-Hurúf (Arab.) tr. "Notaricon," 60.

"Ikhbár" (= mere account of the discourse, oratio indirecta, etc.), 27.

Impotence, Causes and cure of, 201.

Indecencies of Bhang-eaters, 150.

Indian hemp, 149.

"In lam tazidd Kayní" = lit. unless thou
oppose my forming or composing (tr.
"unless thou avert my shame"), 6.

"Ishá" prayer, 233.

Ishári, a word which may have many
meanings (tr. "a white cock in his
tenth month"), 270.

Istiláh (Arab.) = Specific dialect, idiom
(tr. "right direction"), 80.

Istinshák (Arab.) one of the items of the
Wuzú or lesser ablution (tr. "water"),
42.

Iyálah = government-general, 190.

Iyás al-Muzani, al Kazi (of Bassorah) the
Model Physiognomist, 83.

"Iz lam naakhaz, wa-illá," etc., a fair
specimen of Arab. Ellipsis, 236.

JA'AD = a curl, a liberal man, 9.

Ja'ad al-yad = miserly, 9.

Ja'ídiyah (Arab.) a favorite word in this
M.S. = "Sharpers," 9, 220.

Yughaffiru (probably for yu'aftíru) = raising a dust cloud (St.), 207.

Yughaffiru wa yuzaghdimu = raising a
dust cloud and trumpeting with rage,
207.

"Yumázasa-hu fí 'l-Kalám," evidently
a clerical error for "Yumárasa-hu,"
= he tested or tried him in speech
(St.), 242.

Yumkinshayy = "Is it possible," 180.

Yuzaghdimu, a quadriliteral formed by
blending two tri-literals in one verb,
to intensify the idea (St.), 207.

Zabh (Zbh) (*Arab.*) = the ceremonial killing of animals for food, 21.

Zadig (Tale of), 3.

Zaghárit (*pl.* of Zaghrútah) = loud lullilooing, 209.

Zahr (*Arab.*) lit. and generically a blossom
(*tr.* "orange flower"), 37.

Zahr al-Bahr = the surface which affords a
passage to man, 97.

Zakát = legal alms (*tr.* "poor-rates"),
267.

Zamán, Al- (*tr.* "A delay") prob. an error
for "Yá al-Malik al-Zamán" = "O
King of the Age" (St.), 252.

Zardakát (for "Zardakhán") = silken napkins, 40.

Zard-i-Kháyah (*Pers.*) = yoke of egg, 40.

Zifr = nail, claw, talon, 190.

Zill (*Arab.*) *lit.* = "Shadow me" (*tr.* "solace me"), 42.

www.ingramcontent.com/pod-product-compliance
Lightning Source LLC
Chambersburg PA
CBHW060537030726
47498CB00004B/1230